MW00527522

STARRY WISDOM

THE LOVECRAFT TRILOGY
by Peter Levenda

BOOK ONE
The Lovecraft Code

BOOK TWO
Dunwich

BOOK THREE
(this book)
Starry Wisdom

From Ibis Press

STARRY WISDOM

PETER LEVENDA

WITH AN AFTERWORD BY

SIMON

EDITOR OF THE NECRONOMICON

IBIS PRESS
Lake Worth, FL

Published in 2019 by Ibis Press
A division of Nicolas-Hays, Inc.
P. O. Box 540206
Lake Worth, FL 33454-0206
www.ibispress.net

Distributed to the trade by
Red Wheel/Weiser, LLC
65 Parker St. • Ste. 7
Newburyport, MA 01950
www.redwheelweiser.com

Copyright © 2019 by Peter Levenda

All rights reserved. No part of this publication may be
reproduced or transmitted in any form or by any means, electronic
or mechanical, including photocopying, recording, or by any information
storage and retrieval system, without permission in writing from
Nicolas-Hays, Inc. Reviewers may quote brief passages.

ISBN: 978-0-89254-186-7
Ebook: 978-0-89254-681-7

Library of Congress Cataloging-in-Publication Data
Available upon request

Book design and production by Studio 31
www.studio31.com

[MP]

Printed in the United States of America

The fictions of genius are often the vehicles of the sublimest verities, and its flashes often open new regions of thought, and throw new light on the mysteries of our being.

—W. E. Channing, "On the Character and Writings of Milton"

We have left the land of the probable, and are journeying in the regions of the possible. The footprints here and there are of mortals, but of those who have beheld the hidden mysteries of Eulis, who are familiars of the Cabbala, who have raised the veil of Isis, and revealed the Chrishna, the— YAE or the A.A.

—P. B. Randolph, *Eulis*

A NOTE ON THE SPELLING OF FOREIGN WORDS

ONE OF THE CHALLENGES FACING AUTHORS of both fiction and non-fiction is the correct spelling of foreign words and phrases. Where there is a long literary history in a language that uses the Roman alphabet the challenge is not as great as it is for those languages that have their own alphabets ... or no alphabets at all. At that point, one tends to rely on the kindness of strangers: experts in foreign orthography. And none are stranger than they.

"Voodoo" presents just such a challenge. Spelled that way, it has too many associations of witchcraft, black magic, and "voodoo" dolls. It's a Hollywood word, with all that implies. Instead, we wanted to apply the expert advice of specialists in this area only to discover that they do not agree, not even with each other.

One scholar in the field—Donald J. Consentino—as the editor of the massive *Sacred Arts of Haitian Vodou* has come down firmly on the side of *vodou*, while acknowledging that the late Haitian anthropologist Rachel Beauvoir-Dominique preferred *vodoun*. As the latter was not only an anthropologist specializing in Haiti but was also a priestess of the religion and daughter of famed *houngan* Max Beauvoir, we decided that discretion was the better part of valor and went with the spelling *vodoun*.

That said, it will be noted that the title of Michael Bertiaux's most famous work, *The Voudon Gnostic Workbook*, provides an alternate spelling. Wherever his book is mentioned or his system is referred to specifically, we will use his spelling. Otherwise, we will be sticking with vodoun.

The reason for this confusion is the lack of an authoritative Kreyol-English dictionary. The linguists are still in the process of standardizing Kreyol terms, some of which came from French. In addition, the difficulty of approximating the nasal French pronunciation of some words which are African in origin, and from various different African languages as well ... you can see the problem.

You will also see words in Arabic, which use a somewhat standard Romanization and should be easy to identify. Also Bahasa Indonesia is used in some conversations, and we use the standard spellings since Bahasa Indonesia has adopted the Roman alphabet and most of its pronunciations with the notable exception of the letter "c" which is pronounced "ch."

As for the correct pronunciation of *Ph'nglui mglw'nafh … Cthulhu R'lyeh wgah'nagl fhtagn* … boys and girls, you're on your own!

PROLOGUE

April, 2015
Brooklyn

THE CRIME SCENE WOULD NEVER MAKE IT onto the television screens. *Investigation Discovery (ID)* would never showcase it on cable, as much as its owners lusted after it to make their Fall ratings that year. The clampdown by the "powers that be" would be absolute. Nothing to see here. Move along. Have a nice day.

Details did leak, as they always do, but they were so outlandish that no one took them seriously. A headless, naked corpse sitting in a chair in a Brooklyn doctor's office, back straight, arms positioned neatly on the armrests, legs man-spread wide like every asshole on the subway. Male genitalia removed with surgical precision. No sign of blood. No sign of a struggle. No sign of forced entry. No murder weapon. Nothing. Nothing but the doctor's head, defleshed, positioned on a clean paper sheet on the examination table midway between the stirrups.

It looked as if an invisible mother was giving birth to a skull.

★ ★ ★

There was not a drop of blood on the clean white paper sheet. The entire sheet was taken as evidence, of course, but it would reveal nothing. The ob/gyn's body—for the victim was a gynecologist—was eventually removed on a gurney but only after it had been photographed from every possible angle in the rather tight quarters. Homicide detectives would go through the paper files in the doctor's office and would notice eventually that several were missing. This would take time, for it did not appear at first that anything had been moved or removed. It was only when the doctor's files were matched against digital copies on the "cloud"—a remote server— that it was noticed that some files on the cloud were not found among the hardcopies in his office.

Someone had gone to considerable effort to remove specific sonograms and other evidence of the doctor's pregnant clientele.

Among them had been a file on a patient identified only as "Gloria."

★ ★ ★

Homicide detectives would ponder the meaning of the missing genitalia. Had the doctor been diddling his patients, and then providing abortion services when they got pregnant? That could account for the weirdly-positioned head on the examination table. But how do you account for the missing blood? The body had been drained, and it had to have been off-site. And the sharp, clean cuts in the groin. Whoever did that had to be an expert. A surgeon, or a butcher at the very least. Maybe another doctor. A competitor with a gruesome sense of humor?

They would do a tox-scan, looking for drugs of various kinds—was the doctor roofied, or hit with a dose of sodium pentothal?—but would find nothing. There were no fluids to test, anyway, as the blood and even the urine were missing; so they were reduced to testing tissue samples from the organs and the vitreous humor in the eyeball. The tests would take weeks, but they would come up empty.

There were no bruises on the head they could find, but then they didn't have a lot to work with. There was no flesh on the skull, but the skull itself did not show evidence of a blow by a blunt—or any other—instrument. No knife scrapings or other trace. No fibers. The ritualistic and pristine nature of the scene suggested that this was not the killer's first victim, and that the office was not the primary crime scene. The doctor had to have been killed somewhere else, and then the body staged in his office for maximum effect.

★ ★ ★

About an hour into the autopsy the detectives got a call from the medical examiner. It was unorthodox, but she liked to poke the tigers in their cage.

"His rib cage was crushed," she started. "As if someone had been standing on his chest, or maybe jumping up and down on it. Weird, right? Thought you should know.

"Oh, and another thing," she added. "His anal cavity is missing, too. Removed with a scalpel or some other sharp, precision instrument, right from the perineum. What, you guys didn't turn the DB over for a look?" She hung up with a grim chuckle.

What the hell?

★ ★ ★

Fingerprints confirmed that the DB—dead body—in the ob/gyn's office was indeed the doctor. A class ring on his left ring finger was further proof. The missing patient files were the only lead they had to a killer and a possible motive, so they began a systematic search for the patients themselves.

Most were easily located, including one poor woman who showed up that morning for her routine exam. She was at least six months pregnant and moving slowly down the street when she saw the police vans and the squad cars. They stopped her at the yellow tape and held her until a gold shield could come out to talk to her.

When she identified herself, one of the other detectives went through the paper files in the office and did not find hers. That is when they started to wonder if the doctor had been hiding some of the patients' files for reasons known only to him. They took her details, and told her what had happened (omitting the gory details, of course). She nearly collapsed and had to be gently seated on one of the plastic chairs in an outside waiting room while they looked for her file in the office. While her file did not show up in any of the file cabinets, they did find some notations with her name on it on the doctor's computer. That eventually led them to some encrypted files and a stash of sonograms held off-site on a remote server.

And that is when all hell broke loose.

★ ★ ★

Detective Lieutenant (Retired) J. Wasserman was roused out of bed in the middle of the afternoon by a phone call from a homicide detective in his old precinct. He had gotten used to taking naps during the day and looked forward to the time alone with his thoughts, if not his memories. He always got up early, before dawn, an old habit he couldn't quite shake, but found himself getting sleepy—or maybe it was just the depression of a retired cop with nothing to do—a few hours after noon.

"Loo? Is that you? Is this a bad time?"

They still called him 'Loo', short for 'Lieutenant', even though he had been out of the game for months now. And they knew that his wife had passed away recently, so they treated every conversation with him like a minefield.

"Yeah, it's me. What's up, Danny boy?"

"We caught a weird one, Loo, and I thought I would run it by you. Get your opinion. Maybe some advice, too."

"A weird one? Why me?"

"Remember that case you had a while back, just before you put in your papers? That apartment in Red Hook? The one the Feds jumped all over?"

How could he forget? It was a year ago. The Syrian landlords, the empty apartment with the sounds of chanting coming from it— and no radio, no television to account for the sounds. And then that clay bowl spinning in the middle of the table …

"Yeah, think so. What about it?"

"That address came up again in a homicide here in the Seven-Six. Doctor's office."

That spinning bowl. A spirit bowl, he was told it was. Spinning by itself …

"The doctor had a patient at that address. The apartment upstairs."

"Uh, okay. So?"

"The doctor? He's an ob/gyn. A baby doctor. The patient is a young woman. Arab, I think. Due in about three months. With twins."

"*Mazel tov.* What do you want from me?"

Spinning … spinning…

"That's the thing, Loo. She says she's having twins. The file says she's having twins. The first sonogram shows twins…"

"Danny, can you get to the point? I'm not getting any younger here."

Spinning …

"The most recent sonogram … the one taken only a week ago … there's a twin missing."

Spinning … *crack!* The bowl had shattered right down the middle as he was looking at it in that professor's apartment. Was it a year ago already?

"What do you mean, there's a twin missing? She hasn't given birth yet, right?"

"That's what I'm trying to say, Loo. There's an empty space in the sonogram. And the doctor was trying to hide it. He kept those files off-site. Or we think he did. They're missing from his office."

"Wait. What? What do you mean 'they're missing'?"

There was a silent moment on the other side while Danny tried to frame his response carefully.

"He had a lot of patients, this guy. He was investigating something. He had a special file with certain patient records in it. Encrypted. Maybe a dozen, we think, so far. All the same. Women who were pregnant with twins, and who now are pregnant with only one baby. Missing fetuses. It's just not possible, right?"

Something occurred to Wasserman. Something Danny wasn't telling him.

"What does this have to do with *me*, Danny? Just the address? Of the one patient? There's gotta be more than that, right?"

"Yeah, Loo. There is. Maybe just a coincidence. Maybe not. The name of the file, the one where the doctor kept all these weird sonograms and shit? He called it 'The Angel File.' Angel. Wasn't that the name of the guy in the apartment in Brooklyn, the one with the same address as this Arab patient?"

But Wasserman had already hung up, his mind spinning like the Syrian spirit bowl he couldn't get out of his head.

★ ★ ★

Red Hook was in the Seven-Six. It bordered on the Eight-Four, which was Brooklyn Heights, on the north and the Seven-Eight that was Park Slope on the east. On the west you had the East River, and on the south you had the Erie Basin and the Gowanus. Wasserman's last post was the Seven-Six, in the administrative region known as Brooklyn South, and before that the Eight-Eight out by Fort Greene in Brooklyn North. No matter how you divided it up into precincts, it was Brooklyn—Kings County—all the way. Until just before the turn of the century, when it officially became part of New York City, Brooklyn had been the fourth largest city in the United States. All by itself. Wasserman knew the borough like the back of his hand. Every street, every cross street, every bodega and Arab restaurant, and Caribbean holiday. He knew Bed-Stuy and Ocean Hill-Brownsville as well as he knew Sheepshead Bay and Bay Ridge and Gravesend. Once out of the academy he had landed feet first in Brooklyn and never looked back. The politicians at One Police Plaza could jockey for the choice postings all they wanted, but for Wasserman it had been Brooklyn or nothing.

He rose up through the ranks—not too fast, not too slow—and got his gold shield, working narcotics and vice first and then moved on to homicide, where he made detective first grade at Brooklyn South Homicide Squad, which had a grand total of sixteen detectives the year he left. He would still be on the force had it not been for mandatory retirement at age 63, a milestone he hit last December.

He looked at himself in the bathroom mirror. He had already shaved that morning. Showered. Had coffee. Then watched cable news for awhile. Then just sat on his couch and stared at the space in front of him. He became drowsy, and lay back down on the bed, fully dressed, and fell asleep like someone had turned off the light in his brain. Then the phone call from Danny, and now he was completely awake.

He guessed he looked okay, good enough for government work. He pulled on a jacket and left the apartment, locking the door's several locks, and then headed for the subway. After he met Danny on Atlantic Avenue in the Heights he would stop by the precinct and see if he could be of any assistance. He knew no one liked to see the retired guys stick their noses into ongoing investigations, but Danny had called *him*. It would give him something to do.

★ ★ ★

When that professor, Gregory Angell, had disappeared from his apartment in April of last year he had fully expected that the landlords—Syrians who had immigrated decades ago—would have rented it out before you could spell "Damascus." He had stopped by a few weeks later, and was told that the rent was being paid by some government agency in Washington, and that they were to leave the apartment alone. They said that someone had come by with a van and removed most of Angell's belongings—papers, and some artifacts and books—and then left a receipt. Wasserman asked to see the receipt, and they showed him something torn out of an invoice book you could pick up at any stationery store in Borough Hall. The fields were scribbled in, illegible, probably on purpose, but there was a phone number he could make out easily with a 202 area code. Washington, DC. He copied the number into his notebook at the time and forgot all about it. He figured he would look it up later and see who answered. For now, though, he had to stop by his old office and act like he belonged there.

★ ★ ★

As he stepped out of the subway station and onto the street he heard the distinctive sound of a high-powered rifle. Ahead of him, people started screaming. Instinctively, he looked to where he thought the shot had come from and reached for his weapon.

As a retired NYPD police officer, he had applied for—and been granted—a permit to carry a concealed weapon. He still favored the old blue steel .38 caliber Ruger revolver that he had used for decades, not trusting the 9mm semiautomatics that now were standard issue on the force. He had heard too many stories of them jamming when you needed them most. His six-shot revolver never jammed. And you never had to police up your brass, either.

He scanned the rooftops on the other side of the street. Nothing. But further down, near State Street, there was a brief flash of movement from the roof of the law school student dorm at Feil Hall. It looked like a woman, but he couldn't be sure. Something about the way she moved, the economy of gesture, made him think of his late wife. But she—if it was a she—was too far away to be seen clearly, maybe twenty stories above the street. He had to be hallucinating. He couldn't possibly make out a human being at that distance, and anyway Feil Hall was a block north of Atlantic Avenue. If she was the shooter, what the hell was she shooting at?

The answer came sooner than he thought. A crowd had formed on the sidewalk in front of a Yemeni restaurant on the other side of Atlantic. As he got closer, his revolver hanging down at his side in his right hand, he saw the expanding pool of blood and heard the sirens in the distance. He quickly holstered his weapon so as not to alarm anyone or give them the wrong idea, and pushed his way through the onlookers to find himself staring down at a face that he recognized...

...that *everyone* recognized, everyone who saw a newspaper or the local news on television or on the Internet. A visiting politician and statesman to some; a terrorist leader to others. A former officer of the Iraqi *Mukhabarat*, or secret police, under Saddam. A suspected member of ISIL, the Islamic State. The leader of a Sunni peace delegation to the United Nations from the contested area north of Mosul.

But to Jamila—a young Yezidi woman and experienced sniper with a price on her head, who at that moment was breaking down her beloved Dragunov rifle from her perch, her "God spot," twenty stories above the Brooklyn streets—he was better known as Ayman Hasan, the Butcher of Sinjar.

Or he had been, anyway, she thought. *Now he is just a statistic.*

BOOK ZERO

AFTERMATH

It was November of 2014. A mysterious but powerful secret society—the Order of Dagon—had organized a ritual designed for the purpose of opening a Gate between this world and Another, to allow the Old Ones (an alien race that had predated the evolution of human beings on this planet) to penetrate completely into this world. To accomplish this, they had made arrangements with terror groups in the Middle East and Africa to abduct young girls for the performance of the ritual. The girls had to be virgin: that was essential. Hundreds of girls had been trafficked this way, and out of the hundreds fewer than sixty were eventually selected for the ritual. Although the ritual was being duplicated in Dagon lodges all over the world at precisely the same moment, the central rite took place in a remote location in Florida. At this ritual, the youngest of the girls would be used as seers: to enter a trance-like state in which they would communicate with the Old Ones. The older girls—those who were fertile and of child-bearing age—were to be used to incarnate the Old Ones as cult members deflowered them during the ritual. The younger girls, once their purpose had been served, would be sacrificed during the ceremony. The older girls would be removed to another remote location in order eventually to give birth to their hybrid—human and alien—offspring, after which their fate was as yet unknown.

An element of the American intelligence establishment got wind of this ritual before it took place. It coordinated with agencies involved in monitoring human trafficking and terror operations worldwide. Eventually, the ritual sites were identified and the lodges raided by law enforcement and military units, their members arrested. The leader of Dagon—a woman who herself was believed to be the incarnation of one of the Old Ones—was killed in the raid, but others around the world had escaped and were being hunted down.

★ ★ ★

Behind all of this, however, was the single most important aspect of Dagon and one that had been missing during the ritual—which some observers claimed was the reason for the ritual's failure and the success of law enforcement. That was the loss of their most important text: the *Necronomicon*. It had been seized by a professor of religion who was now at large and in hiding. The professor was the descendant of the one academic who had identified the cult of Dagon a hundred years earlier, Professor George Angell of Brown University, Providence. His descendant—Gregory Angell—was believed to be somewhere in Southeast Asia. What was left of Dagon was intent on finding both Angell and the *Necronomicon,* and to conduct the ritual that finally would open the Gate and turn this world into an abattoir of souls.

Pinecastle Bombing Range
Ocala National Forest, Florida
November 12, 2014

She heard the gunfire and saw the searchlights. There were helicopters overhead. Men with guns. Everyone running. Screams.

She had been through this before. At her home. When the men dressed in black uniforms and with the black flag with words written on it that she did not understand rolled through her village, shooting at the fathers and the brothers and the uncles, and grabbing the mothers and the sisters and the aunts.

Now she wanted to run, but she was frozen to the spot. The man in front of her, the one who was in control, raised a sword over her head.

That had happened to her before, too. In her village. On the mountain top known as Sinjar. A man in black clothes and a black mask had raised a scimitar over her until another man told him to stop. That she was more valuable alive than dead. And not for the usual reasons.

She froze. It was the darkest night she had ever seen. She was in a strange country, with strange smells and strange food. She had been taught how to *see* in the big black mirrors they used. To reach out with her mind to touch the faces of demons and *jinn*. It was like make-believe, except there was no playing or joy in the pretend games that they learned. And what she saw had terrified her. And then became a part of her.

Nalin. That was her name. She barely remembered it. The people who took her spoke some Kurmanji, but not much. They gave her something to make her sleep, and she slept for hours or maybe days. She awoke to a strange place, with a strange sun and a strange moon. She was fed strange food, and made to concentrate, *concentrate*, until she could see things in the mirror. Bad things.

And then those things would be inside her. Making her talk. Making her point and command and scream in words she did not understand. Like those flags with the curvy writing and the bad men with the guns. But different. Maybe ... worse?

She froze to the spot. The man in front of her, the one who was in control, raised a sword over her head and then fell backward. The sword dropped to the ground not two feet in front of her. She stared at it, and then felt arms around her as she was picked up by another man who spoke to her in another language she didn't understand.

Another man. Another sword. Another gun. Another language. Another pair of arms.

"You're okay now, little girl," the voice said. "You're safe."

Had she understood English, she would have laughed at the words. And then she would have wept.

★ ★ ★

The leader of the Order of Dagon—a woman who her followers believed was the incarnation of an ancient god—stepped on an unexploded bomb and was killed instantly as a SWAT team descended from stealth helicopters over a bizarre ceremony of ritual magic designed to open a "Gate" between this world and the next. Her brother, who was also her lover and her partner, died in the same explosion. It was the middle of the night in a heavily-restricted area of the forest, and no one knew how she and her entire entourage managed to set up an elaborate ritual on the arcane target area of the bombing range—replete with an enormous pentagram and hexagram, visible only from the air—without the US Navy (who now owned the site) knowing all about it. Obviously, the Order of Dagon had excellent connections, even within the military.

Other cult members were killed when they tried to resist, but most were apprehended alive and eleven girls were rescued. Some of them—called "seers" by the cult—would have been sacrificed at the culmination of the rite had it not been interrupted by the raid. The others—the "breeders"—were being deflowered in an act of ritual sex so that they would conceive human-alien offspring of the Old Ones as a consequence of the ritual.

At the same time, and around the world, other Dagon sites were being raided. The others had been designed to draw attention and fire away from the central ritual in Florida. It was only due to the inspiration of a handful of analysts meeting in an apartment in a suburb of Fort Meade that the Florida site was identified and the precise time of the ritual calculated.

Dwight Monroe, the unofficial leader of the unofficial group and a man with more than sixty years of service in intelligence, was relieved to know that the ritual had been aborted. As the calls came in to his encrypted cell phone he learned that dozens of innocent children from Africa and the Middle East had been trafficked by Dagon for use in this ceremony, a fact that initially had come to the attention of a sharp-eyed photo analyst called Harry. Together with Harry's boss at NSA, Sylvia Matos, and Dwight's long-time colleague Aubrey, they met at the apartment of another old hand, the enigmatic scholar Simon, to plan their attack.

On the same evening, the leader of the New England lodge of Dagon—the somewhat sinister Vanek—had been arrested in Whately, Massachusetts where he was to oversee another of the rituals timed to take place at the same instant as the Florida ceremony. Three more small children, all girls, were rescued at the time. All in all, a total of twenty-three more children were saved during raids on Dagon sites globally.

While the team had celebrated their victory over the cult, Monroe knew that the fight was not over yet. There were still many Dagon initiates at large in the world, and they had the resources to strike again. While US intelligence and law enforcement, and those of allied countries were busy rolling up Dagon's human trafficking networks, Monroe knew all too well that fanatics never surrendered. How else did the postwar Nazi underground last as long as it had? And Dagon was older, more sophisticated, and had ties to terror cells the world over. The loss of their leader would stop them for only so long; another leader would rise to take her place, of that Monroe was certain.

He had only one ace up his sleeve, and that was the fact that he knew the most crucial element of all of Dagon's rituals was so far out of their grasp. He was sure that they would blame their failure on the loss of this artifact, the Book that was now in the hands of a renegade university professor somewhere in Southeast Asia. They had lost their leader, and the only way they could recoup their losses would be to acquire the most sacred text of their cult, the twisted scripture known as the *Necronomicon*. They most certainly would redouble their efforts to find that professor and seize the Book for themselves as they plotted their third—and final—attempt to open the mysterious Gate.

Dwight Monroe knew that, no matter what, he had to seize it first.

"Strawberry Fields"
CIA Detention Site
Guantanamo
April, 2015

The American leader of Dagon's New England branch was languishing in an isolation cell. He had been arrested in Whately, Massachusetts in November 2014 as he was on his way to a ritual that would involve three small children—courtesy of Dagon's international circle of human traffickers—and his own coven of initiates. Vanek's allegiance, spiritual and temporal, was to a man he knew only as the Dark Lord who at the time of the bust was safely in Europe somewhere in the embrace of Dagon leadership. When he was first arrested he heard a rumor that the Dark Lord had escaped apprehension and was hiding out in Prague, according to one source, or in St Petersburg according to another. Now, though, he was not getting any information from anyone anymore.

When the main ritual was raided in Florida, Vanek had already been picked up and interrogated by some old fuck with a patrician accent, and so much juice with the authorities that he was sure he could have been wasted on the spot and no one would have seen a thing. Old Fuck knew about Vanek's parents and his weird-ass twin brother who was in some kind of mental hospital back in the UK. Twins. In the end, this whole thing came down to twins but he was not about to educate Old Fuck on that score. Anyway, he seemed to know about it already. He probably had maybe half the story, but not the whole story or Vanek would be dead by now. Shot while trying to escape. Like that.

Monroe. That was the old fuck's name. Like that actress. The one they killed back in the 1960s. "Candle in the Wind" and all that.

And he had been in custody since that November evening, on some kind of bullshit national security warrant. He had no idea where he was, or even if he was in the United States. He had been sedated, a hood thrown over his head, and transported somewhere. He had been interrogated on and off since then, always with a different spook. He didn't know what else to tell them. They already raided his apartment back in New Bedford and removed every stick of furniture and every scrap of paper. Or that's what they told him, anyway, and why would he doubt it?

They knew how he communicated with the Dark Lord, using that old "save email as draft" technique. But most of their comms were hard copy anyway. They didn't trust email or anything electronic.

Dagon had strict rules about that, which meant they would find very little in his apartment that they could use.

His devotees, though, that was another story. He knew they would fold under questioning. They were not exactly the cream of the crop, that lot. They had only been in the Order a short while, and they spent more time worrying about tattoos and fake swords than they did Order procedures and ritual. So he knew that they would tell Monroe whatever he wanted. But that was why there were degrees in the Order: the lower degrees knew nothing of any importance, and Vanek never initiated high enough that he would have to divulge anything interesting. The Dark Lord wanted cannon fodder, not initiates.

He had no idea of the passage of time. There was no radio, no television, no computer or smart phone where he was. Wherever that was. The guards spoke very little, some of them not at all. There were no newspapers or magazines. No books. Vanek was going out of his bloody mind in his cell, and had to rely on his training to keep from chewing off his own face.

He was reasonably adept at meditation, including asana, prana-yama, and dharana, as required in *Liber E vel Exercitiorum*. He had committed the Tree to memory, including all the paths on the reverse side of the Tree: the Tunnels of Set and their associated Qlipoth. He knew, but dared not recite aloud, the chants specific to Cthulhu, Shub Niggurath, and Yog Sothoth. He knew enough Babylonian to be dangerous; the Sumerian was more difficult. And he could do gematria in his head.

He would do Tarot spreads with an imaginary deck, just to keep in shape. And he tried to send telepathic messages to the Dark Lord but he never heard back. His next step would be an out of body experience, but he was timing the arrival of the guards and the meals so that he would not be vulnerable when they showed up or opened his cell. They seemed to come and go at odd times though, as if to thwart his attempts to measure the passing of days and weeks, so he would have to wing it when he was ready. Just wait for them to show up, and then begin immediately when they left, figuring he would have at least an hour to himself, which would be all that he needed.

It was the target of his OOBE that was yet to be determined. He didn't want to just "show up" in front of the Dark Lord. That was certain to get him terminated in a very ugly way. Instead, he needed information and that could come only from Monroe or one of his minions. He had no idea if Monroe was "protected" in such a way, but there was that other bloke who was with him that night in Whately. What was his name?

Harry. That's right. It was Harry.

Detention Site Green
Somewhere in Thailand
April, 2015

Maxwell Prime paced the few feet from one wall of his isolation cell to the other. The cell was so small it was impossible for him to lie down on the filthy, bug-infested floor, and he was not a tall man. He varied his routine by walking heel to toe going one direction, and then pigeon-walked the other. Sometimes he counted his steps— three—and sometimes he counted in different languages. He knew how to count in English, German, Spanish, French, Mandarin, Russian, and Arabic. His facility with languages was one of the reasons why he had been picked for his last assignment: tracking a university professor named Gregory Angell all over Asia, from Beijing to a ship in the South China Sea. His methods had been ... unorthodox ... and the professor got away. Prime himself had been detained in Singapore on the orders of Dwight Monroe, acting through his flunky, that guy named Aubrey, and tossed into a black site for interrogation and whatever else they wanted. And here he was. He wasn't sure where, but from the smells, the heat, and the humidity it had to be in Asia. The Five Eyes had arrangements with friendly governments all over the continent, so it could be anywhere.

A lesser man would have given up by now, would have crumbled, lost hope, begged for mercy. But not Prime. He was still plotting his revenge and his move up the IC ladder. He wanted to get rid of that old fossil, Monroe, and his asshole buddy, Aubrey. But first he had to find a way to get out of this place.

Wherever it was.

No worries, though. He knew how to manage his interrogators. He knew how to feed them just enough inside dirt that they would be coming back for more. They wanted to know what he knew. They wanted to hear all the gossip, all the rumors around the water coolers back in Maryland or Virginia or DC. Eventually they would begin to see that he might be more valuable to them on the outside rather than rotting in this filthy cell that was used to warehouse Al Qaeda alumni back in the day.

He was good at playing one side against the other. He was even better when his life was at stake.

He might have lost twenty pounds. He still might be wearing the clothes he was picked up in months ago. And he needed a *shave*. And a *toothbrush*. And *nail CLIPPERS. And SOAP!!*

Oops. That's when he realized he was shouting all of this out loud in his empty cell.

Back to the count:

Eins … zwei … drei … Un … deux … troi … Yi … er … san …

The Alchymist Hotel
Prague, Czech Republic
April 30, 2015—Walpurgisnacht

The Dark Lord was holding court in the fireplace room in a hotel a short walk from the Street of the Alchemists. Soon, Prague would be unlivable once the tourists descended. But for now he was comfortable and the spring temperature was still cool enough that he could sit for an hour or so and regale his companions with tales of occult intrigue, most of which he had invented so as to make himself appear more interesting. Best of all, the wine tasting was complimentary.

"Yes, indeed, I was present at that biker bar in Virginia when the

Caliph himself decided to initiate everyone there into the Minerval degree. Imagine, a bar full of skinheads and every one of them an initiate!"

There was the obligatory amused chuckling from the assembled guests. He sensed that perhaps he had told this story before, or maybe once too often. After all, it wasn't about *his* Order precisely so it was not germane to the topic at hand—duplexity be damned—but it helped get everyone in the mood.

★ ★ ★

He had managed to escape an Interpol dragnet the previous November in Turin. Heavily-armed and Kevlar-jacketed cops had descended on the church, known as "Granma" to the locals, with the intention of breaking up what they thought was either a satanic ritual involving children or a terrorist cell trafficking in children. He had gotten the word only minutes before the raid. There had been a spotter in Whately, Massachusetts who had been posted a block away from where his subordinate Vanek was to meet with the local Lodge prior to the ceremony. When she saw the police arrive in force she sent an encrypted text message to the Dark Lord's phone. That was enough to call off the ritual and save the European initiates from being arrested. Over the next few hours, sporadic reports came in detailing the wholesale suppression of Dagon's most ambitious ritual since that fiasco in Nepal. The main rite in Florida was raided, and the ancillary rituals in different towns in different countries— designed to throw off law enforcement –were all rolled up with ruthless efficiency. Even the ritual in Java had been stymied, and that was not easy to do.

The American operations had been nominally under his administration, so he bore the brunt of the anger of Dagon's leadership. He knew that they would move the next attempt out of the United States, but the options were limited due to their idiosyncratic calendar/topology system. The next ritual would most likely be held somewhere in the Caribbean, or possibly elsewhere in Latin America. The hot points kept moving. Dagon was not including him in the discussions, however, so he had no idea of the timing or the exact location, and would not be told until the last possible moment. That stung, but not as badly as what they had done to him when the Florida ritual was quashed. They lost their most powerful initiates during that raid, a deeply creepy brother and sister team whose initiation level was far above his own, killed by automatic weapons fire even as the seers and breeders were being rescued. Dagon took out its fury on him, which is why he was holding court in Prague minus his left arm.

He kept telling himself it made him all the more interesting to the Zelators.

The Dark Lord held the wine glass by its stem and swirled the deep-bodied burgundy within it. It had legs, that was for sure. He looked up and saw all eyes were fixed on him, waiting for the next morsel of gossip or wisdom.

"Magister," began one of his guests, a beautiful woman of about forty from Lebanon who had recently been elevated to the rank of Practicus. "We have studied the calendar and the maps, and while we understand the system theoretically we are having a difficult time doing the calculations."

He nodded in her direction, and then with a glance took them all in at once.

"Is this true for all of you?"

There was a murmur of agreement.

"It is difficult, I agree. One has to change one's way of thinking about time and space, which are constructs of consciousness anyway, and not to be found in nature. We all know that time is an illusion; it seems to go too quickly when we are expecting something unpleasant, or too slowly when we anticipate pleasure. What we are not used to seeing in this way is space: the distances between ourselves, between cities and countries, between one building and the next. That is because we are thinking in terms of the Earth-bound beings that we are. The Old Ones are not so inhibited. They

see everything on Earth from the vantage point of the vast distances
of interstellar space. They also remember what the planet looked
like aeons ago, before the current landmasses were formed. They
superimpose the topology from an ancient time onto the space
we know today. They see our planet completely differently, with
different reference points, many of which are under the seas and
invisible to us but quite prominent to them. Dagon, after all, is an
amphibious God."

"You say time is an illusion?"

This, from an older gentleman whose pedophilic tendencies
were well-known to the Order.

"Yes, from the point of view of mathematics, anyway. The passage
of what we call time has no effect on an equation, for instance. One
plus one equals two is the same as two equals one plus one. The
arrow of time can go in either direction and you get the same result.
The electron field around the nucleus of an atom is unaffected by
time. Atoms don't get 'old.'"

"Then, what does the Order say about astrology, for instance,
which is concerned with nothing so much as the passage of time?
One's birth time, the transits of the planets, and so forth?"

The Dark Lord took a sip of the burgundy before setting down
his glass. He settled back in his comfortable chair and smiled.

"Irrelevant to the Old Ones. The details of our births and lives
have no meaning to the Gods. Imagine an ant farm, and trying
to keep all the natal charts of all the ants organized! And to what
purpose? But to answer your question more specifically: the entire
conceit of astrology is based on having the Earth at the center of
the universe. The Old Ones find that humorous. We have known for
centuries that the Earth revolves around the Sun, but we still behave
as if we are the center.

"Imagine, for a moment, astrology on the planet Mars. Someone
is born on Mars. How does one construct a natal chart for that
person? Does the position of the Earth take over from Mars in the
chart? Is one born with Earth rising, or Earth in the first house? If

so, what is the characteristic of the planet Earth in the chart? Do we simply switch out Mars for Earth? Does Earth then contain all those martial qualities we have for millennia assigned to the Red Planet? And what about the Zodiac? Is it still the same?"

There were murmurs of interest among the assembled guests.

"We are fast becoming a space-faring race. We may indeed see human beings born and raised on Mars in the near future; or on our Moon, or Europa, or Enceladus, or one of the other moons of the other planets. We will be forced to consider these factors, to derive an entirely new astrology that is centered on other celestial bodies.

"That is what the Order has already done. That is why you are having a hard time doing the calculations. Our system is the one the Old Ones use, which is the only way we can predict their arrival and the location of the Gate. Their system is based on conditions in the trans-Yuggothian—excuse me, the trans-*Plutonian*—realm which is their stepping stone into our solar system. Once they have landed there, they measure distances and times appropriate to this system, using our Sun as the reference point, not our Earth."

"Thank you, Magister. That was clear."

He nodded, then pointed to another guest.

"You have a question?"

"Yes," replied a man of about sixty with a shock of white hair framing a youthful face. He had been one of those recruited from the States, with a long background in American esotericism. A dilettante, then.

"What you said about time. My question concerns the Aeons. According to Crowley, there was an Aeon of Isis followed by Osiris, and now the Aeon of Horus. According to Achad, we are now in the Aeon of Maat. Who is right, and why?"

The Dark Lord snorted.

"Again, this question presupposes the legitimacy and even the supremacy of an Earth-based system of measurement of time and space. An 'aeon' of barely two thousand years is not an 'aeon' to be respected. It is hardly a blip in the grand scheme of things. The Old

Ones experience millions of our years as an aeon. And even then, it is barely enough time for them to boil an egg."

There was appreciative laughter around the room. But then the Dark Lord became serious and the laughter subsided.

"Remember what our Book says: *That is not dead which can eternal lie, And with strange aeons even death may die.* Strange aeons—not those of the Crowley cult, or of Achad, or any of the others who play at magic and at contact with the Old Ones. The stumblers and fumblers may at times succeed, almost in spite of themselves, like your Jack Parsons and Ron Hubbard in the Mojave Desert, but when they succeed they fall back on their asses and become terrified. With us, terror is sanctity. Terror is a sacrament. Arthur Machen wrote that there are sacraments of evil as well as of good. Evil is a value judgment that has no value for *us*, but you get the idea. What the others fear, we embrace. What they avoid, we celebrate."

There was silence for a moment, and then the inevitable question. This, from the Lebanese woman with the riot of long black hair and kohl-accented eyes.

"The Book. Do we have it, at last?"

The Dark Lord noticed that the wine was finished, so it was time to close the meeting.

"No, *Soror*, but we are close. We have located the thief, and the Keepers are closing in."

There was a general sigh of pleased anticipation from the guests, and the Dark Lord rose from his seat.

"I believe dinner has been prepared in our usual place in the Old Town. Forgive me if I must arrive later than all of you. There are a number of issues for me to address. Please start without me, and I will join you in about an hour."

They all rose and, one by one, shook his remaining hand. As the last one left, the Dark Lord frowned and turned on his heel, heading for his room upstairs. He had lied to his followers. They *had not* located Gregory Angell, but they *were* closing in. As usual the professor was one or two steps ahead of them. Their reach in the Islamic countries of Southeast Asia was not as great as in other areas. Indonesia, for instance, had its own ideas about religious orthodoxy and extremism, which were not always in synch with the terror groups Dagon worked with in Iraq and Syria. That meant that cooperation was not always guaranteed in that part of the world. The Saudis were doing their best to radicalize the region, but there was still a lot of pushback from long-standing political parties and religious movements, like Nahdlatul Ulama, or NU, which had embraced the Javanese approach to Islam rather than the seemingly orthodox Wahabism of the Saudis. NU was particularly strong in central Java and especially in the university town of Yogyakarta, which is where Dagon's sources believed Angell to be hiding.

Once in his room, the Dark Lord pulled out the handwritten sheet of paper that had been left for him as planned. All communications until further notice were by hard copy, and electronic comms of any kind, including phones, were forbidden under pain of death. His mail drop was a small recess in the statue of Saints Cosmas and Damian on the Charles Bridge. Here he had secured the latest report that very morning. He felt that the choice of that particular statue was appropriate, as Cosmas and Damian were said to have been twins, and Arab twins at that.

The report was brief, and written in a day code based on the short story by Lovecraft entitled "The Whisperer in Darkness." It was all very old school, very John le Carré, time-consuming and labor-intensive, but it worked.

Decrypted, it read:

Angel believed to be in Java. Keepers on the way.

(They had decided to use "Angel" to refer to Gregory Angell, using only the single "L," because … well, because they were the Demons, weren't they?)

They had his general location, and they knew he still had the Book. That was a step in the right direction. Their local chaps had done the right thing and were waiting for the Keepers to arrive rather than try to take the Book themselves. That was important, for reasons they were not cleared to know.

Because they needed not only the Book. They needed Angell, too.

Or, at least, his DNA. They weren't fussy about how to obtain it.

Yogyakarta, Indonesia
May 1, 2015

Gregory Angell, the fugitive professor of religious studies and troubled possessor of the Black Book of the Dagon cult, had managed to live for several months in relative peace and obscurity on the island of Java in Indonesia. The food was healthy, the landscape amazing, the weather was hot and humid, and the people were curious but friendly. There was a mosque on every street corner, and for the first few weeks he would awaken before dawn to the cry of the muezzin to come to prayer. To many Americans, reared on a diet of Islamophobia since 9/11, this would seem sinister or even hostile, but to Angell—who had survived many attempts on his life by non-Muslims since leaving the United States for Iraq the previous year, and who had traveled from there to Iran, Afghanistan, Nepal, and China (among other places)—Java was heaven, and the five-times-daily reminder that "God is great" was eerily comforting. It reinforced the idea that there was a pattern and a rhythm to life that was predictable and inevitable, and this reassured him that peace—the inner peace he desperately sought, with or without a God—was possible.

But he was starting to attract too much attention. He was a *bule*—a foreigner—and even though he had excellent documentation (courtesy of a crooked but kindly sea captain and a windfall of stolen gold) he knew he would soon outstay his welcome. So he had to make arrangements to slip out of the country. Once in an environment where he could blend in more easily, he would consider his next move.

He was fearful of returning to the United States. He knew that the people who had sent him to Iraq were still looking for him, and they had the resources of the entire US government behind them. He couldn't trust Monroe or Aubrey to do right by him. They wanted the Book above all else, and in the last few months of relative isolation and inactivity with nothing to do but read and think, Angell began to realize why.

The text—known as *Al Azif* in Arabic, or *Necronomicon* in Greek—was the survival of an ancient Mesopotamian tradition of magic and spiritual manipulation. It had been confused with the Black Book of the Yezidis: that mysterious clan that lived primarily in northern Iraq, and which had been the target of genocide by both ISIL and by local groups hostile to the people they considered "devil worshippers." The Yezidis claimed the origin of their people and their religion was in ancient Sumer: the same lost realm whose rituals and mythologies formed the basis of the *Necronomicon*. The book was pre-Islamic, a text burned into its pages by a madman and a seer who desired above all else to preserve the old wisdom from the torches of the new faith and its austere leader.

Reading the text, Angell was not so sure the madman was right. The formulas detailed in the *Necronomicon* represented a system of contacting non-human entities from beyond the stars. It might have been better to forget about this idea, destroy the book, and carry on as if it had never existed. Angell had studied religion all his life. He knew its dangers and its limitations. He was aware of the hypocrisy of many religious leaders, and had no answer for those who claimed that priests were pedophiles and ministers were greedy capitalists who robbed their followers of money they desperately needed for food and rent. If religious education and belief failed its own leadership, how could the faithful be expected to keep *their* faith?

To Angell, religion was a work in progress, one that he no longer believed in, just as he had abandoned his faith in God that one terrible afternoon when he witnessed the massacre of Yezidis in Mosul by an angry Muslim gang. But *this*? The *Necronomicon*? It represented a rebellion against religion, certainly, but also against the state and against human civilization and society itself. It was a *cri de coeur*, a cry from the heart, but from the heart of a terrible darkness. To invoke *those* gods, the Old Ones as described in the book, was to invite wholesale destruction upon the peoples of the Earth.

God was a loaded gun, Angell thought. You could admire its design, its intricate workmanship, the bluing of its steel, its history, the names of those who had come before, the designers, the manufacturers, the gunsmiths. The smell of the cordite incense, the Gregorian chant of a round being chambered … but in the end, it was pointed at *you* and you would be blown apart, killed, deformed by the bullet.

God was nothing more than a gun aimed at center mass.

The *Necronomicon* admitted this. Accepted it. One could say even embraced it. There was no nonsense about it. Angell had never seen a purportedly *religious* text so open about the fact that God wanted to kill you.

The central theme of the book involved the survival of an ancient being called Kutulu, the Cthulhu of H. P. Lovecraft's short stories. The Arabic term was *al-Qhadhulu*: a word that appears in the Qur'an as "the Abandoner." The entire text was an effort to call back this being who had abandoned its followers at some point in the distant, pre-historic, past. It was an attempt to roll back civilization to a time when humans were slaves to non-human masters. Why would anyone want to do *that*?

Most books of magic from the same period and region involved commanding angels and demons in the name of God. Magic is not about obedience or worship, but about control over natural (and supernatural) forces. It places human beings squarely in the center of Creation: in a sense, a return to the state that Adam and Eve were in before the expulsion from Paradise.

The *Necronomicon,* however, seemed to represent a craven act of submission by human beings to prehistoric, pagan deities who had enslaved them for their own purposes or who even had created humans as beasts of burden. The ancient Sumerian creation texts suggested just that, and the *Necronomicon* took the idea to its logical conclusion: the Old Ones had created us, and then abandoned us to our fate. The future of a planet mired in violence, waste, pollution, and greed was indeed dark, but the conjuration of the old gods to return and save us from ourselves did not seem like a good alternative. Was religious violence in the twenty-first century a sign that religion had failed us, that God had failed us, and that the only option was the caveman approach of murder and torture? If so, then maybe the author of the *Necronomicon*—the "mad Arab"—had a point after all.

These thoughts and many more just as depressing filled Angell's days and nights in a small house south of the Kraton—the Sultan's palace—in Yogyakarta. Each morning brought the sound of the call to prayer from the local mosques, loudspeakers blaring in cacophonous counterpoint to each other, until after a few weeks he managed to sleep right through them. He bought batik on Malioboro Road, ate *nasi goreng* at open air stands, or *rendang* upstairs at Legian or *gudeg* at the antique Cirebon *resto* and tried to act like a tourist, all the while looking around him at the faces and the body language of the people in the crowds, alert to anything that might signal that the Keepers of the Book—the hit squad of the infamous Order of Dagon—might be in the area.

He walked the streets of the city, his shirt sticking to his torso in the relentless heat, and strayed into small *kampungs* where the lives of the local people touched him. Kampungs are villages or neighborhoods, sometimes with their own security guards and headmen, and are as typical of traditional Javanese life as the *hutongs* of Beijing are typical of Old China. He bought a phrasebook to learn basic Indonesian, and found himself hanging out at *warung2 makan*, attempting to chat with the other diners at those outdoor eating establishments with their charcoal grills and bowls of noodles, soup, and satay. He almost felt human in those moments, and then realized that he was doing himself more harm than good by advertising his presence as a foreigner in their city. His cover story that he was a visiting professor was a very convincing one for someone who was, indeed, a visiting professor, albeit an involuntary one. There were a lot of foreign academics in Yogyakarta, a city which boasted many universities as well as the "Harvard of Indonesia": Universitas Gadjah Mada. However, he steered clear of other foreigners, fearful that they would blow his cover once they realized he was not really attached to any of the colleges. He was concerned lest his identity had become known already, either through news reports or the usual academic gossip.

Instead, he spent some time at the House of Raminten—a restaurant owned by the cross-dressing proprietor of the multi-story Mirota Batik on Malioboro Road—and ate *bakso* and *pecel* while being acutely aware of the horses kept in stalls on the other side of the wall, as the somewhat frightened-looking wait staff in traditional attire moved like cautious sentries through the crowded tables, mirroring his own anxiety. The full-size portraits of Hamzah Sulaeman, the owner and creator of the restaurant and its associated batik store, in complete drag as his character Raminten, were a revelation to Angell, as they were to most foreigners (and even Indonesians) who frequented Yogyakarta: easily the most tolerant and diverse city in Java. This astonishment was increased by the way drinks are served in the House of Raminten: in large ceramic mugs shaped like female breasts.

Angell knew there was a lot to discover about Yogyakarta— "Jogja" as it was commonly known—and the rest of Indonesia, but time was running out for him here. Eventually he would come to the attention of either the authorities or of the Dagon crowd, and either way it would be fatal. He had money, and could live comfortably in Indonesia for many more months, but he knew that would mean growing careless and lazy about security. He hadn't stayed alive this long by being lazy, but security was a problem the longer he remained in one place. He had to find safer circumstances but that was hard to do when he didn't know whom he could trust.

★ ★ ★

All the same, in the back of his mind and working within him like a slow-acting medicine, was his experience on Parangtritis Beach south of Jogja. There in November he had had the most intense spiritual awakening of his life. It was a stark counterpoint to the terror and disgust he felt at witnessing the massacre of the Yezidi workers in Mosul: the event that had made Angell lose his faith in God forever. The experience on the beach resisted definition or characterization, but at its heart it had to do with a goddess, a female saint of some kind, the mysterious Lara Kidul: the spirit bride of the Sultan of Yogyakarta, a protector of the city and the other end of a supernatural axis that stretched from the summit of the active volcano Mount Merapi in the north to the turbulent seas at the south, an axis that ran right through the heart of Yogyakarta and the Sultan's Palace.

He had seen the Goddess of the Southern Ocean, Lara Kidul, stand before him. But behind him had stood none other than the Kutulu of the *Necronomicon,* the Cthulhu of Lovecraft. She was the Goddess rescued from the depths of the Sea where the sarcophagus of Kutulu was said to be buried, and he the High Priest of the Old Ones himself, still dripping wet from the sunken city where he lay, dead but dreaming. It was *all* about Death, somehow, and the sheer mathematics of it made his head hurt; but at that moment, in that shamanic ritual on the beach, the Goddess and the Old One were like particle and wave, two forms of a central premise that could not be embraced or identified until one was destroyed and the other survived.

The collapse of the wave function.

Which was pretty funny, Angell thought. Because, well, both Lara Kidul and Kutulu lived beneath the waves.

He was frightened by the Goddess, but felt protected by her. He had spent his lifetime studying and teaching religion until one tragic afternoon when he found himself disgusted by it. He had become full of hatred towards God and denied any kind of spiritual reality. He had studied a phenomenon that had persisted for thousands of years, something people all over the world believed in, lived for, and killed for, and there had never been any actual proof that this phenomenon—religion—was based on anything even remotely *real*. He had never, in his entire life, experienced the supernatural directly until a misfired ritual beneath a mountain in Nepal caused him to kill a man, and which was when and where he acquired the *Necronomicon* … and had never experienced the Divine directly, until that day months later on Parangtritis Beach when an alien Goddess blessed him with her severity. A part of him knew that he was falling apart; on the verge of a mental breakdown. But another part of him knew that he was coming together, on the verge of a mental breakthrough.

Now, if he could only survive long enough to enjoy either one.

Book One

Verschränkung

("Entanglement")

Blake choked and turned away from the stone, conscious of some formless alien presence close to him and watching him with horrible intentness. *He felt entangled with something—*something which was not in the stone, but which had looked through it at him—something which would ceaselessly follow him with a cognition that was not physical sight.

—H. P. Lovecraft, "The Haunter of the Dark," 1935 (emphasis added)

CHAPTER ONE

Brooklyn

WASSERMAN SHOULD HAVE WAITED AT THE SCENE for Patrol to arrive, even though he was no longer on the force, but he knew that time was running out. He scanned the rooftops across the street, but was convinced about what he had seen the first time. Someone had been on top of Feil Hall when the shot was fired. Maybe it was just kids, law students taking a break. Was there a sitting area on the roof? He had no idea, but as he was thinking these things he was running.

In the distance he heard a voice calling after him.

"Loo! Loo! Where are you going?"

"This way, Danny! Call it in. I think the shooter was on the roof at Feil Hall!"

Danny was on the other side of Atlantic Avenue, arriving just in time for his meet with Wasserman, and in time for the crowd that had gathered around the dead terrorist. He pulled out his phone and called Dispatch.

Wasserman was not in the best physical shape of his life. He was already out of breath and had hardly gone a block. He would have to cut north to get onto State Street and maybe cut her off—he still thought of the shooter as "her"—if she tried to blend into the street traffic heading for Borough Hall.

That's when he remembered that Feil Hall was across the street from the Brooklyn House of Detention.

★ ★ ★

Danny got off the phone after asking for backup at the law school dorm. He advised that a former Homicide detective was already at the scene, but privately he thought his old lieutenant had lost it. There was no way your average shooter could have made the shot from that distance. It had to be, what, a hundred, a hundred and fifty yards? More? With the target walking on a crowded city street, with traffic? And not hit anyone else? That was police sniper territory, not some damned terrorist assassin or drug cartel hitter. Sure, you had military snipers who could hit a moving target at two miles or more in their sleep, but in Brooklyn? In broad daylight?

Response was fast. New York City is the target of choice for the world's angry and dispossessed and that meant that the reaction time of its law enforcement agencies was nearly instantaneous. The uniforms started sorting out the crowd and running sawhorses and yellow tape around the scene. An ambulance barged its way onto the sidewalk, waiting for permission to remove the body. Patrol cars with flashing lights were staggered all up and down Atlantic. News vans had arrived. Danny was Homicide, so he might as well make his presence known. But he knew this was going to be a high profile case, which meant the brass at One PP would take it away from him the first chance they got.

Still, he might as well get his picture in the paper while he could.

★ ★ ★

Wasserman knew a guy at the jail. He pulled out his phone and found the number as he half-walked, half-ran towards the dorm, his eyes raking all the windows and rooftops around him. Within seconds, the street in front of him starting filling up with corrections officers who started scanning the block around Feil Hall. This wasn't exactly kosher, but ever since 9/11 there were emergency protocols in place, some written down and some not. Whoever was loose and not engaged at the moment in the exercise of critical duties had poured out of the gates in response to Wasserman's call to his friend, the duty officer. There were now maybe five men and three women in uniform all along State Street in front of the jail. He saw at least two shotguns.

"Watch the exits," he shouted. "But use caution. The suspect may be armed."

"What are we looking for?"

Good question. What did he tell them? He had no idea.

Just then, a slender young woman with striking blue eyes stepped out of the main door of the dorm, carrying a package under her arm.

★ ★ ★

Something about the way she looked at him. And the package, which was rectangular and suggestive of a long gun in a flower box. Their eyes met, and her expression actually softened. None of the tightness he would have expected from a cornered criminal, the sign that violence was about to erupt.

He reached for his service revolver and simultaneously called out to her.

"Ma'am. Please stop where you are! Police business! Stop, and put down the box! Slowly!"

The corrections officers all jumped at the sound of his voice and looked where he was pointing. They began to form a cordon around the block and the young woman.

But Wasserman *wasn't* a cop anymore. He was a civilian, with a weapon pointed at a young woman and the sound of sirens everywhere as his backup had arrived.

"Put down the weapon! Put it down!"

The street was full of nervous cops who didn't know what the hell they were looking at. There were Corrections officers all over the place, but that was normal as they were outside the House of Detention. And there was this old guy holding an even older piece, looking like he was about to shoot a student coming out of the law school dorm.

Wasserman realized they were shouting at *him*.

He looked around and saw that about a dozen patrolmen were pointing their 9mm Glocks at *him*. He had no choice.

He gently put his revolver onto the sidewalk, speed-talking all the while.

"I'm a retired detective from Brooklyn South. I saw a shooter on the roof of this building. This woman is a suspect in a homicide...."

Before he could finish, he was on the ground with his hands

behind his back. A patrolman fished his wallet out of his back pocket and found his ID.

"Detective Lieutenant Wasserman, retired," he read aloud.

They lifted him up and apologized for the confusion.

But the young woman with the flower box and the brilliant blue eyes had disappeared.

CHAPTER TWO

Brooklyn

WASSERMAN FOUND HIMSELF SITTING ALONE in an interrogation room.

This was a little insulting considering he was a veteran of NYPD, a gold shield no less, with a lot of friends at One PP. But he was not only a witness to the shooting of someone with a diplomatic visa, but had pulled a gun on the street in front of civilians. And then there was that issue with the Department of Corrections and their officers flooding onto State Street.

Finally the door opened and an officer he did not recognize entered the room. He appeared about forty, florid-faced and sweating. An Irish cop out of Central Casting, maybe from some Seventies-era movie about corrupt policemen and a hero detective, or something. Wasserman sympathized. The guy had a dead diplomat on his hands, even if said diplomat was a terrorist, and a retired cop on the scene who may have lost them the perp.

"My name is Beauchamp. I'm with the CT," he said, without preamble and with an attitude.

"The Counter Terrorism bureau."

"That's correct. Working with the Joint Terrorist Task Force. I understand you were on the job?"

"All my life."

"Gold shield? Homicide?"

"Right on both counts."

"Then what the fuck were you thinking?"

Wasserman looked pointedly at the file Beauchamp was carrying.

"You have my statement."

"This piece of shit?" He waved Wasserman's hand-written account of the event in his face.

Wasserman just looked at the man in the eyes.

"It says here you saw something on the roof of Feil Hall. That law school dormitory. Right?"

"Yeah. So?"

"There's no way you could have seen anything that far away. Roof's like twenty stories up. You were blocks from there, on Atlantic. You trying to tell me ..."

"Look. I saw what I saw. I had Danny—Detective Dugin—call it in. I ran towards the building ..."

"And called the DOC while you were at it ..."

"I thought they could help."

"Being they are, like, actual law enforcement officers and you aren't? And what do you mean, you had Dugin call it in? He works for you?"

"We used to work together, at Brooklyn South."

"What were the two of you doing at the crime scene?"

"I was gonna meet him there, on another case."

"What *case*? You ain't working for us no more!"

"He asked for my opinion on a homicide, that's all. It's related to an old case of mine from last year."

"And the two of you just happened to be on the same block in the same neighborhood as what might be the City's most high-profile assassination in decades? And then you move half the fucking Department to a law school dorm blocks away from the scene on a hunch? You gotta take this act to Vegas, Wasserman. The Amazing Fucking Kreskin or some shit."

"Why don't you ask Danny? He'll fill you in."

"I *am* asking Detective Dugin. He's in the next room, trying to save his job. See, he still has a job to save. You, on the other hand, you're just a tourist these days. You understand me?"

"I know what I saw. There was a shooter on that roof."

The detective sighed, and slammed a file on the desk in frustration before his tone softened.

"I know. We got CCTV footage."

"*What?* So why are you busting my chops?"

"We got a dead diplomat. Or terrorist. Or whatever the hell he is. And we got you, Detective Retired Kreskin, in the right place at the right time. Maybe *you* wanted the guy dead. You're Jewish, right?"

Wasserman was stunned.

"What does that have to do with anything?"

"Dead guy was an Arab. Used to belong to the Iraqi army back in the day. Then he joined ISIS or whatever the hell they call it. ISIL. Maybe you figured, what the hell, chalk one up for Israel. Maybe you were running interference for the shooter."

"By leading the whole Department to the God spot?"

The 'God spot' was jargon for the sniper's nest, the place where the sniper could see all of creation before selecting the target. But it conjured up the lyrics to an old song in Wasserman's mind as he said it: *What if God was one of us?*

"By then it was empty. The perp was long gone."

"Just tell me one thing."

"You're in no position to demand anything, Wasserman."

"The shooter. Was it a woman?"

The detective looked up from his file, and took a moment before answering.

"Yeah, it was a skirt. Skinny little number. Face was obscured. She was wearing one of those veil things. But it was Atlantic Avenue, so there's a lot of that going around."

"Old, young?"

He shrugged.

"We got photo analysis working on it, but the consensus is young. Probably under thirty."

"What young woman gets that kind of training? Israeli Army, maybe?"

"Why not the Arabs?"

Wasserman shook his head.

"They use women as human shields, or as suicide bombers. They don't put them in combat. They sure as hell don't want them handling firearms. But you know that already. It's what you do." He sighed. "I don't know. I'm out of my depth on this one."

"Just what I wanted to hear. You'll go home, right? Stay away from this thing now that we've caught it. Play golf, or whatever you old fucks do."

"And Danny?"

"Dugin's alright. We know about the dead baby doctor and all that. He's been cleared."

"So you were just fucking with me."

"I'm in the Counter Terrorism bureau. It's what we do."

★ ★ ★

Wasserman stepped out onto the street. They gave him back his piece and told him to scurry on home, he might be in time for the early-bird special at his local diner. He smiled good-naturedly, but inside he was seething. He knew that a lot had changed since the old days on the Force, but this counter-terrorist environment was poisonous.

He passed by a newsstand and saw copies of the *Daily News* and the *Post*: the alpha and the omega of the New York City media world. Or the Mutt and Jeff. They both carried stories of the shooting on Atlantic Avenue, with photographs of the dead diplomat. He heard Beauchamp telling a guy in the hallway outside the interrogation room that they pulled a slug from the guy's skull. Head shot, from that distance? This was a professional hit, and it was carried out by a young woman. That had to narrow down the list of possible suspects, he thought.

But then he remembered why he had been there in the first place. It was that homicide Danny was wrapped up in.

He reached into his pocket for his phone and his fingers felt a scrap of paper. Pulling it out, he remembered that he had written down the phone number of that agency in DC, the one that was paying Angell's rent. He had wanted to call them and find out what was going on, but now he wasn't a cop anymore and moreover the CT people were probably monitoring his calls. He didn't trust Beauchamp's dismissal of himself and Danny as immaterial to his case. Maybe he should find a payphone. There still must be one somewhere in Brooklyn.

CHAPTER THREE

Fort Meade, Maryland

AUBREY WAS EXPECTED. Monroe opened the door to his office and let his old friend into the windowless inner sanctum.

"I have the final report on the Nepal and Pinecastle arrests."

The ritual in Nepal had been raided by government agents a year earlier. There were bodies, and some of them had taken months to identify. Other participants in the ritual had been apprehended at the scene, but they were not carrying identification. Officials had to rely on fingerprints and other means of determining identity. Some of those apprehended alive had no criminal or government or law enforcement profiles so fingerprints alone were not useful.

It had been a long, tedious process that was complicated by the addition of suspects picked up in the Pinecastle raid, plus the raids on other Dagon sites worldwide: including on Long Island, in Massachusetts, and elsewhere in North America, as well as other sites in Europe.

The suspects were held for their role in human trafficking, which gave Monroe and his team the legal justification for the raids; the added discovery of terrorist connections to the human trafficking rings gave them the ability to hold several of the suspects in isolation in various black sites.

It had been a large, well-coordinated series of police actions across international time zones, involving law enforcement as well as intelligence agency elements. And they were only just now getting a handle on all the ramifications. While the raids had been successfully executed, the sharing of intelligence after the fact was not so seamless and cooperative. Even within the American intelligence community there was a reluctance to share information across agencies and jurisdictions, and Monroe knew that some data was being withheld from his people. It wasn't particularly fair, but as an old hand at this sort of thing Monroe knew what to expect.

"What do we have?"

"Well, we've identified many of those picked up in Nepal, but not all. You have some celebrities of various kinds, financiers, corrupt politicians, that sort of thing. Most of them are not names that would be familiar to the average American. We have mid-level politicos from India and Nepal, as you would expect from the location of the first raid. There were two officers from ISI, Pakistani intelligence, found at the scene. One of them had been killed in some kind of explosion before the team arrived. The other was taken alive as he was trying to escape."

He handed a dossier over to Monroe, with photographs of the two officers and one photo of a dead body.

"There was a Bollywood actor as well, and a Chinese actress from Hong Kong. Both were taken alive as they tried to flee. Then you've got three Eastern European businessmen, a Croatian woman active in the arts scene in Zagreb, and a Russian oligarch with ties to Zhirinovsky, Dugin and their associates, the occult Nazi types. They are all at black sites now. As their arrests were never made public, no one knows where they are or what happened to them. Not too many news crews up there in the Himalayas. And their respective governments do not want the publicity in any case."

Monroe studied the files as they were handed to him.

"Any connections between these people besides Dagon?"

Aubrey shook his head.

"Not that we can find. There are a few financial transactions that are suspicious, some property here and there owned by interlocking shell corporations, and we're working on that. But nothing so far."

"Okay. What about the Pinecastle raids?"

"There's considerably more intel on that little episode. Since several of the raids took place in the United States, we were able to do a lot more digging. Having living suspects has also made the research a little easier, though not by much. Dagon has maintained its policy of leaving no digital footprint, so there is very little in the way of emails and no social media profile at all. Their members have been instructed to stay off the Internet or risk ... well, whatever Dagon metes out by way of punishment for infractions. It's serious enough that most everyone obeys. But there have been a few exceptions. Once the raid was taking place, someone notified a European contact so that they could escape the raid in Turin. That was important. It is believed we just missed apprehending a senior member or two there, just by minutes."

"But the high priestess was killed on-site in Pinecastle, right? Shouldn't that mean that Dagon is finished?"

"From what we have been able to determine from prisoner interrogations—those who dropped hints here and there, or who were just bragging—Dagon is organized like an ancient city-state in some ways. There is a high priest or priestess, in charge of the religious functions, and a kind of monarch in charge of the political or purely organizational functions. Now they mat have lost their religious leaders, but there is evidence that their political structure survived, at least as a skeleton crew. These are the people in charge of communications, finding real estate they can use to hold the ceremonies, that sort of thing."

"Who's in charge of timing the rituals and selecting the sites? Wouldn't that be a purely religious function?"

"I see where you're going with this, Dwight, but the short answer is I just don't know. And how could they conduct a ritual of any kind without their religious leadership?"

"We have to assume that their political leadership is composed of initiates. Nothing else would make sense. They don't control any actual territory, like a city-state. They are a floating kingdom in that sense. And why would anyone belong to Dagon who wasn't an initiate?"

"All good points. If they have been deprived of their priestess, my assumption is that they would simply try to replace her from within their own ranks. But there is another issue to consider."

Aubrey flipped through some of the folders, and then just set them all down on Monroe's desk as he gathered his thoughts.

"There is the genetic component."

"Explain, please."

"It's really for the same reason Dagon needs Angell as well as the Book. The high priestess and her consort were believed to be descendants, in some way, of the beings they call the Old Ones. Hybrids, if you will. Part human, part whatever-the-hell the Old Ones are. They were probably conceived through a similar ritual. That was the point of Pinecastle, after all. First, to provide a means for the Old Ones to penetrate the sphere of the Earth, and second to impregnate the girls they called the 'breeders.' The whole operation was conceived as a kind of stud farm for aliens."

"You have a way with words. So what was the point of the Nepal ritual?"

"They thought they could 'open the Gate' and let the Old Ones in without going through the breeder route. It was a shotgun approach to the problem. Find the point on the surface of the Earth with the most direct connection to their leader—Cthulhu or Kutulu—and then drag It up from the depths of Hell to breach the Gate by force. When that didn't work, so they went to Plan B."

"Open the Gate wide enough to allow the Old Ones to procreate with humans. As had been done at least once before, with their high priestess as the result."

"Precisely."

"But now that the ritual failed, what is Plan C?"

"Well, that's the problem. The ritual didn't fail. Not completely. Some of the girls are pregnant. We just don't know what the eventual outcome of that will be. But their time is drawing near. Those girls will be giving birth shortly. We have no backup plan for this ourselves, and I think we're going to need one."

CHAPTER FOUR

Secure location, Virginia countryside

THE MORE THEY TRIED TO MAKE IT LOOK CHEERFUL, the more it just made them miserable. The huge decals on the walls of cartoon characters unknown to these children from villages in Iraq and Syria loomed menacing and sinister. The desperate, toothy smiles of animals painted onto the cinderblock walls in hallucinogenic colors were seen as threatening to some of the kids, or like some kind of cynical joke to the older ones. Maybe it just seemed worse because of the noise.

The sounds never stopped. Clanging, banging, and the loud, boisterous speech in languages they had never heard before and could not understand. The smallest ones stood like statues in the corners of their chain-link cages with haunted expressions. The older ones were sullen and unresponsive.

And then there were a few that were pregnant.

Harry and Sylvia had taken it upon themselves to visit periodically the secret facility in northern Virginia where the eleven survivors had been assigned after the raid on the cult ritual in the Ocala National Forest in Florida, northwest of DeLand. The ritual had been an elaborate ceremony involving these kidnapped children from a variety of countries who had been sold into slavery to the cult by a sleek operation headquartered in Turkey and run by Daesh: the terror organization known to the world as ISIL or the Islamic State of Iraq and the Levant. The two officials from the National Security Agency had been instrumental in locating the site back in November. In fact, it was Harry—whose specialty at NSA was analyzing child pornography—who had brought the existence of the cult to the attention of his superiors at Fort Meade.

It took a while, but eventually the small ad hoc group within NSA headed by Dwight Monroe—the "Ancient of Days" as he was known, behind his back anyway—and bolstered by his longtime associate Aubrey and the eccentric Simon, had figured out what the cult was going to do and how they would go about it. The ritual involved opening a kind of supernatural "Gate" between this world and ... well, some Other World ... that would permit evil entities access to the planet. While no one at NSA took that possibility very seriously, what they did treat with sober attention was the requirement that the cult perform ritual sacrifice using these kidnapped girls. Whether or not one believed in occultism and magical powers was irrelevant: the girls really were going to be killed or raped as part of the ritual, and that is what Monroe and his colleagues were going to stop.

While they had saved the girls from being slaughtered, they were not able to save all of them from being sexually abused. To make matters worse, there was no way the government would be able to send the girls back to their home countries without sending them back to die. Some of the girls from the other cult sites in the US and Europe were from Nigeria and had been abducted and sold into slavery by Boko Haram; the girls from Syria and Iraq, largely Yezidis, had been abducted by ISIL. There was literally nowhere for the girls to go, and no way to identify their families.

After a month or two of frenzied paperwork and database searches, they were no closer to solving the problem than they had been on the night of the ritual, but there had been a development anyway. Three of the girls were found to be pregnant. And two of the other girls had developed special ... abilities.

"I didn't sign up for this," whispered Harry, the analyst, to his boss Sylvia Matos during their latest visit to the facility. He was staring at the rows of children—all young girls—and shuddering.

"They didn't, either," she responded. She was just as disgusted and horrified, but tried not to show it. She wanted the girls to see her as sympathetic, even maternal. They needed a friend and an ally in this desperate place.

"How can we get them out of here?"

Sylvia shook her head. "The red tape is unbelievable. It's only because we identified all of these girls as material witnesses in a federal investigation that we were able to save them from being deported, or worse. But now ..."

"Now we've got three of them due to give birth in a few months."

Sylvia didn't need to be reminded. Those girls were already quite large, and she didn't want to think what kind of monstrous future they and their offspring would have.

Abortion had been considered, but there was nothing they could do. The Nigerian victims were mostly Muslim with one or two Christians, and the Yezidis were, well, Yezidis. There were a lot of religious and cultural issues concerning virginity, marriage, rape, sexual abuse, and abortion. When gently asked about it, the girls looked confused and terrified. No one could predict if it would be better for them to carry to term, or not. No matter what choice was made, the psychological trauma for these victims would be enormous. Generally speaking, Islamic scholars permit the abortion of a fetus conceived through rape up to four months, but that would have accounted for only one of the girls, a young Nigerian named Chisimdi being held at a separate facility in Massachusetts, and by the time they knew she was pregnant it was too late.

And then there is the Helms Amendment.

It is official government policy to prohibit US foreign assistance to be used for abortions, even those caused by rape and war abroad. It was introduced by Jesse Helms in 1973 as a reaction to *Roe vs Wade*, and attempts since then to overturn the Helms Amendment have been unsuccessful. While the Amendment stresses the intention that abortion not be used as a means of family planning, it has been interpreted in the extreme to include sexual abuse, incest, and even rape: the very situation that the Florida girls found themselves in. Even though the girls were in US custody in United States territory, their legal status was uncertain and no one wanted to make a decision. And what happens when no one makes a decision in the case of pregnancy? Babies.

And then there were the other, younger, girls.

At first, it had been assumed that they were either acting out, or were suffering dissociative episodes due to their emotional and physical abuse at the hands of the cult. Analysis and therapy was made more difficult due to language issues and a woeful lack of cultural knowledge. The child psychologists they had on staff were at a loss to account for all of the symptoms, but once the preliminary report had crossed Monroe's desk he recognized the problem immediately.

The girls would lapse into trance states and begin channeling the very Old Ones that the cult had been trying to contact.

The damage had been done.

★ ★ ★

Sylvia noticed one girl standing apart from the others. She could not have been more than ten years old. She was one of the Yezidi children. Her eyes were glazed over, and her shoulders were slumped. Although all of the children were being taken care of, dressed in neatly-washed and pressed clothes and given hot showers daily, there was something about this girl that was unclean and somehow … diseased. There was an odor coming off of her that was not due to poor hygiene. Sylvia had heard that certain neurological disorders could generate bad smells as a symptom, but she wasn't sure if this was settled science or not.

"Hypermethioninemia," came a voice from behind them.

They turned to face one of the doctors who was assigned to this case. She was tall, serious-looking, and about forty-five. The name tag on her white lab coat said *Devata*.

"You noticed the strange smell? Like boiled cabbage? It may be due to a genetic deficiency. We are still running tests, but so far they are inconclusive."

"Could it be neurological?" asked Sylvia.

Devata shrugged. "It could be. She is unresponsive most of the time. It's a question of whether a genetic condition causes the hypermethioninemia or if there is some other etiology to consider."

"Does she talk at all?"

"Meyan? Only sometimes, and then it's not in response to questions or to any of our staff trying to communicate with her. She starts speaking for a few moments, sometimes in a whisper and other times in a loud voice, almost a growl, and then stops and goes perfectly silent again, often for many hours. Unfortunately, there is no one here who speaks her language, so we don't know what she is saying. We taped her during one episode, if you would care to listen to it. I know there is a security issue, so we have not been able to send it out for analysis."

"What about the others?"

Devata frowned. "The youngest ones are all about the same. They don't communicate very well. They never smile. The older ones are more *present*, but they are obviously very traumatized. The pregnant girls are another story, though. They are in a constant state of anxiety. Of course, they are way too young to be mothers but that's beside the point. These girls were forced into sex under heinous circumstances from what I understand, and they … I don't know how to say this … they seem to be *afraid* of their own babies."

This was shocking to Harry, whose entire mission within the vaults of Fort Meade was hunting child traffickers and pornographers but who was unprepared for this face-to-face confrontation with the results of the evil he tracked through the Web. "Jesus. I mean, have they tried to harm them? The babies, I mean?"

"No, not so far. But they seem to create a kind of distance between themselves and their babies. There is no tenderness, no maternal emotions that we can detect. It is as if the fetuses are tumors: growths of tissue that are foreign to them. I can't quite explain it. I know I am not communicating this well. But they seem to regard their swollen bellies as creatures external to themselves."

They continued to walk down a long corridor with a series of cage-like cells on one side and the garishly-decorated cinderblock wall on the other.

"Do you have a list of the children we brought you back in November?" Sylvia was worried about something.

"Yes, of course. It's in my office."

"There seems to be fewer of them now than in November."

Devata shook her head. "No, I don't think so. You brought us a total of eleven children. Of those, three turned out to be pregnant. Another three had been sexually molested to various degrees. The remaining five were the youngest ones, the least responsive of the lot. They are all still here."

"I only counted nine so far."

"Oh. Yes, well. The other two are in isolation."

"Isolation? Why is that?"

"You'll have to see for yourself, I'm afraid."

Devata pulled out a set of keys from her belt and stopped in front of a steel door that was embedded in the cinderblock wall. It had been painted the same color as the wall, so they hadn't noticed it before.

She unlocked the door and stood aside to let the two NSA officials inside.

"This is one of the two. Each is in her own room. We let them out one hour a day, but always when the others are not around to see them. That means during lunch, when we try to get all the girls to eat together in the lunch room."

In front of them, sitting on a narrow cot that was built into the wall, was a Kurdish girl of about thirteen years old. The only light came from a fluorescent bulb behind a wire cage in the ceiling. There were no cartoon drawings or cheerful decorations here. Only industrial grade grey paint, and a toilet and sink in one corner.

The girl acted as if she was completely alone. She didn't seem to stir at their arrival, or give them any indication that she knew they were there.

"Yasemina? How are you feeling today?"

The girl named Yasemina did not respond. Her eyes were open, but unseeing. They were not even sure she was breathing.

"Yasemina was one of those captured by ISIL. She was sold into slavery in Libya. The people who arranged that were careful not to touch her sexually. For some reason they needed her intact, you understand?"

Sylvia and Harry understood, all too well.

"But something happened to her in Florida, as you know."

"She told you all this?"

Devata nodded. "When she was first brought to us, back in November. One of our guards speaks Kurdish. But then something happened. One of the other girls, a much younger one, began talking to her. And Yasemina stopped speaking. Withdrew completely. Wouldn't eat or sleep. And then one day soon after she attacked the guard and almost killed him. That was about two weeks ago."

Sylvia stared at her in disbelief.

"This small child? She can't weigh more than seventy pounds!"

"It took three strong men to get her off him. She bit off half his face before we were able to rescue him."

That is when they noticed that the girl was shackled to the cot.

"This isn't right. Why weren't we notified? You can't keep her chained to the bed, for chrissakes. She's just a child! A child who has gone through a terrible ordeal."

"You *were* notified. We sent word through channels. And she may be a child, but she is also homicidal. You have your orders, but we have our protocols. We keep her sedated for most of the day. Those shackles are for her protection as well as ours."

"And the other girl? The other one in isolation?"

"This way."

Devata led them out of the cell and locked the door behind them before walking a short distance down the same corridor to the next nondescript door.

This cell was the same as the first, almost a mirror image with the cot on the left side of the room instead of the right. As they opened the door, a whiff of that same odor they noticed coming from Meyan assailed them like a fist. They could hear sounds coming from a far corner.

"This is Nalin's room."

The sight of the catatonic Kurdish girl was bad enough, but this time it was a younger girl—a Yezidi—who sat in the corner of the bleak cell and rocked back and forth, humming. Her eyes were wide and staring, even as her mouth was twisted in a hideous half-smile. One could say that the girl was glaring at them, as if they had committed some horrible affront by coming there. The overall impression was one of madness erupting from a deep well of hatred. Whoever or whatever it was that rocked in the corner and hummed, it was not Nalin. Not anymore.

The three—Devata, Sylvia, and Harry—just stood in the room close to the door as if ready to run if they had to. They did not get this feeling of dread and violence in Yasemina's room even though the Kurdish girl had become violent and tried to kill a guard. Nalin, though, seemed about to spring at them, and something inside Sylvia broke at that moment as she realized she was looking at a girl no older than eight or nine as if she was a wild animal.

Then, she felt the hairs on the back of her neck start to stand up as Nalin slowly turned to face her directly.

She started to speak, in a husky, almost guttural tone, first low in volume, wheedling, almost flirtatious, but gradually working up to an angry howl. The syllables at first were indistinct, like baby talk, but then took on a more unsettling shape.

"*Ia. Ia. Ia. N'gai, n'gha'ghaa, bugg-shoggog, y'hah', Yog Sothoth. Yog-Sothoth!*"

As Nalin reached a crescendo they could hear an answering scream from the room they had just vacated, and then the scream was picked up from everywhere at the installation, as if wolves or coyotes were responding to each other across lonely desert sands or the vast frozen wastes of interstellar space.

★ ★ ★

They were sitting in Devata's office, trying to collect themselves, as the doctor explained the situation the best she could.

"You have not had much experience with the mentally ill, I assume."

All Sylvia and Harry could do was nod, each wrapped in their own reactions to the screaming children.

"It's worse with children. This degree of psychosis is not only unusual, it's … it's unnatural in someone pre-pubescent. Of the two children in isolation, it's the younger child who is in control. The older child merely follows orders. That's why we keep both of them isolated, from each other as well as from the others."

It was Harry who spoke first.

"You said that you were keeping the older girl sedated. Yasemina? Why not the younger girl as well?"

"We tried that with Nalin, of course. It didn't work. The sedative wore off almost immediately. Since she wasn't violent, didn't attack anyone and didn't try to harm herself, we had no reason to keep her sedated. Anyway, it's dangerous for a child that small to be kept on anti-psychotics for any length of time."

"What will happen to her?"

Devata looked down at the file in front of her, but wasn't really reading it. Her mind was far away.

"Without a diagnosis that makes any sense, a prognosis is impossible. Nalin has been with us since November, and in that time we have seen a gradual deterioration of her mental state. We are worried about her effect on the other girls, especially the younger ones. They are already starting to exhibit signs of dissociation that they did not have when they first arrived."

"Are you saying that somehow Nalin is … is *contagious*?"

"No, Ms. Matos, not at all. This is not an organic illness, something communicable like a microbe or a bacterium. But there have been cases of mass hysteria in children …"

"Like the Salem witchcraft trials."

Devata looked up at Sylvia with a hollow expression, and Sylvia realized that she had struck a nerve.

"Yes.You could say that.We don't have a lot of data on that case. It was three hundred years ago ..."

"But you looked into it.You thought it might be relevant.Why?"

The doctor took a breath before answering.

"Scholars are divided as to what transpired in Salem in 1692. Remember that people actually were executed for witchcraft in Salem. Nineteen of them, to be exact. And all on the basis of spectral evidence. In other words, evidence that could not be seen or measured by anyone except the accusers themselves. It was enough for one of the girls to claim that someone had possessed them, or caused demons to persecute them, and that testimony was considered evidence and used to indict and convict innocent persons. But there *was* something wrong in Salem. It *was* a case of mass hysteria, with girls throwing fits and screaming, having seizures. But the adults went along with it. So there were two different conditions taking place there, one among the children and one among the adults. To what degree were the adults manipulating the children, to get the results they wanted? Maybe to get rid of a troublesome neighbor, or acquire a piece of land?"

"What are you trying to say?"

"Look, I don't want to tell you your business. I know that you rescued these girls from some horrible fate. But they were being manipulated and used by adults. They were traumatized. In some cases, even sexually abused and raped. And now, aren't we doing the same thing to them all over again? Haven't you bought into the same mindset as their abusers, believing the same things, feeding into the same hysteria?"

Harry felt himself getting angry at the accusation, and he saw Sylvia tighten in response as well.

But Devata went on.

"These kids need a normal environment. Sunshine. Fresh air.

Love from caring parents. They're not going to get that in here. And they're not going to get that if we send them back. So they have no choice but to relive the circumstances that led to their dissociations, basically creating the only lifestyle they shared in common. And it was hideous."

Harry had had enough. He leaned over and punctuated his remarks with a finger stabbing directly at the doctor.

"You're right. We can't send them back to their home countries, at least not in their present circumstances. They would be ostracized at best, punished severely at worst. Probably imprisoned. Tortured. Killed. What do you want us to do? Put them all on a plane bound for Baghdad or Damascus and wish them the best of luck? They were trafficked, kidnapped from their homes; their families in many cases were slaughtered. If we keep them here, we have to find homes for them. Orphanages. Foster parents. And how are we going to do that, even if we could legally? They don't speak English; most of these kids are Yezidi, which means they are not Muslim, not Christian, not any kind of religion or culture that most Americans can understand. But the one thing we do know—the reason they are here—is that they are material witnesses to one of the worst terrorist networks in the world right now, one that spans the globe and will go to any lengths to achieve their goals. If we send them back out onto the street anywhere on the planet, their lives would be forfeit. The people who trafficked them want them back, for reasons we can only imagine. So while I appreciate your desire to have these kids cavort in the sunshine and fresh air, for the time being we will have to behave like pricks and keep them locked up. And if you find this too demanding, or depressing, no problem. We will find someone else to run this operation. No harm, no foul. Up to you."

Doctor Devata sat back under the onslaught. Sylvia was noticeably silent, but her expression said it all. She agreed with Harry, and was rather surprised at the vehemence with which he voiced the concerns that were on both their minds. He also had absolutely no authority to replace Devata or anyone else for that matter, but she applauded his chutzpah nevertheless.

Taking a breath, Devata responded.

"Your job is national security. Mine is the welfare of these children. I understand we can't send them away, or find homes for them right now. But I have to emphasize that whatever it is they went through last year is still having a serious effect on their mental health. You saw Nalin. You saw her affect, and how she controls the reactions of the others. The other girls display similar behaviors. That's why I have been forced to isolate them. And they are getting worse. They are more agitated every day, as if they are expecting something to happen."

"What do you mean?" asked Sylvia.

"You know how American kids start getting antsy as Christmas or Halloween approaches? More energetic, more aware? Focused on the holiday, the gifts or the candy? These kids are doing the same, except there are no holidays coming up … well, at least none that I am aware of. Maybe on the Yezidi religious calendar? Anyway, they would have no knowledge of the calendar in here. Every day is pretty much the same. We don't let them watch broadcast television, because we find that news programs can be triggering to young children who have experienced trauma. So we play pre-recorded cartoons or something equally innocuous. But these girls … they watch them, but with serious expressions. They're seeing something else. I don't know what. But in the last week or so they have been getting anxious. Worried. Even desperate in some cases. Not the pregnant ones; they seem resigned, somehow. But the others … especially the youngest ones. They're starting to come apart, and I don't know what to do."

After a few more minutes of discussion, Sylvia and Harry felt it was time to leave. They had the information they wanted, and had seen the children again. They got the recording that Devata had promised them on a thumb drive, and got back in their car for the drive to Fort Meade.

Harry plugged the drive into a USB port in the car, and through the speaker system they heard the same eerie chant that Nalin had uttered, the one that caused the whole place to respond in kind. In the silence of the car, it was even more unsettling. Harry unplugged the drive immediately.

"It sounds like the same words, exactly," said Sylvia, when she had stopped shaking.

"Yes. I think it is. Which makes me more nervous. If it was just childish babbling, it wouldn't be so bad. But this means there is a language and a meaning behind it. It doesn't sound like Kurmanji."

Sylvia shook her head as she drove.

"No, it's not."

"Simon will probably be able to identify it, or find someone who could."

Sylvia thought for a moment. The sun was going down and the shadows lengthened.

"Or Dwight. It occurs to me that this is something Dwight might be familiar with."

Harry never knew the extent to which Sylvia knew about Dwight's past, but she always surprised him.

"You know, there is one thing we should address."

"What's that?"

"We have to separate them," Harry said. "We can't have the channeling girls in contact with the pregnant girls."

Sylvia just shook her head. "I know what you're saying, but if we split them up now it might be even more traumatic, especially for the youngest ones."

"But if they stay together, won't the pregnant girls start freaking out when they realize what the others are doing?"

He was right, of course, but they were between a rock and a hard place. Sylvia tried to think of these children as you would survivors of abuse in general. They needed comfort, therapy, counseling, some connection to their own culture. Normalcy. Doctor Devata was right, even if they disagreed on the specifics. If she thought of them as cult members or sacrificial victims to some ancient demonic Being, then she would just freeze up or go crazy and that wouldn't help anyone.

She thought of her own culture and background as a child growing up in Melaka, in the country of Malaysia. Her parents were Portuguese Christians whose ancestors had sailed the Straits of Melaka almost two hundred years ago. She grew up surrounded by Malay Muslims, Chinese Buddhists and Indian devotees of Kali. She remembered as a child being taken to a *dukun*—a kind of shaman— in order to cure her stutter. The shaman was nominally a Muslim, but his indigenous esoteric practice would have been forbidden in a fundamentalist Muslim society. He believed her stutter to be the result of demonic forces, and he channeled a local saint with power over evil *jinn*. Whatever it was, she was cured after that one visit.

Sylvia had watched the girls walk up and down in their cage-like cells. They lacked affect. They were emotionally dark, as if someone had switched off a light inside their souls. They were like ... like zombies.

That's when something clicked, and Sylvia suddenly thought she had found a solution. A temporary one, anyway. She smiled, and grabbed Harry by the shoulder with her right hand as she held onto the wheel with her left.

"I think I know what we can do for these girls."

CHAPTER FIVE

Detention Site Green
Thailand

He heard footsteps in the corridor outside his cell. Probably another meal of some kind. He was not sure of the time of day so didn't know if it was breakfast, lunch or dinner. He lost track of all of that a few days in. The meals were all the same anyway. Boiled rice and a strip of something green. He hoped it was a vegetable.

But it was not a meal that was delivered to his cell this time, but the possibility of salvation.

"Maxwell Prime?"

They didn't use names in here, so that was noteworthy.

"I'll see if he's available."

"What?"

"Yes. I'm Maxwell Prime. Who else would I be?"

"Stand back from the door, please."

There were only three steps in total in the whole cell, so he made use of all of them and backed himself against the opposite wall.

It was dark in the cell. It was dimly lit by a bulb in an overhead cage. It was on a dimmer switch so they sometimes turned it up high and then it was blinding. Other times it was as dim as a votary candle in a vast and empty church.

His thoughts were rambling again. He was losing it. *Keep it together, Maxwell,* he told himself.

The door clanged open. There were three men outside the cell. Two he recognized. They were his handlers. The other man he did not know. He was dressed in a tropical wool blend, light grey, with expensive leather loafers, off-white shirt, and a club tie. He was about forty, and looked like he was at home in the place. That made him nervous. He had to be either Agency, or military intelligence.

The man stepped inside and nodded to the other two who stepped away from the door, giving them a little privacy.

"You don't know me, and you don't need to. But I know you. You have been making some noise that you have something to sell. Information."

Maxwell swallowed, and then answered.

"Yes, that's right."

"Why would I believe anything you have to say? You're a traitor to your country. You misappropriated government funds. You tried to have people killed. Your dossier reads like a bad comic book. Full of colorful villains and extravagant claims. So, convince me that I'm not wasting my time."

"I'll tell you whatever you want to know …"

"No. You don't understand. I have no idea what you want to tell me, so how I can ask you what I want to know? Your background has been scrubbed. I have access to every file notation, the results of every polygraph, your bank accounts, your digital communications, all of it. And it all has been erased. Mr. Prime, you are at present a non-person. You don't exist. All you own right now is your name, and after a few more months in here you will have forgotten that as well. So, why don't we begin with what is not in your file, not in your digital footprint? Tell me something I don't know."

Prime looked around at the four walls of his cell, the place that had been home for … for however long he had been there. He was picked up in, what, November? What day was it now? What month or year? He had no clue. He was thirsty and hungry and constantly exhausted. They didn't let him sleep more than a few hours at a time, and that is if they were feeling generous or simply had forgotten to wake him up.

And this guy, this visitor. He *smelled* good. Like, *clean*. Soap. He sniffed the air. Was that cologne? Some real Hugo Boss shit, none of that Old Spice or Aramis. Fuck, he'd *drink* a bottle of Old Spice if he had one.

Jesus, he *was* losing it.

He snapped back to the present.

"It's about Monroe. Dwight Monroe. And his faithful Indian companion, James Aubrey."

The visitor was silent a moment as he considered what he was being told. Then he spoke.

"As far as I know, you have never met Dwight Monroe."

Max Prime nodded eagerly.

"That's true. I haven't. Who has? But I have worked with Aubrey and it was Aubrey who sent me here."

The visitor sighed in irritation. "Yes, I know. You're not telling me anything new."

"But do you know *why* I was sent here? Do you know what I was working on with Aubrey? Do you know why they had me running all through China as a NOC?"

The visitor shook his head. "Prime, you had embassy cover. You were not under non-official cover."

"That's where you're wrong. I didn't have embassy cover. Hell, I was ordered not to pass the embassy on the street. To stay a mile away from it. I was under deep cover, posing as an FBI agent with a tricked out business card. But that's not the worst of it. I was sent to apprehend a college professor. A freaking college professor. And not a scientist or an engineer but some kind of religion teacher. In *China*. Go figure, right? But the worst part was, I had to make sure to snatch him *and* a book he was carrying."

"A book?"

"Yeah. Can you believe that? I thought maybe it was a ledger. Payments to assets, coded transactions, weapon diagrams, org charts for the PSB, that sort of thing. But no. It was a religion book. Some kind of spooky manuscript from, like, a thousand years ago. It was nuts. But Monroe and Aubrey were all, like, you gotta go get this guy and his book. Do what you have to do, but get them. Don't fuck around. And let us know when you do."

The visitor spread his hands wide. "And, so? Did you?"

Maxwell dropped his head.

"I almost had him, the professor. I tracked him all the way to Shanghai from Beijing. He got on a boat and was headed for Singapore. I had another ship intercept him."

"Another ship?"

"Friends of mine. Previous assignment. Don't worry, no blowback."

The visitor looked like he didn't believe that, but was letting it pass. For now.

"So what went wrong?"

"The other crew resisted. They were heavily armed. They saved his ass. They got the drop on my asset and brought him to Jakarta in irons. And his ship."

"And where were you during all this?"

"Waiting in Sing'. In Geylang. The red light district. Hey, it's legal there. Anyway, I was gonna meet the ship at the port and take the professor into custody. Problem solved. Hail the conquering hero. But Aubrey didn't like my methods …"

"Or maybe the fact that you failed."

"…and he had me picked up in Singapore. The rest is history."

"I still don't understand what it is you have to sell. All I hear is the sad story of how some college professor outsmarted you. Not exactly a bullet point on your resume."

Maxwell nodded.

"You have a point. But what you don't know is why all of this happened in the first place. What you don't know is that Dwight Monroe is insane. Senile. Off the rails. He's running ops from Fort Meade like he thinks he's M from the Bond movies. And Aubrey is his Q. They're using the entire intel community like their personal army. Do you know he fielded a JSOC team in Nepal, just to find this professor? And you think *I* fucked up? They didn't catch him then, and they still can't find him now. And all because of a magic book and some psycho end-of-the-world shit. Ghosts and goblins and space aliens, or some crap like that. And you have me in here and him out there. Who's the real threat to national security?"

"Can you prove any of this?"

"Get me outta here and I will."

CHAPTER SIX

Joshua Tree, California

It was more caravanserai than parking lot. It was an expanse of desert sand split only by some shrubbery here and there with volunteers working as parking attendants waving at the drivers and their dust-encrusted vehicles and pointing to empty slots seemingly visible only to them.

Gloria pushed her little Japanese import as far into the space as it would go. She didn't have a ticket to the event; she would have to walk through a maze of trails between buildings and sand and more sand before she could find the office and the people who sold the tickets. She had called ahead, but was not optimistic that her details were faithfully recorded by the Deadhead on the other end of the line.

She was exhausted. The past six or seven months had been a living hell. She started driving from a motel parking lot in Whately, Massachusetts and now here she was in Joshua Tree, California. The stops she had made along the way had done nothing to alleviate her terror and her desperation, even as her stomach began to grow to an abnormally large size with the strange and gestating fetus within.

She had stopped for awhile in New York City, staying with a high school friend for a few weeks as she pondered her options. She wound up visiting a doctor there, in Brooklyn. A nice man who didn't charge very much and who ran all the usual tests. It was definite. She was pregnant, alright.

With twins.

Her friend insisted she stay with her through the delivery, but Gloria was not enthusiastic about the idea. For one thing, her friend's apartment—like too many New York City apartments—was tiny and overpriced. She couldn't imagine staying there for any length of time, and especially not with a newborn baby. And she couldn't help much with the rent.

For another thing, it was getting harder and harder to come up with reasons why she wasn't with her two sons.

She first told her friend that they were staying with her ex-husband while she figured out a few things. But when she didn't call her kids or get calls from them, it started to look a little suspicious.

And then the bombshell.

The ob/gyn had noticed something unusual with her latest sonogram. She left his office in total shock, walking down the street to the subway station in a daze. Something very unusual had taken place, he told her. His worried expression almost sent her running out the door until he calmed her and said that it was nothing life-threatening, but that her sonogram showed that one of her twins was "missing."

That's what he said. "Missing." How do you lose a twin when you're pregnant with him?

And they were males. She instinctively knew, but he confirmed it. Well, one male now. The other one had already taken off. Pretty much summed up her experience with men up to this point.

That's when she broke down laughing in the middle of the sidewalk. That's when she knew she couldn't stay in New York but had to leave, to find an answer to what was happening to her before she lost her mind.

And now here she was. At a UFO convention. In Southern California. Where else?

Standing in the middle of the desert sand, as if he had just landed there, was a young man who had gone missing from his home in Whately, Massachusetts back in November, on the same day that Gloria discovered she was pregnant; the same day her boys disappeared. Jean-Paul was gaunt and hollow-eyed. He had been off his usual diet of junk food and beer for something like six months or more and had lost a lot of weight. He had had … experiences … and wasn't sure anymore about who he was or what he was doing. He had started off to attend a secret ritual in an old tobacco field outside of town, and suddenly he was missing time. Maybe the ritual had worked? Maybe he was initiated now? Maybe that's how it happened?

He didn't know, but here he was on the other side of the continent and the heat and the light were pounding on his skull. He felt he had powers. Abilities. Could see things. Could hear things. But he had no control over them. Stuff just happened to him. And then there were the weird shapes that sometimes showed up and seemed to delight in taunting him. Or was it haunting him? Taunt, haunt. Whatever.

And now he was seeing things again. A woman that he met while hitching to the ritual. In Massachusetts. And now, here, in fucking California.

★ ★ ★

The young woman who showed up at Joshua Tree National Park was heavily and astonishingly pregnant. She still had two months to go, but looked huge to everyone who saw her. She tried to smile at their inquiries and their well-intentioned remarks—the offers of bottled water, or a place to sit down in the shade—but the unrelenting heat of the desert sun and the carnival-like atmosphere of the gathering were taking their toll.

★ ★ ★

Gloria had come a long way from Massachusetts to be here, her last resort. She had been driving for months, ever since she realized she was pregnant after seeing the pee stick turn positive in that motel room in Whately. She didn't know how she got pregnant, because she had not had time for a relationship of any kind. She had two kids, and a job that didn't pay much back in Providence, Rhode Island. Now her two kids were missing. And a strange man had come up to her in the parking lot of the motel and told her she had to carry her baby to term and then she would get her kids back.

The whole thing was crazy, and made crazier still by the unrelenting efforts of a gene-testing lab in San Diego to get her to show up in California—with her kids—so they could run more tests. How could she tell them she no longer had her kids?

She couldn't go back home to Providence. People would notice that her sons were missing. The school would start an investigation, probably. She didn't know how that worked, but she couldn't afford to find out. They would say she sold them or got involved in some kind of illegal adoption scenario, or maybe killed them and buried them in the woods somewhere. And she was pregnant now, without a husband or significant other. They would say she was a baby factory, just getting pregnant and giving birth to children who later would be adopted by human trafficking gangs.

Or something.

And, in a way, isn't that what was happening? She knew she had not had sex in more than a year. Two years, if she was being honest. She also knew she had those bad—those really bad—experiences at night, the ones where she was taken by someone or something and then these … these things … well, she tried to block it out of her mind, but in the past few months these midnight experiences came to seem more and more relevant. Something had been done to her. Something vile. And now she was pregnant again. And the father … the father had to be some kind of … some kind of *monster*.

And what about her two sons? Who was *their* father? It was her attempt to find out that had started this whole mess. There were anomalies, they said. In the DNA of her two boys. And would she please come out to California so they could run more tests on them? That scared her. She didn't know why at first, but it did. She knew it had something to do with those awful night terrors she had. The weird dreams where she was floating through walls and through space … and then the … insertions would take place. And she would be sore between her legs as if she had spent the entire night having sex with a … with some kind of … *machine*.

So after leaving her friend in New York City she traveled west. It seemed like the right thing to do. She was getting closer to San Diego, and if push came to shove, she would throw herself on the mercy of the DNA testing lab and just surrender. Tell them the whole story. Maybe they knew more than she did about the whole thing. She still had their number, and their address. She carried it around with her like a kind of talisman. Chromo-Test it was called. And in her purse she still had the airline ticket they had mailed her from California. She wondered if she could cash it in.

It was in Phoenix that she heard about this place. There had been some kind of UFO convention there, and they had brochures about Joshua Tree and the upcoming event called Contact in the Desert. It was held out in the middle of nowhere—actually in the desert—and there were cheap motels in the vicinity where she could stay and try to figure out what was going on. She knew that there was some kind of connection between her problem and the idea of alien abductions. Not that she believed in that sort of thing, but she couldn't very well deny the weird midnight sessions with the strange machines and her sudden and unwanted and unplanned pregnancy. Maybe there was a rational explanation for it all. Maybe there was someone at Contact in the Desert who could help her understand what was happening to her.

After all, Contact in the Desert was billed as the "Woodstock of Ufology." Every UFO expert in the United States would be there. Even names she had heard of, from those History Channel shows about ancient aliens and strange artifacts in foreign countries. She knew most of that was crap—she even laughed every time she saw that guy with the weird hair who seemed to think everything was alien—but at the same time there would be serious people there. Scientists, and like that.

It was worth a shot.

★ ★ ★

Damn, it *was* her. Was she one of them? Was she one of the Order? Had she been initiated, too? This was a UFO convention of some kind. What did that have to do with anything? Why were they *both* here?

Fuck, why was *he* here?

He thought back. Thought hard. And came up dry. He couldn't remember where he had been yesterday, much less a week or a month earlier. Since Whately, his life had been one long acid trip of strange roads, lights in the sky, and things plucking and picking at him. He had bite marks on his back and on his feet. His *feet*. What the hell had bitten him on the soles of his *feet*? He had been forced to walk on his heels for miles. That was … when? A week ago? A month? Hadn't there been snow on the ground?

And those dreams. He was never sure anymore if he was awake or asleep. When he lay down to sleep he always seemed to be wide awake, his eyes open and staring into some kind of middle distance in hell. And when he was awake and walking it was like he was dreaming because nothing seemed real, nothing had edges, nothing had sharp corners. Everything was curved into angles he couldn't draw if he tried.

And the noise! It was worse out here, in the desert, where there wasn't any city traffic or construction sounds. It was silent and vast, and that is when it got worse. The pounding noise. The banging on his head. The sound of gongs being struck. Temple bells. Those long, deep trumpets Tibetan monks blew on that sounded like jet engines taking off.

But the times when the sounds stopped—and when they stopped it was sudden, all at once—that was worse. The silence was like a death sentence. It held everything in his life, every stupid mistake, every bad deed, every wet dream, every Tinder swipe (left or right, it didn't matter, because he was fucked up from the start). The silence was an accusation and an indictment and a sentence, all in one.

He had wanted to die, and was afraid that he already had.

But there, in front of him, was that woman. That meant something. He had to find out what.

CHAPTER SEVEN

NSA Headquarters,
Fort Meade, Maryland

SYLVIA AND HARRY SAT ON FOLDING CHAIRS in front of Monroe's desk in his office at Fort Meade. Sylvia was looking optimistic and energetic for the first time since the rescue of the children from the clutches of Dagon, and it was noticeable.

"Dwight, I think I have a possible solution to the problem of the Florida children."

"Florida children" is how they referred to the young girls they had rescued at the Pinecastle Range in Florida. Some of them—the youngest—had been on the verge of being sacrificed once their usefulness to the Order was exhausted. These were the ones who had been trained as "seers": communications mediums who were possessed by the spirits of the Old Ones, the Lovecraftian entities that the Order of Dagon was trying to evoke. The Order would kill them once the ritual was over, so that they could not be used by either other occultists or by the Old Ones themselves.

"Go on."

"It's a question of possession. They were possessed by ... by whatever ... during a ritual of ceremonial magic, a purely Western procedure, but the phenomenon of possession is universal. It exists in shamanism, in Afro-Caribbean religions, in Asian esoteric practices. Virtually in all cultures. I experienced that as a child in Malaysia. In fact, as for Southeast Asia, you know that better than either of us."

She was referring to Monroe's time in Vietnam during the war, when he worked for Psychological Operations.

"Our problem is we are looking at this from a purely Western perspective. Basically, we're trying to play by Dagon's rules. I don't think we are that helpless. What we need to do is enlist the aid of someone who is experienced in possession."

"I take it you don't mean an exorcist?"

"No, not at all. Listen, Dwight, Dagon is a syncretic cult, right? I mean, the whole Lovecraft element of their philosophy and their rituals is really a modern lens through which to view more ancient practices. They use Lovecraft, but also ideas culled from Renaissance magic, the Golden Dawn, and Aleister Crowley. Even Tantra. Right?"

"Yes, that's so ..."

"They've jerry-rigged a system that has Egyptian, Indian, European components, plus Jewish mysticism and Kabbalah, all mixed together with ideas from Lovecraft ..."

"And ancient Sumer and Babylon, don't forget."

"Exactly. It's a bricolage of various disparate and otherwise unrelated elements. But it works because at its foundation there are a handful of universals, and spirit possession is one of them."

"Don't stop now. You're on a roll, Sylvia."

"It's what you've been saying all along, you and Simon, that these rituals are actually a kind of technology. Maybe the heavy furniture of the occult is taking up all the room, but it is basically still a technology. There's a method to it all, a system, that involves the psyches of the people who practice it. Like depth analysis, except in a pro-active way, and not the passive, lay-down-on-a-couch-and-analyze-your-dreams, way."

Harry couldn't contain himself any longer, and jumped into the conversation.

"Sylvia had this great idea that maybe all we had to do was find another ... technician ... another ritual specialist who was familiar with spirit possession to look at the girls and decide if there was a way to free them from the grip of whatever psychological trauma they were going through."

Monroe looked from one to the other while he thought about what they were proposing.

"We had some pretty good remote viewers for awhile."

Sylvia shook her head.

"Not the same thing. We need someone who has been steeped in the same kind of world as the Dagon people. The remote viewers were all G-scale recruits, am I right? Military people or civilian contractors."

Monroe nodded.

"We need to find a reputable sort of occultist with experience in these matters. Someone who understands possession, but who also knows the jargon and the context for the rituals that these girls went through."

"A reputable occultist! CIA tried that, back in the day. They found some pretty good stage magicians, and a gaggle of witches and sorcerers, but no one they could actually work with."

Harry was fascinated by all this, but Sylvia looked demoralized.

"I think that is because they were trying to weaponize the occult, to weaponize the paranormal. MK-ULTRA was all about trying to take it out of the box and use it for purposes it was never designed to achieve. For Dagon, the occult *is* the weapon."

"What do you propose, then, Sylvia?"

"Simon has all sorts of contacts in the occult world. He demonstrated that last year. He knows the groups, the individuals, the ideologies. He speaks their language. Surely there must be someone on that list who understands Dagon without being a member of it? Someone who can give us some advice on how to counteract the Order, if not directly then through releasing those poor girls from the vise-like grip of the trauma they are under?"

Monroe looked a little doubtful. Before he could offer an objection, Sylvia rolled right through him. She leaned over and grabbed him by shoulders and stared into his eyes.

"You *know* what's happening to them. Not just the pregnant girls, but the ones they called the 'seers.' They're in the frozen grasp of something foul, something hideous. I know that we have been focused on fighting Dagon the way we would any terrorist organization, using the tools we have been trained to use since we joined government service. But if you could see those children, look into their eyes, you would know that this is on another level entirely. I've seen what happens to girls who have been rescued from the battlefield, from the viciousness of soldiers who see them as playthings, as sex toys. This is the same, but it's different too. If anything, it's worse. As if that could even be imagined."

She released her hold on Monroe's shoulders but kept her gaze level with his.

"They need therapy, they need counseling, all of that. Of course. And they're not getting it in the holding area we have them in because we don't have therapists who can speak their languages, but even more because the therapists aren't cleared for what really happened to them. They wouldn't be able to help if they were read-in, anyway. What those girls need right now is not our standard crisis counseling, but something far more ambitious. I don't even know what to call it. We lost our vocabulary for that sort of thing a long time ago."

Monroe looked over at Harry, and raised an eyebrow.

"If you could have looked at those girls, Mr. Monroe. If you could have seen the horror in their eyes, as if they were watching something terrible taking place somewhere deep within their minds. And then, every once in awhile, one of them would say something and it was in no language we've ever heard. But it made your skin crawl anyway. I mean, we fought those bastards to rescue these girls. That was months ago. But they're still being held hostage. And we're not doing anything about it."

Sylvia nodded, but then said something that shocked everyone.

"And, anyway, have you ever considered that these girls can be used against us? That while we have their bodies locked up, their minds are gateways for the so-called Old Ones? We have no idea when Dagon will try their ritual again, but when they do, what is to stop them from using the girls in our custody as the point of the spear?"

"Damn, Sylvia." Harry was surprised by his boss's sangfroid.

"It's true," she said, looking from Monroe to Harry and back to Monroe again. "If we believe that *they* believe what they are doing, then we have to assume they have a plan to keep on using the girls. Especially the pregnant ones that I'm sure they want to get back, to see if their ritual worked. But the other girls, too. If word got back to them that some of the seers survived, they will want them. After all, they were going to kill them during the ritual precisely to keep them from falling into our hands. Once they know these girls are safely in our custody, what's to stop them from using any means at their disposal to seize them?"

"And break into a secure United States Government facility?" Monroe was dubious.

"What if they have pre-programmed the girls, with a command prompt of some kind? You know, a … a trigger word? Or some kind of post-hypnotic suggestion? What if they are time bombs in that facility waiting to go off? We saw what happened to one of the girls who was manipulated by a child no older than eight or nine."

"It's been months already, and …"

"And we don't know their timetable. They could be prepping an attempt now, or next week, or whenever. We don't have the luxury of waiting for them to move, since we don't know when or where that might be."

"What are you suggesting?"

"If they haven't moved already, it might mean that they don't have the Book. Or Angell. Or maybe they have one but not the other, assuming they need both."

"They do. Angell is the genetic component they need to make the ritual work."

"So if we can't find Angell on our own, then we need another way to smoke them out, to force them to act and get them in the open."

Sylvia stared at Monroe, looking him straight in the eyes. Daring him to understand what she was trying to say. Not wanting to say it aloud herself.

She saw realization dawn on him, but it was Harry who broke the silence.

"Jesus, Sylvia. You want to use the girls as bait!"

CHAPTER EIGHT

Crofton, Maryland

SIMON HAD SLEPT LITTLE IN THE WEEKS AND MONTHS following the Pinecastle ritual in Florida. While he was satisfied that the main thrust of the Cult of Dagon had been thwarted, he knew that they would just regroup and try again: in a different place, and at a different time. But he ran the risk of total exhaustion. He was not a young man anymore, and neither was his friend Dwight Monroe. They had worked day and night with their small team cobbled together from different departments at NSA, and had identified the time and place of the Cult's ritual: a noxious enterprise that involved the violation and sacrifice of young girls.

He kept current with the disposition of those victims, and knew that some of them had been kidnapped from the Middle East and been sold into slavery by Daesh. That meant that not a few of them were Yezidi, from Iraq. There were still others from the hundreds of girls that had been snatched by Boko Haram in Nigeria. Others still came from the slave dens of Libya and other sites along North Africa's Mediterranean coast.

And still others had come from Eastern Europe and Asia. Simon knew that Monroe was cooperating with the CIA and the FBI on identifying the routes the girls had taken in an effort to identify and apprehend the kidnappers and slave-traders, but he also knew that it was a long and frustrating task they had in front of them. More importantly was the physical and psychological well-being of the victims themselves, and to his dismay he learned that—at least in some cases—the ritual had been successful.

A few of the girls were pregnant.

★ ★ ★

To distract himself from dwelling too long on the implications of that fact, he dived into the most complicated and arcane of all of the tools at his disposal for discovering Dagon's next move. This involved a map, and a prodigious memory of religious and esoteric practices from around the globe. The latter was easy: it had been his career after all. The former, however, was resistant to all the usual techniques of logic and reason.

The map had been essential in identifying Dagon's selection of Pinecastle as the locus of their central or core ritual. It involved the application of a form of non-Euclidean geometry, a kind of algebra that used an arithmetical system that was not base-10, and a knowledge of star maps that had been created from data collected off-planet.

Most maps are based on the idea that the Earth can best be measured from a place somewhat above the Earth: in other words, maps are always bird's-eye views of the planet, whether of a country or a town or even just the highway going through it. It's a top-down perspective. It's also a system that does not include the dimension of time as one of its coordinates. A map of New York City today is pretty much identical to a map of New York City made a decade ago. The same basic land mass, the same rivers, the same boroughs.

Dagon used a different system altogether.

The priests of Dagon revered a being known to them as Cthulhu or Kutulu: the high priest of the Old Ones. The Old Ones according to this belief were non-terrestrial entities that had once ruled the Earth long before humans evolved. Kutulu was said to be buried in a sarcophagus somewhere below the surface of the Earth: either below the seas, or below some land mass. But Kutulu was their connection—their gate or portal—to the domain of the Old Ones: supposedly a distant star system.

How one could be below the Earth and simultaneously connected to a distant star seems counter-intuitive today, but in ancient times the Underworld was often located both in the heavens *and* below the Earth. Distances were collapsed this way, and a point on the Earth— or, more likely, in the bowels *of* the Earth—was equivalent to a point in deep space. This was a geometry of both space *and* time, and if time is computed as the distance it takes to travel between point A and point B in space, then an alteration of time would also result in an alteration of space—according to the theory in use by Dagon. To go more slowly from A to B would mean a greater linear distance between A and B; to go more quickly, i.e. in less "time," would mean a shorter linear distance between A and B. This is nonsense in the world we live in, but the concept of collapsing time and space was central to the physics of the Dagon Cult for without it their rituals would not work. For Dagon, the cosmos is a torus.

The Pinecastle ritual had resulted in several of the young girls who had been abused as part of the rites becoming pregnant. This had been the intention of the cultists all along, of course, and the success of this part of the ritual was deeply troubling. It implied that these victims were now vehicles for some kind of hideous Being or Beings: supernatural forces that had been evoked by the Rites of Dagon and the *Necronomicon*.

Once it was known that some of the girls were pregnant there were heated arguments between Simon, Monroe, Aubrey, and Sylvia over whether or not the fetuses should be aborted. After all, the girls had been raped and their rapists had intended for them to conceive monsters. The girls should not be expected to carry the fetuses to term. In the first place, several of them were little more than children themselves.

The ritual had taken place towards the middle of November. It was now May. That meant the girls were a little over six months' pregnant. One of the NSA's assigned doctors with top secret security clearance had examined the girls and determined that they would be due on or about August 1, 2015. Simon knew that the girls were currently being held in a facility in Virginia as agents attempted to identify and locate their families in the Middle East, Africa, and Asia. As each month went by, the girls became more and more pregnant. It was unfair and even a little surreal, and both Sylvia and her associate Harry insisted that they be allowed to visit the girls and to monitor their wellbeing. This they had done periodically, and their most recent visit had revealed a disturbing escalation of "high strangeness," one that inspired Sylvia to ask Monroe to take more decisive action to protect not only the girls themselves but to thwart the possibility of a new Dagon attempt to "open the Gate."

Monroe had phoned Simon on the new encrypted cell phone he had obtained in the weeks after the Pinecastle ritual. The call was brief, but to the point. Simon had been asked to determine if any of his contacts were experienced in methods of spirit possession and/ or exorcism. The idea was to see if it was possible to find out what the girls were experiencing, and if it was possible to free them from the grip of their possession (if that is what it was), or even to use their condition against Dagon in some way, as if the girls could be "turned" into double agents. Or even used as bait to lure the Order into the open. It was a bizarre request, but one that Simon seemed to understand, if not to agree with. As worrisome as the idea was—to use these minor children as pawns in some kind of weird intelligence game against a very dangerous and wholly immoral adversary—it gave Simon something to do, and a goal on which to focus.

Which is why the sudden interest in Afro-Caribbean magic, and voudon. It represented a tradition of spirit possession that was neutral in the sense that it was not considered demonic possession (a problematic concept that carried a lot of baggage from Abrahamic religions that could be counter-productive). In Haitian voudon, for instance, possession by the gods was considered largely voluntary or at least temporary. It occurred within the confines of a ritual space and at the control of a ritual specialist: a *houngan* or voudon priest. In cases of demonic possession, there was no willed conscious attempt to invoke the possessing demon. Demonic possession could be a permanent state, or nearly so, without it being combatted by an exorcism or series of exorcisms taking place over days, weeks, months, or even years. What happened to the girls at Pinecastle was somewhere between the two: they were not volunteering to be possessed, but the process was under the control of human agents, the Dagon initiates. What was needed was not so much an exorcist but another expert in spirit possession. A shaman, maybe. Or an experienced magician.

Simon knew that in documented cases of poltergeist activity the presence of pubescent children was often noted, and it had been theorized that something about a child undergoing the change to adulthood—with the resulting surge of hormones in the blood stream—might activate some kind of latent psychic ability. It is possible that Dagon was aware of this as well, or that they simply were following an ancient formula that had been tried and true for millennia. The use of children as seers was noted in the medieval grimoires as well as in more ancient texts. Something about children and their susceptibility to psychic manipulation—from demonic possession to poltergeist activity to precognition and mental telepathy—fascinated him, for it teased at a possible biochemical aspect to the paranormal, something he had always suspected.

One did not normally find children present at the *hounfort* or the ritual site for practitioners of vodoun, except sometimes as bystanders. It was usually an "adults only" affair, particularly in Haiti, although traditions were different in Benin and Togo, in Africa, where what we know as "voodoo" originated. In Benin, for instance, "voodoo" is the national religion, and children are present for many of the ceremonies as one might expect. Simon was curious if they were as subject to trance possession as the adults but was never able to get a definitive answer. He did know that the indigenous religion of Maria Lionza in Venezuela, for instance, used one or two young girls as trance mediums during their rituals on the El Sorte mountain. (The Maria Lionza practices are similar to those of Santeria and Vodoun, mixing African and indigenous Indian elements with Catholicism.)

Just the previous year—in 2014—the United Nations warned the British government that numbers of children from Africa were being trafficked to the UK for the purposes of occult rituals, during which the children would be tortured and killed. This was precisely what Dagon had been doing, although in a much more organized way. Dagon's intention was to open a Gate between this universe

and another; while those who were trafficking African children to
the UK were using them for rituals designed to bring wealth, or to
cure someone from an illness, or to curse a rival: the goals usually
associated with popular ideas about witchcraft, sorcery and "black
magic."

Knowing all this, however, made Simon and his companions even
more determined to stop Dagon. Success in their rituals would only
make them bolder and more aggressive, regardless of whether or not
you believed in Gates or multiple universes. Although Dagon had its
roots in the ancient Middle East, it was still largely a Western occult
Order and secret society, and its leadership—while varied ethnically
and racially—still adhered to Western forms of esotericism. They
were well-organized and sophisticated, with multiple connections
to political movements and terror groups around the world. It was a
machine, and a machine like that could afford to traffic in thousands
of men, women, and children for whatever purpose they desired.

So they had to be confronted on multiple levels. While standard
counter-terrorism and counter-intelligence procedures had their
place and were certainly warranted by Dagon's actions and alliances,
it was Dagon's peculiar and unique characteristic as an occult
operation that merited a different approach. They were not in this
for the money. They were not trying to support one religious or
ideological movement against another. They had no territorial
designs (other, one could argue, than the entire planet). Like many
terror groups around the world, they did base their violence on old
historical grievances; but these were pre-historical grievances, dating
to before there were humans on the Earth.

Their value system had to be understood if there was any chance
at all in defeating them, and with that their worldview had to be
understood as well. The adherents of Dagon were human, but only
barely. They claimed a hybrid quality, with lineages that were mixed
human and extra-terrestrial. The Old Ones—their primogenitors—
were from elsewhere in the universe. But they had one terrestrial

connection that was essential to their success in opening the Gate and turning back the cosmic clock to a time when there were no human beings and no primates at all on the planet. That connection was their dead but dreaming high priest, the creature known only as Cthulhu.

★ ★ ★

Simon sat back from his desk and the pile of arcane literature that covered every square inch. He had re-read the entire Lovecraft canon, every story and even all the published correspondence, looking for a key to understanding how this racist, misogynist recluse had managed to wield such amazing power over generations of readers during the last hundred years. A few themes kept coming up, and Simon made meticulous notes of their occurrences. One of them was telepathic communication between the Old Ones (including Cthulhu) and his followers. Another was the aspect of twins, a theme that was especially important in "The Dunwich Horror." Monroe had asked him to look into the possibility that a specialist in trance possession could be recruited to their operation in an effort to free the girls from the grip of whatever entity or entities were now dwelling within their consciousness—or that of their soon-to-be-born babies—and that suggestion was becoming more and more plausible now that he had time to think about it.

The other theme was that of a universe roughly parallel to this one, a place where extraordinary beings lived and extraordinary powers could exist: a place that could be entered through the use of technologies that we are only guessing at today, but which were commonplace among initiates aeons ago. Dagon trafficked children from one country to another, that was true; but they also trafficked in extra-terrestrial forces from one universe to the next. They abducted human children for use in rituals; but wasn't that a simulacrum of the other kind of abduction, the one of humans by non-humans?

Alien abductions?

Simon had an idea of who to contact, but it had been decades since they had been in the same room at the same time. If he showed up alone, there was every possibility that he would come away empty-handed. But if he sent someone else—someone with government credentials and a scary persona—he might be more successful.

He made up his mind.

He phoned Aubrey.

CHAPTER NINE

Yogyakarta, Indonesia

GRAY-HAIRED AND GRAY-BEARDED, THIN to the point of emaciation, Bill Moody was one of those American college professors who spent as much time as possible outside the United States on one overseas posting or another—because who needs to deal with the office politics of an American university or the boring social life on campus? In his case, he had studied as an undergrad with Clifford Geertz, a famous anthropologist and probably the best-known twentieth century expert on Javanese culture. Moody came up through the ranks of academia, became proficient in Indonesian and Javanese, as well as Dutch, and wound up spending a lot of time at mosques without officially ever having converted (or, at least, that was the impression his colleagues had). He was polite and ingratiating, stuffy when he thought he had to be, and engaging when it suited his purposes better. He wore batik shirts and blue jeans, and read copiously in the local Indonesian newspapers every day. He was current on the politics and cultural events of the time, and could discuss them all in any one of at least three languages.

One might think he had the perfect makings of a spy, and one would be right.

Moody managed to wrestle a multi-million dollar grant from the Department of Defense in order to study those Southeast Asian environments that give rise to terrorist ideologies. The grant was under the DOD's "Minerva" program, which was a controversial idea that the Pentagon developed in the years after 9/11 for recruiting American academics with in-country expertise and experience. It was basically a boondoggle for those academics who enjoyed suitably fluid ideas about the ethics of their profession. The American Archaeological Association was under no illusions about it and condemned it roundly. No matter, the money was good and having DOD protection even better. To add insult to insult—the injury was yet to come—Moody was also a member of several Washington, DC think tanks that specialized in defense-related programs and projects. Moody was, quite simply, spooked up.

That is why, months ago, he received a communication through DOD concerning another professor—one Gregory Angell, formerly of Columbia University—and the desire of the Pentagon to identify and detain him. Unknown to Moody, that request had originated with Dwight Monroe at NSA. Under most circumstances, Moody would have been more than happy to oblige, but in this particular case … well … no. This is because he had received another communication through his friends at a mosque on Jaliurang that Dagon was also looking for Angell. He tried his usual connections, spread the word discretely that he was looking to contact an "old friend" from the States who was also a professor, etc. etc. but kept coming up empty.

After having spent the better part of three decades in Indonesia, Moody was—how to put it politely?—compromised. One of the reasons he was so valuable to DOD was his deep involvement with the local culture and its languages, political and religious groups, and personalities. One of the reasons he was so dangerous to DOD was the same deep involvement. He had managed to straddle the line for years without getting caught by either side, but where Angell was concerned Dagon had no sense of proportion. They wanted him found and his whereabouts signaled to their agents in Jogja. Moody figured he would do that first, and then wait an appropriate amount of time before notifying DOD. This was so he would be covered on both sides.

The life of a double agent is, in reality, a steaming pile of nerve-wracking crap.

And now the messages from Dagon were even more urgent. They had reason to believe that Angell was there, in Yogyakarta, in the same town as Moody and they wanted to know his progress. Like, yesterday.

As he walked out of his newly-purchased bungalow—bought

with Minerva gold—near UGM, lost in thought, a neighbor passing by wished him "Good morning."

"*Selamat pagi, pak,*" he said.

"*Selamat pagi, mas,*" Moody replied. The gentleman was younger than himself, a doctoral student named Iqbal at ICRS, the International Consortium for Religious Studies at Universitas Gadjah Mada (UGM), "*Apa khabar?*"

"*Khabar baik, pak.*"

They continued to exchange a few more pleasantries this way, Moody was eager to hit the usual tourist areas to seek this missing Angell guy, when Iqbal handed him the professor on a silver platter.

Switching to English, he said, "Do you know this new professor? He has been in Jogja a few months, but no one knows where he teaches."

"*Orang Amerika?*" An American?

"Oh, yes. But none of the students I know have classes with him. I checked UGM, and there is no one new here. Then I checked some of the other universities, but the same thing. Maybe he is on a research trip?"

Moody nodded, but he didn't believe it. Even when professors go abroad on research junkets they check in with the locals. No one just shows up quietly, stays a few months, and then leaves without a word.

Not unless they were on the run.

"Where does he stay?"

The student shrugged.

"Sometimes they see him on Malioboro Road, or around the Kraton. He eats at *warung makan*, usually, or at some *kopi* place. But he never seems to go north of Malioboro area."

"Big guy? Blonde hair, blue eyes? Typical *orang belanda*?"

"No, no. Short for an American. Dark hair."

Moody knew it was his guy.

"Maybe he needs a tour guide. What do you think?"

"Yah, *pak*. Maybe. They say he is a religion professor, but if so then we should know about him."

"If you see him again, you should call me. I can go to see him."

"Yah, *pak*. I will do that."

"*Selamat jalan, mas.*"

Iqbal took off in the direction of the ICRS building. Moody just stood there for a moment and considered his options.

He knew all the places the tourists went, and he knew all the places the longer-term foreign residents would go. He knew that Angell had not shown up at any of the larger mosques, or he would have been seen and Moody would have gotten word already. But the student said that he hung out around Malioboro Road and that made sense if he was trying to blend in. The place was popular with foreigners, and no one would notice one more. But the student said he had been in Jogja for months. If he was the guy they were looking for, why would he hang around town for months? Wouldn't he just pass through to somewhere else? He must know he is being hunted by the US government and by Dagon. Just being sought by one of those two was bad enough.

The more he thought about it, though, the more it made sense. Indonesia is the fourth largest country in the world, with over 220 million people spread across more than 17,000 islands. It has a growing economy, but large parts of the country are still undeveloped. It was inexpensive for a foreigner to live there, but residency visas were hard to obtain and required a lot of paperwork: something a professor on the run would try to avoid. And if he got picked up for anything at all, with no visa he would be deported at best or imprisoned at worst. Deportation for Angell meant he would fall into the hands of the US government, and probably wind up at some black site somewhere; imprisonment meant he would fall into the claws of Dagon.

Yet here he was. That meant he had connections, or was being protected somehow. Moody would have to be cautious in his approach. He was told specifically by Dagon to take no action against him, just to report his whereabouts and another team would take care of it.

He shuddered. He knew what the "other team" meant: the Keepers of the Book. They didn't play around. They made the SEAL teams and JSOC look like boy scouts on a jamboree by comparison.

Well, that was Angell's problem. His problem was in locating him and reporting back to his handler.

And he suddenly had a good idea where to start.

CHAPTER TEN

Brooklyn

IT HAD BEEN AN IMPOSSIBLE SHOT, AND SHE KNEW IT.

She sat, freezing and wet, on the rooftop across from an Arab restaurant on Atlantic Avenue in Brooklyn, for two solid days. She had experienced worse in Nepal and northern India, and certainly in the refugee camps in Iraq and Turkey. She had faced every kind of privation, including hunger, thirst, frigid temperatures, and scalding heat. The only thing that had saved her from being raped was her special ability, the one Daesh feared as much as her own people did. She had almost been raped and killed as a child in Iraq, when Fahim had been arrested by the *Mukhabarat*, the secret police, in the last days of Saddam's regime. But her special ability had saved her, and the ceiling came down around the policeman. She and Fahim had managed to escape all the way to the camps.

What was her special ability? To be sure, she didn't know. She had blackouts. She knew voices not her own had spoken through her at those times, speaking in languages she had never learned. Well, none of that mattered now. Now she was one of the *jin*, the special female soldiers who fought Daesh in Iraq and Syria. And she had a new special ability. A somewhat more reliable one.

She was a sniper.

★ ★ ★

Her people had moved her into the United States specifically for this one shot. She arrived first in Europe, through Turkey and into Albania, and then across the sea to Italy with a boatload of Syrians escaping the civil war. She found herself in a detention center, but not for long. Her local contact got her out and she made her way across Italy through a series of safe houses run by the Peshmerga—the Kurdish revolutionary group—until she boarded a commercial flight for New York.

Her passport and identity papers had been "borrowed" from a young woman of Kurdish extraction living in France as a citizen of that country. French citizens can enter the United States under the visa waiver system, provided they apply online three days or more in advance of travel. This was done, and Jamila—a young Yezidi woman with more than thirty kills to her credit with a Russian-made Dragunov sniper rifle—entered the United States at JFK International Airport in late April, 2015. Her beloved Dragunov was shipped separately, disassembled and packed safely in a wooden box with bubble wrap and RIG gun grease, in a container full of automotive parts destined for Mercedes dealerships nationwide.

Her contact in New York transferred the rifle to her in a motel off the Brooklyn-Queens Expressway, along with a photograph of the man she was to kill and some brief details about his schedule. She didn't need the photograph, though. She knew exactly what he looked like.

★ ★ ★

She waited on the rooftop of that dormitory for privileged American law school students and kept her eye on the Yemeni restaurant two blocks away. No one had seen her go up to the roof, or if they had they had not bothered to give her a second glance. She knew her clothing would have seemed cheap and artless compared to theirs. Although she understood she was pretty in an exotic sort of way for America, she kept her hair covered in a scarf and that helped to hide her face as well. It was not a hijab, such as the Muslimahs wear, but it was close enough.

What was a revelation to her was America. Especially New York City. She had not known that such a place existed. This was the city that Al Qaeda had tried to destroy with their planes and their suicide pilots. At least, that is what she had heard. She could understand why. It stood for everything that Al Qaeda was against. This was not a capital of nationalism, or fundamentalism, or homogeneity. Everyone was here. She heard every language spoken in its streets, once even her own.

It was in a place called Queens. On a street called Roosevelt Avenue. There were Tibetans and Pakistanis and Indians, all mixed up with Colombians and Salvadorians and Brazilians and Argentines. There were Asians and Africans of every origin. So many Filipinos and Koreans and Chinese. Senegalese and Ghanaians. It all felt familiar and strange at the same time. Surely, New York City was an affront to religious and political fanaticism.

So, she felt more than justified in removing the Butcher of Sinjar from its streets.

★ ★ ★

Then she saw him, on schedule. He had been part of a "peace mission" from Iraq and was going to attend a meeting at the United Nations. But he had an invitation to lunch in Brooklyn first. The problem was her contact did not know if it was one day or the next. The target had kept the appointment fluid, most likely as a security measure. But he had kept to the original plan and she watched him enter the restaurant on time.

After about an hour, he emerged. Alone. That was interesting, but she had no time nor inclination to wonder about it. She took a deep breath, let it out, and fired.

★ ★ ★

She took the stairs down a few levels, and then the elevator the rest of the way. She knew that no one would think to look at that building for the shooter. They would assume it was just another New York City act of violence.

That is when she emerged and saw an old man panting in the street, holding a gun and demanding that she stop. All around her, other people—some in official looking uniforms—were emerging from a large building on the other side of the street, some with weapons. But then police cars showed up and everything stopped. The old man was arrested. And she kept walking as if nothing had happened. Had the police stopped her because they saw that she was carrying a long flower box, they would have found nothing but long-stemmed roses. They would have asked her forgiveness and let her go on her way.

Her beloved Dragunov was in a safe place behind a pipe in the stairwell. Moments after she left the building it had been retrieved by her contact and was even now on its way back to Kurdish territory in Iraq, eager for her embrace once more.

★ ★ ★

She made her way back to Queens by subway, possibly the most dangerous part of her mission. She was due to catch a flight to Frankfurt in the morning, and from there to Istanbul. From Istanbul she would meet her fellow *jin* at a camp on the Syrian border and rejoin the fight to rescue her sisters from sex slavery at the hands of Daesh.

Not a bad occupation for a Yezidi woman who was still a virgin, and who sometimes even now fell into a brief trance of which she never had the slightest memory.

CHAPTER ELEVEN

Yogyakarta, Indonesia

MOODY'S SUDDEN INSPIRATION HAD PAID OFF.

If Angell was hanging out around Malioboro Road and had been there for months, there was one place he was sure to be from time to time.

Foreigners needed money, and that meant either money changers or ATM machines. There were too many of both and he couldn't keep an eye on all of them, so that was out.

Then there were newspapers and magazines. Angell was an American and supposedly spoke English as his native language, and there were not that many places in Jogja that had a good selection of English-language newspapers. Around Malioboro Road, that meant Periplus in the basement of the Malioboro Mall. Again, he couldn't stake out the bookstore for hours at a time, especially as it would only take a minute for Angell to pick up the latest copy of the *International Herald Tribune* and then he would be gone.

But there is a public place where a foreigner could be expected to spend an extended period of time in order to catch up on news and make contact with other people if so desired, and do so relatively anonymously.

An internet café.

And the best selection for foreigners would be along Jalan Sosrowijayan: a well-known backpacker street right off Malioboro Road, replete with low-cost lodgings called *losmen*.

Moody had used the computers there himself from time to time. You paid a small fee—a few rupiah for a half-hour, nothing onerous—and had a pretty good internet connection that allowed you to get your email as well as check on some news sites. Angell would want to know if he was still being sought by American intelligence or law enforcement, and he might even be in contact with friends or colleagues, probably using a pseudonym or some other cloaking device.

The street was full of foreigners, young and old, and Angell would fit right in and not be noticed except by the touts offering tours to the more popular sites like Borobudur or Prambanan, or rides on *becak*: the bicycle-powered rickshaws that are ubiquitous in Jogja. Moody wandered up and down the street that morning, at a time when he knew the internet cafés would be less crowded. Angell would know that, too, as someone who had been in town for a few months.

Presumably Angell would not use a cellphone or a laptop or tablet, because they could be traced. He would stay off-grid as much as possible. That made it even more certain that he would feel the need to use an internet café from time to time. Today was Monday, and it seemed logical that the professor would start the week by checking his notices.

It took only about a half hour of hanging around at the sidewalk café of the Bladok hotel on Sosrowijayan, having coffee and pretending to read something on his cellphone, and bingo, there he was. He looked like the photo his handlers had given him, except maybe thinner and somehow more gaunt. But it was he. It was Angell. He looked furtive as he checked both sides of the street and clocked every face he saw, as if he was an agent in training at the Farm. Moody saw that he was wearing a backpack, and it seemed heavy on his shoulders. He probably had his whole life in there, ready to bolt at the first sign of trouble. Just before he turned to enter the café, Moody took a fast photo of him with his phone. Then the target ducked into the café and Moody waited a few moments before paying his bill and casually walking up to the same place.

Moody got a machine far enough away from Angell so as not to appear too noticeable and rented it for thirty minutes. He logged on to his email account and drafted a note to himself with the date, time and place of the sighting. He didn't send the email, but saved it as a draft. His handler would get it and tell him what to do in person.

He stretched, looked at Angell for a moment, and then got up to leave, sauntering casually out of the café. Angell had been hunched over the computer and seemed to be focusing intently on what he was reading. Moody wondered what it was. No matter. He was certain his surveillance had been successful and that Angell was oblivious to his presence.

He walked out onto Malioboro Road, which was getting busier by the moment, and blended into the foot traffic. He ignored the *becak* drivers and their endlessly repeated invitations—*transport? transport?*—and found a place to stand across the street where he could watch Angell if he started walking that way.

★ ★ ★

Angell closed the browser and looked up in time to see the other American leave the café. He had been spotted, he was sure of it. It had to happen sometime. It was inevitable.

Before he knew for sure he was under surveillance, he had been searching a few Sumerian language sites to identify some of the phrases he had come across in the *Necronomicon*. He suspected that they were Akkadian and not Sumerian, not that it would make a big difference in his research, but it could give him a clue as to when and where the author of the text had encountered them. He had come to the realization that the Dagon was working according to a timetable that had little in common with Western calendars, and believed he had found evidence that they had been so active the past year or so because of a peculiarity of their schedule.

Most calendars are linear. They go from past to present to future. You can purchase a calendar for this year or next year or even last year, and see that it runs from day to day, week to week, month to month, in a straight line. But Dagon used a kind of astral calendar— one based not on the revolutions of the sun or the moon but—based on an astronomy from the vantage point of someplace else in the solar system or even outside it. It was as if the calendar was being twisted the way one would twist a wet rag to squeeze out the water.

Once it was finished twisting it would revert to its original shape and the twisting would begin again. It was a pulse, like the beating of a hideous heart.

A phrase he kept coming back to was the injunction that the "Gate" would open when "the Great Bear hangs from its tail in the sky." There was something funny about that statement, because he knew that the circumpolar asterism known as the Great Bear—*Ursa Major*—hangs from its tail once every day of the year: at least from the point of view of an Earthling. Yet it was doubtful that someone on some other planet somewhere would even know what the Great Bear was. The constellations would have to be entirely different when seen from the perspective of another planet, not to mention another solar system. They were different even when seen on Earth: not just between the northern and southern hemispheres, but within the same hemispheres. The ancient Chinese gave different names to many of the constellations because they arranged the stars into shapes differently. They certainly didn't use Greek mythology the way the West did.

As he was working on this problem, he began to wonder if maybe Dagon interpreted the Great Bear differently, and that is when he began to worry that their ritual timetable had been moved up faster than he had previously suspected. For people on Earth—and in the northern hemisphere—the Great Bear is a kind of cosmic clock. It makes one complete revolution in the sky around the Pole Star every 24 hours, give or take a few minutes. That loss of a few minutes each day means that it points down at midnight one night, but points up at midnight months later. So the ritual didn't have to take place at night, but it was possible that there was a daylight schedule as well: a time when the Great Bear hangs from its tail in the sky but during the day when it is not visible to those on Earth without a telescope or … or a computer program, an astronomical app that would show the relative positions of the stars on any day of the year at any time.

That is when he did a quick search at the internet café and

found such a program online. He plotted in some coordinates—date, time, place—and quickly discovered that the Great Bear instruction was a moveable feast, indeed. So there was a missing piece to the puzzle, something that Dagon worked with in conjunction with the Great Bear requirement: a way to bring together two different astronomies from two different worlds.

A way to open the Gate.

Before closing his browser, though, he did a quick search of his university's website to see if there was any notice of his disappearance, but he found that it was as if he had never taught there. He thought of trying to contact his old colleague Professor Hine, who had done so much to help him get out of China last year, but he knew that would only call down the heat on the Asian Studies scholar so he refrained from sending him an email. He saw that Hine was still listed on Columbia's website, with descriptions of his classes and an old photo of the man making him look much younger than his fifty-odd years.

Angell smiled to himself, and then wondered if he would ever see Hine again, or anyone else for that matter. He made sure to wipe the history on the computer, and then got up to leave. Whoever that American was who was shadowing him, it could only mean one thing: the enemy was closing in. His time in Indonesia was coming to an abrupt end.

He had to flee the country.

Now.

CHAPTER TWELVE

Brooklyn

WASSERMAN FOUND A PAYPHONE and dialed the number on the piece of paper he had written down at that apartment in Red Hook a year ago. He had been mystified by the weird, spinning "spirit bowl" in Angell's Red Hook apartment and all the chanting sounds coming from his room when there was no one there. Angell's Syrian landlords had been spooked enough to call the cops, and Wasserman had been in the area and just showed up. That was in April of 2014. And now there was this homicide of the baby doctor who had a file marked "Angel" of some creepy medical condition in which twins started disappearing. Or, at least, one twin from each mother. And one of the doctor's patients was living in the same apartment building as Gregory Angell. It wasn't a big building, just your average brownstone. There probably weren't more than six or seven apartments in the place. The odds were spooky.

The phone rang on the other end, then stopped ringing. He didn't hear anyone answer. He was about to hang up when a voice came on. It sounded muffled or electronically modified in some way. Hollow sounding.

"Please state your name," it said.

He gave the voice his name and his old badge number.

"Where did you obtain this number?"

He gave the address of Angell's apartment.

And then the voice hung up on him.

Wasserman muttered to himself. "Friggin' government assholes …" he started to say, and then the payphone rang.

He picked up the receiver gingerly, as if it was wired to a bomb.

"Detective Wasserman?"

"That's right."

"You were at Gregory Angell's apartment on …" the voice gave the date and time when Dispatch had called him a year ago.

"That is correct."

"How may we help you?"

"Uh, well, first of all, who is 'we'?"

"Excuse me?"

"With whom do I have the pleasure of speaking?"

There was a moment of silence on the line.

Then: "This is a US government agency, Detective. That is all you need to know."

"Well, US government agency, we have a situation."

Silence.

He waited for a minute, but there was no response, so he soldiered on.

"There has been a homicide connected to the same building. A baby doc ... an ob/gyn. One of his patients is a Syrian woman who lives at that address."

More silence.

"The doctor had a file on her and on a number of other patients. The file was marked 'Angel,' which is the name of the renter of the apartment at that address a year ago. I don't know if these cases are connected in some way, but I thought I should let you know."

More silence. Wasserman was about to hang up in disgust when he heard a different voice come on the line.

"What information does the Angel file contain, Detective?" Wasserman swallowed.

"Well, I haven't seen it yet, but I understand that all the patients in the Angel file were pregnant with twins."

Another period of silence, but Wasserman could tell that he had just laid a bomb on that "US government agency," whatever the hell it was, so he stayed on.

"Twins?" came the eventual request for clarification.

"Yes, that's what they said. Twins. Sonograms or ultrasounds, whatever you call it, of twins. But with a twist."

"And that would be ...?"

"In each case, one of the twins is missing."

"Where are you?"

"In Brooklyn."

"No. Specifically, where are you?"

He looked up at the street sign. He wanted to say he was on the corner of "Telephone" and "Telephone" but he doubted they would get the joke. Or anyone under the age of fifty, for that matter.

He told them.

"Wait right there," came the unbelievable reply.

"Wait … *what?*"

A moment later a black SUV pulled up next to the phone booth. The voice on the phone said, "Get in the car. We will bring you back to your location after we've had a chance to speak."

Wasserman slowly hung up the phone. A man in a dark suit and aviator sunglasses got out of the front passenger side and opened the rear door and just stood there.

"Detective Wasserman? *Retired?*"

"Fuck you."

"Please get in the car, sir. No sarcasm was intended."

"Aren't you going to frisk me first?"

"No need, sir. You're one of New York's Finest. We trust you."

"Now *that* was sarcasm," he muttered, but got in the car anyway.

★ ★ ★

As he settled into the back seat, he noticed that there was no one else in the car. There were two men in the front seat, but he was alone in the back.

Just as he was about to ask where they were going, a video screen rose up from a center console and flickered to life.

"Detective Wasserman, please make yourself comfortable."

He was looking at the image of an older man with white hair combed straight back, dressed in a dark blue, pin-striped suit with a powder-blue shirt and a school tie.

"My name is Aubrey. I am sorry we have to meet this way, but I am not in New York at the moment. This is a secure line. For all practical intents and purposes the vehicle you are in is a SCIF. That means ..."

"I know what it means. A Sensitive Compartmented Information Facility. Like what they have in embassies and in government offices."

"It is necessary that we speak at once since you may have some information that we need, hence the need for urgent communications."

"Who do you work for, Mr Aubrey?"

"Just Aubrey, please. And I work for your government, Detective. That is all you need to know at present. I realize that is irritating, but I have my orders as well."

"How do I know you are really working for my government Mr. ... uh, Aubrey?"

Aubrey shrugged.

"We can waste some time with passwords and telephone numbers, the color of the day, things of that nature. But what we are asking you is not a danger to your security or the nation's, so you shouldn't feel as if you are cooperating with an enemy. And, anyway, *you* called *us*."

Wasserman was not convinced, but he didn't know that he had any choice. He had dialed a number in DC and now he was talking to the people he called. He knew that, no matter who these people were, they were working for the government.

"Okay, you've made your point. What do you need to know from me?"

"You had reason to investigate a disturbance in Red Hook about a year ago."

"Yes. I happened to be in the area. I had attended a retirement party for a friend from the force."

Aubrey nodded. "And then?"

It was Wasserman's turn to shrug.

"And then I investigated. I heard noise coming from the apartment in question ..."

"The apartment of Professor Gregory Angell."

"Right. Angell. And the landlords were upset. There was chanting and what sounded like a parade going on in the apartment. So I called for backup and when they arrived we entered the apartment."

"And what did you see?"

"Nothing. There was no one there. Not a soul. It was a small apartment. A lot of books as I remember. No electronics to speak of. Nothing that would have been making that sound."

"Is that all?"

The detective hesitated. He didn't want to tell this Aubrey guy about a spinning spirit bowl in the center of the table, or else the guy would think he was crazy.

"There was nothing else to do. The noise had to have been coming from somewhere else. But it stopped when we entered the apartment and that was the end of it."

Aubrey was silent a moment, but stared into the screen at Wasserman as if accusing him of holding something back.

"And then today."

"Today?"

"Today, Detective. You were present at a shooting. In Brooklyn, I believe?"

"That's right."

"Was that in any way connected to your experience of last year?"

"Not that I know of. I was there by accident. I had a meeting with a homicide detective about another case."

"The one about the gynecologist who was killed."

"The same."

"Tell me about that."

"There isn't much to tell. I haven't been able to connect with Danny … with Detective Dugin … yet."

"But the doctor had a patient at the same address as Gregory Angell." It was a statement and not a question, but Wasserman answered it anyway.

"That's right. Same address. And the name on the file was 'Angel.'"

"Was that the name of a patient?"

"I don't think so. It seemed to be the name of the entire file containing records of more than a dozen patients."

"Why do you think it was named 'Angel'?"

"I haven't a friggin' clue. Look, what's this all about?"

"Detective Wasserman, we need to find Professor Angell. As soon as possible."

"Who's 'we'?"

"*Again*? We, the *government*, Detective. And we need your help to do this. He may be in the United States, or he may be abroad. At this point, we are not sure where he is or even if he is still alive. So we need you to find out as much as you can about this case from your friends on the force."

"Why don't you do that directly?"

"Because the Department leaks like a sieve, and because we don't want the counter-terrorism people distracted from their regular duties. We need an independent agent working for us in the City, keeping us apprised of the case of the murdered doctor and any connection it might have to Professor Angell. And to the shooting this morning."

Wasserman was startled.

"You think they're connected?"

Suddenly he noticed that the car had stopped.

"We expect your discretion as this is a matter of national security. We'll be in touch," replied Aubrey. And the video screen went black and descended back into its slot.

And Wasserman looked out the window and saw that they had driven him straight to his apartment. His "location," indeed.

Spooks. He hated spooks.

CHAPTER THIRTEEN

The Occult Book Store
Wicker Park, Chicago, Illinois

Aubrey hung up from his conversation with Detective Wasserman and got to the airport just in time to make his flight to O'Hare. He was following up on a suggestion made by Monroe's friend, Simon. A few hours in the Windy City and a civilized dinner and he would be back in DC the next morning.

He could use the change of scenery.

He was certain that Monroe didn't remember—if he ever knew—but Aubrey had been raised in Chicago. It was a long time ago, but the memory of that three-floor walkup on South Escanaba was seared into his mind. It had been a firetrap: a wooden apartment house with porches in the back, facing onto a primary school named for a Civil War general. He had not been back in decades.

But that was in South Chicago. Today, his destination was Wicker Park—a kind of hipster area now, much like Williamsburg in Brooklyn—and the landmark Occult Book Store on Milwaukee. That is where he was to meet his contact, arranged for him in advance by Simon at the suggestion of Monroe: an enigmatic occultist named Michael Bertiaux.

Bertiaux became famous among the occult cognoscenti when he was written up in books by Kenneth Grant: the English-born protégée of Aleister Crowley. His "Typhonian Trilogies"—a set of nine volumes based on Crowleyan magic, the Lovecraftian "mythos," and hard-core Tantra—were popular among serious occult scholars and practitioners alike. The many references to Bertiaux, and to something called Voudon Gnosticism (a mix of Haitian voodoo, Western ceremonial magic, and an idiosyncratic system composed of elements of both of these plus much else besides), assured the Chicago-based adept of a devoted following.

Bertiaux had spent time in Haiti and had been initiated by adepts in that country before returning Stateside to begin formulating a system of magic that included art, spiritualism, Lovecraft references, and Crowleyan Thelema. His *Voudon Gnostic Workbook* is a massive affair, and was originally published in book form by Magickal Childe Publishing: the company that was started by Wiccan high priest Herman Slater back in the 1970s in Brooklyn Heights, only a few blocks from the apartment where Lovecraft himself had lived for a short time in the 1920s. It was the Magickal Childe bookstore—formerly the Warlock Shop—that had been targeted by investigators as a possible locus for the infamous Son of Sam cult of the 1970s.

The threads that connected all of these individuals and their work were tight, indeed. From Crowley to Grant, Grant to Bertiaux, and Lovecraft through it all. Throw in Afro-Caribbean religion and you had the mix that Monroe and Simon had identified as the environment that Dagon would use to further its noxious ends.

Monroe was certain that Bertiaux had valuable information to share concerning the latest iteration of Dagon and their final project for incarnating the high priest of the Old Ones, Kutulu, in corporeal form in this Earthly dimension. While Aubrey had his doubts about the purely esoteric aspects of this business, he had to concede that Monroe had been right about the seriousness of the threat to innocent lives posed by the fanatics of Dagon and their Keepers of the Book. He had already spoken to such illustrious personalities as Umberto Eco and Alexander Grothendieck over the course of this operation; Michael Bertiaux would simply round out the collection.

He stepped through the glass door of the storefront bookstore and was greeted by a counter on the right and a long corridor running through the center of the store with bookshelves on either side. He was reminded of the labyrinthine library at Umberto Eco's residence, but this store was considerably smaller and with a focus on the arcane.

A young man behind the counter looked up as Aubrey walked in. They got all types in there, so he wasn't startled by Aubrey's urbane and polished appearance. He saw a tall, slender man of advanced years—a little like Michael Rennie from the original *The Day The Earth Stood Still*—carrying a leather satchel and an air of resignation.

Aubrey looked up and down the store, seeking alternative exits, and quartering the space in his mind so that he could recall important details, all the while remaining aware of the man behind the counter.

"May I help you?"

"I am waiting for someone," Aubrey managed to respond, politely.

"Oh. You must mean Ari. He said someone would be coming by."

At that moment, the door to the shop opened again and in walked a youngish man with unruly hair and casual attire in hues of brown and yellow, with a T-shirt that had the logo of something called the Black Lotus Kult.

"Are you Aubrey?"

★ ★ ★

The two left the store for a location Ari identified only as Zothyria, with Ari driving for about fifteen minutes in light traffic. "Zothyria" turned out to be a high floor in an apartment building on South Michigan Avenue that was used by Bertiaux as living space, art studio, and temple, among other things, with an excellent view of Lake Michigan. Ari and Aubrey did not exchange many words on the way there, although it seemed as if Ari had a lot of questions for Aubrey, but was hesitant to ask them out loud. He was used to interviewing people for some online publications, but there was an air about Aubrey that made him think a question would simply curl up and die around him, as if the elegant old man emitted a negative force field.

They took the elevator up and Ari preceded Aubrey into the apartment after a soft knock on the door to announce their presence.

Aubrey was greeted by a man of approximately 75 or 80 years of age but who looked younger. Bespectacled, he sported a generous white beard and a kind of tonsure, with a ring of white hair encircling a bald crown. In fact Michael Bertiaux was a bishop in a Gnostic church, among other dignities.

The studio itself was cluttered with paintings of startling color and composition, all—or most—by Bertiaux himself, designed to illustrate one or another of the themes and entities reported in his textual and ceremonial work.

"You must be Aubrey?"

"Indeed."

"Please, have a seat." Bertiaux looked up, and Ari nodded and left the room.

"May I offer you some tea, or perhaps coffee?"

Aubrey declined, and decided to get straight to the point. There was something about the studio and the odd paintings that was unsettling, even to someone such as Aubrey, who had been on battlefields and in prisons and who had seen the worst that humanity has to offer. But the wide, staring eyes of some of the "entities" gazing out from the riotous colors of the artwork seemed to suggest a living darkness from a deeper place than even human depravity could imagine. It was not darkness as evil, but as a kind of sub-basement of the psyche, where disused, broken, and diseased things were not so much stored as tossed and forgotten. Aubrey had a brief thought of someone selling their home and being forced to clear out the cellar first. Was that what death was like?

★ ★ ★

"Sorry?"

Aubrey blinked. Somehow, he had drifted off in the middle of a conversation.

"Forgive me. Something had occurred to me as you were speaking. You write of a Universe B. In other words, a Universe somehow parallel or even perpendicular to our own ..."

"It is a common idea in esotericism, though perhaps not stated in quite the same way. There is a dimension from which illumination may be found. It certainly doesn't seem to be falling off the trees around here, wouldn't you agree?"

All Aubrey could do was nod.

"When one meditates, or performs occult rituals, one is crossing over from our world to another, if only briefly. The occult author of the nineteenth century, P. B. Randolph, laid all of this out quite clearly for the time. The idea of a magic circle, within which the magician must stand as he summons angels or demons, is a place between the worlds, between this Universe and the Next. Thus there are access points in this dimension that enable one to jump into the next dimension more easily."

"*Les points chauds?*" Aubrey suggested, using the French pronunciation.

Bertiaux was somewhat startled that this stranger was familiar with his work to that extent.

"Yes, actually. The *points chauds*, or 'hot points,' serve as gateways to Universe B."

"Can you explain that?"

Bertiaux was silent for a moment.

"We are talking about the physics of the *Necronomicon*."

It was Aubrey's turn to be startled. Why is he *always* hearing the name of that book no matter where he goes? And no matter with whom he is speaking?"

"You mean, the *Necronomicon* as invented by Lovecraft?"

The old magician smiled owlishly behind his glasses.

"Invented? Perhaps. But I consider the *Necronomicon* to be a *terma* and Lovecraft himself to be a *terton*. Are you familiar with these terms?"

Aubrey nodded. "If you had asked me that a year ago, I would have said no. But I have been getting a crash-course in Tibetan religion lately."

"So you know that a terma is a discovered text, and that a terton is the person who discovers it. A terma can be a physical object that was buried, like a book, or it can be its spiritual equivalent. At any rate, the physics represented by the *Necronomicon* is what concerns us here. Are you a member of the Brotherhood?"

"Pardon?"

"No, perhaps not. No matter. You appear to have a grounding in the essentials. When you contacted me, I understood you to be a friend of Simon?"

Aubrey nodded.

"Well, he wouldn't send me someone completely ignorant of the basic facts of the Gnosis. To be brief, then, there are power zones. They are on the Earth, but not always in the same place at the same time. That is because geography and topology depend upon physical laws, and the physics of the three-dimensional world are not the same as the physics we are discussing. Once you change your perspective to take in another dimension, the topology undergoes a transformation. In other words, your maps and globes become useless even though you are still physically present in this world, on this planet. The relationships—spatial and temporal—between yourself as the observer and another person or thing as the observed event are re-oriented, so to speak. A different 'orient': a different East, a different cardinal direction. Not only in space, such as north-south-east-west, but in time, such as past-present-future."

"If that is the case, then how would it be possible to … to work within such a different dimensional environment?"

Bertiaux sought a way to explain in the vernacular what occultists and sorcerers know in their own specialized jargon.

"It can be described as vibrational, but not in the New Age way of talking about 'vibes' and such. If the string theory people are correct, then reality as we know it is the result of the vibrations of extremely tiny strings. These are purely mathematical 'strings,' of course, as no one has ever seen one. Put another way, we know that light and sound are vibrations. Color is a vibration of light at different frequencies. Even the esoteric language provides guidance for that. The magic 'spell' for instance refers to the words of a chant designed to cause change to occur, like the Indian mantra. The word 'grimoire' for a magician's workbook comes from the word for 'grammar.'"

"I'm not sure I follow. How does any of that answer the question of how one navigates between dimensions?"

The magician folded his hands across his stomach and smiled benevolently. Aubrey was struck by the image of a Buddha.

"It is written that in the beginning was the Word. And the Word was with God. Surely you remember that from your Bible?"

"Yes, but that seems a bit theoretical. How does one actually employ that knowledge ..."

"The ancient Egyptians used to open the mouth of the mummy in a very specific ritual," Bertiaux interrupted. "It was done using a device that was crafted from a piece of meteoric iron. A magnet. An instrument that they knew pointed to the North Star. So the dead being reborn; the opening of the dead person's mouth; the use of a magnet that points North, and moreover crafted in the shape of the Big Dipper, part of the Great Bear constellation. The same constellation mentioned in the *Necronomicon* as the indicator of the Gate between the two universes. All you need to know is in that ritual. Or in the divine trances of *le peristyle*."

Aubrey was totally at sea. He had sparred with philosophers and mathematicians, with spies and double agents, with commandos and neurotic professors. But he was ready to throw in the towel with this old man in an apartment in Chicago who seemed to be speaking in tongues, all of them English.

"I think I will have that coffee," he surrendered.

★ ★ ★

Aubrey made his way to his hotel, the newly-opened Virgin Hotel in the Old Dearborn Bank building (which he remembered from his childhood as just that, the Dearborn Bank Building, where his disabled father had worked during the war pushing a broom). He was exhausted from his hours-long conversation with the Magus of

Michigan Avenue and needed a shower, a nap, and a stiff drink. He assumed the Virgin would provide all three.

There was no reception desk, evidently. A young lady with an English accent walked up to him with an iPad and checked him in. Ah, yes, the place was named Virgin because it was owned by Richard Branson, the Brit of Virgin Airways fame. Aubrey looked up and remembered some of the details from the old bank lobby, and was surprised to see that the plaster ceiling had been restored. The building was an Art Deco masterpiece, dating from 1928, and had those weird mythological creatures in the façade. Bertiaux would have felt right at home, he thought.

He received his room key and found his way to his "chamber" as they were called at the Virgin. Another Hogwartian touch, like the original façade. Aubrey allowed himself a brief flight of fancy as he imagined his own room to be the "chamber of secrets" considering that he, himself, was a keeper of secrets.

He removed his jacket and tie, and sank gratefully into a chair and surveyed the last three hours in his mind. He had his notebook in front of him, but needed no prompting to remember the high points. He would refer to his notes later, for clarification or expansion, but right now he wanted to recall the mood, the impressions, of the meeting.

As with Umberto Eco in Italy, and Alexander Grothendieck in France, Bertiaux had been tricky. All three men had waltzed around what he wanted to know. No one had been direct, or seemed to know how to respond to a straight question with a straight answer. Aubrey was used to intelligence debriefings and even to hostile interrogations, should the truth ever be known (and he hoped it wouldn't be). He knew that debriefings often could be embellished to make the speaker appear more knowledgeable than he or she was; he also knew the perils buried within any hostile interrogation, where a subject would invent information to please his or her captors, or would simply lie to conceal important data as they were taught to do. It was amazing how little truth could be found in everyday conversation; how much less in an intelligence environment, when lives or even nations depended on it. It all came down to words, to language, even to semiotics, and Aubrey trusted none of that.

When you came to the occult, however, all bets were off. He got that from Eco, certainly, and also from Grothendieck who— even though he was a world-renowned mathematician—was heavily invested in occult theories and mysticism. But Bertiaux was the culmination of all of that.

He suspected that Bertiaux was being honest with him, even voluble. But context was everything, and even after years of association with Monroe and his weird fixations, Aubrey was still on shaky ground when it came to occultists and their jargon and their "field" to use a term borrowed from Pierre Bourdieu, the French sociologist. All this about the *Necronomicon*—which is what started this whole mess with Gregory Angell back in Red Hook—was at its heart incomprehensible to Aubrey. He recognized that it was a kind of religious text in its way, and he well knew how that was enough of a motivation for some people and groups of fanatics to go absolutely ape-shit and start killing innocent people. It could have been the Bible, or the Qur'an, or any other sacred text. The gods all seemed to require massive infusions of blood, preferably from human beings who were not on the same cursed page as their fellows. Jefferson said that "The Tree of Liberty must be refreshed from time to time with the blood of patriots and tyrants," or some such foolishness. Aubrey had seen the folly of that sentiment more times than he could count, from Vietnam to Chile, from Nicaragua to Afghanistan.

What about the Tree of Life, though? Why does *it* need to be watered with the blood of children, of the innocent? What sick fuck came up with that theory? What deranged deity? What "blind idiot god of chaos," to use one of Lovecraft's images?

He was wandering in his mind, going from locked room to locked room and trying all the knobs. He was tired, obviously, and could use that drink. There was a mini-bar in his "chamber" and he decided to go in that direction rather than order something more exotic from room service.

He opened the mini-bar and then just sat and stared into it.

He realized that he understood Angell. He understood the professor's initial reluctance to assist Monroe in his arcane mission of finding the *Necronomicon* before the "Mad Arabs" did. He understood Angell's disgust with religion in general, his loss of faith: in God, in religion, in government. Angell was at large somewhere in the world, and for a moment Aubrey wondered if they should just leave the bastard alone. His job, though, was to find him before the "others" did: the fanatics, the terrorists, the child-snatching cultists. He would do that. It's what he was made for, what he was tasked to do.

But he wasn't sure what he would do when he found him.

There was some cognac in the mini-bar. That would do for now.

BOOK TWO

SPUKHAFTE FERNWIRKUNG

("SPOOKY ACTION AT A DISTANCE")

There seemed to be an awful, immemorial linkage in several definite stages betwixt man and nameless infinity. The blasphemies which appeared on earth, it was hinted, came from the dark planet Yuggoth, at the rim of the solar system; but this was itself merely the populous outpost of a frightful interstellar race whose ultimate source must lie far outside even the Einsteinian space-time continuum or greatest known cosmos.

—H. P. Lovecraft, "The Whisperer in Darkness" 1930, pub 1931.

CHAPTER FOURTEEN

Yogyakarta, Indonesia

ANGELL GLANCED AROUND FOR A LAST LOOK at the place he called home since landing in Indonesia. There wasn't much there—everything he owned fit into his backpack—but he had been happy there for the first time since Iraq. He had made peace with that part of himself that had begun to hate God, religion, and the world after witnessing the massacre of the Yezidi in Mosul. Back then, he had been sleeping in his apartment in Red Hook with a gun under his pillow, not so much for protection as to remind himself that he always had a way out of the madness and the despair. He had been suicidal, and then Aubrey had appeared and offered him a mission, a purpose to his life. He had not wanted to take it, but something about the offer and the possibilities made him consider it, and then accept it. He had been told that a terror group was planning a major terrorist attack that would dwarf anything that had happened so far, including 9/11. He was told it had to do with a book, and that he had to do whatever he could to find and retrieve it.

He wound up at a refugee camp in Turkey, where he saw an amazing young woman who seemed possessed by a strange demon. He saw her again, in a cave under a mountain in the Himalayas, somewhere in Nepal, where she was possessed once again. The entire room began to tremble with the force of something that he could not name, could not identify, except through the book that she held: the book he had been sent to find.

The force of that experience—the sensation that something unbelievably evil was rising up from the bowels of the Earth to threaten the world—was enough to shatter his atheism. Maybe it wasn't God that was trying to rend the veil between the worlds, but that wasn't the point. Whatever it was, it wasn't human and it was powerful in a way that no human experience—not love, not hate, not desire—was powerful. It shook him like a baby's rattle, and he fled the scene with the accursed book and a need to disappear somewhere in the wilderness until he could get his mind around what had happened, and what had happened to him.

And then there was that incredible experience on the beach the week he arrived in Indonesia. The ritual with the book. With the old shaman. He saw—with his eyes but with more than his eyes, as if his optic nerves were located somewhere in his chest—a goddess or a female spirit or something like that, Lara Kidul, the Goddess of the Southern Ocean, and she somehow poured a balm on his soul that was both bitter and acrid, but also healing. And, at the same time, he felt the Shadow grow across his shoulders: the existential threat that was the Thing they had been summoning in that cave in Nepal. The Thing that had possessed that poor young Yezidi girl until her face and voice began to transform into something hideous:

Cthulhu.

And now he was planning to leave once again. He felt like that guy in the old television show, *The Fugitive*, who was always in a different town every week. But he had changed since this same time last year. He was less cynical, less pessimistic. His self-loathing was dissipated. He felt empowered in a way that he never had before. He felt … he felt for the first time that he was actually *in* his body. Extended through all of it. From his inner organs to the tips of his fingers. He was *incarnated.* A complete human being. Not just a human with a body and a mind, but a *soul.*

He knew he shouldn't dawdle but that small room in an Indonesian *kampung* was the only real home he had known in years. The apartment in Red Hook was never really the sanctuary that he wanted it to be. It was more like solitary confinement, if the prisoner was allowed to keep a firearm.

He had always been impressed by the fact that Muslims had to pray facing a specific direction: the Ka'aba in Mecca. The direction was called the *qibla*, which is Arabic for "direction." Every mosque had a spot on the wall or ceiling that served as the direction of prayer. Many hotel rooms around the world, and especially in Africa, the Middle East, and Asia, had the same: a small plaque with an arrow pointing towards Mecca. He used to picture it in his mind: millions of the faithful, all facing the same direction towards Mecca all at the same time. There were more than a billion Muslims in the world, and of course they did not all pray at the same time due to time zones, but at any given hour there would be millions…

The Islamic calendar was lunar, but the time for prayer is solar: based on the division of hours between sunrise and sunset. This blend of lunar and solar influences was distinctly alchemical, if not even Tantric, in nature, at least according to Angell's recent, albeit solitary, ruminations. And the fact that the Ka'aba contained a meteorite, a "stone fallen from the sky," made the whole thing even more mystical.

He had to pay attention to these details because it was the context in which the *Necronomicon* was written: by a supposedly "Mad Arab," named Abdul Hazred, who hailed from Yemen, a part of the world notorious for antinomian sects, and which was now being targeted by Sunni Saudi Arabia for its distinctly Shia loyalties. Angell remembered that the family of Osama bin Laden—this century's ultimate "Mad Arab"—also has its roots in Yemen. So, for all of these reasons, Angell's sojourn in Indonesia had paid off in terms of a much-needed refresher course in the theory and practice of Islam.

★ ★ ★

His thoughts went back to those first days a year ago when a strange, older—albeit well-dressed—man named Aubrey paid him a visit in Brooklyn and told him that his country needed him to go back to the war zone. Since then, his life had been turned upside down. Not that it was great to begin with, with him sleeping with a gun under his pillow and having Mosul flashbacks at three am. What Aubrey did was give him a purpose. Angell was aimed at a problem like a heat-seeking missile and he found his target.

And then he went walkabout. To Mongolia and China, and from there to Java. All because of a book, which—if he thought about it for any length of time, which he did every day—was pretty cool. In this era of digital everything, with entire libraries, paintings, and compositions available as .pdf files or on websites, with streaming films and music and podcasts, to have the world in an uproar over a hardcopy, hand-written manuscript was gratifying to a scholar, especially one who specializes in ancient religions from the days when they didn't even have books much less Kindle.

And that was it, wasn't it? You could photocopy the thing or digitize it, scan it even, and for some reason it wouldn't be the same. They had to have the original, the actual one he was carrying around with him and never left out of his sight. Angell thought maybe that was because they—whoever "they" were—needed to be sure they had the actual volume and not an altered version. Angell went so far as to check the pages under different lighting sources to see if maybe there was something embedded in the pages, or an old erasure, or something. That maybe the *Necronomicon* was a palimpsest: a manuscript written over the erased pages of another, more important, manuscript.

But, no. It had to be the book itself. It had to be the contents, the text, what it actually *says*. They had to be sure, those murderers from Dagon, that the calculations were correct. That there weren't lacunae in the text. No marginalia.

They had to know if the stars were right.

Problem was: Angell had done his own calculations, had covered dozens of pages of cheap paper with them. Had tried different textual analyses and translation strategies. And he still couldn't figure out how Dagon's system worked .

But he had the distinct impression—heightened by seeing the surveillance at the internet café—that whatever was going down, was going down soon. Within weeks at most. Maybe less.

And who the hell was he going to tell?

CHAPTER FIFTEEN

New Orleans
Same Day

IN THE LAST YEAR, CUNEO HAD CLEARED all of his cases with the exception of the two biggest ones: the murder of the old lady in Belle Chasse in November, and before that the weird double homicide in the Lower Ninth with the victims penned up underground in some kind of Faraday Cage. At least that's what it looked like.

The two cases were connected. There was a lot of weird voodoo shit involved in each one, and that last one spooked him completely. It was not easy to spook Cuneo, an Italian-African American from the Bronx who worked cases out of the Ninth Precinct in Manhattan before putting in his papers and taking this relatively cozy position—he thought—in laid-back New Orleans. But for him the Big Easy had turned into the Big Queasy. He had a suspect in the last homicide but he was like a wisp of smoke. He left a "smiley face" calling card behind, but that went nowhere. He wasn't linked to the other "smiley face" murders that had occurred at different spots in the United States over the years. Cuneo guessed it was just his sense of humor.

And then there was the kid.

They had discovered a child buried alive in a box in that house in Belle Chasse. Cuneo still could not understand how that baby managed to stay alive in what was a kind of sarcophagus behind a wall in the basement of the house. *Basement.* In *New Orleans.* The whole thing made no friggin' sense.

But they rescued the child and brought him to the hospital in an ambulance with all the lights and sirens because they thought he would die at any moment. And while they were doing that, Cuneo realized that there had to be another baby in a box in another part of the basement and they broke down the wall, found the sarcophagus, and it was empty. But not before Cuneo had been attacked, and knocked unconscious for a short while as the attacker escaped through a basement window. An impossible escape, especially as Cuneo suspected that the attacker was ... ah ... the other baby?

Yeah, it didn't sound better to him either. He kept that little fact to himself. Him, and his colleague Lisa Carrasco. Lisa seemed to have a natural instinct for the case, though, and she had managed to trace the original builders of the house to a firm in Providence, Rhode Island. It seemed that a religious community—the Church of Starry Wisdom—had been forced to abandon their original building due to some unpleasantness with the local population. They used the same architects, though, when they moved to New Orleans before the turn of the century, sometime in the late 1800s. Lisa had been trying to get more information on the architects, but it had been a long time ago. And, anyway, Lisa had other duties and was only really a part-time assistant to Cuneo.

Still, he now had two homicide cases in different parts of town that involved occultism and possibly ritual sacrifice. This in a city as well-known for voodoo as for Mardi Gras. He had tried to keep as many of the details of both cases away from the public, but a chill had descended on the French Quarter and the voodoo shops anyway. The local Masonic lodges were also affected, as it seems the old lady from Belle Chasse was known to them as well. Women are not initiated into regular, Blue Lodge, Masonry but they are in what is known as Co-Masonry (which has a more pronounced esoteric flavor, too). It seems she was a full-fledged Co-Mason, whatever that meant in the grand scheme of things.

The house she lived in was owned by a front corporation that was headquartered in the Cayman Islands, which was itself a front for another corporation headquartered in the British Virgin Islands, and from there to ... outer space somewhere. One interlocking corporate relationship after another. For a house in New Orleans. The companies didn't seem to own anything else that he could find. The house itself wasn't particularly valuable, and the furnishings were nothing to write home about. The only unusual aspect of the place—aside from the sarcophagi in the basement—was the book collection and the associated esoteric artifacts.

Cuneo wanted them seized as evidence, but he had a hard time convincing a judge until he showed her photos of the basement, the boxes with their strange hieroglyphics, and the spines of just one book shelf with titles like *The Book of Black Magic and of Pacts, Aleister Crowley and the Hidden God, The Black Pullet, The Sworn Book of Honorious, The Gates of the Necronomicon,* and *The Picture Museum of Sorcery, Magic and Alchemy.*

"What?" said Her Honor. "No *Long Lost Friend?* No *Sixth and Seventh Books of Moses?*" She knew her New Orleans hoodoo real estate, that was for sure.

"Actually, Your Honor, she had those, too."

Smirking to herself, she signed the warrant.

Now Cuneo had a stack of very suggestive literature on his desk, sprinkled with a variety of color-coded adhesive bookmarks. He was getting closer, he felt, to understanding the strange writing he found all over the walls and the boxes in the basements but they didn't seem to be from a single source. They were mixed Egyptian, Sumerian, and Tibetan scripts and diagrams, along with some he could not place in an esoteric context but which made sense in a purely mathematical one.

There were a lot of those cube-type figures, the kind you used to draw as a kid to show all the sides of a three-dimensional six-sided cube in two dimensions. But they weren't always cubes. In fact, most of them were oddly-shaped, but still wire-framed so that you could use them to depict multi-dimensional space. Instead of the usual Latin or Greek letters that mathematicians would use at the corners of the diagrams, Cuneo found Egyptian hieroglyphics in places; Sumerian cuneiform in others; and Sanskrit in still others. There were some letters that looked like Aramaic, too, but Cuneo had called it a day by that time. He remembered that movie with his hero, Denzel, about the demon that possessed people just by touching them. *Fallen,* it was. The creepy serial killer in the opening scene was speaking Aramaic then, too, as Denzel and John Goodman found out later from a local university professor.

Cuneo knew that was where he was headed, eventually, once he had this material a little better organized.

"Any luck?" Lisa's voice jolted him out of whatever reverie it was he allowed himself this late in the afternoon.

"Hi, Lisa. No, not really. I mean, a lot of data, but nothing that makes sense or hangs together very well."

"So, we're no closer to finding this guy?"

"Not today, anyway. I keep getting other cases, ones that are usually a little easier to solve—gangbangers and domestics—so this one gets pushed back from time to time until I can focus on it again."

"You'd think a serial killer case like this one would get a task force, or something," she said, as she made herself at home on the one spare swivel chair she could find.

"They don't wanna use the 's' word just yet."

"Well, you had two in the Ninth Ward and the old lady in Belle Chasse. That's three, so that's a serial, right?"

"As far as the FBI is concerned, I guess, but we haven't brought them into this one. They may not even be aware of it, anyway." Cuneo sounded doubtful about the whole thing. "How about you? Any news on the architect front?"

"No more than we had last time we talked."

Cuneo shook his head and stared at a photocopy of the floor plan of the Belle Chasse house. "I sure would like to know why they built tubes in the house that go nowhere."

Each of the two sarcophagi had a tube running into it from the ceiling of the basement, but there was no indication that the tubes served any real purpose. They seemed to dead-end at the ceiling, and then another set of tubes was discovered that ran from the ceiling of the ground floor to the floor above: only a few inches. It was maddening.

Lisa shrugged. "It's almost as if the tubes were there first, and they built the house around them."

"It's N'awlins, cher. Anything is possible," he replied in his best bad New Orleans accent.

Lisa smiled, and then got up to leave.

"Let me know if you need my help on anything, *cher.*"

"You bet," he replied, already lost in thought.

Lisa kept smiling as she left. He was completely at sea, and for reasons known only to her she enjoyed it.

★ ★ ★

The sarcophagi in the Belle Chasse place had occupied most of his attention, but he found himself going around in circles. He turned his attention to the first crime, the dead bodies in the Faraday Cage in the Ninth. He suspected they were connected because of the similar occult diagrams and the overall weirdness of the crime scenes. There was also the deeply unsettling finding by the medical examiner that the old lady—Mrs. Galvez—who had her neck broken in Belle Chasse had given birth recently. Galvez was about a hundred years old. Something like that. It should have been biologically impossible for her to conceive or to bring any kind of fetus to term even if she could conceive. He thought of his own Catholic upbringing and the idea of the Virgin Mother. In that case, the virgin—Mary—was capable of conceiving and bringing to term but she was unmarried and, well, a virgin. But according to Catholic doctrine she gave birth to Jesus.

Now here was a much older woman who gave birth. It was like two women at opposite ends of the spectrum, neither of whom should have been capable of conceiving and bringing to term. As far as he could tell, there had been no males present at either scene.

And then you had the case in the Lower Ninth. Two bodies found by accident in a concrete bunker underground. And the metal rods that formed a kind of cage around them. Again, there was a ritualistic component as well as a sexual one.

It made his head hurt.

And somewhere in the pile of paperwork on his desk was a

report he asked for on the structure of the underground bunker. A lot of engineering and geological terminology he didn't understand and had to look up. But basically it seems that the metal rods had been custom made. There were plugs made of something called magnetite at each end of each rod. It was weird. It was as if the design of the cage was based on magnetic principles.

Who the hell would go to that kind of trouble, unless it was for some off-the-wall ritualistic purpose?

He had the coroner's reports on the bodies, too. More weirdness. Cause of death was undetermined, but when they examined the brains of the two victims they found an abnormal amount of a metallic substance in the slices. Spherical. Tiny. But unmistakably there.

Magnetite.

"Shit," he said aloud, surprising everyone in the office. The old lady, Galvez, she had owned the house in the Ninth. Or her husband had, or was the caretaker, or something. The house in the Ninth had exploded shortly after the bunker had been discovered, and after he—Cuneo—was forced to shoot a wild man in the street waving a machete. A man whose name and photo matched one in the files from 1907.

He had the post-mortem on old Mrs. Galvez. He had to see if they did the same test on her brain that they did on the two DBs from the Ninth Ward bunker.

He found the folder and flipped through the pages. There were scans, as he had hoped. Same results. The medical examiner's opinion was that the presence of the microscopic spheres of magnetite might have indicated Alzheimer's.

Cuneo thought back to the interview he conducted with Mrs. Galvez at the time they had discovered the underground bunker and the fact that she owned it. It was a strange discussion, to be sure. Galvez had hinted at all sorts of dark secrets, membership in arcane societies, and the rest. She confirmed that the society she referred to was the same one he had been looking at in the archives, a case dating back to 1907.

She sure sounded crazy, but he didn't think she had Alzheimer's. But then, what did he know about Alzheimer's? Nothing. All he knew was that she was lucid and aware and was able to hold a conversation; she seemed perfectly present. But then, one with Alzheimer's could go in and out, right? Sometimes fine, sometimes absent?

He sighed. He didn't know. He would have to ask around. In the meantime, that had nothing to do with the two bodies in the Ninth Ward. They hadn't died of Alzheimer's. Whatever they had died of, had to do with the weird bunker and the metal rods and the occult symbols all over the place.

They had been sacrificed.

He sat back in his chair and considered his options. He knew nothing about whatever weird cult was involved in this thing. He had approached this case the wrong way. Forensic evidence would only become useful once he had a suspect, and right now he had none. The old lady, Galvez, was the closest he came to a suspect in the Ninth Ward case and she was dead, murdered, possibly another sacrifice.

There was a cult connection there, too, as Lisa told him. Some religious group called Starry Wisdom. From New England. And Galvez had told him she belonged to something called Dagon. Neither of these were familiar to him at all. He knew Jonestown, the Manson Family, Scientology, Haitian vodoun, Santeria ... but Starry Wisdom? Dagon?

He could find no trace of these groups in any database.

His last investigation had resulted in a guilty plea in exchange for a reduced sentence. He figured he had maybe an hour before another slew of homicides landed on his desk. He might as well take advantage of the lull and make a few calls.

CHAPTER SIXTEEN

New York City
Same day

RETIRED NYPD DETECTIVE WASSERMAN sat with his old colleague
Danny at the counter of a coffee shop in Brooklyn Heights, with a
view towards the Brooklyn Bridge. They were drinking coffee and
poking at sandwiches. Danny had just come from a meeting on the
case of the murdered gynecologist, and wanted to bring Wasserman
up to date. It was a case that so far was going nowhere. But first, they
had some unfinished business.

"You're in the clear on that assassination thing, Loo. Whoever
that shooter was, he's long gone. He—or she—left no brass, no
prints, no hairs or fibers. We can't even trace the weapon, except it
was some kinda fancy sniper rig. But you knew all that."

"Yeah, Danny. I did. They laid it out for me when they picked
me up at the scene. So there's no leads?"

Danny shook his head.

"They're working on your idea that the shooter was a woman.
They got some CCTV on the suspect, but she was wearing one of
those veil things and it hid her features. You put together a sniper
rifle and a woman in a veil, and you feel like that should narrow it
down a little, right?"

"It doesn't?"

"It should, but they don't seem to know what to do with the
info. I think it's all going to the Joint Terrorism Task Force, and
they're keeping us out of it. A high profile case like that, I don't give
a fuck. Let the Feds handle it, and they will, eventually, no matter
who ID's the perp."

"Who's got custody of the body?"

"We do, for now. Eventually it'll be returned to the Iraqis. Guy
was a Muslim, and they're supposed to bury him right away. The

Mayor's office rushed the autopsy and they'll give the body back to their officials tonight."

"What are they gonna do? Fly him back to Baghdad?"

Danny shrugged. "Damned if I know. Or care, at this point."

"The guy was a terrorist, though, right?"

"Depends on who you talk to. Seems like the guy was ISIL for awhile, but defected or something and wound up with a post in the Iraqi government. What's left of it."

"Weird."

"Weird that he defected, or ...?"

"Weird that ISIL let him live."

"Well, like I say it depends on who you talk to. Could be just rumor at this point."

Wasserman knew that the shooter was the woman he saw getting out of the law school dorm. He tried to replay those moments over in his mind, to get a better picture of her. Something. But it all "happened so fast" as eyewitnesses always say, and now he was one of them. It still bothered him, though. Here he was, a decorated if retired police detective, and he was useless. So he decided to change the subject to the case of the murdered and mutilated ob/gyn.

He didn't mention his strange phone conversation with the voice in DC, or the car that had picked him up, or the even stranger video call that took place in the SUV with a guy who could've doubled as Peter Cushing, the guy who called himself Aubrey. He had no idea how much Danny already knew, but he was sure he had to keep this episode to himself. Somehow Danny's dead doctor had some connection with the Angell character from Red Hook last year, and Danny already was aware of that, but not of the deeper links back to mysterious G-men in tricked-out SUVs. Better to keep him in the dark a little while longer while he tried to figure out the angles.

Danny was already fidgeting at the mention of the dead doctor.

"See, Loo, we know that the office could not have been the crime scene, right? No blood, no sign of a struggle. No trace evidence of any kind, which is damn near freaking impossible. Or so they tell me. The whole thing was staged. But for whose benefit? Us?"

"Who else?"

Danny shook his head.

"Damned if I can figure it out. It looked ritualistic, they say."

"Who's 'they'?"

"Ah, you know. The freaks from the Bureau."

"Oh. The profilers."

"Yeah. Profile is right. Everything they do is in silhouette."

Wasserman looked a question at him.

"You know. Silhouette. Everything is two-dimensional. There's no depth to what they tell us. I can write the damned profiles myself at this point."

"Danny, you amaze me."

"Fuck you."

"No, I mean it. I never heard that silhouette thing before. I like it."

They were both silent as they contemplated their coffee and their future.

"What about the mothers? The ones who lost their … whaddaya call it … fetuses?"

"We're talking to all of them. All we can find, anyway. There's one or two in the wind. We'll find them."

"And what are they telling you?"

"Some of them didn't know shit. They didn't even know they were missing an embryo until we told them. We thought they knew. You can imagine the scene. We had to bring in therapists for some of them. They were, like, losing it even though they were as big as houses with the one."

Wasserman shook his head at the callousness of his old partner. "And the fathers?"

"We interviewed the ones we could find. Some of these mothers were doing it all on their own. Husband died, or they got divorced, or were never married in the first place. You'd be surprised how few actual couples we found. Except for one or two lesbian couples who got pregnant through …unconventional means. Anyway, seems this doctor specialized in hardship cases, so word got around."

"Did you get a consult from another doctor? Just in case?"

"Yeah. There was this one guy. A Doctor Neal or Nile or something like that. Specializes in 'missing fetus' cases. Can you believe it? Like it's a medical specialty or something?"

"Is it?"

"Well, kinda, yeah. He says it's a 'natural phenomenon'. A lot of potential twin births end up that way. One twin sorta consumes the other in the womb, or something. Showed me some photos. Freaky as shit."

"Jesus."

"Yeah, really. Who knew?"

"But then … why would this Brooklyn gynecologist keep this, like, super secret file on them? If it was so natural?"

Danny leaned over the table and spoke under his breath in a hoarse whisper.

"That's just the thing. It gets worse. This Neal or Nile said that there was a big flap some years ago about this 'phenomenon' among members of the '*U—F—O* community'."

Then he sat back against his seat and folded his arms across his chest.

"You're shitting me."

"I shit you not, old son."

"What did they think? That a little green man took their baby? And only one fetus of the two? Like he wasn't tryna be greedy?"

"Like a friggin' dingo."

"What?"

"You remember. 'A dingo ate my baby.' That Australian broad."

"Damn, Danny. You are a veritable fountain of trivia."

"A Fountain of Trevi of Trivia."

"Indeed. But … I don't get it. What's the connection to this case, then?"

"The doc? The dead one? There was all this correspondence between him and some flying saucer group about the cases. Seems that some of the ultrasounds were taken only a few days apart. One day, everything is fine. Twin fetuses. A day or two later, and one of them is missing. He felt that the usual explanations didn't cut it. That the missing fetus couldn't disappear that fast, or something. So he started researching other cases and came across the UFO stories. There were clippings in his files from the newspapers about UFO sightings in New York around the same time as the fetuses go missing."

"Oh, man. Come on, Danny. Don't tell me *you* are falling for this crap?"

"Hey, I ain't saying nothing one way or another. But I gotta follow up, right? The clippings, the ultrasounds, the missing twins. And let's not forget the dead and mutilated doctor. Maybe he was offed by some UFO nut. Or one of the mothers went apeshit. Is there such a thing as *pre*-partum depression?"

"I don't have a clue, Danny. I guess it's possible, right? She gets the bad news and then kills the guy. But the crime scene … the posing of the body … that's not a rage kill, Danny. That was calm and controlled. Organized. And I don't care how big or strong the woman was, she needed help to move that body around the way she did even if she killed the guy herself. Like you said, that wasn't the primary crime scene. He was killed and decapitated—and his head *defleshed*—somewhere else. Expertly. With forensic counter-measures. And this was all done without any witnesses."

Danny just nodded, morosely, and picked at his sandwich.

"What about the ones that got away?"

"Whaddaya mean?"

"You said there was a couple of moms you can't find. One of them must know something. If I was involved in the kill, I would take off for parts unknown, too. If you found everyone else, and they're alibied up, then whoever is left must have some knowledge of the case or maybe she's even the perp. Or her husband or significant … whatever."

"Yeah, of course. But we don't know who they are. Well, the one. There's one I know is missing for sure. I mean, we have her file and her ultrasounds but there is no last name. No real phone number or address."

"She left fake contact info?"

"We figured it was an immigration thing, you know? Most of this guy's patients were foreign."

"This *is* New York. Almost everybody here is foreign."

"Hey, I'm from Yonkers. What does that make me?"

"A fucking tourist, what else?"

"Oh, like *your* people came on the Mayflower. On the Matzoh Ball, is more like it."

"Hey, watch it. Remember that old beer commercial? 'There are more Jews in New York City than there are in Tel Aviv'?"

"That, I believe."

"Do I detect a note of anti-Semitism, Danny, Old Boy?"

"A *note*? A whole friggin' *concerto*, you unrepentant rabbi."

"Golda Meir was born in Brooklyn. Did you know that?"

"Only every time you tell me. Which means, at least once a month."

★ ★ ★

They went on like that for awhile so they could return to their lunch and put the murder behind them. But as their plates were cleaned away and they settled in on another cup of coffee, the case again came up in their conversation like something from their lunch they could not quite digest.

"You gotta find that missing mother. What was her name?"

"Gloria. I only got the first name."

"Hey. Don't doctors these days run DNA from the fetuses, to check for congenital illnesses, birth defects, and like that?"

Danny shrugged. "Sounds familiar. Maybe they do. But like I said, this doctor seemed to specialize in hardship cases. Aren't those DNA tests expensive?"

"Sure," he nodded. "But he was looking for something. He thought there was something weird about some of his cases. Maybe he woulda paid for the tests himself."

Danny smiled.

"That's why you're the Loo, Loo. You got the best ideas. I'll run it down, see if there are any DNA results in his files and, if not, see if he maybe contracted with a DNA lab somewhere and get a subpoena for their records. Maybe there's some way to use the DNA to identify the missing mother."

Danny picked up the tab for lunch, saying it was a business expense and knowing that since his old lieutenant was Jewish he wasn't going to pay anyway.

They bickered good-naturedly like that on their way out of the diner, never noticing that someone in another booth had followed them all the way with his eyes and a friendly smile.

CHAPTER SEVENTEEN

Simon's Apartment
Crofton, Maryland

Simon began to laugh, quietly and reservedly at first but he couldn't stem the flow and he eventuallsy collapsed onto the couch.

★ ★ ★

Aubrey was non-plussed. He arranged his leather satchel in front of him and began to withdraw some papers with his notes of the meeting with Michael Bertiaux.

He had just flown in from Chicago and drove himself from Dulles to Simon's apartment. At least it was a domestic flight. He had been flying all around the world in the last year and it was getting old.

He arrived at the apartment and was surprised to see that no one else was there. The others, he was told, were still at Fort Meade. They were analyzing some data that had come in concerning the current whereabouts of the Dagon leadership.

So Aubrey sat down and began to recount his bizarre meeting with Bertiaux. What started as the regular sort of debriefing that Aubrey had done so often throughout his career had slowly morphed into a deadpan comedy routine as he tried to describe the Occult Book Store, the apartment building, the Ari fellow, the weird paintings and statues, and most of all the pleasant but inscrutable Michael Bertiaux.

★ ★ ★

"I'm sorry to have put you through that!" Simon managed to get out, between gasps.

"No, you're not," corrected Aubrey, with an arched eyebrow.

Simon nodded, still chuckling. "You're right. I'm not. But it was necessary."

"I'm sure," Aubrey replied absently, staring at the papers in his hands.

"Something wrong?"

"I am reading these notes. They're my notes. I took them. I wrote them down. But I don't understand a single word." He looked up at Simon, helpless.

"Maybe you can figure them out. I'm old. I'm tired. I need a nap."

With that, Aubrey stood up and left the apartment. His notes were in a pile on the chair he had just vacated. Simon picked them up and began to read.

★ ★ ★

After about fifteen minutes, he realized that there was no way Aubrey could have understood them. They would make no sense to someone who was not immersed in the subject like Bertiaux was, or Simon himself. And even then ...

It dawned on him that the Chicago mage had deliberately made his explanations obtuse. They obviously were not meant for Aubrey at all. They were meant for him.

★ ★ ★

"They're practically in code. Decipherable, of course, but impenetrable to most people, even well-educated people. If you didn't have a background in this particular and peculiar mix of western esotericism, Lovecraftian literature, and quantum mechanics, you couldn't even begin to translate this."

"Is that why you said it was intended for you?"

Monroe and Sylvia had arrived at Simon's apartment about two hours after Aubrey had left. Monroe had spoken with Aubrey by phone, and was told that Simon would be able to fill them all in.

"Yes, Dwight, I believe so. He could have explained this more plainly to Aubrey—well, a little more plainly, anyway—and didn't have to resort to some of the terms he's throwing around here. He's trying to tell me something, and couching his language in a way that's designed to resist an eavesdropper figuring it out. He must be worried about something. Probably the same thing we are."

He picked up one of the pages bearing Aubrey's notes, and pointed to a diagram.

"You see this? Aubrey didn't draw it. Bertiaux did."

"What is it?" asked Sylvia, who up to now had been silent as Simon rattled on about what he had discovered. She could tell that Monroe was focused entirely on his old friend's narration, and she didn't want to disturb the flow.

"It's a *vèvè*. An occult diagram. It's used by *vodouisants*, followers of *vodou* in Haiti. Actually, they are usually drawn by the *houngan* or the high priest of a vodou circle. In Bertiaux's interpretation, however, they are more than symbols of the Haitian gods, the *loa*. They are geometric pathways of force. This one is of the Marasa, the Twins, and seems to be related to the information he was giving Aubrey."

He traced the design on the paper with his finger.

"Each of these designs is different, one for each of the gods. The gods themselves are said to represent primeval forces. Before Bertiaux, there was another author on Haitian religion called Milo Rigaud, equally controversial, but he insisted on the same thing. He said that these diagrams were geometric forces that depicted various relationships between space and time, intersections between space lines and time lines. All very fanciful, of course, until a similar conclusion was reached in the twenty-first century by an actual mathematician."

Monroe nodded. He was in familiar territory now.

"That would be Benjamin Tippett. I believe he teaches in Canada. A few years ago he published a paper analyzing some of the themes in Lovecraft's stories from the point of view of mathematical theory. The geometries described by Lovecraft were taken apart by Tippett and shown to be decipherable by someone with a working knowledge of Riemannian theory. The paper was written tongue-in-cheek, of course, but the math was solid. Lovecraft's descriptions of weird geometries and their effects on the human psyche seem to align with modern theories of spacetime curvature."

Simon nodded. "It's what Bertiaux calls 'Necronomicon physics'. It's what he was getting at during his meeting with Aubrey, but it went over Aubrey's head."

Sylvia laughed. "Seriously? Aubrey was the guy who interviewed Alexander Grothendieck!"

"Oh, Aubrey can follow the math alright. It was the magic he was having a hard time understanding," answered Monroe.

"But is this getting us any further along in our mission?"

There was a moment or two of silence as all assembled pondered Sylvia's question.

"Well, I'm still not finished going through Aubrey's notes, but there might be an answer in here somewhere. Remember when we worked out when and where the Dagon cult was going to perform its ritual last November?"

They nodded, and groaned inwardly. They seemed to have found the solution to that problem while fueled with adrenaline and Simon's exotic meals. They were not sure they could do *that* again.

"The cult is restricted, in a sense, to its own system. The schedules and topologies they employ are idiosyncratic to them. Or so it would seem. By comparing what I know of the systems of Aleister Crowley and H.P. Lovecraft to the Afro-Caribbean sources represented by Michael Bertiaux and Milo Rigaud, as well as the virtually impenetrable material published by Kenneth Grant, a great deal of similarity is discovered. Aubrey's notes are very helpful in that regard. Bertiaux was in contact with many organizations and individuals globally during his career, which began in Haiti in the 1960s and which included groups as diverse as the Theosophical Society, the Old Catholic Church, various Eastern churches, and of course the Martinist groups he encountered in the Caribbean. Add to that his background in western philosophy and his career as a social worker among the Haitian population in Chicago. The material he gave to Aubrey is a kind of summary of all of that, as well as a virtual password to Dagon's system."

"All of that? Really?"

"It's in esoteric shorthand, of course, but the elements are all there. If we maintain strict vigilance on our contacts both here and abroad and scoop up any chatter we can find, we might be able to tie all of this together."

"It would be a lot easier if Dagon used electronic communications of some sort."

"That is a problem, of course, but not an insoluble one. It means they can't act quickly, and must rely on slower communication systems to set up their next attempt to open the Gate. Snail mail, for instance. Ads in print media. Face to face contact. That sort of thing. That could work in our favor."

"But they've had six months already. They could have arranged anything in that amount of time."

"That ritual in Florida took a lot out of them. It resulted in the sweep of some of their major players, maybe most of them. Cultists were arrested all over the world, all at once. It didn't put an end to them, but it slowed them down considerably. They would have had to regroup, maybe even find and train new initiates."

Sylvia shuddered. "Not again. Those poor girls, Simon. You should have seen them. They're traumatized, probably for life."

"But it was your inspiration that got us going in the right direction, and you wouldn't have seen that if you hadn't gone to visit them."

"Possession is similar the world over. It's what occurred to me when I saw the smallest girls. We had cases like that in Malaysia, where there is a culture of supernaturalism and shamanism. In the west, it is common to think of possession as the demoniacal version, like *The Exorcist*. But possession can also take place with different kinds of spiritual forces. If we can find people who understand spirit possession, they might be able to help those girls. At least the ones they called the 'seers.'"

Monroe thought for a moment, and hesitated before saying out loud what he was considering.

"The Dagon people don't know about the girls. They don't know how many survived, or even if any survived. They don't know we have them in custody. And they don't know that some of them are pregnant."

It was Simon's turn to look worried.

"What are you thinking?"

"What was Dagon afraid of from the very start? That the seers could be used in reverse. That the Old Ones could use them as gateways into this world. In that case, they would go looking for the ones who let them in. And as for the others, they *wanted* the girls to become pregnant. What was their long-term strategy then? Would they raise these girls in some kind of orphanage or group home? Does Dagon have assets like that? Think of the personnel they would need, and the cost of housing, food, etc. plus security. They would need a remote location far from prying eyes, not only of nosy neighbors but also of the state. And that is if they were planning on keeping them all in one place. If they were distributed around in different locations, think of the logistical issues."

"But how could we possibly locate …?"

"We can't. Not without a lot more data. And we don't know how much time we have left. I imagine the target location would be in the States, if only because their central ritual took place in Florida. It would be easier to move them around in this country just the way they had gotten them to the site. Vans with blacked-out windows, that sort of thing. But where would they have gone?"

"How about Mexico?"

They were startled to hear Aubrey's voice come from the doorway to the apartment.

"Sorry. Didn't mean to startle you."

"I thought you were home, taking a well-deserved rest?"

"Oh, I cat-napped. That's pretty much all I need these days. And I kept going over the interview with your Chicago occultist in my mind. It was driving me insane, so I decided to give up on sleep and come over to see what progress we were making."

"How did you get past the downstairs door?" Simon was puzzled, and not a little concerned.

Aubrey only smiled.

"I've been in this business a long time. Some fancy electronics won't stop me."

"So someone else let you in?"

He shrugged.

Monroe jumped in before they all got sidetracked.

"What were you saying about Mexico?"

"Remember the Finders case from some decades ago?"

Monroe winced.

"Yes, I think we all do. It made headlines briefly, until the Agency pulled the plug."

"That had a Florida connection, and a DC connection, and in the end the children said that they were going to a special school in Mexico."

Sylvia alone looked puzzled.

"What was Finders?" she asked.

★ ★ ★

Simon had brewed a fresh pot of coffee, a Viennese blend he favored, and offered around a tray of warm Portuguese egg tarts which thrilled Sylvia no end. Egg tarts may have their origin in Portugal, but they are well-known all over Southeast Asia.

Once everyone had their coffee and desert in front of them, Monroe settled back in his chair and began to recite the history of the Finders cult and its mysterious aftermath.

"It was thirty years ago, or so," he began. "In Tallahassee, Florida. Concerned citizens reported to the local police that two well-dressed men seemed to be in charge of a group of small children who were playing in a park. The children were filthy and badly-clothed. The police responded, and took the children and the two men into custody. The children said they were on their way to a special school in Mexico."

"This was in 1987," Simon chimed in. "We were in the midst of the satanic cult survivor scare during which the whole country was under the impression that a nationwide ring of Satanists was kidnapping and sacrificing tens of thousands of children or more during their rituals."

"So, like the Pizzagate hoax?" asked Sylvia.

"Indeed. The same idea. Eventually the authorities would discover that there was no nationwide ring of child-abusing Satanists, no millions of missing children, and no graves full of dead babies. With a total lack of forensic evidence and no corroboration, the hysteria eventually died. It was odd, then, that the Finders case did not go much further in strengthening the conspiratorial nature of the scare."

Monroe continued in his summary of the case. "The evidence in the Finders case *was* quite strong. Identification on the two men in the van led the police back to Washington, and an informant led the Metropolitan Police Department to two addresses in the District. One was the cult's headquarters and the other was a warehouse where some very suspicious items were stored. The group was known as the 'Finders' but it was unclear what that signified. What the authorities found was a cache of documentation that demonstrated the involvement of Finders in human trafficking, child abuse, animal sacrifice, and the like. There were numerous contacts worldwide, including in China and Hong Kong. Visas for Eastern European countries. Travel to Moscow, North Vietnam and North Korea during the time period from roughly 1950 to 1970. There were also photographs of rituals, including animal sacrifices, involving children. The MPD and the Customs Service began an intensive investigation only to be shut down by CIA as a matter of national security."

"Jesus ..."

"And this was a story that was carried in all the major newspapers and news magazines at the time. Oddly, it never really caught the attention of the satanic cult survivor crowd. Here was hard evidence of an actual child-trafficking cult, and although it was picked up and reported widely the story simply disappeared."

"I imagine because it was easier, or at least more fun, to focus on the stories no one could prove but which could be embellished as one wished."

Monroe simply shrugged. "CIA had used Finders as a sub-contractor in cyber affairs, data mining and cyber security and the like, which was a young field in the 1980s. It was in the Agency's best interests to ensure that law enforcement did not have access to the documents and files held by Finders. But that meant covering up for some very strange behavior on the part of the cult's leadership."

"What about the school in Mexico?"

"No one was allowed to follow up on that. There have been rumors of such a school in Mexico for decades, though. It is believed to be located on a ranch or farm close enough to the border to enable quick runs back and forth. The *maquiladora* area, perhaps. Or Matamoros."

"Wasn't there a drug cult operating out of Matamoros at the same time?"

Simon chimed in. "A cult that used *Palo Mayombe* as their cover: an Afro-Caribbean religion, originally from the Congo, that is well-known for its use of an iron cauldron called a *nganga* or *caldero*, usually filled with all sorts of natural ingredients. The Matamoros group you refer to filled the cauldron with human blood and other body parts, but their leader was not considered a genuine *palero*. That said, a palero *was* arrested in Miami for hoarding human skulls, and another in New Jersey in 2002 who had a nganga similar to the one used by the Matamoros crowd."

Aubrey interrupted the flow which he knew could get out of hand very quickly with a question.

"Does any of this have anything to do with Dagon?"

Simon gave a meaningful look in Aubrey's direction before answering.

"Your notes give us every reason to think so. And you were the one who brought up Mexico. It is actually a very good possibility. Had the ritual in Florida been successful last year they easily could have driven down along the Gulf Coast to Louisiana and then Texas and crossed over into Mexico from there. Figure two days' drive, max."

"So why didn't they just hold the ritual in Mexico itself?"

"Your notes say it all. It was a question of time and place. There was nowhere in Mexico at that time that would have been suitable for the kind of ritual they were performing. There was no *point chaud* or hot point in that country. There wouldn't be for a number of years yet, according to their peculiar spacetime geography."

"So they could be there now. Regrouping."

Monroe nodded. "It's a possibility, of course. But remember one very important fact: as far as we know, they do not have the Book. They didn't have it in Florida, and they will probably chalk up their failure to complete the rite to that single element."

"And not our raid on their location?"

"Well, that too, of course! But they would have calculated that we were able to determine their location and schedule for the ritual due to the fact that they did not have the physical Book in their possession. That this lack made them more vulnerable, or somehow that gave us the edge." Monroe looked at them all significantly. "They won't make that mistake again. Which is why we *have* to find Angell. And we have to do it before they do."

CHAPTER EIGHTEEN

Yogyakarta, Indonesia
Next day

"Captain, I think it may be time for me to leave here."

"What do you mean, Pak?"

"I have noticed men following me. This morning, there was a man watching me at the internet café on Sosrowijayan. A *bule*."

"A white man? Is that all?" The Captain laughed. "There are many *bules* on Malioboro Road, Pak!"

"Sure, of course. But this man was not sightseeing. He was watching."

The Javanese ship captain had met Angell for *kopi* at a *warung* off Malioboro. It was their usual meeting place, a habit they had developed since Angell started living in Jogja. They would catch up every few weeks. It was more to keep a watchful eye on Angell and his security than anything else. If the captain was at sea, of course, then they did not meet, but usually his voyages lasted only a few weeks at a time as he plied the shipping routes between Hong Kong, Singapore and Jakarta. He had saved Angell's life and now felt proprietary towards him. Also, they had shared quite a significant booty when another ship tried to apprehend Angell and wound up being boarded by the Captain's men and taken to Jakarta as salvage.

This time, however, Aji had answered Angell's cryptic text message and waited for him at their usual warung while Angell watched from a safe distance to be sure he wasn't followed.

"I see. If he was not shopping or taking tourist photos then I can understand what you say."

"He was just standing there, staying in the shadows. I saw him in the same internet café earlier this morning. And then after I left. He was watching."

The captain nodded. He had learned to respect Angell's instincts. It was too dangerous not to do so.

"I will be sorry to see you go, Pak."

"I am sorry to have to leave, but I don't want to get anyone else in trouble and, anyway, I think that the people who have been trying to catch me are working on some kind of timetable."

"A schedule, you mean?"

"In a way. Not a normal one. I mean, not a calendar timetable. Something to do with astronomy. The stars. I know it sounds insane, Captain, but that's how I got into this mess in the first place. The people who are after me are a little … *gila* … crazy. They work with a different calendar and believe all sorts of strange things."

"Not so crazy, Pak. This is Java. We have all kinds of crazy things here. Many different calendars, too. Not just western and Islamic calendars but Javanese calendars. Did you know that in one system the Javanese week has only five days?"

Angell smiled. "Yes, Captain. I have been reading up on your culture. I am fascinated by your *primbon*, your almanacs. There are Sanskrit prayers next to Arabic ones, Hindu and Buddhist deities, and incantations in the old languages. All mixed together."

"That is the beauty of our culture. We don't throw anything away. If it is useful, we keep it. Even if it is not useful now, it may be useful later. We call it *kejawen*. It is the essence of being Javanese. To accept everything, to respect everything. But does this have anything to do with that book you carry with you all the time?"

"Everything, Pak Aji. It has everything to do with the book. The people who are hunting me are obsessed with it. And they are obsessed with me. There is something that connects me to the book in their eyes."

"What could that be?"

"It has something to do with my ancestors, one of my distant relatives who once owned the book, and with a writer who made up stories about it and got everyone upset."

"Ah, I see. *Kejawen*, again. We Javanese understand about ancestors, obligations, and karma."

Angell was taken aback for a moment. He had never associated what was happening to him because of the book as "karma" but it kind of made sense. What did it say in the Bible about the sins of the fathers being visited on the children, "even unto the third and fourth generations"? If a generation is twenty years and it all began with the murder of Professor Emeritus George Gammell Angell on the Providence docks in 1927, then Gregory Angell is in the Biblical ballpark.

"I think you may be onto something, Captain. Not karma, exactly, for who knows another's karma? But something else … something more tangible, measurable. They need me *and* the book. Together. At least, that's the way it seems now."

"And you, Pak? What do you need?"

Angell gave him a rueful smile. "I'm not sure, Captain. I thought I knew, a year ago. Now, I am not so sure. My point of view has changed a lot since that day on the beach."

That was the day a local shaman introduced him to the Goddess of the Southern Ocean. It caused a polarity in Angell's consciousness such that whoever he was, or whoever he thought he was, became sharp and clear as if everything extraneous to himself had been burned away. But what neither the shaman nor Captain Aji knew was that the Goddess did not show up alone.

"Do you know how you will leave? Do you need help in arrangements?"

"I'm not sure yet. I was thinking of going to South America, somewhere the Americans don't have an extradition treaty or where the people following me would lose me. Brazil, maybe. They have a treaty with the States but you can disappear there. Somewhere like that. But not directly."

"I have a cousin in Garuda. Maybe he can help."

The national airline did not fly to Brazil, but connected in Qatar or Dubai. Angell was not sure he should risk flying back to the Middle East after everything he had been through the past year. And he didn't want to go through a Chinese connection for the same reason. Aji read his mind.

"Don't worry. We can arrange something through Singapore. They have flights everywhere and we can avoid some trouble areas."

Angell nodded, gratefully, but was still not sure he should be flying out of Indonesia. Well, he certainly couldn't walk. And a voyage by ship seemed out of the question, too.

"You're thinking to sail? It's possible, of course. At least, part of the way. We can get you to Borneo, and from there you can sail to the Philippines. From Manila you can fly to Brazil, I think, by way of Tokyo to Dallas."

"No, that won't work. I can't risk flying into the States."

"Ah, of course. So ... the only way is to try through Singapore and from there to Europe. From Europe you can get direct flights to Brazil. We can get you to Kalimantan, and from there to Singapore. I will call my cousin."

Aji got up from the wooden table and they shook hands. "If I were you, I would go now to the airport and wait for my cousin to show up with a ticket to Kalimantan and onward booking. It is not safe for you to go back to your place. Do you need anything from there?"

Angell shook his head. "I have everything on me."

"Very good. Get to the airport and wait there. There are many flights from Jogja. There are some cafés there. Find one and be patient. My cousin's name is Ali."

They embraced one last time, and Angell once again expressed his thanks to Aji for all he had done for him. Aji placed his hand over his heart and bowed, and disappeared into the crowd.

★ ★ ★

Adisutjipto International Airport is a small, regional airport but a very busy place nonetheless. There are no jetways. It is the type of airport where one walks out onto the tarmac to board the plane, like a character in a movie from the 1950s. There are direct flights to many cities in Indonesia, but also to Singapore so there is a small

Immigration and Customs presence for the international passengers. Usually, though, one has to connect in Jakarta for the overseas flights.

Angell took a taxi from the Malioboro area to the Affandi Museum, acting like a tourist and watching to see if anyone was following him or showed any unusual interest. After a half-hour of wandering around, he hailed another taxi and this time went straight to Jalan Raya Solo and the entrance to the airport.

There are, as Captain Aji mentioned, a number of cafés at the airport serving local food so Angell found one near the terminal entrance, ordered some *nasi goreng*, and sat with his back to the wall looking out onto the parking area.

So much of his life had changed in the past year that he hardly recognized himself. The peace he had found in Jogja was an illusion, he knew, a temporary respite like any vacation. He was back in the game, now, and on the run again. He knew Dagon was gearing up for another try at their ritual, and if you had asked him about that a year ago he would have shrugged his shoulders and said "So what? A bunch of crazies having a kegger in the desert ... who cares?" Now he knew better. And he knew that he was somehow still part of all of that. He also knew it was not as crazy as it would seem to any sane person. He had witnessed that ritual in Nepal. He had seen the impossible on the beach at Parangtritis. He had felt the ... the Thing ... that Dagon worshipped rise up behind him and *speak* to him. He was a scholar of religion; he knew how these experiences happened, there were scientific explanations, all sorts of rationalizations ... but he knew that his life had changed because of these experiences and he could only imagine how the lives of those who courted these experiences, who specialized in them, would be changed and how they would be motivated to change the lives of everyone else around them. Dagon was dangerous not just because they believed in impossible things and crazy ideas and were willing to enact these ideas on the rest of the world. Dagon was dangerous because the experiences were *real*, because they were evidence of a deeper fissure within the human psyche that threatened to open wide and swallow them all.

And now he had to find a way to warn Aubrey and his people without giving away his position or getting himself into more trouble than he was in already. He trusted Aubrey to do the right thing where Dagon was concerned, but wanted to keep a lot of daylight between them anyway. He knew that Aubrey or whoever he worked for would use him just as they had when they sent him after the Book. They knew his weaknesses and his vulnerabilities and they exploited them for their own purposes. Even though he was a different person now, he wasn't sure he could take a chance with them again.

"Pak Gregory?"

The human voice shook him out of his reverie. That was dangerous in itself. He should have been alert.

"I am Ali, a cousin of Aji. You know Aji? I am his cousin." The small man in the brown and gold batik shirt and black pants and sandals could not have been more than twenty years old, it seemed. He held out his hand and they shook.

"No, please, sit, sit. We should talk here." Ali sat down at Angell's table and produced a thin plastic folder. He began to speak softly so that no one in the café could listen in.

"Pak Aji tells me that you need to get to Brazil. He also tells me that you need to avoid connections in the States. That is easy to do." He pulled out an itinerary from his folder and pointed to it as he spoke. "You can fly from here to Singapore directly with Air Asia. In Singapore, you can connect to a flight to Frankfurt. From Frankfurt there are direct flights to Sao Paulo and Rio de Janeiro." He looked up, expectantly.

"I thought I was going through Kalimantan."

He shook his head. "Bad weather right now. Sepinggan is closed for the rest of the day."

"Haze?" Slash and burn farming had contributed to a growing

problem of smog in the region. At times it was so strong one could smell wood burning as far away as Singapore.

"We can wait another day or so," offered Ali.

"No. I should get out of Indonesia today, if possible. Singapore will have to do. Will my documents hold up?" Angell whispered.

Ali nodded. "They'll get you as far as Singapore, no problem. We have made other arrangements for your flight to Frankfurt." He withdrew a small envelope from his folder and slid it over to Angell.

"You will use this passport in Singapore for your onward flights. Just a precaution, in case anyone is monitoring the manifests. Destroy the other one at Changi Airport before boarding your flight."

Without opening the envelope, Angell smiled his thanks at Ali. "Thank Captain Aji for me. I hope to see him again very soon, in better circumstances."

"Pak Aji has told me very little about you, Pak, only that you are a good man who studies religion and who is in danger from his own government. Almost all of Pak Aji's friends are in similar dangers, I think. Your ticket to Singapore is in the envelope as well as the information you need to pick up your ticket to Frankfurt and Sao Paulo. You can change from Sao Paulo to Rio if you wish. There will be no extra charges."

"What do I owe the Captain?"

Ali shook his head. "He says he made a lot of money with you, Pak. These arrangements are his gift to you. Only come back to visit with him when you can."

★ ★ ★

An hour later, Gregory Angell—as Richard Raleigh—was on his way to Singapore, non-stop. In his pocket was another passport, this one made out to Lawrence Appleton. Each had the same passport photo, taken in Jogja months earlier when Aji was arranging Angell's Indonesian visa. The Richard Raleigh passport was American. The Appleton passport was Canadian. Angell was pleased with that, as a Canadian passport was almost universally respected. An American passport these days … not so much. The details were the same, except for his place of birth which was listed as Montreal, Quebec. Angell had friends at McGill University there. He could wing it if he had to.

In less than an hour, he landed in Singapore. He passed Immigration easily and was tempted to take a taxi into the city and see the sights. Some *roti paratha* and maybe *hokkien mee* would not go badly, either. But he realized he had to keep moving and get out of Asia as quickly as possible.

He checked the details he had been given by Ali, and saw that he had a reservation in the name of Appleton for a flight to Frankfurt that left in two hours. He took the rail shuttle from one terminal to the next and made his way to the reservation desk and got his boarding pass as well as a ticket for Frankfurt-Sao Paulo.

Changi Airport is one of the world's best airports, continually rating in the top ten—or even the top five—of international airports. There are drug stores, grocery stores, numerous restaurants for every type of cuisine, bars, and every convenience. Angell stopped in a food court on the lower level of the terminal that offered a selection of typical local food prepared in large woks right in front of him and managed some *char kway teow* and a *teh tarik*. As he sat there, he considered his options from then on.

While he trusted Captain Aji with his life, he didn't know the cousin well enough (or even at all). Plus, he knew that between American intelligence and the Dagon goons he would be watched, monitored, and traced. So he decided on the instant to change his travel plans. Rather than fly into Sao Paulo he would switch to Rio.

And rather than fly from Frankfurt he would fly out of Heathrow.

British Airways had a nonstop to Rio from Heathrow. All he would have to do is fly into Frankfurt as scheduled but disappear for awhile and turn up in Heathrow at the last moment. He knew that Ali had told him to destroy his current passport in Singapore and use the Canadian one for Frankfurt but he would hold onto the

Richard Raleigh passport for now and maybe use that one for the Frankfurt-Heathrow leg and revert to the Appleton passport for the nearly twelve-hour flight to Rio. An additional amount of confusion would help him cover his tracks.

Having made that decision, he got up from the table and made his way to the gate. His flight to Frankfurt would be boarding in thirty minutes.

★ ★ ★

The name "Richard Raleigh" did not turn up any flags, nor did "Lawrence Appleton." The names and passport numbers sailed through the computer systems of countries, airports, and Interpol. No wants, no warrants. The names did not appear on any watch lists anywhere. The itineraries from Yogyakarta to Singapore, Singapore to Frankfurt were innocuous enough as well. There was a lot of traffic from Europe to Southeast Asia, and Yogyakarta was a well-known destination for tourism as well as for university scholars attending any one of the city's dozens of colleges or doing research at the historical sites.

But there *was* a flag for one of the other passengers flying from Changi to Frankfurt. He didn't realize it, but Professor William "Bill" Moody—anthropologist, guest lecturer at UGM, spy for the Minerva Project, and informer for Dagon—was on a very secret but very serious watch list.

CHAPTER NINETEEN

Malpensa Airport
Milan

THE DARK LORD HAD BEEN SUMMONED. The pain in his left arm still bothered him, even though the arm wasn't there anymore. Phantom limb, they called it. The nerve endings had been cauterized, of course, but they were still sending signals to his brain.

Or something.

He wasn't that clear on the science.

★ ★ ★

So he had a single carry-on bag in his right hand, and his boarding pass sticking out of his shirt pocket. It was awkward getting around this way, but he was still alive. It could have been so much worse. The lack of the arm really impressed all the little Practicuses, though. He had been fitted for a prosthesis, but there was something about the sight of that artificial hand at the end that unsettled his stomach. He had waved off the psychotherapy at the time, and maybe that had not been a good idea after all.

He told the emergency room staff that he had lost the arm accidentally, in a traffic accident, and that the limb had been burned completely and could not be reattached. In actuality, Dagon had severed the limb just below the shoulder and had thrown the severed arm into a furnace in front of his eyes. It was a simple ritual, refined and unsentimental. He had no idea who had wielded the sword, as everyone was masked as was typical of these sorts of things. One did not know the names or faces of those who meted out punishment. It was all very medieval, and he could appreciate the taste with which the ancient ceremony was conducted. It was like those excommunication rituals of the Catholic Church, like the one in the movie about Thomas à Becket. Very dramatic, very arcane.

A lesser man would have screamed and begged for mercy. Well, a man on a lesser quantity of drugs, perhaps.

They then drove him to the hospital and got a gurney for him before disappearing into the night. It took weeks to heal from the amputation, even though Dagon had used a very sharp instrument and a single, clean cut. It took another few months to recover completely, but his powers of concentration were considerable and honed by years as a Zelator in the Order and that facilitated his recovery. And his good humor.

★ ★ ★

He liked the dining options in Italian airports. All those sandwiches piled up in the glass cases, full of cured Italian meats and cheeses and all of it on that excellent fresh-baked bread. He had to keep away from flesh these days, though, as he was in the middle of preparations for the Last Ritual. Dagon had summoned him to the ancient site in Al-Qadisiyyah governorate in south-central Iraq. It was in Shia territory, which was good for them as they had always had better luck with the Shia than the Sunnis.

This would be the first time in millennia that the Ritual of the Gate would be held at the place where it all started: the ancient site of Nippur, known to the Sumerians as Nibru: the Throne of Enlil … and the Kingdom of Dagon.

There had been controversy among scholars as to the true nature of Dagon. While some recognized that Dagon was the head of a Cult of the Dead—linked to the ancient Sumerian god Enlil—there were others who resisted that concept and thought of Dagon only as an agricultural deity.

The fools.

Dagon's title was transliterated as *dgn-pgr* in Ugaritic, the chief language of his cult before it had been polluted by the Philistines and replaced by Aramaic. *Dagan Pagrê*: Dagon the Corpse; Dagon the Cadaver; Dagon the Dead. And his book was the Book of Dead Names. The coveted and elusive *Sipru Dabahi almi*, known to the vulgar as *The Necronomicon*. Odd how Lovecraft knew all of this before the scholarship was done, before the ink on the obscure papers written by even more obscure scholars, such as Paton and Quell, was even dry. Lovecraft—in "The Shadow Over Innsmouth"—knew of Dagon and reported his worship the way it had been since antiquity, the way the Dark Lord himself understood it to be, the way they had all been taught. Lovecraft had known of the mysterious beings called *kulull* , the half-man, half-fish beings of ancient Mesopotamian lore that comprised the race of Dagon, beings whose name recalled the central character in the rites of Dagon—aside from Dagon itself—Kutulu.

The Tantric interpretation of the terms "Shadow" and "Innsmouth" was a key to the understanding of how the Order was to open the Gate during the previous ritual, but that rite had failed and the Dark Lord was one of those held responsible. This was his chance to right that wrong, and to show the Keepers of the Book that he was someone upon whom they could rely, a man of trust.

The opposition, who had tried so successfully during the past two attempts to thwart the rituals of Dagon, did not understand a crucial aspect—the core aspect—of what it was they were trying to do, what they had to do. This was something it was impossible to understand if all your knowledge of religion and esoterica came from books, or from those wife-swapping witchcraft cults on Long Island, or those desperate Crowley-worshipping Hippies in Southern Fucking California. They didn't understand that it was Aiwaz alone who held the power and the legacy, an unbroken line straight back to ancient Sumer. If all you knew was the name Aiwaz, you had the key. You could use Tantra, Voodoo, Wicca, ceremonial magic … it didn't matter. Crowley could teach you nothing of any value if you were already an adept of Tantrika or a vodouisant and could make contact with Aiwaz using the arcane formulas of those disciplines.

And Dagon was the connection to Aiwaz. Even the verbose and incomprehensible Kenneth Grant understood that one could not approach the one without the other. The Deep Ones and the Old Ones were the twin poles of Zothyria.

★ ★ ★

"Your boarding pass, sir?" The flight attendants on Emirates were polite and accommodating. He tried to reach the boarding pass in his shirt pocket but the flight attendant simply said, "Permit me," and retrieved it for him and led him to his seat.

"Welcome aboard, Mister ... Gunnar Nordström." It was a close equivalent to his birth name, but not too close that someone would recognize it. And the passport was Finnish. Not something the authorities would be looking for. Dagon had the best document service, and they should: they hired former members of the Iraqi Mukhabarat after the fall of Saddam. He nodded to the flight attendant with the appropriate amount of false gravity.

He was able to put his carry on in the overhead bin single-handed without any difficulty, and sat back in his aisle seat with a sigh of satisfaction.

There was no direct flight from either Turin or Milan, so he was prepared to connect in Dubai. This would be his first time in Baghdad, where he would be picked up by a Dagon agent and taken to the site. He wasn't particularly happy about doing this in a war zone, and without one of his arms, but the honor and the prestige overwhelmed all other considerations.

The arm was bothering him. It itched sometimes, even though it was no longer there. It made him wonder about the Old Ones. Were they the "phantom limbs" of humanity? Lost, severed from civilization so many aeons ago, but still present in our deepest unconscious layers? The difference would be that his arm would not grow back or be returned to him, but the Old Ones ... the Old Ones were on their way back to Earth.

Their voyage back to this world began in 1945, two years before the death of the Old Master.

He asked for a glass of cabernet sauvignon, inhaled its bouquet, and then—satisfied—closed his eyes and recalled to mind his satanic catechism.

The New Mexico Desert
1945

The Trinity test had been successful, and Oppenheimer, the lead scientist on the Manhattan Project, was pleased. "I am become Death," he wrote. "The Destroyer of Worlds."

Now they knew the bombs would work. And just in the nick of time, too. Truman was due to meet Stalin to discuss carving up the post-war world between them. He had to demonstrate that he had the atomic bomb, and that Japan would fold like a cheap suit. Otherwise, Russia would have to worry about Japanese troops on their border with China.

What Stalin didn't know was that Oppenheimer had solved the last nagging problem of bomb design with a little help from the Third Reich.

It was the U-Boat that was captured in the Atlantic and sailed down the coast to Portsmouth, New Hampshire in May of 1945. U-234 was loaded with over one thousand pounds of uranium, blueprints for weapons systems, and even a few engineers who were being sent by the Nazis to the Japanese to help them put it all together. There was also a complete, disassembled Messerschmitt Me262 jet fighter. And there was a Luftwaffe general on board, who would serve as liaison with the Japanese.

Had the U-Boat made it to Japanese territory, there is no telling how the war would have ended.

Oppenheimer had been stuck at a critical stage of the bomb design. When it was seen that the U-Boat contained large quantities of uranium, the people in charge of the Manhattan Project were notified and Oppenheimer flew out immediately. He was seen boarding the captured submarine, and then a security lid was clamped down hard on the event (like everything associated with the Manhattan Project). Oppenheimer later flew back to New Mexico, newly-inspired by what he had seen, and the rest is history.

The explosions over Hiroshima and Nagasaki in August, 1945 were enormous and unprecedented. Entire cities were wiped out. The world had never seen a weapon of that magnitude before. Oh, Tokyo had been fire-bombed, and so had Dresden. Those were bad enough. Inhuman. Hideous. But this new weapon … atomic bombs, they were called. Something to do with splitting the atom and releasing vast amounts of energy. It had begun as mathematical equations, and then within a few years … the arcane Kabbalah of theoretical physics had become very real, very fast.

What no one knew—except for the scientists and a few military personnel, and the President of the United States—was that the type of uranium found aboard the U-Boat indicated that the Nazis had, indeed, already become a nuclear power and were entirely capable of producing their own atomic bomb. The decision to bomb Japan was done in desperation rather than calculation, for Allied intelligence did not know at the time if any other U-Boats—carrying similar cargoes of uranium and the technical information necessary to weaponize it—had made it to Japanese territory. If they had, the Japanese would have had the bomb and no doubt would have used it.

Be that as it may, Oppenheimer read Sanskrit in his spare time. He was doing his own translation of the Bhagavad-Gita. He was something of an esoteric scholar himself. In other words, he should have known better. He should have realized that such a massive explosion involving the basic building block of all life and all matter in the universe—the atom—would have had spiritual consequences as well as purely physical. The Earth is a delicate organism, surrounded by fields both magnetic and atmospheric. Blowing a hole in the atmosphere with an atomic blast was equivalent in human terms to severe psychological trauma, the kind that begets psychosis.

In the American euphoria that greeted the end of World War Two no pause was given to a consideration of the devastation wrought everywhere else on both hemispheres. Japan had fallen and was in total disarray, with starvation and disease rampant. Its government was replaced by an Allied occupation force. The same was true in Germany, where Soviet troops had gone on a rampage, raping and murdering their way to Berlin. China had a bloody revolution, and Mao Zedong became its supreme leader. Korea was split in two by 1950. Vietnam was in revolt against the French. Indonesia against the Dutch. India and Malaya against the British. And on and on. The war did not end with the two atomic bombs over Japan. It had just entered a different phase.

Over the Mediterranean
May 2015

His flight now over the Mediterranean, the Dark Lord sipped his wine with gratitude. He had not been alive at the end of World War Two, but his parents had been. For him, the war was this supernatural event that took place *in illo tempore*, in some kind of mythic time when there were forces of good and evil fighting a cosmic, even Manichaean, battle. Everyone felt nostalgic about that time, even those who had not been born yet. It seemed simpler in some ways: the Third Reich and the Japanese Empire were evil kingdoms that had to be destroyed. There was no moral ambiguity, no hesitation.

What they didn't understand—the antagonists during that conflict and during every other conflict in world history—was that there was another side, a side that always won, regardless of how human beings tallied up the score. It was the side that feasted on the blood of the battlefields, on the tears of widows, on the pain of wrenched limbs, sucking chest wounds, and missing organs. It didn't matter who was fighting, or which side won or lost. The Old Ones always won in the end. They always got their banquet of human misery. It was the missing piece of the puzzle, the one that the do-gooders never understood.

If the Old Ones are not fed—if their rites are not performed, and if the sacrifices are not made—they will take out their wrath on the entire planet. The Aztecs knew this with their dread Temple of the Sun, and so did the Maya with their sacred calendar. The Jews knew this, and practiced it, as long as they had their own Temple intact. The Muslims know this still, as do all the religions and sects that still practice animal sacrifice. Altars must run red with blood, otherwise what are they for?

So, the Dark Lord reasoned, the Order of Dagon performs a service necessary to human survival. If the sacrifices stop, then the Old Ones will make the planet suffer in ways no one could possibly imagine.

The problem was: the Order had become too greedy.

The problem was: someone had opened the Gate too soon.

Traffic between this world and the next had been frequent but manageable over the centuries. Dagon had ensured that the Old Ones were fed; and the "other ones"—their sworn enemies, that simpering gaggle of astral cannon fodder known as the Church of Starry Wisdom—facilitated the gradual introduction of the Old Ones into the human space, neutralizing their impact by creating generations of hybrids, of alien-human DNA. The idea was that when the Old Ones finally did return, they would find the planet heavily defended by Starry Wisdom and its bespoke beings that preserved the best of both blood lines.

But a previous leader of Dagon had become alarmed when she noticed the exponential increase in hybrids on the planet, realizing that the Masters she served would not be able to invade and conquer as had been planned in the aeons before *homo sapiens sapiens* evolved. So a different culture had taken over Dagon sometime in the early twentieth century. A decision was made to open the Gate as quickly as feasible, and everyone could just take their chances with the outcome.

So … atomic bombs. Wars. Genocide in Africa, in Asia, in Europe. The Holocaust. Revolutions. Ritual magic in California: Jack Parsons, and his buddy L. Ron Hubbard who would eventually go on to start Scientology, one of Dagon's better inventions. UFO sightings in the Pacific Northwest.

Then … Roswell, New Mexico. The location of the air field that was home to the 509th Bombardment Group, the very same group that had dropped the atomic bombs on Japan. Roswell: the site of the secret laboratory of Robert H. Goddard, the father of the liquid fueled rocket, who died the day following the atomic bomb strike on Nagasaki. Roswell: the site of the iconic "flying disc" crash in 1947 that became synonymous with Ufology. The Old Ones had a sense of humor, anyway. Or was it a sense of justice? Or revenge?

Then, the discovery of the Dead Sea Scrolls the same year. And the death of Aleister Crowley that December.

Then, brainwashing. Bluebird and Artichoke. MK-ULTRA and the Manchurian Candidate.

The UFO overflights in Washington, DC in 1952. Parsons dying that same year from an explosion in his home in Pasadena.

Then: Kennedy. Vietnam. The Summer of Love. Martin Luther King. Another Kennedy. Charles Manson. *Hollywood Babylon.*

★ ★ ★

"Gunnar" knew that it all had been a mistake, but a mistake made long before he was born. It was his generation that had to deal with the fallout. Lovecraft had tried to warn everyone about the problem, knowing that the Old Ones were gathering themselves for a final assault on the Gate and therefore on the planet Earth. How Lovecraft knew all this had been a mystery to the Dark Lord for most of his life. It was only with his latest initiations that he had been allowed to see a glimpse of the truth.

Some slight turbulence as they neared Sicily. He held onto his wine glass with some effort, but then the plane leveled out and everything returned to normal. The flight attendant returned with more wine, as if reading his mind. He smiled at her in gratitude, and resumed his musing.

Lovecraft. How he would have loved to have been a rat in his wall.

★ ★ ★

The turbulence that shook his flight coincided with turbulence felt by another aircraft at the same time, thousands of miles apart. Gregory Angell's flight was just leaving the airspace over India and heading over the Arabian Sea as the Dark Lord's plane headed towards Dubai. Moody, also on Angell's flight, had never met the Dark Lord but knew him by reputation. Had he known that their planes were in the air at the same time there is no saying how Moody would have reacted.

As it was, he was making his way up the aisle and towards Angell's seat. The backpack was within reach in the overhead compartment.

Moody could put an end to this once and for all.

CHAPTER TWENTY

Singapore to Frankfurt

ANGELL SETTLED IN FOR THE LONG FLIGHT to Frankfurt. All he had was his backpack, and he resisted the temptation to open it and remove the Book and his notes. Instead, he closed his eyes and tried to sleep. He knew he would have to be alert and quick-witted once he arrived in Brazil. He had enough cash to facilitate a cheap berth somewhere in Rio, and would need a few weeks to acclimate himself and get oriented. During that time, though, he had to act on the information he was accumulating about Dagon and what he believed their next step would be. The more he thought about it, the more he realized he had no time to waste.

He had an aisle seat in the forward section of economy. There was no one in the middle seat next to him, and a tired looking woman with her head on a pillow against the window. The plane was peaceful, so far. In another hour or so the beverage service and then the meal service would begin. He figured to take advantage of the lull and rest his eyes.

Three seats behind him Moody sat, restless and anxious, reading and re-reading the in-flight magazine without registering a single word. He would be out of communication with his masters at Dagon for the duration of the flight, but they would expect a report from him upon his arrival in Frankfurt. He would be met by someone he knew, they told him, without telling him who it would be.

He tried not to stare at the back of Angell's head, but as he was the only reason Moody was on this flight it was hard to ignore him. He thought about getting something to drink, a stiff Scotch maybe, and then thought better of it. He had to remain sharp. If he screwed this up, Dagon had ways of making him regret it.

★ ★ ★

Angell's cat nap became a deep sleep. He slept through the beverage service and the meal service. The lights in the cabin were dimmed and the plane grew quiet as the passengers spent their time either reading or sleeping. If he thought about it, he would have realized that he hadn't really slept well the past few nights as he became aware that his movements were being tracked.

He hadn't noticed Moody on the plane, or recognized him as the man who had been following him to the internet café and then who turned up smoking cigarettes on Malioboro Road, or he would have been more alert. The other passengers were a mix of Asians and some Europeans and Americans, and Angell had noticed nothing suspicious about any of them. He realized he wouldn't have known a Dagon member anyway, not unless it had been someone from the scene in Nepal.

Instead, he relaxed into a comfortable slumber, or as comfortable as one could be in an economy class seat on a long international flight. The deeper he descended, the more elaborate his dreams became. He normally did not dream of people he knew or had met; mostly they were just anonymous faces, strangers. But this time he dreamt of a succession of familiar people which made his dream seem more real than usual. He saw Aubrey, of all people. He saw Adnan, the man who died in his arms in Nepal. He saw Jason Miller, the man he killed in that same underground chamber. He saw an old Zoroastrian priest, dying on top of the Tower of Silence in Iran.

And he saw a young Yezidi woman. Jamila. The strange person who had channeled a god, an Old One, and who had handed him the Book and called him "Terton": one who discovers a *terma*, a hidden text, a revealed scripture.

And Jamila became Lara Kidul, the Goddess of the Southern Ocean. And as he gazed with awe at the Goddess rising from the sea a deep sense of foreboding turned his dream into a nightmare. Something was wrong. Very wrong.

The plane dipped and swayed in some turbulence over the Arabian Sea.

Angell awoke with a start to see a man standing over him.

★ ★ ★

It was worth a shot, Moody thought. Angell was fast asleep, even snoring slightly. His backpack was in the overhead compartment above his seat. If he withdrew the book now, Angell might not notice it was missing until after they landed and by that time Moody would be long gone, handing the prize in triumph to the Keepers of the Book: Dagon's version of a SWAT team.

He opened the overhead compartment and saw the backpack at once. There was a zippered section and one that was only flaps and buckles. It was quite full, and he didn't want to waste time standing there and rummaging around. The book had to be quite large, at least the size of A4 paper, he thought to himself. So it was most likely in the bigger, zippered compartment.

He looked up and down the aisle. The flight attendants were congregated in the galley, and the other passengers were either asleep or ignoring him completely.

He reached for the knapsack.

★ ★ ★

The man standing over him was reaching into the overhead compartment. *His* compartment. He was holding onto the compartment to steady himself in the turbulence.

"Can I help you?"

Moody started.

"Oh, uh. Just looking for a blanket. It's cold in here."

"Yes, it is. I don't think you'll find one up there, though. There was just enough room for my backpack."

Moody smiled apologetically, and closed the compartment. He turned to walk back to his seat, and Angell closed his eyes again and in a moment was back on Malioboro Road, staring across the broad avenue with its becak drivers and horse-drawn carriages for the tourists and the blaring taxis. And he saw him. He saw the man who was standing over him. He had been across the street. And before that, in the internet café.

Whoever he was, he had followed him from Yogyakarta and was now on the same plane going to Frankfurt.

Angell was not a commando. He was an academic. And until his trip to Iraq last year with Aubrey he was pretty much out of shape. The last eight or nine months had toughened him, from his trek out of Nepal and across parts of China to wind up in Mongolia and then to Beijing, and his confrontation on the high seas with the mercenary captain Arthwaite who had tried to capture him on behalf of a strange intelligence officer named Maxwell Prime. These events, some of them harrowing, meant Angell had learned some basic things about how to defend himself. But he was stuck at 35,000 feet for another few hours with a tracker of some kind: Dagon or American intelligence? Who could tell?

Angell ran through the combinations in his mind. The guy was in his forties, at least. Pushing fifty. He had a lot of grey in his hair and his face was lined and wrinkled, possibly from spending a lot of time in the sun. He had the broken capillaries in his nose of a dedicated drinker. He spoke English with an American accent, so there was that.

He knew the type. If the guy was an academic, like him, then he was in archaeology or anthropology. Something that would keep him outside. He couldn't be an action officer with CIA as he seemed physically unfit and a little sloppy when it came to tradecraft. He could be a contract agent of some kind, though, a guy they hired on a kind of contingency basis.

But that meant he could be working for almost anyone. Whoever it was, they had deep enough pockets to pick up the tab for airline fare from Jogja at least as far as Frankfurt at the last minute. That meant that they knew where he was going and were probably waiting for him at the airport.

Okay. Change of plans.

CHAPTER TWENTY-ONE

The French Quarter, New Orleans

THE PROFESSOR WAS WILLING TO HELP as long as Cuneo protected her identity. Cuneo thought that was strange, since every academic he ever ran across wanted as much publicity as possible, giving "publish or perish" a whole new meaning. But Cuneo agreed, and met Dr. Francine LeRoux over coffee in the Quarter.

It was the kind of spot Cuneo loved, and associated with New Orleans. It was paneled in dark woods and fragrant with the aroma of freshly ground coffee, and located on a side street so that it was not crowded with tourists in the middle of the afternoon.

As they sat over *café au lait* and beignets, they had an illuminating conversation.

"My department is Liberal Arts, as you know."

Cuneo nodded. The woman at the table across from him was about forty, forty-five. She was tall, slender and had arresting dark brown eyes and skin the color of the coffee they were drinking. She had a shoulder bag as well as a purse, and the former was stuffed full of books and papers that she set down next to her chair, keeping her purse on her lap. She was scattered and natural at the same time, a woman who had some of the characteristics of an "absent-minded professor" mixed with movements that were fluid and sensual. She had a tomboy quality that Cuneo found endearing and an easy way of speaking that was part scholarly and part self-deprecating and aware of the absurdities of life. Speaking with her was like sharing a secret no one else could know.

"We don't have a religious studies department at Tulane per se, but we offer a religious studies minor with courses mostly in Buddhism and world religions, that sort of thing. Some of us come from backgrounds that combine religion and culture, the arts: intersectionality if you want to call it that. In my case, I'm a native of New Orleans and there is a tradition in our family that one of our ancestors was Marie Laveau, the Voodoo Queen." She smiled. "I know, I know. Virtually everyone in the Quarter claims that."

"Didn't Marie Laveau have something like a dozen or more kids?"

"Probably fewer than that, and most of her children died before they reached maturity anyway. But she did have one daughter who survived, and she became Marie Laveau the Second after her mother died, picking up the baton as it were and conducting rituals. But what about you? You have an Italian name, but …"

"Yeah, I know. My father was an Italian from the Bronx. My mother was Haitian."

"Ah, so you have some background in *vodoun*," she said, giving "voodoo" the Creole pronunciation.

"Well, not a lot. Just the usual stuff. My mom burned candles, had a bag she wore with roots and herbs in it from time to time. But her husband, my father, was Catholic and she was kinda Catholic, if you know what I mean."

"Sure. The Haitian approach to these things is rather flexible. African spirits masquerading as Catholic saints, that sort of thing. But I don't think you wanted to talk to me about Afro-Caribbean spirituality."

Cuneo realized he had already eaten two beignets and the powdered sugar was all over the front of his shirt. He brushed it off, slightly embarrassed, as he conceded her point.

"No, that's true. Well … actually, I don't know if that's true. I'm a little at sea with all of this, and before I start wandering the Quarter looking for *gris gris* and John the Conqueror root, I thought I would try to get a second opinion."

She sipped her coffee thoughtfully and looked at him over the rim of her cup.

"Why don't you start at the beginning?"

Over the next thirty minutes Cuneo gave the professor a summary of the two, interconnected cases: the first, the double homicide in the Ninth Ward and the second, the murdered woman in Belle Chasse and the strange child now at the hospital ICU. He kept the gruesome details to the minimum but focused instead on the occult aspects of the case and especially the strange designs and sigils from both cases. He showed her a few of the photos he had taken at both crime scenes, just of the weird drawings and not of the bodies of course.

"This is not *vodoun*," she offered, right away upon seeing the artwork.

"No, I realize that. I was pretty sure, anyway. It looks more like western ceremonial magic, but I can't place the system."

She looked up at him, startled.

"Wow. You have been doing some reading, haven't you? I never thought I would hear a homicide detective use the term 'Western ceremonial magic.' I'm impressed!"

He shrugged. "Well, I had a case with occult overtones when I was back in New York a few years ago. That, and my mother's influence, I guess. When I came across that strange concrete bunker in the Ninth Ward I started doing some serious research."

He passed a photo across the table of the bookshelves in old Mrs. Galvez's house.

"What do you make of all of this?"

She examined the titles on the spines of the books carefully. "That woman was no amateur. Some of these titles are hard to come by. Expensive. And you wouldn't know to look for them if you weren't already deeply involved."

"She was a Freemason, if that is any help."

"A Co-Mason, most likely. They're the ones that accept women as members. They're also a little more occult-oriented. Some of the lodges, anyway. But I don't think this collection reflects that tradition. Not really. What secret society did she tell you she belonged to?"

"Dagon. The Order of Dagon, or something like that."

"Dagon? Like the Biblical Dagon?"

"Don't know."

"Dagon was mistakenly thought to be a fish-god, you know,

half man, half fish, or something like that. It was a linguistic error, though. Dagon was actually more of a death god."

"A death god?"

"Well, like a lot of agricultural deities. You know, you plant a seed and it's like burying a body. And then a plant grows, and it's like resurrection."

"Ah."

"According to Jewish tradition, Dagon was the name inscribed on the breastplate of Goliath."

"You mean, like David and Goliath?"

"That one. Goliath was believed to be a worshipper of Dagon. In fact, there is the Biblical story of how a statue of Dagon kept falling down and breaking in the presence of the Ark of the Covenant."

"So, for sure, Dagon is the bad guy in this story?"

"Depends on your point of view, I guess. I don't want to make a value judgment here—I am an academic, after all!—but, yeah. Dagon was considered to be one of those bad pagan gods that had to be vanquished by monotheism. Like that."

"More coffee?" Cuneo saw that she had finished her coffee and the rest of the beignets. He got up to go to the counter and place another order, and as he did so he noticed that she looked at her phone.

When he came back with a tray, he asked her: "Hey, am I holding you up? You have to be somewhere?"

She gave him a rueful grin. "Sorry. I forgot I was having coffee with the cops."

"It's okay. I get that a lot. Or, actually, never."

"Well, I did have to leave for another appointment but I checked my phone and it got postponed, so if you have time …?"

"Sure. I only have a few more questions, actually. I'll make them quick."

"Shoot."

"So you haven't heard of an Order of Dagon?"

She shook her head. "That's a new one on me, but I can check it out. I have access to all sorts of academic databases that you guys probably don't use."

"I'd appreciate it. The diagrams, the occult … what do you call them? Sigils? Seals?"

"Well, some of them are definitely in the style of vèvès, but they are not familiar to me from any of the major rites. They're not Petwo, for instance. But there's someone who could help you out with this, who lives in New Orleans. He was a houngan, a priest of vodoun, in Haiti who came here after the earthquake destroyed his hounfort, his temple. He's a very unusual guy, but he knows all there is to know about this stuff and could probably identify the signs that don't look familiar to me."

She wrote down his name and contact info on a napkin and slid it over to Cuneo. He saw the name Hervé, and a phone number.

"The other signs, though, are the ones you recognized, right? The Egyptian-looking one, and some of the others?"

Cuneo appeared a little uncomfortable, talking with an expert in this stuff, but he had to admit that the Egyptian hieroglyph for the placenta jumped out at him.

"It was a kind of sudden inspiration. I stopped looking at the symbols like some kind of incomprehensible … I dunno … forensic countermeasures? And started seeing them as trying to say something to me. As if they represented actual things or people or something. And, like I say, I did have some experience back in New York with a cult that operated in Lower Manhattan. I started my research into this stuff at the time. Didn't think it would come in handy years later and far away, though."

"What happened to the boy?"

Cuneo just shook his head and looked down at the table before answering.

"That's a hard one. There is something genetically wrong with him. He's suffering from all sorts of congenital defects. He's covered with hair, he's growing at an alarming rate, and sometimes is violent."

"Jesus."

"Yeah, well. The staff doesn't know what to do with him. They can't put him into the foster care system, for sure. And they don't really have a handle on his condition since it seems to change every so often."

"And they can't identify his actual parents?"

Cuneo looked away, out the window of the café, and then back again.

"If I didn't know any better, I would say that the box we found him in was his mother. I mean, what else did all those symbols mean? How else did I find him in there? I think that when old Mrs. Galvez was murdered that somehow he started to die in there, too. You know, the way a fetus dies when its mother dies."

She just stared at him, open-mouthed.

"I know, I know. It sounds really crazy. First, she was over a hundred years old. Second, she obviously wasn't carrying a child. Third, the baby was found in a box! None of it makes sense unless you stand away from it and try to figure it out based solely on the evidence we found at the scene. Which, of course, leads to all sorts of impossible conclusions. I know, I know."

"Do you think she was murdered in order to … I don't know … kill the baby, too?"

"Wow. Now you're starting to sound like me."

"Look, the woman was killed and the baby would have died unless you had that sudden inspiration, right? The murder of the woman was also an attempted murder of the child."

"That would only make sense if the mother was carrying the child at the time of the murder, right? But she wasn't. She was upstairs and the baby was in a box behind a wall in the basement."

"But from what you say the baby has congenital defects of all kinds. If the murderer knew that but couldn't get to the baby itself …"

"Because it was in a box behind a wall …"

"Then killing the mother—I mean, if she was the mother— would have killed the baby, too. The goal was not to kill the old woman, but to kill the baby. The murder of the old lady was just a means to an end."

Cuneo sat back in his chair and regarded the professor with newfound respect, even a little awe.

"I never actually thought of it that way. Brava, professor."

"I have my moments," she smiled.

"But that means whoever knew about the baby had to know about the weird occult involvements of Mrs. Galvez, or how else would he have known anything about it?"

"Your suspect, then, has to be one of the cult people she hung around with."

"But if so, then why would he have gone against her? Especially to the extent that he would commit murder?"

"And, just as importantly, why do you keep saying 'he'? Your perpetrator could just as easily be a woman."

"Touché."

"What if it was a rival cult, though? Or a breakaway group, something like that? The history of secret societies is rife with internecine struggles, especially over leadership positions and bragging rights."

"That complicates things, of course. I'm still trying to get my head around Galvez and her library and her hidden boxes behind walls. This throws a whole new level of total confusion at the case."

They were both silent a moment. Cuneo realized that he was comfortable around the professor, and enjoyed talking with her. It was almost like two grad students discussing a course they were both taking, instead of a homicide detective and his consultant trying to solve a grisly crime.

"Of course, we're back to the single most inexplicable fact in this case. How did a baby get into the box?"

The professor flipped through the crime scene photos Cuneo had placed on the table between them.

"The two bodies in the concrete bunker ... they're unsolved, too, right?"

"Sure. They're connected. Mrs. Galvez had some kind of title to the place."

"So, did the same person who committed those murders also kill Galvez? Is that what you're thinking?"

Cuneo spread his hands.

"Look, I'm not really supposed to be discussing details of these cases with anyone, except to get some different angles on the whole cult aspect."

"I get it. It's just that you have two bodies—a male and a female, right?—in this weird occult-like contraption underground, and then you have another underground scene miles away, and they're both connected to Galvez. A man and a woman, and a baby. You see where I'm going with this?"

"Okay. Sure. You're saying …"

"In both cases you have this weird architecture. In the first case, it's an underground concrete box. You called it a Faraday Cage?"

"Something like that." He wasn't telling her about the magnets. He had to keep as many details as he could out of the public view. But since the news media had already covered the general details of each crime, he could confirm what everyone already knew.

"And in the case of Galvez, you have another box. With a body inside it."

"Where are you going with this?"

"I'm not sure. But it seems like part of the same ritual. Or, at least, the same ritual tradition. You're familiar with Wilhelm Reich and the orgone boxes?"

It sounded familiar to Cuneo. Something to do with layers of metal sheets.

"Wasn't Reich put in jail? Something to do with mail fraud?"

"Something like that. He claimed to be able to cure cancer. It had to do with harnessing the sexual energy of the human body and permitting it to flow unimpeded."

"Aha."

"Yeah, it was a little out there, but practitioners of kundalini yoga do pretty much the same thing."

"So what was it about the boxes?"

"I'm thinking there's a connection there. What you were looking at in the Ninth Ward was maybe a kind of orgone box instead of a Faraday Cage ... or maybe both at the same time. A way to collect and concentrate biological energy. Reich used the box to heal wounds, regenerate the cells of the body, that sort of thing. I don't know if he ever tried putting two people in the box to have sex, but it seems like the sort of thing someone would have tried eventually."

"And if conception occurred inside the box ..."

"You'd have a kind of super baby. At least, if we took Reich's theories seriously and pursued them to their logical conclusion."

"So ... forgive me for being dense, but orgone is biological energy?"

"It was more than that, actually. Reich believed it was everywhere in the atmosphere. He even built machines to collect orgone from the air, or something." She lowered her voice. "He was also interested in UFOs."

"Oh, boy."

She laughed.

"He used to shoot them down, he claimed, with his cloudbusting equipment, machines based on his orgone principles. He believed that the UFOs were piloted by aliens who were trying to destroy the planet with negative orgone."

"I think I'm in information overload right about now. Wilhelm Reich, UFOs, voodoo, mysterious babies, ritual magic ... and I'm still no closer to solving three homicides."

"Call the number I gave you. He's got his ear to the ground in the Quarter, and is an encyclopedia of information on the occult scene around here, and not just the *vodoun* aspect."

"Will do. And thanks very much for all your help. I really appreciate it."

She got up and collected her massive shoulder bag and her somewhat smaller purse.

"Let me know if you need anymore information or just want to try out some theories."

"I surely will."

"And let me know if you don't," she said mischievously with a wave, as she walked out the door.

CHAPTER TWENTY-TWO

The Mall in Columbia Maryland

MONROE WAS IN CONFERENCE WITH AUBREY.

That generally meant he would meet his colleague away from the office where they could converse in peace. In the movies, that meant a park bench with the Washington Monument or the Lincoln Memorial brooding in the background to give the scene some gravitas. In real life, it was a busy mall or shopping center, or maybe a food court. Ambient noise made it more difficult for electronics to pick up their conversation; well, more difficult than an isolated park bench anyway.

The other alternative was a bit more comfortable. That would be Simon's apartment. But Monroe did not want to presume upon his old friend's hospitality (or his kitchen) more than necessary. There would be time enough for that later.

So Monroe and Aubrey met at the Mall in Columbia. It was a twenty-minute drive, but Monroe liked the anonymity. Had they gone to the Fort Meade Post Exchange, which was a lot closer of course, they would have run into people they knew.

Rather than go to one of the restaurants they opted for the food court. It was crowded and noisy at that time of day, which suited the two old men just fine.

"Anything new on Angell?" This was always his first question, and it had taken on an almost ritual significance.

"Same as before. We have picked up some indications that Dagon's people are more active than usual in the Southeast Asian sector, but we have nothing definite. If Sylvia was right that Indonesia was one of the ritual sites last November then it is possible that Angell was there or was apprehended there. However, there has been no word on his capture or that of the Book. It's quiet."

Monroe thought about that for a moment. "And Prime?"

"Maxwell is still being held at the black site, and still not talking. I think his usefulness may be at an end. Quite possibly he is as ignorant of Angell's whereabouts as we are, once he lost him after Shanghai. Anything new on Vanek?"

Monroe shrugged. "Vanek's information is dated, as well. He was not brought in on the Angell operation at all. His job was to recruit bodies in the States. What he has on Dagon is pretty much what we already know."

"In what is possibly unrelated news, that assassination in New York City has NYPD going in circles, it seems. The Joint Terrorism Task Force seems intent on saying it was the work of Kurdish extremists, YPG if you believe the Turks, but neglects some intriguing evidence. I spoke with a detective who was on the scene. Well, retired detective. He just happened to be there, and saw the shooter."

"And?"

"It was a woman. A girl, really, according to him."

"A girl shooter?"

"Yeah. And if she was YPG, then we're talking Kurd or even Yezidi."

"Remember that girl at that refugee camp in Turkey? The one you took Angell to?"

"A bit of a stretch, connecting the two, but for some reason she popped into my mind, too. Her, or her sister. If she has one. The man who was killed was responsible for the massacre of her village. The girl—the trance medium, or seer, or shaman, or whatever you want to call her—was Yezidi. From what we have been able to piece together, that same girl showed up later in Nepal after disappearing from the camp."

"But how does she go from being a teenage trance medium to a professional sniper in less than a year?"

"I'm not saying they're the same person, of course. And there's something else."

"I'm going to need to eat something. What do they have around here anyway?"

They made for the establishment that had the shortest line. It was some kind of Tex-Mex affair. They ordered their food and returned with their trays to the table which had remained blessedly unoccupied in their absence.

"You were saying?"

"The murdered gynecologist. That was the reason the retired detective was there in the first place. He was consulting on the case. Seems the doctor was keeping a secret file on his patients who exhibited something called missing twin syndrome."

"What the hell is *that*?"

"It's when a mother seems to be carrying twins early in the pregnancy, but one of the twin disappears later on so she gives birth to only one infant. From what I understand, it isn't that rare. The missing twin is somehow absorbed back into the body, or something. But for some reason this ob/gyn was keeping tabs on about a dozen of them or more."

"Strange, sure. But I'm not really sure how it relates to our case."

"It's like this. The retired detective? He was the one who showed up at Angell's apartment in Red Hook last year when the landlord heard those weird noises. Remember?"

"Ah. That is relevant. Maybe."

"And one of the mothers of the missing twins? Her address is the same as Angell's."

"Jesus! That *is* strange. That's way too many coincidences, all in one day. The girl sniper, the assassination of a man who killed Yezidis, the detective from the Angell apartment. The mother from the Angell apartment. What was her name? Was she Syrian or Iraqi?"

"I have it written down." Aubrey reached into his pocket for the slip of paper that had the names on it given to him by Wasserman.

Rather than read the name aloud, he handed the paper to Monroe so he could read it for himself.

But before Monroe could find the name of the mother from Angell's apartment building he saw something else that stopped him in his tracks.

"This name? Who is that? Where did she come from?"

He pointed to the name "Gloria."

"No idea. It was missing her family name. I don't have much more than that."

"There's no phone number, no home address. It's the only one like that."

Aubrey nodded. "Yes, I noticed that, too."

"I wonder…"

"You're not thinking it's that woman from … Boston?"

"Providence. She was from Providence."

"Did she ever show up at Chromo-Test?"

"No. She never did. In fact, she disappeared from her home in Rhode Island back then. In November. I forgot all about her."

Both men were quiet a moment. The food court continued to bustle all around them, and in the mix was a large number of students milling around. Gloria. What had happened to her? Monroe thought briefly of the girls they had rescued in Florida, and marveled at the tremendous distance—in culture as well as geography—that separated the two groups: the Yezidi children who had known only war and exploitation, and the American kids who knew only privilege and indulgence. He wondered if there was a middle way, or if the world had always been like this.

I must be getting old, he thought to himself, and not for the first time.

"There have been some interesting developments from left field, however," said Aubrey, diverting his old friend's morose thoughts for a moment. "I am not certain they are relevant to our case, but they may be. My contacts at Langley were eager to court my favor for some reason and they were practically falling all over themselves to let me know that our Pinecastle adventure has tentacles reaching into some strange and nefarious places."

"No pun intended?" asked Monroe.

"What? Oh. Tentacles. Indeed." Aubrey poked at something on his plastic plate called a burrito. It bore little resemblance to anything he had dined upon in San Miguel de Allende when he was infiltrating student movements there in the Sixties. He was reluctant to imagine what sort of protein would be concealed by something called "little donkey."

"Yes, as I was saying. Our friends at the Agency have let us know that there has been considerable fallout from the operation. They were actually contacting me to congratulate us on rolling up so many human trafficking rings abroad. I told them I had no earthly idea what they were talking about. I knew about a few in the States, of course, and a few in Europe. The ones we're still watching. But they seemed to imply I was being modest for not taking credit for some cells in Latin America."

"Really? Latin America?"

"They mentioned Bolivia, for some reason, and the Caribbean. I was led to believe there was a ring operating out of Leogane, in Haiti."

Monroe thought for a moment.

"We know there are human trafficking rings in all those places, of course. Some large, some small. We don't have assets in either of those countries. So why does the Agency think we had anything to do with rolling them up?"

"What they call the 'religious angle.'"

"The religious angle?"

"Yes. In other words, there are cultic connections to these groups and they stumbled upon references to Dagon."

"Good Lord."

"No one outside of our little circle was supposed to know about that. Not since Angell disappeared."

"That was the plan, anyway."

"So they put two and two together, based on what was uncovered at Pinecastle and at the other locations, including the interrogation of suspects."

"But if we were not involved in Bolivia and Haiti, and neither was Langley, then who was?"

Aubrey gave up trying to coax a confession out of the burrito and pushed his plate away.

"There can be only one conclusion. There is another group out there working from the same hymnal we are. And they are one hymn ahead of us."

He let that sink in as Monroe thought about the implications.

"There is an angle we can explore. Sylvia and Harry brought it up to me a little while ago. It's a little off-the-wall, but then so is everything about this case. What do we know, really, about spirit possession?"

Aubrey rolled his eyes.

"That there is no such thing? Not really? That it's a form of psychosis or group hysteria or something. A neurological disorder. Temporal lobe, like that?"

"Those are the scientific reactions, I suppose. You know I've encountered a lot of what they refer to as 'paranormal' phenomena in my career."

Aubrey nodded, and started looking around the food court for a replacement for his abandoned burrito.

"Well, what these Pinecastle girls are suffering from can be diagnosed as mania, or hysteria, or even some form of dissociation. But that doesn't get us any closer to solving the problem. What if we approached it from a purely … I don't know … supernatural point of view?"

That got Aubrey's attention.

"Dwight, you've sent me all over the world chasing all kinds of ghosts. I think I'm used to the supernatural point of view by now."

"But you've been interviewing respectable sorts like Eco and Grothendieck."

"There have been others, you recall."

"Oh, yes. That unfortunate couple in Wales. Vanek's parents? And just now that guy in Chicago. Bertiaux."

"Among others."

"Who was recommended by Simon, you recall. Maybe we need

to do more work in this area. There might be a UFO connection to all of this, as well. I don't mean actual flying saucers, but maybe the UFO world is a kind of cult in and of itself and may be a recruiting ground for groups like Dagon. What if that murdered doctor in Brooklyn was the victim of Dagon, concerned that he was onto something about their own genetic experiments?"

"Dwight, that's a Pandora's Box of crazy you want to open up there. All kinds of people claiming all sorts of wild experiences."

"That's why I need you to work with Simon. He'll have an idea as to reputable lines of inquiry in this area."

Aubrey groaned.

"Look, I know you don't like Simon particularly, but he's a good source for this type of material. Look how he was able to help us in the Pinecastle affair."

"I know, I know. It's just that … he really doesn't have any kind of operational background, no training in intel, no security clearances. Plus, he's … well, weird."

"Cooks good, though?"

Aubrey stared dejectedly at the burrito, growing cold and greasy on its paper plate.

"I'll grant you that, anyway. But look, you and I have been through a lot together in our careers. There are things that someone like Simon would never understand. I don't know how much we can trust him. He's not had any military experience either, from what I can piece together. He's from a different world."

"And that is precisely why we need him. We need access to that world. His world. The evidence we gathered from the Pinecastle scene—the magical implements, the seals and sigils, etc.—all seem to point to a definite western approach mixed in with the Tantra and the Lovecraft. We just need the benefit of another perspective on this thing."

Monroe got up from the table and stretched.

"And what will you do in the meantime?"

"I'm going to go back to the Codex. I know I'm missing something, but I don't know what it is."

"Good luck. I'll try to find something edible, then give Simon a call."

Monroe turned and walked away, waving as he did so. Aubrey watched him go. Monroe had a few years on him, but he still walked with the energy of a younger man. He didn't know how much longer that would last.

Aubrey stood up and strolled over to a Chinese counter in the food court, and then gave up when he saw what they were offering by way of Chinese food.

What he really wanted was a hamburger. A real hamburger. Not a fast food imitation. He wondered why it was that America not only offered imitation Chinese food, and imitation Mexican food, but also imitation American food.

I must be getting old, he said to himself, and not for the first time.

That is when he felt his smartphone vibrate in his pocket. It was an encrypted text, and its contents made him lose all thoughts of lunch and begin to run after Monroe.

Prime is in the wind, it said.

CHAPTER TWENTY-THREE

Arabi, St Bernard Parish
New Orleans

TWINS. IT ALL CAME DOWN TO TWINS.

In vodoun, the Twins were present at the Creation. They hold a place of importance above the other gods. They are sometimes thought of as the two poles of existence, of good and evil, darkness and light. The mythology of the Twins is deep, mysterious, and resists all attempts at easy formulation. It is not something an academic would understand because any purely intellectual explanation is bound to fall short. One has to experience the power of the Twins to understand why they are revered. And feared.

No one understood that better than Hervé.

Once the houngan of his own peristyle in Port-au-Prince, demolished in the earthquake that devastated Haiti in 2010, he left that country shortly thereafter and went to Miami along with other refugees. In Haiti he had studied his own religion at the feet of other houngans and came up gradually. But there were problems.

Hervé was transgendered. While that was not a problem for the *vodouisants* in general it was a problem for some people in Haitian society. Homosexuals and transgendered people were being harassed at best and murdered at worst in the streets of Port-au-Prince and other cities. Within the sacred precincts of the peristyle, he could dress in any clothing he chose and was mounted by loa both male and female (as were the vodouisants in general anyway). The possessing spirits did not discriminate between physical genders; a female loa could possess a male, and a male loa a female. It made no difference. Gender was seen as a quality of expression and not as a biological characteristic. The loa did not ascend from the depths of the ocean all the way from Guineè to suddenly become picky as to whom they mounted. One could be born that way as well: with a male body and a female spirit, for instance.

This gender fluidity was reflected in the Twins. One was male and the other female, but they had to be together and honored together or else there would be trouble. Hervé knew that he contained both Twins within himself, and that sometimes he was Taiwó, the boy, and sometimes Kehinde, the girl, to give them their Yoruban names. Together they are known as Ibeji and are usually addressed as a single orisha or loa. The Yoruban people come from Nigeria which, for some reason, has the highest birthrate of twins in the world. In some villages, there are as many as 150 twin births for every 1000.

In the Congo, when twins die the parents carve small figurines to represent them. These are cared for as if they were human children. They are fed and bathed every day. They are put to bed in clean sheets every night. To do otherwise is to invite disaster.

Although the Ibeji are considered a single loa, they have different personalities. They represent the chaos of small children: the playfulness, the tempter tantrums, even the wisdom. The violent actions of poltergeists in the West would be seen as the mischief created by the Twins in Afro-Caribbean cultures.

Hervé had studied all of this for years. He knew that he was a child of the Children, a child of the Ibeji, of the Twins. He/she felt that fluidity within himself/herself depending on the state of the presence in the peristyle. Certain drums spoke to the Twins directly and on hearing the right beats, the right rhythms, they would appear. But Hervé never knew in advance which one of the Twins would show up, or perhaps they both would.

There are photographs of men who are possessed wearing women's clothing, and women wearing men's clothing. There are some *vodouisants* who wear a special costume of which one half is male and the other half is female. This was normal.

Once in America, Hervé began to study gender fluidity in other cultures and discovered to his amazement and pleasure that this was not uncommon among shamans and other ritual specialists. There was a long tradition of transgendered priests in Indonesia, for instance, and among some Native American tribes. There were

Siberian shamans who were cross-dressers. In some areas, they were referred to as a fifth gender: after straight male, straight female, gay male, and gay female.

Among the Fon-speaking people of Dahomey and Benin—where voodoo is the national religion—the chief deity is Mawu-Lisa, a being that is a male-female composite. Of that composite, it is Mawu—the female deity—who is supreme. In addition there are no gender pronouns in the Fon language, no "he" or "she." Hervé began to understand how powerful language was in establishing channels and levels of power, division, and perception. In some languages one is forced to refer to someone not by their gender pronoun (since none exist) but by their given name. In other languages, every noun has a gender. In French, which he learned in school, everything was either *il* ("he") or *elle* ("she"). In English, there were no gender pronouns for objects—such as table or chair—as there were in French and Spanish. It was all very confusing, but also very revealing. Translation becomes so problematic when you either have to add or subtract gender from conversations.

And then, in the New York Public Library on Forty-Second Street in New York City, he managed to see illustrations in a book on European alchemy and saw many depictions of a luminous being that had both male and female characteristics and understood that this was an essential phase in something called the Great Work, in the development of the Philosopher's Stone: an object of some kind that could cause transformations in matter, in physical material. Hervé was stunned. He stared at the picture for a long time in complete silence and wonder. If he could discover the Philosopher's Stone, he could cause transformations. *Transformations.* It seemed like the next step after possession by the loa. He could become whoever, whatever, he wanted. Wasn't that the dream of his brothers and sisters, to wave a magic wand and have their bodies and their souls be the same?

Or, even better: wave that wand and transform the society around them so they wouldn't have to do anything else, be anyone else, except whatever, whoever they actually were.

When he was mounted by the loa, he was immortal. His limbs and his mind stretched throughout the universe. At first he felt it like a hood being thrust over his head in a kind of cosmic kidnapping. Then it was like he was blind drunk, and would wake up without really remembering what he had said or what he had done as a god. With time, having the loa possess him was like being penetrated by a lover: he lost all sense of time and space and was nothing but sensation. Flying, sometimes. Dancing. Deranged.

No wonder it said in the Bible that the stone the builders rejected was the chief stone of the corner. That was how he felt, exactly. A rejected stone, but an essential one. A Philosopher's Stone.

He knew he saw the world differently from others. He certainly experienced it differently. He could see powers and spirits that others could not. He resonated with images and sounds and smells in ways that others—male, female, gay, straight—could not feel, or see, or hear, or understand. Or believe. Except for the children. The children—the pre-pubescent children—in every culture seemed to share this ability, only to lose it when they achieved adulthood. Only when they were possessed, mounted by the loa in love and in violence, in joy and in terror, did they begin to remember who they really were.

If *les blancs* could experience that sensation, wouldn't that cause them to understand how insignificant is their insistence on proper gender roles? If a big, fat, sweaty American preacher was possessed by Erzulie, or Yemaya—female loa of various traditions, including Hervé's own—would he not finally understand that gender was not the same as sex? As he pranced coquettishly and red-faced around the peristyle, flirting with every man in the temple, sashaying and primping like a downtown debutante, thrusting his hips and his breasts out for maximum exposure and the appreciative murmurs of the crowd, would he not come to the realization—not at that moment, of course, with the loa riding him like a prize pony, but later, after he collapsed onto the dirt floor with exhaustion, his energy lost to the goddess like white milk through a straw, but later that night or early the next morning as bits and pieces of the ceremony came back to him or were remembered for him by his friends—would he not realize that everything he thought he knew about gender was nothing more than ideology, bad science, and propaganda?

But it was futile. The houngans would never permit a *blanc* to be possessed by the loa. And with reason: vodoun was the field of their pain and their despair. It was the religion of the slave trade in the Americas; in Africa, it was the religion of the indigenous people, before Christianity, before Islam, before the genocides. Why would they surrender their identity and their culture to … to *tourists*? Slavers? *Missionaries*? He knew of some houngans who had no problem initiating whites because they knew the whites would not understand what had happened to them anyway. But possession? No. No way. That was off-limits. The *blancs* would never understand about the Twins, for instance.

Or about the city of the dead beneath the sea.

Or about the ritual known as *Wété Mo Nan Dlo*, (or, in French, *Retirer d'en bas de l'eau*) the ritual of reclaiming the dead from the water.

And that is what he told the scary *blanc* who was now holding him at gunpoint.

★ ★ ★

He was taking that shortcut through the empty lot between Royal Street and St Claude, in Arabi. He was headed for the Lower Ninth and was planning on crossing Angela Street at St Claude, maybe stopping first at the Waffle House because it was cheap and they didn't hassle him there. He was on his way to meet some detective about some of the stories floating around the Quarter about dead Satanists or something, when he was jacked by this white guy in a blue-and-white seersucker suit—a fucking seersucker suit—and Panama hat holding a nine like he knew what to do with it. It was a scratched up piece, too, as if to advertise its own experience in the world of bullets, cartridges, and dead people.

"Where you going, Hervé?"

"Do I know you?"

"I know you, *cher*, and that's what matters."

"What do you want?"

"A little conversation is all. I heard you got yourself a new gig, up in the Lower Nine. Nice little place. A peristyle, some fags— excuse me, flags—and a goat or some such. Sounds real pretty. Like you, Hervé."

It was late in the afternoon and the lot was quiet. He couldn't hear anyone coming down the path between the bushes. And if he hollered out, it would just be written off as some kids playing in the lot. Or maybe a romantic tryst. He still didn't know who the guy was or what he wanted.

"You a cop?"

The man laughed.

"A cop? That's what you think? No, *cher*, I am not a cop. I am not law enforcement. At least, not of man's law."

He started to panic.

"You … you mean God's law?"

The guy was probably some religious fanatic who hated "voodoo" and gays with equal passion. He knew it was pointless to point out that he was transgender and not gay.

"No, not of God's law, either. There are other laws in the world. The law of the jungle, for instance. But we don't have time for a lecture on the varieties of jurisprudential experience, do we? No Karl Llewellyn. No William James, either. You didn't get that reference, did you? Anyway, it's just you and me and this here Glock. And a question. Answer it truthfully and you can go skipping home to your loas and your hoodoo spirits and play dress up. Answer it false, and they'll be burying you in pieces. You're a tiny little thing, and I dare say this weapon weighs about half of you."

"What is your question?"

The man pointed with his gun towards a small group of bushes off the path. Hervé walked in front of him until told to stop.

"Sit down on that stump there."

He did so.

"I want to know something, and I think you are the person who can clarify some matters. Anyway, that's what I heard. I've been following you around town for a few days, trying to see if the rumors were true. I guess they were. That's why I'm here. But I also know how everybody lies in the Quarter. I know how the voodoo queens operate and how people get ripped off all the time with false promises and cheap hopes."

"I'm not from the Quarter. I'm …"

"From Haiti. I know. I checked you out. You had quite the operation down there. You had some respect from people. And a lot of hatred from others. Mostly 'cause of the way you are, I expect. But I don't care about that. I want to know about the dead. About the ritual of reclaiming the dead from the water."

That was when Hervé's heart sank. He suddenly knew where this was coming from, and why this scary *blanc* had been trailing him for days.

"Who did you lose?" he asked the man with the gun.

"What do you mean?"

"You lost someone. In Katrina. Someone who … who was lost beneath the waves. When the levee broke. And you think that *vodoun* can bring her back. Your wife, wasn't it?"

The man's eyes were full of hate and sorrow. Hervé couldn't predict which one would win out in the end, even though the outcome was life or death for him.

"No," he said through gritted teeth. "It wasn't my wife. It was my little girl. My little Penny. She … I … she was gone before I knew what was happening."

"I'm sorry …"

"And they say you can bring her back. You can bring back the dead."

Hervé immediately started shaking his head.

"No, it's not like that…" he tried to explain.

"Don't tell me that! They say you can do it. The ... the ... what do you call it ... the *Retirer d'en bas de l'eau*. You call up the dead from the waters!"

It was then that Hervé saw something he did not want to see. He saw this man in the seersucker suit holding the hand of a small child. A girl of about eight years old. Penny. And she was sad. Sad and terrified. There was wind. Rain. The power was out. They were going into a darkened room. Alone. Again.

And the levee broke.

★ ★ ★

"She wasn't afraid of the storm."

He looked up, the muzzle of his gun pointing at the ground.

"What? What did you say?"

"Penny. Your daughter. She wasn't afraid of the hurricane. She wasn't afraid of Katrina. She didn't believe something with such a nice name would hurt her. Katrina. That was her mother's name, wasn't it?"

"How did you ..."

"She wasn't afraid of Katrina. She was afraid of *you*. She was afraid that all the power going out in the city, all the flooding, you would have her all to yourself for days. She was afraid you were going to do things to her again. Hurt her again. Make her bleed again. Over and over until the power was restored. Only you didn't expect what happened next. You didn't expect the levee would break and the waters would come and ... and *retirer* your daughter. I will not help you. Penny is safe where she is, with the loa."

"You little cocksucker! I'm going to blow a hole in your diseased balls ..."

He raised his gun to fire but Hervé just stood up and looked him in the eyes. The man heard a voice coming from somewhere. The still, small, quiet voice of a little girl. A prepubescent girl, whose trauma had given her paranormal abilities along with tremendous grief and physical pain.

"No, Papa. Please, Papa. No."

Whether it was a memory of the last time he tried to molest her, or a voice coming to him from beyond the watery grave, *retirer d'en bas de l'eau*, it didn't matter. It had its effect.

He gave a groan and fell to the ground, dropping the unloaded weapon that had not been cleaned in years. Hervé hadn't heard the girl's voice, but he did hear a ringing sound. The sound of bells. Church bells? No. It was his cell phone. A number he did not recognize.

Detective Cuneo was leaving him a voicemail.

CHAPTER TWENTY-FOUR

Singapore to Frankfurt

ANGELL GOT UP FROM HIS SEAT to stretch his legs. The guy who had stood over him to look into his overhead compartment wasn't in his seat, and presumably was in the lavatory. Angell walked back to the galley area where an exit door was located and stared out its window for awhile at the night sky over India.

It was a clear night and anyway they were above the clouds. The stars were visible and the view outside the port was peaceful and even a little otherworldly. Angell thought of how few people in human history had been able to do what he was doing: look at the Earth from 35,000 feet up. Since the days of the first Wright brothers' flight it had been just a little over a hundred years. Millions of people had flown on aircraft since then, but considering the Earth's population—in the billions—it was a drop in the population bucket. No one had been able to do what he was doing for thousands of years of human civilization, not to mention hundreds of thousands of years of *homo sapiens* walking the planet. Walking, not flying.

Walking. Not flying.

At that moment of reflection, Angell realized what he had been missing in his efforts to understand the *Necronomicon*. The calculations were made not by people who had been restricted to walking the Earth, but by people—creatures, beings, aliens, whatever you want to call them—who had flown *over* the Earth. People who had come down from the heavens and who therefore had a markedly different perspective on the planet from those who had never been higher than their local mountain or hill. The garbled instructions in the Book for calculating the Opening of the Gate were not garbled at all, not really. They were just incomprehensible to an Earth-based intellect rather than a Sky-based one. Like a fish trying to draw a map of the Himalayas.

The Book was clear: the Gate was opened when the Great Bear hung from its tail in the sky. That was what was confusing him.

The book's intense focus on the Great Bear had never made much sense to him.

Because the Great Bear hangs from its tail every day—*from the perspective of the Earth*—specifically in the northern hemisphere. In other words, the Great Bear makes a complete revolution around the North Star once a day. That is because the Earth rotates on its axis once every twenty-four hours, give or take.

The Great Bear is only visible in the latitudes above the equator. In the southern latitudes the Great Bear is replaced by the Southern Cross constellation. In fact, in the southern latitudes even the Moon appears upside down from the perspective of their northern neighbors.

But from what perspective would the Great Bear be visible but not rotate so frequently, or even at all?

From space.

These measurements ... the occult calendars ... all of that, would no longer obtain if the practitioners were *space-based* and not Earth-based. It would be an entirely different system!

With a feeling of triumph Angell rushed back to his seat. He would take advantage of the next few hours of relative peace and quiet and recalculate everything, using the ritual in Nepal—the one where he acquired the Book during a firefight that took the life of a friend and which re-introduced him to the young Yezidi woman, the trance medium—as a baseline from which to figure out the next date on which Dagon would try to open the Gate. Whether you believed in a Gate or not, Dagon did: and that meant they would try something equally grand and criminal to ensure their success. That must be why, he thought, that guy was following him all the way from Indonesia to Frankfurt. They are on a tight schedule, and they need the *Necronomicon*.

The grimoires—the workbooks of the magicians—were always specific as to time. The hours of the day were assigned to the planets, and had their own mystical names associated with angelic forces.

Each day was ruled by its planetary force, and the hours of the day and night were divided accordingly. Thus, a ritual for love would take place in the day and hour of Venus, the planet most associated with love. A ritual of aggression or violence would take place on the day and hour of Mars. And so forth. It was a primitive system, and charts were included in the grimoires to guide the aspiring sorcerer, and with the magical purposes all very mundane and relevant to basic human desires.

Sophisticated magicians would apply their knowledge of astrology for a more precise and accurate timing of their rituals at hours when the actual positions of the planets were known from the elaborate star charts and tables of houses that astrologers employed for their natal and transit analyses. This was an echo of how the ancient sovereigns of cultures as diverse as those from Babylon and Egypt, Mexico and China, would have their heavens plotted by specialists to predict success in war. The more sophisticated the ritual the more it was elevated out of the realm of spell-casting and bewitchment and towards loftier, transcendental ends that could only be understood by those who had spent a lifetime studying the arcane arts, but which at its heart concerned contact with non-human intelligences: angels, demons, spirits, gods.

The system of Western ceremonial magic is predicated on the assumption that there is an intimate connection between events in the sky and events on Earth; that the cosmos is a kind of giant clockwork, with the gears moving according to a fixed pattern that is discernible by the wise. This was the way the world worked, and magicians—who were observers of nature—knew that in order to attain the maximum benefit from their rituals that they should be synchronized with the vast machinery all around them.

Angell had a cursory knowledge of all of this from his studies of ancient religion. Such a theme was always present, even though it was often overshadowed by theology, or the attributes of various deities, or conflicts between priests and sects. Now that he was forced to look at this more closely he became amazed at the degree to which the concept of time and calendars and schedules was so prominent.

That Stonehenge was created as a kind of cosmic sundial is now taken for granted; that many ancient monuments were aligned with constellations or with the movements of the Sun and the Moon is a given. Even many of the cave paintings going back to Neolithic times now are understood to be depictions of constellations. It goes without saying that this theme was based on how the heavens were perceived from the vantage point of anyone *on the surface of the Earth.* There was a Sun and Moon, and they both "rose" in the east and "set" in the west, as did the planets, in their "zones." There were fixed stars that were the constellations of the Zodiac, against which the movements of the planets and the Sun and Moon could be tracked.

So he thought he understood at least *this* aspect of the Dagon system until he realized that their timing methods were based on a different perspective altogether. They had not devised hourly and daily planetary tables based on the positions of the heavenly bodies from the point of view of someone on the Earth. Their perspective was completely foreign, as if it was from a telescope based somewhere else in the solar system ... or maybe even beyond. It was an astrological system—maybe—in which the Earth was one of the planets. It was crazy. But it was also a revelation.

When he realized that whoever had composed the *Necronomicon* some 1200 years ago was using a system that could not have come from the Earth, it meant that the system of magic described in its pages was extra-terrestrial. The days, hours, and planetary assignments made no sense otherwise. The "Mad Arab" was "mad" because he had been in contact with non-humans. In modern parlance, he was a contactee.

Once Angell realized that, it was only a matter of revisiting all the calculations and making them consistent with the ritual he knew had taken place already, the one he gate-crashed in Nepal. By collating that date and time and place with what he already knew about the system in the *Necronomicon* he was able to define a new timetable, at least in broad strokes.

★ ★ ★

The calculations were excruciatingly difficult without a scientific calculator or at least a slide rule (not that Angell had ever learned how to use one), so the best he could do was approximate the timing. There was another aspect to the Great Bear that he had neglected to include in his research, and it was so obvious he hated himself for having missed it (him having a PhD in Religion, after all).

And that was the reason why the ancient Egyptian mummification ceremony had made use of an adze: a ritual implement that was used in the "Opening of the Mouth" ceremony, to give the mummified pharaoh the power of speech in the afterlife as he traveled to the North Star.

The adze was in the shape of the Big Dipper: the seven-starred asterism that is part of the Great Bear constellation. That was deliberate for it was made of magnetite or magnetic iron, probably from a meteorite. The Great Bear was not only a marker of time, it was an indicator of direction: in this case, due north. The North Star is so named because it occupies the northernmost position in the night sky, and the Great Bear points to the North Star.

Due north and magnetic north are not the same but—as Aubrey would say—it was close enough for government work. The relationship between direction in space and the magnetic field was a deep one. There are four basic forces in the physical world: the strong nuclear force, the weak nuclear force, gravity, and electromagnetism. The Earth is enveloped in a magnetic field, and the location of magnetic north changes all the time—but so gradually that one would never know it. There were ages in the history of the Earth when the poles shifted, or even switched places with magnetic "north" in the south, and vice versa. In fact, the current path of magnetic north shifted in 1904 to the straight, linear path it is on now after several centuries of meandering around the Arctic Circle. Angell thought that was relevant somehow, a thought nagging at him from the back of his head, but he couldn't place it. Instead, he focused on the idea of the magnetic adze in the mummification ceremony.

But there was no evidence that the ancient Egyptians were aware that magnetic iron pointed north. The use of a compass to find one's direction did not come into use until about the fourth century BCE, and that was in China. So how were the ancient Egyptians aware of the relationship between magnetic iron or lodestone and the Big Dipper?

And what was the relationship between magnetism, the North Star, and speech? Was there some understanding among the Egyptians that cognition was somehow related to magnetism? If so, what was it?

Angell realized that these were significant factors in the *Necronomicon* "algorithm," for he was always confused by the idea of the Gate, and when it was open, and why Dagon made such a fuss over it. But now that he had collated two seemingly minor pieces of information—the idea of the Earth as seen from the vantage point of a space-faring civilization, and the idea of the shifting magnetic field of the Earth—he knew he was closer to the answer, and that meant closer to discovering the secret at the heart of Dagon. The problem was he didn't have enough science to figure out the rest. For that, he would have to enlist the help of an expert.

★ ★ ★

Behind him, Moody stood up to stretch his legs. He glanced over at Angell to see him scribbling furiously in a notebook. He could not see the *Necronomicon* from where he was standing, and figured that Angell had it hidden in his backpack which he could see was now stored beneath the seat in front of him instead of in the overhead. No matter. When they arrived in Frankfurt the book, the notes, and Angell himself would fall into the possession of Dagon. He had been stupid to overplay his hand earlier and try to steal the book from the overhead compartment. There was all the time in the world, and when they left the arrival gate at the airport he would have fulfilled his duty to Dagon and maybe be free of them at last.

CHAPTER TWENTY-FIVE

Arabi, St. Bernard Parish
New Orleans

THE GUY ON THE PHONE SAID TO MEET HIM at a Waffle House near the Lower Ninth. Odd that he would have picked a place so close to his first weird crime scene.

Cuneo hadn't been to a Waffle House in ages, not since he first drove down from New York to take up his position in New Orleans. He remembered them as a little depressing, but at least they were open twenty-four hours. Which is probably why they were depressing. He hadn't had lunch after that meeting with the professor, so at least he could get something there.

He parked next to the restaurant and walked through the glass doors, looking up and down to find his appointment. He started to wonder if he was early when a thirty-something black woman gestured to him.

Cuneo shook his head, figuring her for a working girl, but then she said the most amazing thing.

"Cuneo? You're looking for Hervé?"

He walked over to her booth.

"Yes. Do you know him?"

She made an extravagant gesture with her shoulders.

"That's an existential question. The easy answer is I am Hervé. Dr. Francine sent you?"

"Ah. Aha. But your voice on the phone …"

"Protective coloration," he replied, in a more masculine-sounding voice. "I am trans. She did not mention?"

Cuneo smiled, and almost laughed.

"No, she didn't. But then, I'm from New York."

What Cuneo saw was a Haitian woman with short-cropped hair, fine-boned, wearing a kind of colorful turban and an equally colorful shirt in a tropical design. Hervé could not be much more than five-foot four or five, and spoke fluent English with only a slight accent.

"But your name is Hervé?"

"Yes. It is thé name on my passport and my green card. I was born with both male and female characteristics but the doctor decided I was male. It was a *fait accompli*, at least legally. So I use that name for official purposes." She added, with a raised eyebrow, "I have other names."

Cuneo sat down across from her and considered the laminated menu.

"Waffles? I guess?"

"The specialty of the house, detective."

Cuneo ordered. He saw that Hervé was already halfway through a plate of waffles swimming in maple syrup.

"Were you waiting long? Sorry if I was late …"

"Oh, no. Not at all. I was close by when you called. A man tried to murder me, actually. In that lot in back of the restaurant."

"What!"

She shrugged. "Nothing to it, really. He had a gun, but it wasn't loaded. He was a little crazy, you know. He lost a … a loved one in Katrina. He thought I could help."

The waitress brought over a plate of waffles and some coffee. After the *café au lait* in the Quarter with Francine, this tasted like something found in a shower drain but he gulped it down anyway.

As he did so, Hervé began talking to fill the silence.

"Do you know where Arabi got its name? No? It was from a man the local people had heard about. A crazy man in Egypt who tried to burn down Alexandria in 1882. He wanted Egypt to be free of the British. The people liked his style, so they named their town after him. They wanted to be free, too. They still do."

"So, Arabi actually means 'Arab'?"

"Yes, and no. It could also be a mangled version of his name, Ahmed Urabi. Urabi, Arabi. *Comme ça.* The only thing we know for sure is that he was a 'Mad Arab.'" She looked at Cuneo to see if he reacted to the phrase, but he didn't seem to. She sighed.

"Francine told me that you wanted to ask about things I may have heard about a strange cult operating in the city, killing people?"

"Well, briefly, yes. You've heard about the homicides last year? The one here, in the Lower Ninth, and the other one in Belle Chasse?"

"Yes, I know of them. They were in all the newspapers and online. But the details were sparse. Even so, there were many rumors among the *vodouisants*. The practitioners of *vodoun*," she clarified.

"Yes, I am familiar with the term. What do you think about the case? What have you heard?"

Hervé looked behind her and got the waitress's attention for more coffee.

Turning back to Cuneo, she said, "You are out of your depth here. There is a whole world beneath the streets of this city that you cannot imagine. The cemetery is the entrance to that world. In what other city on earth is a cemetery its very heart? Only here, in New Orleans. People come here from all over the world to visit St. Louis Cemetery Number One."

"Yes, I know. Marie Laveau is buried there."

Hervé sniffed. "So they say."

"But what about Dagon? The Order of Dagon? Have you heard of it?"

She nodded. "About a hundred years ago, they came here. Not to the city proper, but out in the bayous. South of here. Barataria, they say. There is an old burial mound there, put there by the Indians aeons ago. Lafitte called it the 'Temple.'"

"Lafitte? Jean Lafitte, the pirate?"

"The same. He hid out there. Some say he buried treasure there, too, but no one has found it so far."

"What about Dagon?"

"It was mixed up with some *bokors* from Leogane, you know,

black magicians. But the real leadership came from the desert. Mesopotamia. Babylon. They held a big ritual out there one year, on the Day of the Dead. Followers came from all over the world. That was Dagon. From the Fertile Crescent to the Crescent City. Funny."

"What happened?" Cuneo asked, although he knew the answer already.

"They got raided by the police. The leaders escaped, but many of the followers were arrested. They were looking for missing children. They didn't find any."

"Did the group survive? Are they still here?"

Hervé shrugged and sipped more coffee before answering.

"They all left town after the raid. They say some stayed behind, but the police inspector at the time would have known about it if they did. Anyway, they were international."

Something occurred to Cuneo.

"That raid was a long time ago. But someone got the police to go to the bayou, to raid the ceremony."

"Ceremony! It was no ceremony, *m'sieur*. It was an orgy. Dagon was about sex, about using sex to control people's minds and actions. No self-respecting *vodouisant* would be involved in something like that. But Europeans, yes. Anyone with … *comme dit-on* … 'issues' about sex would be attracted to the kinds of rituals Dagon performed. Pedophiles, for instance."

"And homosexuals? The transgendered?"

"Careful, *officer*."

"No offense intended, but in those days wasn't any kind of sexuality that wasn't mainstream suppressed and repressed, if you get my meaning?"

"I understand you perfectly, *sir*. But Dagon in those days had a very narrow understanding of their own magic. They thought that the only power that could be raised was that between male and female. Biological male and biological female. You know, to make baby? Age was not the barrier, therefore *les pédophiles*. But homosexuality would have been seen as ... as counterproductive. It was a position very unsophisticated."

She leaned forward to make an important point.

"You know I have my own *hounfort,* here in New Orleans?"

"Yes, I gathered that."

"I am what is called *ounsi.* An initiate. *Ounsi asogwe.* The word *ounsi* means a spouse of the loa. A *spouse.* Husband, wife, it does not matter. I am married to the spirits. Gender is not relevant."

"What was the purpose of the ritual, then? The ritual in the bayou?"

Hervé set down her cup and stared at Cuneo.

"You mean you don't know?"

Cuneo spread his hands. "How could I know?"

She leaned over and angry-whispered the answer to Cuneo so that no one else in the nearly empty restaurant could hear.

"To open the Gate. The Gate between this world and the next. To let them in!"

"The Gate? Between ... between the living and the dead?"

"No! Not between the living and the dead. No. The Gate between us and *Them.*"

"I'm ... I'm sorry. I don't understand."

"Between the people on the Earth. *Us.* The human beings. And *them.* The people from the Stars. The people not from here. And not people, either."

At this point, Cuneo was certain that she was insane. Maybe drugs? Trauma from the earthquake? But Francine had sent him to her, respected her as a source. An informant, in anthropological lingo. Come to think of it, in cop lingo, too.

But something she said ...

"You said the Stars. People from the Stars. Have you heard of another group like that, called Starry Wisdom?"

"*Sagesse étoilée.* Yes, I have heard of Starry Wisdom."

"What happened to them?"

"Happened? Nothing. They have been here for a long time."

"You mean they're still here?"

"They never left."

Cuneo was reminded of what the Smiley Face guy had said to him last year, outside the Galvez house: *I never left.* It was an eerie coincidence.

"So, you know where they are right now?"

Hervé shrugged. Cuneo didn't like that. There was way too much shrugging going on around this case.

"I can take you in for questioning. You know that, right?"

"May I finish my waffles first?"

"Look, I don't want to hassle you. You're a friend of the professor, and she recommended you highly to me because of your background and your knowledge of the … of the field I'm interested in. But this is a homicide investigation, and New Orleans is knee deep in homicides, so I pretty much have carte blanche right now."

Hervé grinned. "So, you mean, we can do this the hard way or the easy way?"

Smart ass.

"What I mean is, if you want to contribute to lowering the crime rate around here you can help. I don't want you to violate any kind of religious principles or like that, but I do need to make contact with these people. Their members have been getting killed and I need to know why and I need to put a stop to it."

She pushed her plate away and beckoned to the waitress to clear the table and bring more coffee. The way she did it was almost regal, as if she was sitting in a Michelin five-star on the Côte d'Azur rather than a Waffle House a few blocks from the Lower Ninth Ward. Cuneo noted the sense of command she had, her total self-possession. He had the sense, watching her, that she morphed in front of his eyes into different people. Some male, some female, and some whose gender he couldn't place but it didn't matter. Some were older than she was, some younger. A turn of her head and she was someone else, someone wiser and tougher. Another turn, and she was coquettish and sly. He couldn't get a fix on her, and that bothered him and intrigued him. It was like questioning someone with multiple personalities.

"Starry Wisdom exists, as I have said. But they don't publish their locations. Only members know, and only when they have to know. That house, the house where the lady was killed, that house was important to them. It was a ... ah, I don't have the right English words, forgive me ... a ... *bien, une alembique.* We don't have a Creole word for this."

Cuneo asked her to repeat the term, and thought he recognized it.

"You mean an alembic?"

"Ah, yes. So it is the same word? *Alembique?*"

"Yes, I think so. But I don't really know what that is. It's laboratory equipment? For chemistry?"

"Yes, like that. An *alembique* is a kind of condenser. For condensation. You know?" She made trickling movements with her fingers, which Cuneo noticed were long and thin and ended in nails painted mauve.

"Okay, but how is their house a condenser? An alembic?"

Cuneo always knew when someone was lying to him, and he also knew when someone didn't want to answer a direct question and instead waltzed him around the dance floor a few times. This was one of those times.

"Well, in fact, every house, every building, is a condenser. The people who live there or work there concentrate their *élan vital*, their life force, inside the walls. The roof of the building acts to contain that energy and it condenses and falls back into the rooms of the house."

Cuneo raised an eyebrow at this description. "But surely the circumstances are different with different buildings. Is your hounfort a condenser? Does it have a roof?"

Hervé looked at the homicide detective with a little more respect at this question.

"And what do you know of the hounfort?"

"My mother was Haitian."

She sat back in her seat and drew a long breath. "When did she leave?"

"At the time of Papa Doc. She was a young girl and was being harassed by the *tontons macoutes*. She came to New York, to the Bronx, and met my father."

"Was she beautiful?"

"Yes. Very much. You look a little like her, actually."

At that, Hervé didn t know how to react. It was a compliment, one of the highest, but she was very aware of the disparity in power between them, as well as the difference in culture. She did not know if he was playing her like a criminal, or simply being honest. She had to be careful around this one.

"How much did she tell you about *vodoun*?" she asked, focusing on the reason they were sitting there.

"Oh, just basic stuff," he answered, dismissively. "The hounfort, the houngan, the peristyle. The loa."

"So she spoke to you of possession, of how the loa ride the *vodouisants* like a horse?"

"Yes, sure, but there has been a lot of that in the media, too. Movies, television programs, books ..."

She flicked her fingers as if removing dirt from her blouse, a deprecating gesture including everything the culture of the *blancs* had to say about *vodoun*.

"What is important to know is that possession is real, and it is voluntary. If you attend *un service* ..." she said, using the Creole pronunciation, "... then you are vulnerable to possession. It is an accepted thing. The loa come up from the ground, under the Earth, all the way from Guinee, and take hold of you. It is how we know our faith is real. No other faith can claim such a thing, that their gods can appear and demonstrate their powers to the devotees on a regular basis. No other faith except the ones you ask me about.

Dagon, and Starry Wisdom. If the *blancs* have *vodoun*, it is to be found there. In those groups."

Cuneo felt himself drowning in hyperbole again, so he brought the subject back around to his central question.

"You said the house was an alembic. But I still don't understand. If, as you say, every house is an alembic what makes the Galvez house different or special?"

"It was designed that way, you understand? Some buildings, they are good alembics. Others, not so good. The design of the building is important. It must have ..." she paused as she searched for the word she wanted. "... it must have 'fingers', you know? Fingers that reach to the stars." She pantomimed with her own fingers, aiming them skyward in a grasping motion.

"Like church steeples?"

"Ah, yes! Exactly. But the ... steeples? ... must bring down the energy into the Earth. To ground the energy. There will be conduits, you know, like pipes, that bring the energy down into the building. If you look, you will find them."

Cuneo had already found them, but decided to keep that to himself.

"And then what happens? When the energy is brought down?"

"It must be collected. Like water in a well. And then it goes back up, and comes back down. Condensation. Until the energy has been purified and concentrated. Then the devotees can use it for their own purposes."

"Is sex involved in all of this?"

She laughed at his expression. He was so obviously uncomfortable discussing this, and with her: a transgendered houngan.

"You Europeans are obsessed with sex. You don't know what to do with it, where to put it. How to deal with it. You will never understand it that way. One of your own tried to explain it to you, but you did not listen because he was black."

"I have no idea what you're talking about."

She leaned over the table again, and looked into his eyes as she spoke.

"New Orleans has a long history of strange societies, of Afro-Caribbean religions, but also of Freemasonry and of Rosicrucianism. The Polar Star Lodge of the Freemasons was set up here in 1794, and chartered by France in 1798. Polar Star. Think about that. It is important. *L'etoile polaire*. Like your *Sagesse étoilée*.

"At the same time as Marie Laveau was active here, there was another teacher and leader who brought with him the wisdom of Egypt and Europe and who made the connection between the magic of the white people and the Arab people with that of the African people. Like Marie Laveau, he was also a mulatto. His father was white, and his mother was a slave. Marie Laveau's father was white and her mother was a free black woman. His name was Paschal Beverly Randolph. These were people that the anthropologists might call 'liminal' because of the way they walked the line between two races, two cultures, and even two religions."

She paused to drink some of the execrable coffee, and returned to her theme as Cuneo simply sat and tried to put all of what she was saying into some kind of context he could use to solve the crimes.

"Randolph was a friend of Abraham Lincoln. He wanted to free the slaves, like Lincoln. He was respected by many *blancs*, but especially by the secret societies. He received initiations in the Middle East and in Europe. Freemasons, Rosicrucians, everyone. He created the first Rosicrucian lodge in America. He created the techniques upon which German occult lodges were based. He wrote many books. And he lived here, in New Orleans. He learned *vodoun*. He took some of what he learned and included it in his rituals and his writings. If you are looking for Starry Wisdom and Dagon, you must start there."

She started to get up to leave, but Cuneo wasn't finished yet. He put a hand on her arm, and she looked down at it and then up at him, a question in her glance.

"One more question, please. Are these two groups—Dagon and Starry Wisdom—enemies, or collaborators?"

She smiled and raised a mocking eyebrow.

"It doesn't matter, *m'sieu*. There is no 'good guy' or 'bad guy' here. There are only two forces, fighting over control of this world. Like the loa, sometimes good, sometimes bad. Sometimes on your side, sometimes not. You think there is some benevolent god somewhere, looking down from heaven and loving you? We know better. We *vodouisants* know better. Dagon and Starry Wisdom know better. Your ignorance of this basic fact is the condiment on the feast of flesh that this modern world has become."

As she left the restaurant she stopped for a moment at the door and looked back at the confused detective.

"Read your Randolph, my friend. *And* your Lovecraft. The answer is there."

CHAPTER TWENTY-SIX

NSA Headquarters
Fort Meade

THE BLACK SITES WERE UNDER THE CONTROL OF CIA, in cooperation with the host countries in which they were located. Access to
prisoners in the black sites was, obviously, tightly restricted. Transport
to and from a black site was similarly restricted. The exact location
of a black site was known to only a handful of people, and prisoners
were taken to black sites hooded and blindfolded so that they would
never know where they were.

When Maxwell Prime was taken out of his cell he was hooded
and shackled, wrists and ankles. He was shuffled along a corridor
outside his cell and past the room where he had been interrogated
by an agent sent by Aubrey.

Neither Aubrey nor Monroe was CIA, of course, so their "guest"
was accommodated by the Agency which was not unusual. High
value terror suspects picked up by military intelligence in the field—
Iraq, say, or Afghanistan—were similarly housed in Agency black sites
from time to time. After 9/11, there was a degree of inter-agency
cooperation that had not obtained prior to the attack. Maxwell Prime
was considered an NSA detainee for the sake of the paperwork, but
he was really just Monroe's prisoner. Agency personnel were not
involved in his interrogations, but by an experienced officer sent by
Aubrey to handle the process.

Aubrey suspected that Prime had his own network of operatives,
informers and even enforcers developed over time during his career
in the intelligence field. He could not have pulled off the attempted
snatch of Gregory Angell at sea the way he did without a lot of
resources in the criminal underworld. It took resources and know-
how, the kind that comes only with extensive experience. That made
Prime especially dangerous. He could sell those capabilities to the

highest bidder, and it was clear to Aubrey that Prime had ambitions beyond his G–scale salary and a pension at retirement.

Prime's danger was also his vulnerability: his hostility towards Monroe. Aubrey had no idea where that had come from as there had been little to no direct contact between the two men that Aubrey could determine. No matter, it was there and had to be addressed. Someone had sprung Prime from the black site: an action that could only have been taken with the approval of someone very high up in either the Agency or NSA, and Aubrey knew it wasn't NSA.

Was all that making-nice on the part of CIA a smoke screen to distract Aubrey—and by extension Monroe—from another operation they were planning with Prime?

As Aubrey and Monroe considered the possibilities, Maxwell Prime was on a CIA flight from Bangkok to Ramstein Air Base in Germany, where he would be held until his handlers were satisfied that he gave them what he had on Monroe.

Aubrey was pacing back and forth in Monroe's rather small office.

"I can't understand who transferred him. I got a call back from my contact in the Agency. He claims he doesn't know anything, either."

"Is he telling you the truth?"

"He always has before. But that doesn't mean anything. I don't think he'd color outside the lines for us, is what I'm saying."

"If the Agency is behind this, then that means they are using Prime for something."

"It means they're using him against *us*."

"What kind of damage can he do?"

"To us? Nothing. Our operation is the very definition of compartmented. He was tasked with finding Angell if Angell wound up in Asia, specifically China. He had Angell's description, that sort of thing. He wasn't read in on the details. The problem was he brought in a whole shitload of unauthorized persons on this when he finally did locate him. Contract agents of some kind. He was acting on his own initiative …"

"Do you believe that?"

"What do you mean?"

"Think about it. What possible motivation could he have for acting on his own initiative? I mean, I can understand a little swaying over the center line, but not mounting an entire kidnapping operation on the high seas. In the first place, it costs money. In the second place, he had no cover for that kind of job."

"So, what are you saying?"

"Isn't it obvious? He wasn't working for us. He used what you told him about Angell and offered it to some other spy shop somewhere."

Aubrey nodded to himself and closed his eyes. He took a deep breath, and exhaled.

"That means he was sprung by the other guys," he whispered, half aloud.

"Who has that kind of entrée to a black site?"

"Nobody outside our little community."

"So the opposition has to be one of us."

"You're not suggesting a mole inside NSA or CIA?"

"Not exactly," Monroe shook his head. "What if Dagon has penetrated one of the shops around here? What if they have somebody inside? That would make more sense, even if the implications are hideous."

"The Russians did it with Aldrich Ames. And the Israelis with Jonathan Pollard."

"Not to mention the Chinese."

"If Dagon has a hold of Prime, then God help him. He was safer in a black site."

"But if Dagon has him that may mean they will use him against us in some way we have not anticipated."

"Have you spoken with Simon yet?"

"No, not with all of this going on. But I guess there's no time like the present." Aubrey reached for his phone.

"It's all hands on deck, old son."

"*What the holy fuck?*"

Monroe rarely had heard Aubrey use colorful language. He was a gentleman of the old school, the Allen Dulles–elbow patch–pipe smoking school, if somewhat better dressed than old Al and with a more archaic moral code.

Aubrey was staring at his phone. At his encrypted phone. To which few had the ability to call or text.

There was a text waiting for him.

It read:

The priest dwells in the tunnels of Calabi-Yau, in the topos of the ziggurat. Le Poteau Mitan a rigid rod. Sphere to disc. Disc to sphere. How many points chauds on the surface of the Stone? The Shining Trapezohedron! Calculate, and assemble!

BOOK THREE

DAS GLÄNZENDE TRAPEZOHEDRON

("THE SHINING TRAPEZOHEDRON")

Time and Space are forms by which we obtain (distorted) images of ideas. Our measures of Time and Space are crude conventions, and differ widely for different Beings.

—Aleister Crowley, *Magick in Theory and Practice*

The fact of infestation ought alone to have demonstrated the post-mortem life of humankind long ago; for every age, since the dawn of civilization, has been familiar with it. What else were the oracles of Delos, Delphi, Dodona, and Phrygia? What else the demoniac possessions of Christ's time? What else the obi and the voodoo spells of Africa, the West Indies, Long Island, and New Orleans? What else the secret mummeries of the Druids? And what else is the practice of modern mediumship? From the lips of its oracles you hear the most divine teachings and the next hour the most ribald curses and the most awful blasphemies! Why? Because the unfortunates are in the merciless grasp of the exuvia of the spiritual worlds—the larvae of the starry skies.

—P. B. Randolph, *After Death*

The four-inch seeming sphere turned out to be a nearly black, red-striated polyhedron with many irregular flat surfaces. ... He could scarcely tear his eyes from it, and as he looked at its glistening surfaces he almost fancied it was transparent, with half-formed worlds of wonder within. Into his mind floated pictures of alien orbs with great stone towers, and other orbs with titan mountains and no mark of life, and still remoter spaces where only a stirring in vague blacknesses told of the presence of consciousness and will.

—H. P. Lovecraft, "The Haunter of the Dark"

CHAPTER TWENTY-SEVEN

Contact in the Desert
Joshua Tree, California

GLORIA HAD JUST SHOWED UP AGAIN at Joshua Tree with Jean-Paul in tow. It was going on late afternoon, with the desert sky turning several shades of mauve before settling down to a deep purple, a long strip of dying sunlight in the west waving goodbye and good luck. All around them there were people involved in various stages of discussion on topics dear to those who follow the UFO scene. Abductions, exotic materials housed in government facilities, the machinations of Majestic-12, ancient aliens, cryptozoology, conspiracy theories, and all manner of speculation on all matter of ideas. It was like one long dream interpretation session, like something from a Jungian therapy hour, with everyone on the couch and free-associating, including the therapists.

Gloria figured the crowd divided into two basic groups: those who had direct experience, and everyone else. Those who had direct experience had no way of communicating exactly what they had experienced because there was no vocabulary for it. No context. You started from the premise that what happened could not possibly have happened; therefore, you were crazy, or deluded, or part of an elaborate hoax. Then there were those who believed everything the experiencers said, no matter how contradictory, and who believed they had the answer. When an experiencer spoke, the others would nod and smile knowingly, even if they knew nothing. Or next to nothing.

Gloria found all of that infuriating. She didn't want anyone's acceptance, or support. She wanted answers.

She wanted to know where her kids were. And she wanted to know whose kid she was carrying now. She wanted to know how this possibly could happen.

"Doesn't look too promising around here," she said to Jean-Paul.

"I don't know. There's lots of famous people here. I mean, some of them are whack, but ..."

"You sound like a fanboy."

He shrugged.

"Not really. I mean, UFOs aren't really my scene. I'm more into the occult stuff. You know, witchcraft and magic and like that. I was invited to a ritual the night I saw you on the highway, but ... I don't know ... something happened. Sometimes I think this is all one ritual and it hasn't ended yet. Like maybe I'm dreaming? Or hallucinating? Like maybe they gave me something? I don't know. I wish I did, but I don't."

"Well, you're here for a reason. Somehow you wound up here just like I did. I'm not one of those people who thinks everything happens for a reason. But some things do. And in my case, I can tell you, the UFO thing is real because it happened to me."

"Yeah, pretty hairy stuff. So maybe there's someone here who can help."

"That's what I'm hoping, but ... after getting a look at this crew, I think it's a waste of time. This is like Woodstock, with everyone getting high, except no one is getting high here. And there's no music. At all. That's fucked up."

"Jeez, since you put it that way..." he smiled.

They were walking between the various pavilions and threading their way through crowds of people who were attending one or another of the featured events and speakers. Gloria waddled more than walked; it wasn't really an environment suitable for pregnant women who were that far along. Between the desert heat and the crowds and the long distances between buildings and the confusing maps ... she found a place to sit down and rest while she examined the flyer again and tried to identify someone who seemed saner than the rest.

"Who's this guy?"

She pointed at a photo of a vaguely satanic looking male, with a narrow goatee, whose specialty seemed to be the alien abduction "experience." His name was Alexander Ferguson Blair. His presentation had already begun and it was close enough that she figured it was worth the short walk to another chair indoors, with air conditioning, where she could sit.

"I dunno. I think he was featured once on the History Channel, though. Something to do with DNA or something."

"Okay. Sounds promising. Let's go. Help me up." He reached under her arms and got her into a standing position with a trace of wobble.

They made their way to the pavilion and found seats inside, towards the rear of the room. It wasn't large, and it wasn't crowded, but it was dark and cool. Gloria sensed right away that this guy, whoever he was, was not interested in the flash and trash approach. He spoke softly into a microphone attached to his suit jacket and pointed to a succession of PowerPoint slides as he described genetic "anomalies." Jean-Paul got bored almost immediately, but the idea of genetic anomalies got Gloria's attention. Isn't that what Chromo-Test said she had? Anomalies?

Blair went into some dense material concerning RNA and DNA and chromosomes and how the genetic code was like a program, or maybe it was like an alphabet but an alphabet with only four letters that could make millions and billions of words. He started to sound like Carl Sagan.

"Are you following this?" she asked Jean-Paul, who could only shake his head hopelessly.

But then Blair pointed to a slide that had showed an old statue or something with two serpents entwined around a staff or a wand. Jean-Paul recognized that right away as a mystical symbol. Or maybe it was pagan. Something like that. But he started to focus.

Blair was saying that this ancient design was our genetic code's attempt to communicate itself to our consciousness. That it appeared all over the world in many ancient cultures and was always considered to be an emblem of life and immortality. He then went on to another series of slides, and it seemed as if Blair was trying to convince his audience that the genetic code came to Earth from … someplace else?

Had it been anyone else, Gloria would probably have scoffed. But his presentation was so measured, so self-conscious, so devoid of wild claims or cheesy theatrics, that she found herself paying close attention. It was as if he was describing the past six months of her own life.

When it was over, there was some polite applause but for the most part the audience melted away into the desert darkness in search of other entertainment. Gloria took that opportunity to walk towards the front of the room, Jean-Paul in tow a few steps behind her.

"Um, excuse me? Mr. Blair?"

He was still standing on the elevated platform that served as a stage, unplugging his laptop from the room's audio-visual system. He turned at the sound of her voice.

"Yes, can I help you?" His voice in person was softer and sounded kind, if maybe a little long-suffering and hesitant.

"Um, you don't know me, but …"

"Gracious! You must be eleven months along! Do you want to sit down? Please, take a chair. I'll be right down to speak with you."

She wasn't sure she liked that "eleven months" crack, but she supposed he was just trying to be nice.

And she was grateful for sitting again. *The heat and the hard travel over the past six months must be getting to me,* she thought.

True to his word, he packed up his laptop and came down the side steps to where she was sitting.

"Now, are you comfortable? Can I get you something? Some water, maybe?"

"No, thank you. I have water." She produced a plastic bottle.

"Okay. Well, then, how can I help?"

Suddenly, Gloria didn't know how to begin. So she started with a question out of left-field, as a kind of ice-breaker.

"Have you ever heard of a company called Chromo-Test?"

★ ★ ★

As they were speaking, a shadow crept over the entire event. It moved slowly over Joshua Tree and the buildings and the cars and the participants. It was massive, and silent, and … majestic. It blocked out the stars.

And no one looked up.

No one saw a damned thing.

★ ★ ★

"Yes, I have. Chromo-Test is one of those DNA testing labs where you send in a swab and they tell you if you're descended from an Egyptian princess or something equally exotic. Have you had that done?"

Gloria nodded.

"For my two boys."

"So, this is your third?"

At that, Gloria didn't know how to answer. Talking to Blair was a little like making confession in church, though. He didn't seem very judgmental and she felt that he must have heard a lot worse. So she plunged in.

"Yes, and no. I'm not sure. I mean, I wasn't supposed to be pregnant at all. Not, you know, the usual way."

"The usual …?"

"Jesus, I don't know what I'm saying. I mean, I hadn't had *sex*. At *all*. And suddenly I was pregnant, peeing on stick in a motel room in Whately, Massachusetts, and my boys … my two sons … were gone! Gone! And … and … there were these *anomalies* … and then I was pregnant with *twins*! And now there's only the one. Somehow a twin went *missing*! How does that happen?" She held her face in her hands and started weeping.

Blair was a little taken aback by all of this. He looked over to Jean-Paul and then back at Gloria, as if trying to figure something out.

"So," he began. "Let's start from the beginning. You're from Whately, Massachusetts?"

She shook her head. "No. No, I'm from Providence, Rhode Island."

"I'm from Whately," Jean-Paul piped in.

"You're ... together?"

"God, no. No offense, Jean-Paul."

"Jean-Paul, like ..."

"Like the philosopher. Right. My parents were freaks. But that's beside the point. She needs help. She just doesn't know what kind, or where to go."

"So you wound up here. You met in Whately? And then traveled here?"

"It's too complicated to explain right now," sobbed Gloria. "I just need to know what to do. They told me I had to have the baby and then I would get my boys back."

"They? Who is they?"

"Okay, not *they*, exactly. This guy. In the motel parking lot."

"Had you ever seen him before?"

"No, I don't think so."

"What kind of car did he drive?"

"He didn't. I mean, I didn't see any."

"And what were you doing in Whately?"

"Good question," offered Jean-Paul, who didn't know the answer himself.

"I was running away. I ... Chromo-Test had told me that my sons' DNA had ... anomalies. They wanted me to go there and bring them to be tested again, I think."

"Seriously? That's ... very strange."

"Yeah, I thought so. And suddenly I was worried that maybe they would keep my boys for some kind of experiments or something. So I took off. I still have the tickets they sent me."

"Tickets?"

"Air tickets, for San Diego. For my boys and me."

Blair sat back and whistled softly to himself.

"That's ... that's just unheard of. There should have been no need ... well, you know about Chromo-Test, of course?"

"Know? Know what?"

"No, I guess there's no reason why you should. Chromo-Test was started by some government types about five, six years ago. Defense Department. A lot of people who work for the government find jobs in the private sector later, if they're any good, or if they have marketable skills or contacts. The board of Chromo-Test is almost totally made up of former government officials. Mostly scientists, of course. Some engineers. Like that."

"Awesome," said Jean-Paul, clearly impressed with what sounded like conspiracy talk.

"But I don't understand. Why did you come to a place like this? Why did you think to find answers here?"

Gloria looked up, wiped tears from her eyes and cheeks with a wad of tissues she found in her purse, and handed him the copy of the letter from Chromo-Test and the air tickets for San Diego. He took them and saw that they appeared to be genuine, and handed hem back to her.

"Because it happened to me. It happened. The ... the whaddaya call it ... abduction. It happened to me."

"Ah," said Blair. He was beginning to doubt this whole story. The hugely pregnant woman, the strange kid with her, the confused tale as to how they came to be there. The only thing that held his attention was the fact that she *did* have tickets for San Diego, and the attached letter *was* from Chromo-Test with her itinerary from Providence. That didn't make a whole lot of sense by itself unless at least some of what she was saying was true.

"Do you have copies of the testing that they did? Did they send them to you?"

Gloria shook her head. "All I got was the company asking me to go out there. I just wanted to know who the father was, you know? Because I had my doubts. I was married, and I always thought that he was the father, but when I put it together with everything else ... with the night terrors and the ... the hallucinations of test tubes or flasks or whatever the hell you call them ... and the fetuses ..."

"So, you're an experiencer."

She looked up sharply. "Not like *them*! I don't see any flying saucers, and it always happens at night and I wake up in the morning. There was no missing time. Just me missing sleep. Well, sleep and alimony payments."

Blair gave her a rueful smile. "Okay, look, I believe you. I am intrigued by the Chromo-Test reaction, because that itself is an anomaly. Nobody does that. Nobody sends tickets for a complete family to travel coast-to-coast, all expenses paid, for a DNA test. Something is fishy there. And this other pregnancy. You say you were expecting twins?"

"That's what they told me in New York."

"You were in New York? City?"

"Yeah, I have a friend there, from before. I stayed with her for awhile and went to a local doctor, in Brooklyn. He told me I was expecting twins. That pretty much rocked my world, as you can imagine. First, no sex for like almost a year or more, and then, voila! Twins!"

"And then what happened?"

"I was going to him every few weeks or so, and then one day he told me that one of the twins wasn't there anymore. Disappeared."

Blair nodded. "Okay. And then what happened? Did you call the police about your missing boys?"

"How could I? I was told to carry the baby to term and then I could have them back. How could I possibly tell that story to the cops? They'd have me committed."

"You're probably right."

"You get a lot of cases like this, right?"

He was taken aback. "I don't get cases. I'm a researcher. I don't have ... clients or anything like that. I study genetics in the context of world religions. It has some relevance for the UFO community, which is why they invited me here. But it's not exactly a popular subject."

"Oh. . . . Can you help me?"

"What is it you really want me to do?"

"I just want to know what happened to me, and why Chromo-Test wants me in San Diego, and when I'm going to get my babies back."

"Well, I can do my best. I'll need as much information as you can give me, about yourself, your kids, about Chromo-Test, and especially about that man you saw in Whately who told you about your pregnancy."

Gloria nodded and sniffed into her tissue. Jean-Paul sat there, wondering if there was anything in all of this for him or if he would suddenly disappear again and wind up somewhere else, his job done. He opened his mouth to say something, but got pre-empted by Gloria again. That was okay, he guessed. Her problems were way bigger than his.

Blair asked Gloria, "Will you be here awhile?"

"I'm staying at a motel nearby. I'm not going anywhere."

"Okay. Can you come back to the Conference tomorrow? I'm free in the early afternoon, and we can find someplace to talk. In the meantime, I'll do a little research online tonight. Can you write down the name of that doctor you were seeing in Brooklyn?"

She did that, and he asked for a few more details and then told her to back to the motel and rest. He would have something to tell her the next day.

She got up, grateful that someone listened to her and didn't think she was insane. Or a criminal. Jean-Paul helped her down the aisle to the doors and Blair watched them go.

"Chromo-Test. Really?" he said to himself once they were out of earshot. "And missing twins? Either she has been reading way too many blogs on UFOs, or this is the real thing. And what are the chances of that?" As cynical as he was, he was going to give it a shot anyway.

One never knew.

★ ★ ★

Outside in the cool desert air, a relief from earlier that afternoon, Gloria turned to Jean-Paul.

"Thanks for everything. Really. You've been real helpful."

"No problem, Gloria. Glad to be of help to somebody."

"I'm starving. What about you?"

"I could eat."

"Let's not eat here. My phone says there's a Chili's or an Applebee's or something like that close by."

"Works for me."

"Waddle me over to the car. Let's see what's for dinner in Joshua Tree, California."

Gloria got into the front passenger seat and moved to hand the keys over to Jean-Paul, who would drive. But the driver door didn't open as expected.

"Shit," she said to herself. "Where did he go?"

She waited another few moments and then lifted herself out of her seat and back into the desert air. She looked over the hood of the car, but she didn't see him.

"Jean-Paul!" she called out. But there was no sign of him.

"Oh, crap." She walked around to the other side of the car and let herself in. She couldn't fit behind the wheel, which had been adjusted for Jean-Paul's slender frame, so she had to move the seat back all the way first, which was a mini-ordeal. She got in with a grunt and gave it another minute. Maybe he had to pee or something. But he was right next to her when they got to the car. *Why were men always leaving? Fuck*, she thought. *Even the aliens left*. That thought made her laugh out loud.

She started the car and drove out of the parking lot and onto the highway. *Food first*, she said to herself. But something inside her suddenly filled with sadness thinking about Jean-Paul.

It was if he had just died.

CHAPTER TWENTY-EIGHT

Singapore to Frankfurt

ANGELL COULDN'T SAY HE CRACKED THE CODE but he had come close enough to let someone else finish the job. Plus, time was running out. The plane would be on the ground in Frankfurt and there was no telling who or what was waiting for him there. He had to get the word out, somehow.

He had access to wifi aboard the flight, but he had to use a credit card to access it. Captain Aji had provided him with what was basically a debit card. It was an anonymous credit card with a fixed amount already loaded. In this case, it was five million rupiah, or about 350 US dollars, more than enough to surf the Net.

The problem was: he had no phone and no computer. Those things could be traced and, anyway, he was pleased not to have had access to them while he was on the run. To him, smart phones were like electronic leashes. In the old days, if you were away from home or the office, you simply couldn't be reached. You were free. That was heaven. Anyway, the internet cafés were good enough so far and he never thought to get a burner phone because, well, who would he call?

As he sat there wondering what to do, he looked over at the woman in the window seat. She was obviously asleep and completely oblivious. Without attracting attention, Angell glanced over and saw what he was looking for.

In the seat pocket in front of her was a device of some kind, with a cable trailing out of it and plugged into a power outlet below the seat. It was either a tablet or a smart phone; he couldn't tell from where he was sitting.

He had to warn Aubrey of what was coming. He didn't know how many of them were on this flight, or if more would be waiting at Frankfurt. He didn't know if he would survive the flight itself, to be honest. The enormity of his predicament suddenly hit him. He had spent so many months in pleasant isolation that finding himself back in the game was disorienting. He had information vital to Aubrey and his people, and at the same time he was being hunted down for the kill. They wanted the book, sure, but they also wanted him.

If he used the passenger's device without her being aware of it, the message he sent would be tracked back to her eventually but by that time he would be on the ground and long gone. He had to compose a message that would be comprehensible to only a few people but which would communicate the essentials and the urgency. He didn't know how to contact Aubrey directly and, anyway, that could be suicide.

He would contact Steve Hine, his old colleague at Columbia, and get a message to Aubrey that way. The extra level of separation would give him more time to get away after he landed as Aubrey or his people—whoever they really were—traced the call back to the lady with the smart phone who would know nothing.

With that plan in mind—and acutely aware of the man sitting a few rows behind him—Angell began to compose his message.

CHAPTER TWENTY-NINE

Joshua Tree, California

ALEXANDER FERGUSON BLAIR SAT IN HIS ROOM and struggled with some slow wifi. He had the names of Gloria, her two sons, the doctor in Brooklyn, and the name from the Chromo-Test itinerary. He decided to search for the doctor's name first, to see if such a person actually existed. He was still having a hard time swallowing everything that Gloria had told him, but if the names and dates checked out …

What appeared on the screen of his laptop made him sit back and whistle.

Gloria's doctor did, indeed, exist. Or had existed at one time. He had been murdered according to the *New York Times* website, and not that long ago. He was definitely an ob/gyn and he was definitely in Brooklyn. But did Gloria just lift that name from the same website he was looking at? He had experience with people trying to set him up and ruin his reputation, such as it was, by feeding him false data.

There was the name of an NYPD detective listed in the news story. He performed a search on that name and one or two links came up. The first was to a different story that happened around the same time, the assassination of an Iraqi politician or something. Also in Brooklyn. The second link was to some very brief biographical material. Nothing else.

He checked his watch. It was eight pm in California, which meant eleven pm in New York. Probably too late to call. But he could see if he could get a number for him and call tomorrow.

He tried information, and the number was unlisted. He figured a lot of cops would have unlisted numbers, for the obvious reasons. Especially homicide detectives. Instead, he got the phone number for NYPD general information. He would have to do this the hard way.

Next he searched for anything he could find on Gloria Tibbi. He got the usual stuff from those websites that tracked people, their addresses, and so forth. She seemed to be who she said she was, so that was a relief anyway. He looked for news stories, and was coming up dry when he noticed a small item in the Providence *Journal*. It was an ad paid for by her ex-husband asking for any information concerning the present whereabouts, etc etc. of her and her two sons.

So, she *was* on the run. And she had two kids. And she had those tickets. And the itinerary from Chromo-Test. So far, everything was checking out. The one thing he couldn't check was her story about the abductions.

But the Chromo-Test interest in her case could indicate something serious, at any rate. Maybe not aliens, of course, but something very strange anyway. He would call them in the morning before his next presentation at Contact in the Desert. He would see if he could get anyone on the phone to confirm or deny Gloria's story and see how they react.

He shut down his laptop and debated going out to get something to eat, and then decided against it. He was tired, and he had a long day tomorrow. Going to bed early seemed like a luxurious idea.

Within minutes, he was asleep.

★ ★ ★

But the Internet never sleeps. His search for Gloria Tibbi raised a small flag in the bowels of the NSA. The search was tracked back to the ISP in Joshua Tree. (Blair had not used a VPN, knowing that it would have slowed down his internet connection even more.) So a log had been created showing the search, date and time, location of Blair's ISP, and details of his other searches conducted at the same time. Whoever was watching that sort of thing would have the name of Gloria Tibbi and Gloria's doctor in Brooklyn. The connection between the doctor and Gloria would confirm what Monroe had been thinking: that his missing DNA donor had been going to the ob/gyn who specialized in "missing twins." The *dead* doctor.

And now they had a possible location.

★ ★ ★

Monroe was also in bed at the time the flag was raised. There was no urgency associated with the flag, no request for immediate action. He had put in his request for a flag after his conversation with Aubrey. That meant he would learn of it in the morning, once he logged into the system from his office.

At the moment, he was sleeping peacefully. There was a collection of short stories by Jorge Luis Borges next to his bed, and an empty glass that earlier had held a measure of Armagnac. He found he needed a strong drink just before bed if he wanted to sleep for anything more than two or three hours. His thoughts often kept him awake long after the lights were out. A drink helped to quiet those thoughts and relax his compulsive review of the day's events.

About a mile away, Aubrey was still awake. He had a volume of Clarice Lispector short stories open in front of him but he couldn't focus. That weird text message on his encrypted phone seemed to defy all his attempts at teasing out a a meaning. He knew that he and Monroe would go and visit that insufferable Simon in the morning to get his take on it.

His thoughts kept returning to his conversation with Dwight Monroe. He recalled his interview with the mad mathematician Alexander Grothendieck shortly before his death in France and, before that, with Umberto Eco in Turin. These men were geniuses, albeit as different from each other as they could be. Was Monroe a genius, too, he wondered? We would never know the intelligence geniuses. If they were that good, they lived forever in the shadows and their greatest creations were invisible to their fellow human beings.

Grothendieck told him that all dreams come from the Dreamer.

Now, near midnight, Aubrey allowed himself to wonder if mortal conflict could take place in the dream state. If the New Age people were right, and consciousness was everything, then it stood to reason that dreams were the arena of conflict. What were nightmares if not records of conflict taking place in some undefined territory of time and space? Umberto Eco had told him that most of what Dwight Monroe was worried about—magic, secret societies, fabled and notorious books like the *Necronomicon*—was based on fraud and illusion, phantoms manipulated by cult leaders and conmen. We use the term "dream" to mean things of illusion, of fantasy and of trickery, thought Aubrey. When someone says something fantastical, we say they are "dreaming." Cthulhu, wrote Lovecraft, lies "dead but dreaming." The dream is the channel of Cthulhu's power, with which he manipulates his dreamers.

There is something here, thought Aubrey. *Something profound. Important.* He almost had it but then he, too, fell asleep. Perchance to dream.

CHAPTER THIRTY

Simon's Apartment
Crofton, Maryland

N̲o̲ ̲m̲a̲t̲t̲e̲r̲ ̲h̲o̲w̲ ̲m̲a̲n̲y̲ ̲t̲i̲m̲e̲s̲ ̲t̲h̲e̲y̲ ̲r̲e̲a̲d̲ ̲i̲t̲, it remained nearly impenetrable.

The priest dwells in the tunnels of Calabi-Yau, in the topos of the ziggurat. Le Poteau Mitan a rigid rod. Sphere to disc. Disc to sphere. How many points chauds on the surface of the sphere? The Shining Trapezohedron! Calculate, and assemble!

"What the hell?" Monroe was irritated at the jumble of terms that meant virtually nothing to him. He was getting more and more irritated these days, and those around him—few though they were— had noticed. They began to worry about their old mentor's health: physical and mental.

He shoved the paper in front of Sylvia, whose expertise in all forms of cryptography made her the reasonable source for a reasonable answer. Aubrey was sitting on a chair in a corner of the room closest to the door, as if ready to flee at any moment from the hyperventilation of these over-educated nerds.

"The tunnels of Calabi-Yau? Isn't that from Lovecraft?"

Monroe shook his head. "Doesn't appear in his writings. There may be something in the Mythos, but it doesn't sound familiar."

By "Mythos" Monroe meant the wealth of stories by other authors using the Lovecraft themes as bases for their own work. August Derleth was one of the first. Purists would reject anything Lovecraft himself had not written as being non-canonical, as it were. It was Simon who spoke up at that point, something nagging at the back of his mind.

"Grothendieck died last year, right? At the same time we squashed the Dagon ritual in November?"

"Yes. He was a brilliant and interesting human being. To abandon pure mathematics for a life of spiritual seeking." Monroe sounded genuinely sorry to have lost the eccentric genius.

"Something … something is bothering me, though. We read through what you had of his work on the mutants—those special individuals Grothendieck thought were the next generation of human evolution, or something."

"So?"

"Maybe nothing." Sylvia wasn't sure she knew where she was going with it, either. "Wouldn't that be a reference to alien-human hybrids, at least from the point of view of Dagon?"

"Possibly, sure. I don't think that's what Grothendieck had in mind, not specifically, but a group like Dagon could easily interpret it that way I suppose."

It was Simon's turn to jump in. "See, the fragment you just showed us mentions a 'rigid rod.' That's a common term in geometry, which was Grothendieck's specialty. Of course, his was not the pure Euclidean geometry, but advanced forms dealing with extra dimensions. And then all of that about spheres and discs. And finally the Shining Trapezohedron, which does come from Lovecraft."

"From 'The Haunter of the Dark.' It's about a church in Providence that was abandoned when the locals became concerned that human sacrifices were taking place there. But the congregation left behind a stone of some kind that they called the 'Shining Trapezohedron.' It was a gateway into another dimension. Or something."

"Forgive my ignorance, but what is a trapezohedron?" asked Sylvia.

"It's trapezoid plus polygon, in other words a three-dimensional trapezoid."

"That seems awfully specific for a horror story."

"It does, but then that's Lovecraft. He was a scientist at heart, and brought a scientist's sensitivity to the genre." Simon's tone of respect was not lost on the other guests.

"You think this whole thing is a mathematical expression of

some kind? A way of expressing a formula in plain English?" Monroe asked.

Simon thought for a moment.

"No, not exactly. But the use of rigid rod is peculiar. And the author associates it with the *Poteau mitan*, which is something I do know. It's from Haitian *vodoun*. Voodoo, to you. It's the pillar in the center of the *peristyle*: the sacred space where the *loa*—the Haitian gods—are called up. They are believed to travel from under the ground, up the Poteau mitan, to appear here on Earth ..."

"...where they possess human beings during ritual." That was Sylvia, who was starting to see what Simon was getting at.

Monroe stopped pacing a moment and looked at both of them.

"Right. The gods come from under the Earth. A version, maybe, of the Lovecraft idea about a buried high priest of the Old Ones."

"In a way. The spirits of vodoun, the loa, are said to come from Guinee which refers to their African homeland and which they perceive as being on the other side of the world. So the gods travel down into the Earth from Africa and up the pillar into America. It's like saying you can dig far enough to reach China."

"And once here, in America, they possess the devotees during the rituals."

"That's the idea."

"'Sphere to disc,' it says. And 'disc to sphere.' I wonder if the sphere is the Earth itself? And the disc is, I don't know, a section of the sphere. A reference to their peculiar ideas about geography. The ritual in Florida was an attempt to use a fusion of Tantric and Western magical ritual to cause the Gate to be opened and to incarnate the Old Ones into human form. A ritual based on sex. Am I correct so far?"

"In a word."

"What if they have switched cultural modalities? What if they have abandoned the Indian, Tantric, sexual method and are now looking at an Afro-Caribbean method? Ecstatic ritual, drumming, chanting, to summon Kutulu from below the Earth to possess one of the devotees here?"

"They tried that once before. In New Orleans. Back in 1907. They were raided, and the ritual failed."

"Did someone call the police?" Sylvia blurted out.

No one spoke for a moment.

"That's a good question, actually." It was Harry's turn to get involved.

"I was reading the Lovecraft story where this raid was mentioned. 'The Call of Cthulhu.' It's not clear who dropped a dime on the whole affair. He writes that some local people notified the police since they were terrified at the sound of the drums and the fact that some of their women and children were missing and believed to have been captured by whoever was participating in the ritual. An Inspector LeGrasse shows up and busts the ritual, kinda like we did a few months ago. Would Dagon have taken the chance to hold their ritual where local people would have noticed it? And kidnapping local citizens as well, thus ensuring that the authorities would be called? It doesn't seem likely. Only the participants should have known, and Lovecraft makes a point that these participants were people of color."

"In other words ..."

"In other words, these were not people who would have had excellent relationships with the police, or who would have been motivated to expose them. Especially not in 1907. Only an enemy of the cult would have done that. At least, that's what occurs to me."

Sylvia turned from Harry to Simon. "Is that possible? Would there have been a rival cult in the area?"

He shrugged, noncommittally. "That part of the world was famous as a center of Afro-Caribbean religion, mostly what they call 'voodoo' from the Haitian term *vodoun*. There has been a lot of misconception about voodoo, just as there is about Islam for instance. In the case of voodoo or *vodoun*, we are not talking about a black magical practice but the survival of African religious practices brought over from Ghana, Dahomey, Benin and Nigeria for the most part. Also, we should remember that Haiti actually won its independence from the French in the eighteenth century. In Haiti itself, *vodoun* had no sinister associations. It was, and is, the religion of the people. Catholicism, while strong in Haiti, is seen as the religion of the elite and is often used to conceal the practices of vodoun by substituting Catholic saints for Haitian gods, and so forth. You find that in a lot of Afro-Caribbean religions, such as in Santeria which is the Spanish version."

"Do you always talk in paragraphs and footnotes?" asked Harry, sincerely curious.

"Sorry. I know I tend to lecture if I'm not careful."

It was Monroe's turn to interrupt.

"But the singular thing about *vodoun* is that it is an oral tradition, right? There is no 'black book' in that culture, no *Necronomicon*. There are long periods of initiation in which instruction is given by word of mouth. The emphasis is on direct experience of spiritual states, rather than a more sterile reliance on the written word."

"In which case," added Simon, "they are the more dangerous for it. By not committing anything to writing, these groups can evade detection and eavesdropping a little better than those groups committed to the worship of the text. Let's face it, you can fake a spiritual lineage by quoting the right books and sounding knowledgeable—it happens all the time in occult circles and on social media—but that would never fool a *vodouisant*: a practitioner of *vodoun*."

"Which makes these groups more difficult to penetrate."

"There is also the cultural aspect, as well as linguistic and ethnic, even racial aspects. It would be like a white American trying to infiltrate Boko Haram."

"Like Dagon, which doesn't advertise."

"Exactly," said Monroe. "They have no presence on social media or anywhere on the Internet, which unfortunately is how most people get their information these days."

"Which brings us back to our original question. Who ratted out the 1907 ritual in the bayou?"

That was when Aubrey's phone buzzed again.

"Jesus Christ," he muttered, loud enough for everyone to hear.

"What is it?" Monroe's tone was on edge. He had not shared the Maxwell Prime story with the group as they did not have a need to know, but it was weighing on him and he suspected the worst from Aubrey's expression.

His old friend turned to him with wonder in his eyes.

"It's Gregory Angell. He's surfaced."

CHAPTER THIRTY-ONE

Steven Hine's office
Columbia University, New York

IT WAS FINALS WEEK AND STEVEN HINE, professor of Chinese religion at Columbia University, was busy and distracted. He was in his tiny office with the door closed and locked. He wasn't in the mood to see any students, and anyway his office hours were posted and this wasn't one of them. He had a TA grading papers in another room while he stared at an article by Livia Kohn on Shangqing Daoism and tried to concentrate but it wasn't working. His mind couldn't rest.

It had been months since he last saw Gregory Angell in China, and every time he tried to find out what had happened to him the responses only got more ambiguous. He knew he had to keep a low profile, for his friend's sake, but the lack of contact was making him nervous. He had even asked around, and no one in his department had heard anything about Angell's situation and even looked at him a little oddly when he did ask, so he stopped. It was as if he had become a non-person.

He had had enough. His friend was in considerable danger, somewhere in the world, and he couldn't just sit by and not do anything about it. He knew that he might be making things worse by going to the media, but it had been months now and he was sure that Angell was either dead or in enemy hands ... whoever or whatever that enemy might be. Considering the visit to his hotel in Beijing by a man claiming to work for the FBI, that enemy could be his own government.

It was late last year, and Professor Hine had been on a trip to Beijing to talk about Daoism, Ch'an Buddhism and Chinese alchemy at a university there. Some guy who called himself Maxwell Prime had shown up and asked him a bunch of questions about his colleague, Gregory Angell. He left his card, and then Gregory had shown up looking like he hadn't slept or eaten since the Clinton administration. He had to get out of China, and Hine had helped him. He had some friends in a Tibetan Buddhist temple and they dressed him like a monk and got him to Shanghai and from there onto a ship bound for Singapore. That was the last he had heard from him.

When he tried to trace the ship later, he discovered that it had diverted to Indonesia. That couldn't be a good thing. It seemed suspicious, but his discrete inquiries since then had resulted in no news, no sightings, nothing. He had hoped Greg was safe and sound on some tropical island somewhere—Indonesia had thousands of them—but he thought that wasn't the case. If he was safe and holed up somewhere he would have gotten a message to him somehow.

So he bit the bullet and called the number on the card Maxwell Prime had given him, the one with the US Embassy in Beijing contact info. He asked to speak with Prime without giving his own name. The woman who answered claimed never to have heard of anyone called Maxwell Prime, and hung up on him abruptly. Too abruptly, he thought.

In desperation he went back to the Buddhist temple and tried to see if they had any news. And that is when they told him a strange tale of pirates in the South China Sea and an attack on Angell's ship, with Angell just managing to get away. And the man who had planned the attack?

Maxwell Prime.

That's when Hine lost it. He knew that Angell had either been killed or captured or, at the very least, was cowering in some Southeast Asian backwater without a friend in the world, waiting for the hammer to come down.

The fact that he had called the embassy looking for Prime was duly noted and passed on through channels. A recording of the call made its way to Aubrey, who listened to it several times but could not identify the caller. Prime had been in a black site for months by that time, and Aubrey figured the caller was someone Prime owed money to. He would have followed through on it, but there wasn't much to go on.

But now it was finals week. In another few days, Hine would have a month or so of summer vacation to sit and stew about Angell and wonder what had happened to him. He had this growing sense of unease, as if Angell was reaching out to him in the ether somehow. Unsettling dreams. Strange premonitions. Monsters in the dark. Unfiltered starlight. Rats in the walls. *All that study on Daoism and Chinese alchemy must be getting to me,* he thought. *It's affecting my unconscious.*

And that's when he checked his email and got the shock of his life.

★ ★ ★

Angell had been clever enough to put his name in the subject line of the email, otherwise it might have gone unnoticed for weeks. He was afraid Hine would have some kind of email blocking software so that it would wind up in a junk mail folder, but he was betting that the woman's email address wasn't already listed as "spam."

He had composed his message on paper, reducing its length as much as possible so that he could type it in quickly. He couldn't use one of his own email addresses as they were probably being monitored. But no one would think to monitor, much less block, some anonymous lady's email address. Or so he hoped, anyway.

He waited until she got up to use the lavatory. There was a bit of a line so she would have to stand there awhile, giving him just enough time to access the internet through the plane's wifi. She had a tablet, and her email program was running when she left to go to the toilet. That was a stroke of luck, otherwise he would have had to take a chance using his own—an email address he hadn't used since he left the States a year ago—or, worse, waste valuable time creating a new one.

He typed in his friend's email address, put "Angell" in the subject line, and quickly typed in his message, all the while watching to be sure his neighbor had not returned.

When he finally hit "Send" and returned the tablet to its seat pocket, he turned around once more and saw that she was just getting out of one of the lavatories.

And Moody was just going in.

★ ★ ★

Hine stared at the email with its provocative subject line.

It had been sent to him by someone he did not know, a name he did not recognize, but seeing "Angell" as the subject got his attention. He opened the email and saw that, true enough, it was from Gregory.

★ ★ ★

I am using a stranger's device to send you this message. She does not know me or that I am using her email so responding to this address would be pointless. I have been laying low for months but now I need your help. I am in serious danger. Worse than that is the danger others might be in. I need you to contact a man named Aubrey at the NSA. I don't know how to contact him but if you call asking for Aubrey and mentioning my name I am sure they will connect you. This concerns a possible terrorist attack, and the date and time it will be carried out. This involves some calculations made using the book you saw me with in China. I have done most of the calculations and need to inform Aubrey of what I have. He is to tell you a way for me to contact him. This must be done at once. I will contact you again in a few hours. Thanks for everything and for saving my life in China. Gregory.

★ ★ ★

Angell used the "terrorist attack" angle because anything else would make him look crazy. Everyone took terrorism seriously, and he was afraid that the use of the term in an email might trigger some frenzied reaction from the NSA ... and then thought that maybe that would be a good thing, and would help Hine make the right contact with Aubrey.

They had another two hours or so before they landed in Frankfurt. They had just started the last meal service and the cabin lights were going up, getting everyone awake and ready for the eight pm landing.

Angell wondered if he would make it to breakfast.

CHAPTER THIRTY-TWO

Simon's Apartment
Crofton, Maryland

"A PROFESSOR FROM COLUMBIA, A CHINA EXPERT, called in to the switchboard asking for me. He says Angell contacted him just now. Said to locate me and stand by. Something about a terrorist attack. Something imminent. Then he started going on about ... about a mutual friend."

Aubrey and Monroe were in the room Simon used as a study, and they were alone.

"A mutual friend?"

"Prime. Maxwell Prime. It seems this is the professor that was contacted by Prime in Beijing. Remember I told you that someone called the embassy in Beijing, asking for Prime? Evidently Prime gave this professor some bogus cover story about the Joint Terrorism Task Force. So now we know who it was who called, and why."

"So this professor knows about Angell, *and* about Prime?"

"Evidently."

"Jesus. What else does he know?"

Aubrey looked away at the row of books on Simon's shelves while he tried to formulate an answer that would soften the blow. But there wasn't any around it.

"He knows about the Book as well."

Monroe stared at him, open-mouthed.

"You're telling me there's some professor out there in New York, loose, who knows about Angell, and Prime, and about the Book?"

Aubrey could only nod.

"We've got to get to him before anyone else does. Do you have contact info?"

"I know who he is, and where he lives. But he doesn't have Angell's details. He has to wait for Angell to make contact. He says Angell has done some calculations and knows where or when the next attack will come. It was obvious that the professor doesn't know what Angell is talking about and thinks it's terrorists."

"How did Angell contact him? Phone? Email?"

"Email."

"That means he's left a digital trail. We have to make this priority one and get a trace on that email. The … the … what do you call it … the ISP address. Trace it back to where Angell is located now."

"I've already initiated a trace."

"Without a warrant?"

"Internally. We would have picked it up anyway, especially if it was coming from overseas. I'm doing a search on emails sent to the professor's email address from overseas in the last six hours. We monitor international comms, especially those going to subjects of interest in the US. It's pretty narrow, but should give us the ISP in the next few minutes. If we need the text of the email, we can get a warrant."

"We can simply ask the professor to see the email, but should work on getting a warrant anyway. In the meantime, with any luck we can pick them both up and quarantine them until we know what Angell is up to. And if he knows where Prime is being held, and by whom."

Aubrey's phone buzzed again. He was really starting to hate the thing.

Monroe listened to his end of the conversation with mounting alarm.

"Yes. Right. When will it land? Uh huh. Alright. Get a team to the airport. Orders are to pick him up. Ask the airline to see if he has a checked bag. We need any bag or luggage or anything he might be carrying. He must not be allowed to pass anything at all to anyone at all. Pick him up and hold him. I'll be there as soon as I can get a flight."

He hung up and looked at Monroe.

"They traced his ISP to a wifi system run by an airline. He's using someone else's email address. A woman. Maybe a friend. We'll pick her up when they land. He's on a flight from Singapore to Frankfurt. They'll be on the ground in less than an hour."

"Frankfurt? Any idea what he's doing in Germany?"

"Not a clue. It could be a connection to an onward flight. Frankfurt's a major hub."

"Is he traveling under his own passport? It wasn't flagged if he was."

"Don't really know. We're trying to get his seat number and maybe some confirmation of his ID from the airline."

"It's possible that it isn't him at all. That whoever the woman is, she agreed to send an email on his behalf."

Monroe nodded, talking on the phone as he did.

The two men walked out of Simon's study and into the living room where Simon, Sylvia and Harry were standing, waiting for them, expectant looks on their faces.

"We may have Angell in custody in the next few hours. In the meantime, keep at it. We don't know what Angell knows, and in any case he might have it all wrong, so keep trying to decode that cryptic message and see where it will lead us. See if it meshes with the data you received from Bertiaux in Chicago. You may want to get a forensic document examiner on call, as well, for when we get the Book. Maybe between our work and Angell's we just might crack this thing once and for all."

The two old spies kept walking without losing their stride and left the apartment without a backwards glance.

CHAPTER THIRTY-THREE

Frankfurt International Airport

THE FLIGHT WAS MAKING ITS FINAL APPROACH. It was going on eight pm local time. Angell was ready to jump out of his seat as soon as they landed, but he knew he would have to wait while all the passengers ahead of him made for the exit doors. He wanted to be sure he was in a crowd, though. He could not afford to be a straggler.

Next to him, in the window seat, the woman whose tablet he had "borrowed" was roused from her nap and collected her belongings. He had erased his message to Hine from her "sent" box, so he was confident she would never know how he had used her device.

Behind him, Moody was prepared to do what he had to do to make sure Angell did not escape. He could only imagine what would happen to him if Angell disappeared in the crowd at the airport.

The flight attendant announcement was made, and everyone made sure their seat belts were fastened and their tray tables were in the upright and locked position. Angell had his knapsack under the seat in front of him, ready to be plucked up at once, as soon as he could stand in the aisle. He was acutely aware of the old guy who had tried to take his knapsack earlier. He wanted to put as much daylight between them both as possible. He didn't know if the guy was armed—probably not, not these days—but he didn't want to take any chances.

The plane came in for a smooth landing. There was a light drizzle outside, and they took awhile to taxi to their gate. Angell kept his eyes on the exit doors in front of him, and as soon as the plane came "to a complete stop and the captain turned off the fasten seat belt sign" Angell was standing with his knapsack in his arms in front of him.

As usual, there was a crush of passengers ahead of him, standing and stretching and reaching into the overhead compartments for their carry-ons. It seemed to take hours, but in reality was only less

than ten minutes before Angell started shuffling his way towards the
forward exit. He dared not look behind him at the other guy, but
kept his eyes focused on escape.

Behind him Moody stood with an overnight bag in his left hand,
his right hand free and ready to make a grab for Angell if necessary.
There were six or eight people between them, but everyone was
moving so slowly that Moody wasn't worried about losing him.

Angell had not made a reservation for his flight to Heathrow
as he did not want to alert anyone of his plans. At this point, if
anyone had his itinerary, it appeared as though he would connect in
Frankfurt for a nonstop flight to Rio de Janeiro. He would find a
way to get to Heathrow—there were always many flights between
Frankfurt and London—and from there go on to Sao Paulo.

But first, he had to make contact with Hine to see if his message
had been transmitted. To do that, he would make use of any of the
internet options at the airport.

Off to the side, the woman passenger was surrounded by several
officers in plainclothes from both German and American security
services who demanded access to her tablet and who took her away
to a separate room for interrogation. Angell never saw it happen,
concentrated as he was on getting away from Moody.

Instead he left the plane and walked down the jetway to the
terminal. The airport was busy and Angell did his best to melt into
the crowds and ditch the tail from Yogyakarta. Moody pushed his
way roughly through the line of people when he saw Angell start to
disappear.

Angell saw what he was looking for right away: a small area with
desktop computers and internet connection on a long desk with
stools at which almost all machines were taken. He had to make
a quick decision: keep moving and get rid of his tail, or stop right
there and make contact with Hine.

As fate would have it, Moody seemed to have disappeared. Angell
looked in a circle around him and didn't see the guy. He shrugged,
and sat down at the single available computer.

A few feet away Moody had been stopped by someone he had never seen before but who had placed his hand on his chest and told him "we'll take care of it from here." The man handed him an envelope with an air ticket.

"This is your next assignment. Your plane leaves in forty-five minutes. Run."

He opened the envelope and saw a boarding pass for a flight to Dubai. It would take him twenty minutes at least to get to the gate.

He ran.

CHAPTER THIRTY-FOUR

Frankfurt International Airport

"HE'S MADE CONTACT WITH A GUY CALLED HINE. Steven Hine. His old colleague from Columbia. The guy who actually helped him escape from me in China. Can you believe it? Angell is running his own spy network, the cheeky bastard."

Maxwell Prime was in Germany, being run by Dagon; specifically, by the Keepers of the Book, although he thought he was working for the Office of Inspector General of the CIA, investigating the activities of agents assigned to work with Monroe and Aubrey and building a case against them. He was told it was a joint CIA-FBI task force, and that NSA was being kept in the dark. It was the kind of cover story that appealed to Prime's sense of grievance against Monroe and he was led to believe that this could be a major stepping stone in his career.

As he learned on the flight from the black site to Ramstein, Dagon had no clue how their rituals—they called them their 'operations' for Prime's sake—had been compromised so successfully each of the last two occasions. They were on the ropes, and were gathering themselves for one last attempt. Prime came to their attention due to his failed snatch of Angell and the Book in China. Their success at blackmailing a certain CIA chief of station in Asia enabled them to gain access to the black site in Thailand as if they were legitimate intelligence officers. But they still had no direct line on the person or persons responsible for breaking up their "operations" last year. The compromised station chief had told them that Prime was being held on orders of some Brahmin in NSA: a connection of which they had been unaware. Prime would fill in the details nicely.

"Where is he now?"

"He's right in front of me," he said into the concealed microphone. "He just got off an email exchange with Hine. Hine told him he made contact with the DC guys and that they are waiting for his next communication. Angell then sent Hine some gobbledygook about numbers, literary references, shit like that."

"Can you send that to us?"

"How the hell am I supposed to do that? Your people are probably better equipped for that."

"So how did you know what was in it?"

"Because the asshole told Hine in the email itself. In the clear. I read it over his shoulder, the dumbass. He was looking around, I guess for the other guy from the plane, but didn't notice me."

"So ... not such a good spy, then?"

"He's beaten you so far."

"*Us.* He's beaten *us* so far. Remember where you were sitting twenty-four hours ago."

"Yeah, yeah. Bite me."

"Where's Moody now?"

"Heading off to Dubai like he was told."

His prey had just gotten up from the desk, hefting his knapsack onto his back, and making for another part of the terminal.

"Angell is on the move. Gotta run."

"Keep him in sight. Our people are standing by throughout the terminal. We'll pick him up once we know where he's going."

"What happens to me then?"

"You'll be briefed."

Maxwell Prime broke the connection and started following Gregory Angell down the terminal and past the fast food restaurants and the bars, all the while thinking that these guys needed him more than he needed them.

Always a dangerous attitude to take.

★ ★ ★

Aubrey was in the air. He got a commercial flight out of Dulles and would touch down in Frankfurt in eight hours. It was the only flight he could get at the last minute, no military transport being available. It was decided he should go, as Angell knew him by sight. He was the only person in Monroe's team that Angell had actually met, and

anyway Aubrey had recruited him. He was Aubrey's "asset." In the
meantime, however, he had a hastily-assembled team waiting to pick
Angell up at the airport and bring him to a secure location to await
his arrival. They were not to interrogate Angell, but to keep him on
ice. They were, however, authorized to examine his belongings and
to alert him if they found the Book.

Aubrey had a first-class seat and a wifi connection. He wondered
how he would get Angell back to the States, and figured the trip
back would be in a military transport. He still had no idea what
documents Angell was traveling on, but whatever they were had
to be fraudulent. He briefly considered the possibility of a black
site, but rejected that at once. They needed Angell's cooperation and
anyway he was essentially turning himself in.

He would bring Angell back to DC and they could sort it all
out from there.

★ ★ ★

Angell sensed that he was being followed, electronically if not by
human tails. They had to have traced his email with Hine back to the
plane or at least to Frankfurt. He sent what he knew to Hine now
that he knew that Hine was on board with what he was planning.
He knew his old friend would get the data to Aubrey and whoever
Aubrey worked for, and they could use it to figure out Dagon's next
move. But Angell also had to worry for his own safety. If he surrendered to Aubrey and his people he might never see the light of day
again. They had to be pissed at him for disappearing after Nepal and,
of course, the fact that he had not surrendered the Book. The data
he sent to Hine was his sign of good faith, but he was holding back
the Book as his personal insurance policy. He knew a lot now about
Dagon and about the global network of psychos they represented.
Dagon wanted him, dead or alive, and the Book. So did Aubrey and
his people. He thought of that line from *Casablanca*, and amended it
to read "Seems like as long as I have this Book, I'll never be lonely."

He passed a trash bin and got rid of the passport he used to get on the plane for Frankfurt. He reverted to the one he used to get to Singapore. Lawrence Appleton had become Richard Raleigh once again.

★ ★ ★

In the tiny room used for the interrogation of terror suspects and smugglers, the woman who had occupied the window seat next to Angell had watched as the officers opened her purse, her carry-on, and her one piece of checked luggage. They asked her a hundred questions, repeated over and over again. They were polite and civil, but it was easy to see they were under enormous pressure.

In the end, they could not find any reason to hold her. They examined her smartphone and her tablet, and verified that it was her email account that had been used by the man they called Angell but whose airline manifest showed was somebody called Lawrence Appleton, a Canadian.

They examined her US passport and noted the large number of visas from all over the world, which should have raised red flags. Argentina, Brazil, Chile, Peru, Colombia, Australia, Malawi, Algeria, Egypt, India, Nepal, and Indonesia. And virtually every country in Europe, East and West.

But when they communicated this information to Aubrey, who was still in the air over the Atlantic, they received the curt command: "Hold her! Do not let her out of your sight!"

The Indonesian visa stamp coincided with the Dagon ritual last November, when it was suspected Angell was there after the aborted attempt to snatch him from the ship in the South China Sea. Aubrey suspected she was an accomplice somehow.

But they received the command too late. She had been let go.

★ ★ ★

At the United Airlines desk, she walked right up to the clerk behind the counter and extended her hand with a big Midwestern smile.

"Hi!" she said. "My name is Stacey. What's yours?"

CHAPTER THIRTY-FIVE

Frankfurt International Airport

THERE WERE OFFICERS FROM THE GERMAN SECURITY services doing a sweep of the airport. The Americans had provided a photograph of Angell taken from his passport file, but they were not being too transparent as to why everyone had to drop everything and go looking for this guy. A big shot was expected to fill them in when he arrived from the States but that was hours from now and they needed to act at once.

They had his name, or at least the one that showed up in the manifest. Lawrence Appleton, from Canada. The Germans were told his real name was Gregory Angell and that he might be using fake identification to board another plane, or to pass through customs and immigration in Frankfurt and hit the streets. So the names and the photo were sent to all the immigration officers manning the desks at the international arrivals hall.

As the minutes passed, more American and German officers showed up to assist in the search. CCTV camera feeds throughout the airport were being monitored, particularly those in the region of the arrival gate. They saw someone fitting Angell's description carrying a backpack of some kind, who then disappeared and who showed up again at an internet kiosk. That sent agents racing to the computer to cordon it off and remove it for analysis.

At the same time, another feed picked Angell up walking alongside a food court and possibly being followed by another man they did not recognize.

They went back to the first feed and saw that the same man had accosted another passenger outside the arrival gate and handed him an envelope.

Within minutes they had identified the passenger as William Moody, a university professor. A further search revealed that Moody was booked on another flight, this one going to Dubai. The Middle

Eastern destination raised all sorts of alarms, and agents wondered if this was a feint meant to distract them from their real prey or an actual terrorist operation they were monitoring.

By the time they could organize themselves to stop the plane from taking off it had already left German airspace.

★ ★ ★

Aubrey was getting updates on his phone aboard the flight to Frankfurt and was growing more agitated by the hour. He was helpless to do anything except issue instructions that would not be followed quickly enough to have any real effect. If it was up to him, he would have the whole airport locked down, but that wasn't going to happen. So he had to be diplomatic with the German officials while being a bad ass with his own people. It was exhausting.

He sent a flash message to Monroe, asking that somebody meet the plane in Dubai where this guy Moody was headed. He had been in Indonesia the same time as Angell—why the hell were all these people in Indonesia? Was it a frigging convention?—and was on the same flight to Frankfurt. If there was an Indonesian-Dubai connection, was it Jemaah Islamiyyah or some other radical faction? Had Angell been targeted by a terror group for real? Of course, this Moody character may have nothing at all to do with Angell and it was purely serendipity that they got this guy in their sights.

That's when he was informed that a name search revealed that Moody had a contract with DOD. Something called the Minerva Project. So he was one of theirs.

Maybe.

★ ★ ★

Had Aubrey been able to watch the CCTV feeds from his airplane seat, he would have recognized the arrogant smirk of Maxwell Prime and he would have sounded the general alarm. But he had not, so he did not. That would come later, when it was too late to do anything about it.

★ ★ ★

As for Prime, at that moment he was fast-walking through the airport keeping his eyes on Angell the entire time. He knew that his people were starting to move in from every direction and they would have Angell in their custody in mere minutes.

Thankfully they had let Prime have a quick shower, shave, and change of clothes before they set him on this frenzied chase. He spoke into his mic as he saw Angell take a sudden right. But there was no need. They were watching his every move.

★ ★ ★

Angell saw the Lufthansa desk and made a beeline for it. His initial plan had been to get to Heathrow and fly to Brazil from there, but now everything had changed. Seeing Moody on the plane set off a series of events in a chain reaction that got Hine involved, and now Aubrey as well. He knew he was going to get picked up eventually by someone and had to make a fast decision as to how that would happen, and by whom. His onward reservation to Brazil was in the name in his other passport—Lawrence Appleton—and he couldn't use that one now as that identity was burned and, anyway, he had discarded it already. He had to think fast and find a way to use the Richard Raleigh passport to buy another ticket with cash, of which he had an ample supply for the first time in his life. Because of 9/11, cash purchases of tickets were frowned upon but if he used his passport and had a good cover story he might be able to sort it out.

But as he approached the Lufthansa desk he noticed the clerks behind the counter look at him as if they saw a ghost. They were looking down at something he couldn't see, and then up at him.

That was it. He was made. The airport had suddenly become a trap.

CHAPTER THIRTY-SIX

New Orleans Police Department
At the same moment

LATE IN THE AFTERNOON IN NEW ORLEANS (and about nine-fifteen pm in Frankfurt) and back from his meet with Hervé, Cuneo picked up the ringing phone at his desk in the Homicide department. He had to remind himself that the weird crime scene in Belle Chasse was not only the Galvez homicide but included the baby they found—the one they took to calling "the boy in the box"—who was never far from his mind. When they rescued him from the box in the basement, he was covered in hair and looked, well, freakish. The doctors told him it was a case of "severe hypertrichosis." He didn't know what that meant, but "severe" sounded about right.

The voice at the other end of the phone was from the hospital where they had taken him the day they found him, still alive, in that impossible basement sarcophagus. It was the ICU nurse on duty, Rachel something. They had spoken on and off the entire time.

"Detective Cuneo?"

"Speaking. Hi, Rachel."

"Hi. Listen, it's about the baby."

"What's up?"

"Well, we've been updating you periodically, as you asked. So you know that he has been growing at a pretty steady rate. We can't keep him in the Neo-Natal ICU much longer. He's pretty much outgrown the equipment we have."

"So …"

"He's already three feet long, uh, tall. He weighs sixty pounds. We're going to have to move him to a bed, or maybe to the ICU on the other floor, the one where we treat adult patients."

"Jesus. Does he need to be in ICU at all at this point?"

"See, that's the problem. His vital signs are all over the place. His

BP swings from 200 over 120 down to 80 over 60, sometimes in the same hour, and then back up again. His brain waves ... I don't even want to go there. He's on solid food, Detective. I don't mean just mashed peas or apple sauce. I mean *solid* food. I'm a grown woman and I don't eat that much."

Cuneo thought for a moment, and then asked the question he was afraid to ask.

"Is he talking?"

He could hear the hesitation on the other side as Nurse Rachel tried to formulate an answer that would make sense and still not be horrifying.

"That's the thing, the thing that bothers all of us most of all. He seems to be talking. He's making sounds. But they aren't in English. We have some nurses here who speak Hindi and Tagalog, and they say it isn't any of their languages. I speak French and Creole. Not those, either. But it seems like he is really trying to communicate with us. He stares at us and speaks insistently. Sometimes he slows down and repeats the same thing, over and over, as if he is trying to get through to us. And at other times ..."

"Go on."

"At other times, he cries. He seems to be crying for his mother. Wailing, is more like it. It's loud and terrifying. It is also a pitiable sound, Detective. It tears at us, rips us apart."

Cuneo closed his eyes and held the receiver against his forehead. He felt helpless. He had saved the baby, but now it had become something else. A kind of monster, and he hated to think of any child, no matter how strange, as monstrous.

He knew that in the past babies born with the condition of excessive facial and body hair were often killed by their parents. He didn't want to fall into that category, the category of people who were threatened by the Other. After all, his father was Italian and his mother was Haitian. You can't get much more "Other" where he came from. Before he could speak, Rachel interrupted his train of thought.

"You have to get him out of here, Detective," she hissed into the phone. "Get him out of here. He's scaring the shit out of all of us, and out of the rest of the staff and the patients, too."

"The patients?"

"They can hear him wailing at night. Howling. And last night we found him *walking the halls*. If you can call it walking. He was on all fours, like a … a wolf, or a dog, or something. More like a raccoon. He had become unattached from the monitors. We don't know how. We have him restrained on his bed now, but that won't last. We can't send a seven month-old infant to a psych ward, as much as we would like to in this case. Our doctors are stumped. The weekly consult is going on now. Everyone is in there, including administration and legal, and I know they are going to kick the can down the road until it's too late to do anything. They say his condition is due to some genetic defect, but he's too young to send him somewhere to get treatment, if treatment exists. They are constrained by regulations and procedures, and in the meantime we nurses have to deal with him."

"So what do you want me to do?"

"Get him out of here, Detective. Find a place for him. Find his parents, or a foster home or someplace to send him. But get him out of this hospital."

"A foster home? Are you serious …?"

"And we never had this conversation. I could get fired. You understand?"

★ ★ ★

There was no way for Cuneo to do as she asked. There was a mountain of red tape that would have to be negotiated even if he could, and that would take months. He was fearful that, if left to their own devices, the nurses might contemplate some form of euthanasia and call it an accident. He had seen worse things back in the City.

He had to confess that he had not been back to see the infant since the day he was rescued. The sight of it in that box, and covered with hair, still haunted him. The hospital staff was nothing if not heroic if they had managed to deal with him all this time.

He knew they had tried to get the baby released before, shortly after it was left there. DCFS—the Department of Children and Family Services—were not equipped to deal with the problem, although they monitored the baby's situation and development, waiting for an improvement so that they could move on the case. But as for the hospital, well: no parents, no insurance, no next of kin, an unknown genetic abnormality … it would cost the hospital a fortune. The city had picked up the tab initially, but the costs were astronomical now. They couldn't place the baby anywhere. It was too sick and, anyway, no one would foster such a bizarre infant much less adopt it.

And the homicide that started all this still had not been solved. The house was still sealed. If he could find out how the baby got in that box, who put him there, it might help solve the case, but more especially, it might help him find out what to do with him. He thought back to that moment, coming out of the house, when he saw the strange guy standing across the street, smiling at him. The guy who had cold-cocked him in the basement. The smiley face guy. He had to know something, but so far no one had been able to find him.

Maybe he was due for another visit to the house. He had been putting it off, but after speaking with Hervé and the professor and then that phone call from the hospital he figured it was the least he could do. Maybe there was something there, some paperwork or documents or something, which would shine a light on the baby. Stop thinking of this as a homicide, he told himself. Think of it as a missing persons case.

He was closer to the truth than he knew.

★ ★ ★

At the weekly consult the conference was room full of doctors and administrators. While the nurses had been going nuts with the hairy baby, the doctors had been intrigued and some even obsessed with the case. There had been cases like it before, of course, but they were rare. Severe hypertrichosis was an unusual diagnosis as it was and that, coupled with the baby's enormous size and intelligence, gave the medical professionals a lot to think about. Some of them were even thinking of co-authoring a paper together for the Journal. Reputations could be made on this bizarre patient.

But first, a determination had to be made as to whether—and to what degree—this was a genetic defect, what defect it was, and if it was result of the very unusual circumstances attending the baby's birth.

They all knew what the police had told them: that the baby had been found in a kind of coffin or freezer unit in the basement of a house in Belle Chasse. That it had been some kind of elaborate setup but with no indication how the baby had actually been born and how anyone had managed to put the baby in that box behind a wall. There had been tubes or pipes running into and out of the box, but they were behind the wall, too.

The general assumption was that the cops had gotten some of the details wrong. There had to be some kind of access to the box from outside the basement that they just had not discovered. Maybe the baby had been put into the box to die. Everyone had horror stories of parents killing their kids if they were unusual, or had some congenital defect. That was the most logical conclusion, according to the doctors. The baby's mother had been horrified at the sight of her excessively hairy child and had decided to bury it alive in the house rather than risk burying it somewhere outside where it could be found.

And all that strange writing on the box, the hieroglyphics and symbols and letters: mere superstitious ritual in order to seal the evil inside the box with the baby. This was New Orleans, after all, with its colorful history of voodoo and black magic.

After the doctors had satisfied themselves with these explanations, they next proceeded to an analysis of the baby after the seven months. Unusual growth spurt. Attempts to speak. Breaking free of the monitors in the ICU. All of this suggested an above-average intelligence as well as some kind of glandular problem.

Well, there was no use beating around the bush. Only a complete genetic workup would steer them in the right direction.

The administration approved the decision and agreed to pay for the workup. The baby was sedated—not an easy thing to do, as it turned out—and tissue samples taken directly from cheek swabs as well as blood. Might as well be thorough, since they didn't know what they were dealing with.

Then they got the test results back, and that is when everyone began discussing writing it up for the Journal with their reputations made for life. Maybe even a Nobel.

★ ★ ★

The desk in the conference room was covered with reports and diagrams and charts. A light table had been brought in and more charts were hung and backlit like x-rays.

Specialists were called in. A science reporter—under an iron-clad NDA—sat in a corner and watched, wide-eyed, as one after the other the doctors took a look at the DNA analysis and whistled, or shouted, or staggered backwards in awe.

This was not the usual report one would expect from genetic testing of a deformed or stricken child. Actually, there was nothing wrong with the test itself. No indications of abnormalities at all.

At least, not in the DNA they could test.

They had asked for, and received, both mitochondrial DNA and Y-chromosome DNA. The mitochondrial DNA is inherited strictly from the maternal line. The Y-chromosome contribution comes from the father. The baby was definitely male, of that there was no doubt. The condition known as generalized hypertrichosis terminalis is believed to arise from abnormalities on chromosome 17 and that is where the doctors focused their attention.

Humans have 23 chromosomes in total. Chromosome 17 contains

more than 80 million base pairs. It's a busy place. It takes a great deal of analysis to isolate a genetic defect like hypertrichosis if there is nothing to match it against. Cases of generalized hypertrichosis terminalis are quite rare, making identification even more difficult.

In this case, however, the specialists were faced with a different problem. The Y chromosome was abnormally shortened. It was virtually just a placeholder, or so it seemed at first.

The Y chromosome is the shortest of all chromosomes anyway; it's as if all it is good for is making a baby male. But this specimen was ridiculously small. There was no way to determine the father's haplogroup.

All modern humans are understood to share a common origin in Africa. This "original" haplogroup, therefore, is identified as Haplogroup A. Paternal DNA has been categorized as anything from Haplogroup A to Haplogroup T. Mitochondrial DNA or mtDNA has given us Haplogroups up to X, that last one associated with the Druze of Lebanon.

The DNA obtained from the Boy in the Box did not reference any known haplogroup on the paternal line and, amazingly, the maternal line was equally elusive.

It was the mtDNA that really gave the analysts pause.

The sample taken from the cheek swab was not identical to the sample taken from the baby's blood. It was as if the infant was carrying two different DNA lines, neither of which had exemplars in any of the known haplogroups. In other words, the baby had no human parents.

"Let's not go jumping to conclusions." This was Ward Phillips, the hospital administrator. "We all know that the Human Genome Project mapped the code for only one human being, RPCI-11, an African American who otherwise is not identified. That means we could have been missing essential information in unmapped genes from other individuals. I mean, how much of RPCI-11 is useful when compared to other exemplars? Seventy percent? There's still a lot of the genetic code we don't understand yet."

That explanation seemed to satisfy the administrators but not the doctors themselves.

"Ward, we've got virtually nothing here to work with. We're looking at nucleotides, we've got a double helix, all seems fine at the macro level, but when we look a little bit closer nothing makes sense. How do you account for two different genetic profiles from the same person?"

"Easy. Contamination."

"Seriously? They're both equally bizarre, Ward. I could understand, maybe, contamination of one sample but the other sample should produce a DNA profile we could work with. But both samples—contamination or not—are equally fucked up. Excuse my language, but Ward …"

"I get your point. Has anyone communicated with the lab?"

Another administrator raised her hand.

"I did. They are as puzzled as we are, and suggested that maybe we had been playing a joke on them and created a bogus sample to see what they would do with it."

"I see …"

"They also …"

"Go on."

"Well, they also said … I don't know how to explain this, either, and remember I'm just the messenger, don't shoot me …but they said that when they went to retest the samples to see if there had been a processing error, they found that the samples had … mutated."

All discussion stopped in mid-sentence around the conference table.

"What? Explain, please."

"The samples had changed. Not on the Y chromosomes, they seemed stable. But the X chromosomes had mutated between one test and the next. So they tested again. And again. They changed each time. It was as if …," she sighed and took a deep breath, staring at the floor, and then concluded in a rush of words: "It was as if the Y chromosomes were issuing instructions to the X chromosomes."

She withdrew a sheaf of papers from her briefcase and dropped them unceremoniously on the desk.

"These are the results of the other tests. They're all … different."

★ ★ ★

The assembled staff took another two hours to go over the printouts and discuss the findings and their implications.

"Let's keep cool here, people," said Ward. "We keep saying it's evidence that the baby is not human and that just isn't the case. The baby is obviously human …"

"Not like any human being we've ever seen, and we live in New Orleans."

That got a smattering of laughter, but the gloom and doom settled in pretty quickly.

"Agreed it has hypertrichosis, but that is a human condition, a congenital defect. We should be able to find evidence of it in the code, if we could only make sense out of what we have."

"What about the gigantism?"

"Do we know that it is gigantism? None of the tests came back positive."

Gigantism is a condition in which the pituitary gland is affected, often by a tumor, which initiates abnormal growth in children.

"What about chromosome Xq26?"

"Can't find it."

"What do you mean?"

"Look at the charts, for chrissakes! We can't identify the individual chromosomes! It's nuts!"

"We could be looking at a genetic explanation for gigantism, though. There haven't been any convincing genetic arguments so far. If this patient's condition is connected in some way to his gigantism we may be looking at a whole new syndrome."

"It would be nice if we could identify his parents."

"That was the homicide in Belle Chasse, remember?"

"Yeah, I know, but haven't the police managed to trace the kid's family yet?"

"No. And let's face it, the family probably doesn't want to be found, homicide or no homicide."

One of the lawyers who had been silent the whole time very quietly and unobtrusively got up and left the conference room, reaching for her cell phone to make a call. These were the tests they had been waiting for.

"It's Lucy Shaw," she whispered. "In New Orleans. Chatter confirmed."

CHAPTER THIRTY-SEVEN

Frankfurt International Airport

ANGELL SAW THE SIGN FOR BAGGAGE CLAIM which would guide him through Immigration and then Customs before he would be allowed to leave the airport. He was certain, however, that there would be watchers at the exits so he made a quick decision that he hoped was counter-intuitive to the people looking for him.

There is a "Cloud Transit Hotel" in Terminal One which is where his flight had landed. One can rent a room for a short stay, say three hours or so, or even longer. It was expensive, but Angell figured that three hours was all he would need to out-wait the watchers. If they were looking for Lawrence Appleton they would be disappointed. He was Richard Raleigh now, and an American not a Canadian.

But first, he would have to lose whoever might be tailing him.

★ ★ ★

He walked through the crowd of passengers all seeking either their boarding gate or a bar or café to pass the time until their flight was called. He bumped into a few, inevitably, and found what he was looking for.

Hanging off one purse was a pair of sunglasses. Made for a woman but would do for now. At a bar along the way he found a baseball cap on an empty stool. He grabbed it and kept on walking.

There was a restroom a few feet further along and he ducked into it.

Maxwell Prime was right behind him.

★ ★ ★

Angell found an empty stall and went in and closed the door. He quickly took off his jacket and turned it inside out. It wasn't made to be reversible, but it would have to do for awhile. He then tucked his hair inside the cap and put on the sunglasses. The problem was his knapsack. Probably everybody and his brother was looking for it.

So he decided to remove his jacket, still inside out, and drape it across the knapsack. He looked at it and it seemed to change the appearance somewhat, enough so that if they had already seen it the difference might confuse them for a few seconds, sufficient to get away. He would carry it with the strap wrapped around his arm instead of on his back.

Maxwell Prime had not observed which stall Angell had gone into so he just stood around and waited. Passengers came and went and still Angell had not surfaced. Prime picked a spot near the door to the restroom and leaned against the wall. If Angell was going to wait him out, he could do the same. In the meantime, two other watchers showed up and nodded to him. He nodded back, and they took up positions: one across the way, and the other on the opposite side of the restroom door.

What Prime had not counted on was the presence of an entirely different crew, also looking for Angell and with the added benefit of monitoring the CCTV cameras. These were Aubrey's team and they had spotted Angell going into the same men's room.

Suddenly it was getting very crowded.

★ ★ ★

Prime could not simply snatch Angell and frog march him out of the airport. He had to maintain a low profile. But his associates carried official identification and might be able to whisk him away from public view long enough to put plastic restraints on him and drug him, and then get him to their final destination: a location that had not been shared with Prime. They could not risk pulling that cowboy stuff inside the men's room, however. They would have to wait until he walked out the door. They anticipated he would put up a fight, so they would have to act fast and look like they were authorized to take violent action if necessary.

Prime had been down that road before, and was certain his colleagues had been, as well, so he wasn't worried about the outcome.

But then he looked up and realized another team had just walked onto the field. Prime had no idea who they were or which side they were playing for.

He spoke into his mic: "Guys? We got company. Any of you brought dates?"

"What?"

"I clocked two more players, one in a blue blazer and beige trousers, and the other in a windbreaker holding a coffee cup."

"Copy."

"Are they ours?"

"Negative. A visiting team."

"Instructions?"

"Maintain your positions. Proceed as planned."

"If there is interference?"

"Take them out."

"In the middle of the fucking *Flughafen*? And without a gat? Are you serious or delirious?"

"Follow orders."

The problem was Prime wasn't very good at following orders. It's what got him into this mess to begin with. At the same time, he was pretty good at improvising. He had no time to figure out where the other team belonged. All he could do was assume they were the enemy. He saw his colleagues stiffen and get ready for a fight. He only spotted the two bogies but there could be more.

Okay. No more mister nice guy.

He swung around and re-entered the restroom in just enough time to see this guy who looked like Angell in a pair of shades and a ball cap saunter out of a stall.

"Doctor Angell, I presume?" he said, with mock civility, a Henry Stanley in the covert German jungle. He even clicked his heels.

Angell stopped dead in his tracks. This was it. Dagon or Aubrey? He had no idea.

"You will be so kind as to accompany us?" he said, pointing with his chin at the other two men. "I believe you have something that belongs to us."

They were standing outside the restroom now, dodging men going into it and trying not to block the entrance.

Prime's two colleagues began to approach them but Angell suspected they were not sent by Aubrey. Something about Prime's smarmy delivery. It was familiar. That's when he realized that this was the guy who had been in Hine's hotel room in Beijing last year. The one who said he was FBI.

He braced himself for a fight. He would knee this guy in the groin if he had to. But at that moment there was a scream and all hell broke loose.

CHAPTER THIRTY-EIGHT

Monroe's Office, NSA
Fort Meade, Maryland

ANOTHER CALL CAME INTO THE NSA SWITCHBOARD from Professor Hine. It was routed to Monroe's phone as Aubrey was in the air on his way to Frankfurt. It was about nine pm Frankfurt time, and about three pm DC time.

"Is this Mr. Aubrey?"

"No," replied Monroe. "Aubrey works with me. He is presently unavailable. But I am up to date with the case. You may communicate with me, Dr Hine."

"I'm … I'm not sure …"

"I assure you, I am current with the situation concerning Gregory Angell and his famous Book."

Hine was silent a moment on his end of the line.

"You were the one … you were the one who sent him to Iraq, is that right?"

Monroe took a deep breath.

"Yes. That is correct. He was … he *is* a brave man, Dr. Hine. I am very glad to learn that he is alive."

"Well, he may not be for much longer. He was followed all the way from Indonesia to Frankfurt. He sent me more calculations upon arrival. He said you … well, Aubrey … would understand their relevance. But frankly I am worried about him. He's not exactly a commando, Mr. …?"

"Monroe. My name is Monroe. Dwight Monroe."

"Mr. Monroe. Anyway, he will do what he can to ditch the tail but it has put a crimp into his plans."

"His plans?"

"He was going to travel to another country to lay low after sending you the calculations he made. He doesn't want any more of all this."

"I can understand that, but there is a problem."

"Which is?"

"He has a Book which is a very dangerous artifact that is on the wish list of some very evil people."

"Yes, he knows that."

"What he may not know is that it is not only the Book that these people need. It is Angell himself. They need to have physical possession of Angell as well. Dead or alive, it doesn't matter much to them. So you need to work with us, Dr. Hine. For your friend's sake, if nothing else."

"I'm not sure I agree. It seems to me that Angell isn't safe unless he is miles away from all of you."

Through the phone, Monroe could hear some commotion on Hine's end of the conversation.

"Uh, can you hold a moment? There's someone at the door."

Hine set the phone down, and Monroe closed his eyes and frowned. He knew what was coming.

"*What the hell?* Monroe? What is this all about?" Hine came back on the line, furious.

"We can't have you wandering around loose, Dr. Hine. For your own protection. We need to know what you know, and we need to keep you safe. These evil people I mentioned will be looking for you, too. So I suggest you pack a few things and go with the people I sent to your apartment."

"You bastard…"

"And bring the calculations. Whatever you do, don't forget those."

"Am I under arrest?"

"Think of it as protective custody."

"Mr. Monroe, I know you don't have law enforcement authority at the NSA. You can't arrest me and you can't take me away against my will."

"Dr. Hine, you're a smart man. You know I can get a warrant, and have the FBI pick you up if I have to. National security, and all that."

"Then do that. Until you do, I'm not going anywhere."

"And the calculations?"

"Those you can have. Gregory wanted to be sure you got them as soon as possible."

★ ★ ★

Hine had been warned in advance by Angell that something like this might happen. He held the phone out to the men who had just entered his apartment and who had a black Escalade waiting downstairs. One of them took it and listened to Monroe's instructions. As he did so, Hine went to his laptop and picked it up. He pulled a thumb drive from the USB port and handed it to the agent.

"The calculations your boss wants are on this. Take care of it," he said.

When the men had left, Hine sat down in front of his laptop once again. He knew the men would be back, with a warrant, and this time they would not be so polite. He figured he had at most an hour before it all went south. They had probably posted somebody outside his door or downstairs at the front entrance to the building to make sure he wasn't going anywhere. Angell had told him to do what he had to do in order to save himself. As long as Monroe or his people got the calculations, Angell didn't care what happened to him but there was no reason why Hine should be in trouble.

Hine didn't see it that way, though. Angell was in Germany on the run from a variety of organizations. They were all operating in the shadows. Some kind of rogue intelligence operation, plus a bunch of religious nuts, and God knew who else or what else was after him. Even this guy Monroe. Angell was completely alone, running blind, banging into walls inside a dark box.

Maybe it was time to shed a little light on the situation.

CHAPTER THIRTY-NINE

Terminal One
Frankfurt International Airport

It was a woman's scream, and it galvanized the crowd milling around the various boarding gates and concessionaires. A man was on the floor, grabbing himself between the legs and moaning. People pulled away from him like ripples in a pond.

Maxwell Prime made a grab for Angell but only got a fistful of the professor's jacket as Angell twisted and dodged away in the confusion and turned right down the corridor. That's when Prime realized that the man on the floor was one of his two colleagues.

"*Vergewaltigen!*" screamed the woman in what sounded like freshman German 101. "*Ich wurde vergewaltigt!*" Rape! I've been raped!

It was a setup. Prime yelled at his remaining colleague. "He's making a run for it! Go after him!" And he pushed the man into the crowd.

At the same time, the other team was as confused as he was. One of them leaped over the moaning man on the floor and dashed in the direction that Angell had been going only a second earlier. The other looked around in frustration and then spotted Prime and made to intercept him.

Prime pushed a bystander in between them and started running after Angell. *I have no time for this shit,* he said to himself. *Who the hell was that woman and why didn't I spot her before? How many fucking teams are after this guy anyway?*

Aubrey's people far outnumbered Prime's in the airport, and Aubrey's team had the benefit of working with local law enforcement and intelligence, and access to the camera feeds and other security services. Prime was taking orders from a disembodied voice over an earpiece and had only two other men as backup, men he had never met before that night, one of whom was now out of commission.

There was a moment when he thought that maybe he was being set up by the very people who rescued him from the black site, maybe as a patsy for some other operation that was taking place without his awareness.

All of these thoughts ran through his mind as he chased Angell through the throngs. Angell seemed to be making for Immigration, which meant he would leave the airport. If he managed that, he could wind up anywhere in Germany. The rail line was right outside, and trains from Frankfurt connected to everywhere in Europe.

"The target is making for the exits," he spoke into his mic.

"Impossible. He would have to wait in line, even if he had an EU passport. There's no way he would risk that."

"Agreed, but he's heading there anyway."

"Stay close to him. See what he's up to. Where's your backup?"

"On the floor, counting his balls. Some skirt kicked him in the groin, claimed he was trying to rape her."

"*What?*"

"I'm not making this up. Mutt is down, and Jeff is behind me somewhere." He was panting, trying to run and talk and think at the same time. How had he outrun his backup? What kind of people had they sent him?

"Check out the other team. Find out who they are, and what they are doing here. If they had wanted to snatch the target they could have done so. I'm fucking confused."

"Don't worry about them. We are aware. Just do what we brought you here to do."

Then he saw Angell ahead of him as once again his prey veered off at the last moment and headed in another direction.

Where the hell is he going?

Back at the restroom entrance, airport security had arrived to see what the commotion was all about. They raced from the left as Angell and Prime ran to the right. They found the man on the floor, rolling in agony, but the woman was nowhere to be seen. Eyewitnesses claimed that they saw the screaming woman, but not the actual assault. The security officers got on their radios to call it in, and the one in charge of Aubrey's hastily assembled team heard the description and shook her head in amazement.

"We had her," she said aloud, to no one in particular. "*We had her!*"

"Who?" Her number two looked up from where he was still scanning the CCTV feeds. "Who did we have?"

"The other passenger! Angell used her tablet to send the message to the States. The woman who was sitting next to him on the plane! She's the one who created the diversion just now."

"You're shitting me. We *had* her?"

"Who the hell is she?"

Sitting in an aisle seat on her flight to New York instead of her previous window seat to Frankfurt, the subject of their confusion was looking into a pocket mirror and putting the finishing touches on her makeup. Her mascara had run, but that had been deliberate. It had to look good: a woman crying rape would have been teary-eyed, and anyway running mascara was as good as a ski mask. No one would be able to recognize her again.

The plane backed away from the gate. As they leveled out over Europe, she turned to the man sitting in the seat next to her and gave him a big smile.

"Hi!" she said. "My name's Stacey. What's yours?"

★ ★ ★

At the airport, Prime had just turned a corner after Angell when something big and heavy struck him in the face. He went down for the count, dazed but not unconscious. Angell didn't waste any time but hefted his bag over his shoulder and slipped into a book store, going in one way and taking an exit on the other side, away from where Prime was trying to sit up. He knew that there were others with Prime and he waited behind a stack of books to see what they looked like so he would know them if he saw them again.

Sure enough, a man in a blue blazer ran over to Prime who was pushing him away in irritation. Angell took a brief moment to look at both of them, and then turned away and walked slowly back in the direction he had come.

Last year he had been told by Aubrey that the *Necronomicon* was a weapon, but before now he had never understood its usefulness as a blunt instrument. Well, that and about twenty grand in cash in rubber banded bundles at the bottom of the bag, wrapped in his underwear.

The Cloud Transit Hotel was back down the other end of Terminal One and he would take his time getting there. He still wore the cap and the sunglasses, and was panting heavily from the run and the adrenalin. He tried to slow his respiration and to make himself look small and unassuming. No telling how many others were in the airport, and how many more might show up at any time.

He would stick to his plan and hide in the transit hotel.

Then he looked up and saw that he was surrounded by airport security personnel with guns drawn.

And two American intelligence officers in plainclothes holding badges.

There was nowhere else for him to go. They had him.

CHAPTER FORTY

Queens, New York

JAMILA HAD BEEN TOLD TO WAIT.

Between the eyewitness account of the old NYPD detective and some CCTV footage it was possible she had been identified, perhaps through facial recognition software (something she hadn't known existed). Her contacts weren't sure. But it was considered safer to have her wait in Queens until the dust settled when she could be gotten out of the country more easily. It was possible that she would have to leave out of some other airport, maybe in the South or on the West Coast where surveillance would be weaker. Right now, she was an unknown who committed an assassination in New York City of an important Iraqi politician. All airports would be watched, roads into and out of the City would be checked. She was told to lay low for awhile. She was advised not to go out on the streets in daylight but to wait until dark, but that she should limit her excursions as much as possible. Change her appearance. Like that. They would figure something out.

Jamila was used to hiding behind a stone wall for hours or days and picking off her targets and then retreating. This cloak-and-dagger stuff was outside her experience. And while she trusted the people who brought her here for the impossible shot, she knew that they would sacrifice her if they had to do so to protect their own operation.

So she stayed in her motel room during the day, feeling the loss of her beloved Dragunov which was now on its way back to the Kurdish camps in Syria or maybe Iraq. As long as she and the rifle were not in the same time zone, the authorities would have a hard time linking the two. In Iraq, this would not have been a problem, especially not under Saddam. They would have taken her out and shot her. She was a Yezidi, after all, and automatically considered an enemy of the people. Here, in the United States, they didn't know

Yezidi from baked ziti. When she heard that from her contact, she had to admit she didn't know what baked ziti was, either.

So she watched a lot of cable television and tried to improve her English. She would have bought hair color and tried to dye her hair, but she had no idea how to buy it, where to buy it, or how to use it. She would have to rely on her scarves to cover her hair.

And she would have to wait for the phone call that would give her the next set of instructions. Until, that is, she saw the six o'clock news.

★ ★ ★

Jamila had a name. Steven Hine. A professor at Columbia University. It had taken her the better part of an hour, switching between channels, trying to find a news station that was repeating the Angell story, and then trying to decipher what she was seeing. Her English was the basic, tour guide kind of English in which she had been tutored in while in Europe waiting for her ticket to New York. She was not up to understanding the news. She had a small English-to-Kurmanji dictionary, which helped a little. The rest she had to figure out from context.

What she got was Angell was missing; Angell was from New York; this man Hine had information about him. Hine was in New York.

She was in New York.

But it was while seeing the photograph of Angell on the news that she felt an uncanny feeling come over her, like a bad memory. The last time she had seen Angell there had been violence and death. She was used to violence and death, since her childhood in Sinjar where the Yezidi had been treated like animals, since Saddam Hussein, and long before, but this was different. She had a sense memory of being possessed by some transcendent being, some dark Power that had occupied her mind and body, casting off her soul or her spirit to some abyss where her only companions were loss and despair.

At the same time, she had felt more human than ever before, as if the Being had extended into every corner of her body, filling it out, empowering it. It had been terrifying, but also exhilarating. While it was happening she was frantic and horrified. When it was over, and the Being had left, it was as if her head was floating in the clouds and her feet were huge anchors to the ground. Slowly she returned to normal, almost with a sense of regret.

She had been possessed before, of course. She had entered into those states that always frightened people: her family, her neighbors, the other Yezidi who knew about it. She would prophesy in those states, speak with a different voice—a man's voice, sometimes, a woman's voice at others—and not always make a lot of sense to anyone else. She knew this, but usually had no memory of those episodes once they were over.

It was Angell, in that cave in Nepal, who had stopped the possession of the Being from overwhelming her and from harming the people around her. She had been abducted from a refugee camp in Turkey, identified by people who knew her abilities, and who knew she was a Yezidi from the Holy Mountain. They seemed concentrated on these two aspects of her existence, the two aspects that defined her the most but which were also—to her mind—mundane and not worthy of interest. After all, everyone she knew was Yezidi. That wasn't so strange. And her "ability" was, to her, a curse that set her apart from everyone else and made it so hard for her family to find her a husband.

But these men—strange, foreign men—found her valuable and were impressed by everything about her. They had not tried to get intimate with her, which was a relief. She had heard stories about Daesh seizing young girls and forcing them into marriage with their fighters, or simply raping them and leaving them to die. These men did not do that to her. She was being saved for something else.

Whatever that was, it had not worked. In fact, it had failed spectacularly. She remembered a ritual in the cave; the Being rising from the depths; and then gunfire, and the man Angell—whom she had last seen in the refugee camp—appearing and seizing the Book, the book of evocations of the Being that somehow connected her to a secret cult of some kind. A Book that had roots in the same lost civilization as the Yezidi: Sumer.

So there it was. She was linked to her people's ancestral home not only in body and blood, but in her soul as well. She was a way for Sumer to reappear in the modern world, and that could only mean one thing to her: the return of the Seven Angels to Heaven, and right behind them would be the Yezidi people, *her* people, first among all the peoples of the Earth.

Seeing that image of Angell on television she began to doubt herself and her mission. She had fled Nepal after the failed ritual and wound up in North India, at Dharamsala, where she was mentored by an old Tibetan monk who taught her how to control her special abilities. Then she left India and arrived back in Turkey, and then to a unit of women soldiers who were fighting Daesh to take back their homeland. She became powerful in the world that mattered, the world where murderers had invaded her home and slaughtered her people. She fought back. She killed. She saved. Rescued young women like her. She was respected, if still feared a little because of her occasional "episodes" of trance-like, epileptic-like, states.

Now she was in America, the "Land of Opportunity," and it lived up to its name. She saw her opportunity, presented to her in living color on a flat-screen television in a motel room in Queens. The opportunity to get to the bottom of who she was and why she was here. The opportunity to understand her purpose. And maybe, just maybe, the opportunity to avenge her people once and for all.

CHAPTER FORTY-ONE

Monroe's office, NSA
Fort Meade, Maryland

MONROE HUNG UP FROM HIS CONVERSATION with Professor Hine. He was rattled. While he had to do a lot of unpleasant things in his career he knew he was stepping over the line now. He usually didn't throw his weight around with American citizens. Most of his time was spent on the front lines against foreign adversaries, and he never questioned his motives or his actions in defense of his country. But now he was dealing with a multinational threat: a group that had no national allegiances or indeed any kind of territorial identity that he could understand. He could not characterize it in terms of language, religion, political or economic affiliation. Even its history was murky. With all of that, they were fanatics who had no concern for the value of human life, so they had a lot in common with some of the other cults he had to deal with in his lifetime. But the other cults had identifiable goals or, at least, goals that could be quantified using the normal parameters: a country of their own, or the destruction of the Western way of life, or the overthrow of governments, etc. Dagon's entire *raison d'être* would be incomprehensible to most people.

They measured time in aeons. They measured territory in terms of the whole planet. Their ideology was a fairy tale. Their methods were transnational crime and terror. They revered an invisible and long-deceased high priest who communicated with his devotees in dreams. Their membership crossed racial, ethnic, gender, and political boundaries. And their immediate goal seemed to be doing whatever they could do to make the membrane between this world and the next more permeable. They deliberately courted insanity and violence as technologies to accomplish their goals. They were a threat to every nation, every religion, and every social construct.

★ ★ ★

And they played the long game.

He had a report on his desk now from some hospital in New Orleans. The same type of genetic abnormality that he had been tracking for years had shown up there, in spades. The number of these cases was increasing exponentially, and he knew that this was all due to the growing threat from Dagon. He had another report, an internally-generated one, that gave the location of the woman he had been tracking since last year, the one from Rhode Island with the bizarre Chromo-Test results. And there were others. A lot of others. And now a dead doctor in Brooklyn as well; a horribly mutilated corpse and no suspects. The pace was increasing. A plan was in place and the schedule was accelerating.

He was out of his depth, and it was too late for him to do anything about it. He would have to read in the others because he was too old, and growing too weak, to control this situation on his own. With Aubrey now on his way to Germany, Monroe began to feel a sense of isolation that was almost unbearable. He had recognized the threat long ago, but could convince few others of what he knew to be true: that a cult operated on the Earth that had been around at least as long as recorded civilization, and perhaps longer (if their own texts were to be believed). And that this cult had managed to weaponize the paranormal in ways CIA and the militaries of many countries—including the old Soviet Union and China—had only dreamed of doing themselves.

He knew Simon was current with all of this, and maybe more than Monroe realized. But Sylvia and Harry—even with all their exposure to Dagon over the last six months—would think their leader had gone round the bend if he started to insist that what Dagon believed was literally true. So far they had been able to rationalize all of this because they had the evidence in front of them. They had rounded up actual criminals. They had rescued actual girls. Monroe had demonstrated that it was necessary to understand the weird Dagon belief systems in order to confront them. It was the way the British had "weaponized" astrology during World War II without believing in astrology themselves. They knew their enemy believed in it, and that was all that was required.

But this … this was different. The genetic evidence was becoming overwhelming. And now murder. Angell was back on their radar and Dagon was doing what they could to apprehend him and the Book. Once they had both in their possession, they would go to the next—and perhaps final—phase of their mission. And how could Monroe convince anyone else that the only effective countermeasures would be more of the same: rituals, sorceries, magic?

Strangely, the answer presented itself in the form of a knock at the door.

CHAPTER FORTY-TWO

Same as before

"Sylvia. What are you doing here? I thought you and Harry were working on the Dagon calculations with Simon."

Monroe opened the always-locked door and let her in, clearing a chair for her to sit on.

"I left them to it. The discussion was going way over my head, and I have two doctorates. As I was going out the door it was something about ferromagnetism, lattices, magic squares, and something called the Grothendieck-Riemann-Roch Theorem. I was only slowing them down every time I asked them to clarify what they were saying. And I needed a break anyway. Something has been bothering me about all of this."

"Welcome to the club."

"And Simon was so busy with his calculations and explaining Riemann geometry or something to Harry that he neglected to cook anything, and that's just wrong."

"Don't let him hear you say that. He'll be mortified for days and probably cook enough … whatever … to feed an army."

Sylvia gave an appreciative smile at the tired old expression.

"Do you know where that expression came from, Sylvia?"

"No, but I have a feeling you're going to tell me."

"Humor an old man. It comes from something called Coxey's Army, which was a protest march against unemployment. The first was in 1894 or so, and then there were others. One during 1914, I believe. It was led by a businessman named Coxey. The original expression was 'enough to feed Coxey's army.' The march was observed by L. Frank Baum and became the inspiration for *The Wizard of Oz*. Did you know that?"

Monroe finished speaking and seemed lost in thought. A march on Washington, and *The Wizard of Oz*. There was some kind of resonance there. Magicians in Congress. Vampires in the White House? Spooks who were spies, and spooks who were ghosts. Boo. Something. Something.

"You look exhausted, Dwight. More than that, maybe. Depressed?"

He just shook his head. "Frustrated, is more like it. We are working at the intersection of science—well, science as we understand it—and mysticism, or something along those lines. It has been an obsession of mine for more than fifty years, this intersection. And I still don't entirely understand it. There are concepts ... ideas that demand an enormous effort to understand, even to frame adequately. I feel like I am always just on the verge of a breakthrough that never comes."

He smiled ruefully.

"That wouldn't be so bad—an old man's hobby horse—except that lives are at stake, and maybe even more than that."

"Didn't we investigate this type of material seriously, back in the day? Occultism, ESP, the paranormal? Because we thought the Soviets were doing the same?"

Monroe nodded, clearly surprised that Sylvia would bring up a subject that was something of an embarrassment to the purely technological wing of the intelligence community that was represented by the NSA.

"Yes, it's true. CIA did have a number of projects in the 1950s and 1960s that dealt with aspects of what we would call occultism today. We all know about the ESP and remote viewing experiments the military and CIA had contracted out to SRI during that period."

"Wasn't that called Stargate?"

"That was one of them."

"Rather pithy, knowing what we know now. I mean, really? *Star. Gate?*"

"Yeah, you know ... I don't remember who came up with that one. It does seem deliberate in retrospect, doesn't it?"

"And that was about using only the mind to see what was happening in other parts of the world ..."

"And, if my old friend Ingo Swann was to be believed, on other planets as well."

Sylvia was confused, though.

"If the mind is capable of doing these things all on its own, then why would groups like Dagon need rituals, human sacrifice, and the rest of it?"

Monroe laughed. "If you knew what we went through in those days to get a result that was statistically relevant, you wouldn't ask that question. It was dreary, tedious work with often vague and ambiguous achievements. We proved that something was there, that the human mind was capable of doing things that seem impossible within the parameters of modern science, but that was about all."

"But you did locate submarines, missile bases, and the like?"

"Yes, but the problem was that the phenomenon was not reproducible, not easily and not consistently anyway. Sometimes it worked, and sometimes it didn't. That was when some of the wags in Technical Services over at the Agency decided to enlist the aid of actual occultists. You know, witches and magicians and the like. I mean, they did experiment with using various drugs to expand the reach of the mind, too. LSD, for instance, and mushrooms, peyote, and so forth. The shamans of various countries often employed hallucinogens as part of their rituals. But everyone began to realize that you couldn't just drop acid and then remote view a Soviet missile silo. There were pieces missing in our understanding."

"But the occultists …?"

Monroe nodded again, warming to his subject.

"Sure. They tried to isolate various aspects of what occultists did and how they did it. Ritual magic seemed to have some basic, fundamental procedures across cultural and religious lines and some of that dovetailed with the hallucinogenic procedures. Set and setting, for instance. Setting meant the environmental surround of the ritual along with set: a specific intention. Like guided acid trips." He smiled at Sylvia. "This was way before your time. Very Sixties. Think Jefferson Airplane, Jimi Hendrix, and Woodstock."

"And Timothy Leary. Wasn't he one of yours?"

"Ouch. Well, not one of *mine*, particularly, but ..."

"So let me get this straight, Dwight. I can understand what we did against Dagon because there were human lives at stake, and an international human trafficking ring that was part of it. The ritualistic aspect of it was incidental, and useful to know only insofar as it led us to what they were doing, when they were going to do it, and where. But are you saying that there really is more to all of this than a bunch of crazies out for blood? That they constitute a different kind of threat?"

Monroe steepled his fingers in front of his face and closed his eyes. How to answer this without sounding ... credulous, or feeble-minded?

"You know about my background. You know about Vietnam, for instance."

"Sure."

"So you know I have witnessed paranormal events."

"I don't doubt that you have."

"And you know that remote viewing was an essential ingredient in starting this entire campaign against Dagon a year ago? When we had viewers glomming onto the fact that there was chatter concerning a book whose contents would destabilize the Middle East, even more than it already is?"

"I know only what you've told me, and that the remote viewers confirmed the chatter on the SIGINT channels you were monitoring."

"And you know that I keep this huge file in my safe, the Lovecraft Codex."

"Certainly."

"A core concept that you find in Lovecraft's stories is that there is a race from 'beyond the stars' as he would say that is always trying to find a way into this world, or this planet. These are beings that for the most part remain invisible to us. There are human beings who collaborate with them, and they are the occultists, the psychics, and the artists. Now the ancient peoples of many cultures believed it was possible for some humans to travel to the stars, either dead or alive. The pharaohs of Egypt, for instance, voyaged to the stars after the mummification ceremonies. Siberian shamans voyage to the stars while alive and return with wisdom. The stars represent the world where occult concepts seem to operate: a realm accessible to humans through arcane practices, from meditation and 'remote viewing' to ritual magic, hallucinogenic drugs, and the like. Extreme experiences, of which ritual sacrifice is only one."

"Jesus, Dwight. You're starting to sound like Simon."

"Yeah, well, I guess I have to watch that. One of us is enough! But to get back to your original question: yes, I do believe that there is more to Dagon than the obviously criminal elements of their operation. It was our remote viewers who first became aware of what they were doing, and of their interest in the *Necronomicon*. That indicates a way of functioning on a completely different plane in the world. And the fact that they would go to such an extent, including the expenditure of vast amounts of money and time and effort, to conduct a bizarre ritual in the underground chamber of a mountain in Nepal … well, they are true believers. It's not enough to call them fanatics. They maintain strict operational security. They recruit carefully, and always with an ulterior motive in mind. There are no charismatic leaders that we can identify. The ones we killed or captured in Florida and elsewhere were unknown to us until that night. They don't advertise for followers. They don't promote a lifestyle or a theology or seem to require conversion. They are an anomaly, a complete mystery. They don't even seem to be part of the human community of souls, but are just passing through even though they claim they have been here since before the human race evolved."

"So, that means …?"

"That means they've found something. The key to making it all work. Occultism, magic, whatever you want to call it. Science will one day come up with its own definition and terminology, but right now we are dealing with a group of people who understand the dream state, and how to manipulate it. People who understand about the powers of the human mind and how to enter and leave psychological states at will. How to expand consciousness. How to work proactively with symbol systems. That is why I had Aubrey visit Grothendieck before he died, in order to learn more about the mad mathematician's ideas about the Dream and the Dreamer, and his theories about the Mutants. Why I had him visit Umberto Eco and find out how semiotics and the structure of symbol systems could be exploited by the ruthless. It was as if logical, dispassionate scientists had decided to take Lovecraft seriously and to actually explain him."

"As you have been doing for as long as I've known you."

"That long? I guess you're right."

Sylvia felt she was on to something and tried to take a different approach.

"You know that prosecutors can't take cases like this to trial, right?"

"Thank God we're not law enforcement. We're in intelligence. We collect data, information, track terrorists, smugglers, traffickers, spies. We go from the particular to the general, from what we overhear one spy say to another all the way to predicting the overthrow of governments. It's a black art no matter how you look at it. So why don't we use black arts as a force multiplier for black ops?"

"You're pleased with that analogy, aren't you?"

"Been waiting to use it for weeks. But that doesn't mean I'm wrong or being melodramatic. The world is dangerous on the macro level, but on the micro level it's made up of *people* and there is more to the average human being than politics, economics and religion which are basically the only vectors we ever trace. There's something deeper, a level of consciousness where decisions are made and where words and symbols have more weight than arguments or reasons. I mean passion and inspiration. Giordano Bruno called it 'love' and so did Plotinus. Even Crowley said 'Love is the law, love under will.' In the end, the fate of the world will be decided on emotion rather than reason, on love rather than policy, on the irrational rather than the reasonable. And occultism is the application of that emotion, that irrationality, that dream state, to real world problems. It will be on a scale that we won't recognize until it's too late. Lovecraft knew it, though. It's all in the manipulation of dreams, the crafting of the right fantasy, and the weaponization of nightmares."

And that is when his phone rang again, and he was asked to turn on a television to any news channel.

CHAPTER FORTY-THREE

Wasserman's Apartment
Brooklyn, New York

WASSERMAN SAT IN HIS APARTMENT in his underwear, staring at the window in front of him but seeing nothing but his own thoughts. The strange phone call to DC and the even stranger conversation in Aubrey's mobile SCIF, had caused him to worry that maybe he had stepped in something vile. He should have known better than to call the Feds about anything. That's one of the things you just don't do as a cop, unless you have no other choice. But that thing about Angell and the possibility that there was some weird baby-snatching—or fetus-snatching—cult going around and that there might be a connection to terrorists or at least to Arabs or something ... how could he keep all of that to himself? What if it all blew up in his face? At least this way, he was going by the book.

Yeah, a voice said in his head. *But you're not a cop anymore. You left the 'book' at the office.*

He was trying to convince himself he had done the right thing anyway when he finally had that chat with Danny who was lead on the "baby doc" homicide and learned more details. Once he left Danny at that diner at the end of the Promenade in Brooklyn Heights, he had more than ever been sure that contacting DC was the right thing to do.

For the case. Not for him.

He thought about maybe making some coffee, something to rouse him from his lethargy, something to do with his hands. But that meant standing up. It might even mean getting dressed. Just for appearance's sake. And that seemed like too much work, so he stayed where he was and thought over his convo with Danny.

The doctor—Richard Hill—had been an elderly widower and his estranged family actually thought he had retired long ago. He once had a thriving obstetrical practice on West Seventy-Second

Street, but gave it all up in the late 1960s and moved overseas for several decades, traveling the world, before returning to New York after 2001 and starting a quiet, private practice in Brooklyn. He charged his patients very little and always seemed to have time for them, day or night. He had only one assistant—a young woman named Miriam Asante who also served as receptionist—but they had not been able to locate her. As far as Danny was concerned, she was either their prime suspect or another victim.

Danny said there were a total of twenty-three patients whose ultrasounds showed missing fetuses. That is, the original shows two fetuses, or twins, and the later ones showed only one. He had a discussion with a number of ob-gyns in New York who told him that "missing fetus syndrome" was not that uncommon. It was due, they said, to "fetal resorption" which means that the twin had died in the uterus and had been reabsorbed into the other twin or into the placenta, sometimes leaving a flattened version of itself called a *fetus papyraceous*: a name that for some reason gave Wasserman the shivers, for it meant that the fetus had become like a sheet of papyrus.

No one knows the reason for what seems like a high rate of fetal resorption—some twenty to thirty percent of all multi-fetal pregnancies—but to have a cluster that large in one location is unheard of in the literature, and at least one doctor consulted said it may actually be evidence of some kind of health hazard.

The Center for Disease Control was consulted but they could find no indication that the anomalies were due to a pathogen of any kind, nothing in the air or water supply that would specifically target the fetuses of pregnant women. It would take months, maybe years, before they could narrow down a disease vector if there even was one. In the meantime, Danny and the rest of the Homicide Division had their hands full trying to follow the rest of the evidence.

They managed to locate most of the mothers. A few were still missing or out of reach. One in particular, Gloria, had been in only a few times and then disappeared shortly after her last exam. She gave an address in Park Slope, and when they went there they found she had left long before. She had been living with a friend from Rhode Island when she just picked up and left one day. When they questioned her friend further, they discovered that she had two other children as well, but that no one knew where they were.

This was starting to look a little strange.

And that's when something clicked for Wasserman, which is why he was sitting on the edge of his bed in his Fruit of the Looms and staring out a closed window at the building across the way.

Rhode Island. Isn't that where Angell came from?

Who the hell comes from Rhode Island? It's the smallest damn state in the Union. Whadda they got? Like five residents and a lobster? What are the odds that two cases in Brooklyn not only share the same address in Red Hook but are also two Rhode Island natives?

And now both of them are missing.

He turned on the television for a moment of distraction and then it all became surreal. It was as if what was going on inside his head had been projected onto the flat screen. There he was, the missing professor. A photograph, anyway. And a story that he had been missing for a year and had probably been abducted by terrorists or something.

"Crap," muttered Wasserman to himself. "I guess I gotta go get dressed."

BOOK FOUR

ICH BIN EIN QUANTENGREIS.

("I AM A QUANTUM ANCIENT.")

"This folk," I translated to myself, "dwells in remote and secret places, and celebrates foul mysteries on savage hills. Nothing have they in common with men save the face, and the customs of humanity are wholly strange to them; and they hate the sun. They hiss rather than speak; their voices are harsh, and not to be heard without fear. They boast of a certain stone, which they call Sixtystone; for they say that it displays sixty characters. And this stone has a secret unspeakable name; which is Ixaxar."

—Arthur Machen, *The Novel of the Black Seal*

Properly prepared ... your mirror becomes so amazingly sensitive as to not only receive and retain images of things too subtle for solar light, but to bring out and render them visible. Nor is this all. There is light within light, atmosphere within atmosphere, and intelligent beings who dwell within them, and who can commune with man only through such mirrors, upon which they can photograph the information they wish to convey, either by scenes depicted therein or by words projected thereon. ...

—P. B. Randolph, *Ravelette*

Prof. Enoch Bowen home from Egypt May 1844—buys old Free-Will Church in July—his archaeological work & studies in occult well known. ... Of the Shining Trapezohedron he speaks often, calling it a window on all time and space...

—H. P. Lovecraft, *The Haunter of the Dark*

Ich weiss viel. Ich weiss zu viel. Ich bin ein Quantengreis. (I know a great deal. I know too much. I am a quantum ancient.)

—Wolfgang Pauli

CHAPTER FORTY-FOUR

Esna, Egypt
South of Luxor
April, 1843

IN THE BLISTERING NOONDAY HEAT Professor Enoch Bowen of Brown University wiped the perspiration from his neck with a length of locally-made cotton cloth that was already drenched. His clothes were covered in dust and his boots in a thick layer of sand. He rose from the dig with an aching back and shielded his eyes from the punishing light of the Egyptian sun. They were only thirty-three miles south of Luxor, but three thousand years in the past.

The temple had been partially excavated earlier, and none of it would ever be completely uncovered since most of it extended beneath the town. But he had what he came for, and that was all that mattered.

The temple was dedicated to the god Khnum and was of a late vintage, but the city itself was much older and had once been known as *Ta Senet*: the "Holy City." Khnum was already an ancient god when the temple had been built. He is sometimes shown with a potter's wheel, making the first humans as children out of clay (perhaps a resonance of the story in Genesis of God fashioning Adam from clay). His son was Heka the god of Magic (*heka* means "magic"), who "existed before duality had come into being" and to Bowen this meant that Heka represented the Sanskrit concept of *advaita*, or non-duality. Khnum's consort was Neith, a warrior goddess, called the "mother of mothers." Yet among the stelae and statuary of the temple was the recurrent image of a strange and almost forgotten god called Tutu: an equally ancient deity that was probably the survival of an older cult from the desert to the south.

There were representations of Tutu in various other locations, such as at Shenhur, north of Luxor. Here at Esna, however, there was a wealth of iconographic detail that fleshed out the nature of this wrathful being, and that is why Bowen had traveled here, away from the more heavily-visited sites along the Nile outside of Cairo. There was something about Tutu that troubled his dreams, which was ironic since one of Tutu's powers was to protect one from nightmares.

In the distance, Bowen could hear the call of the muezzin for the noonday prayer. He was working with a small staff of local helpers, mostly Muslim (although there was a Christian community in the town), so he sat down on a large stone at the entrance to the temple and drank heavily from a bottle of clean water while he waited for the completion of the *salat*. In the worn leather dispatch case at his side was concealed the object he had come so far and worked so hard to locate.

This was a strangely-shaped rock or stone, seemingly fashioned with modern, Iron Age tools even thought that would have been impossible for something so old for the ancient Egyptians did not have iron tools. Indeed, rather than the pure symmetry that so many ancient cultures favored, this object was insistently asymmetrical and so bizarre in construction that if one held it at different angles it seemed to change shape in one's hand. An optical illusion, of course, but nonetheless unsettling. It was contained within a specially-constructed wooden box covered with images that clashed remarkably with those carved into the stones of the temple as if designed by a different hand from a different race entirely. Yet, there was enough similarity between some of the designs on the box and some of the depictions of the god Tutu that Bowen had to admit that the connection was there and that the temple's hieroglyphics held the key to the function of the device. He felt certain that it was this device and the powers of which it was capable that gave the sobriquet *Ta Senet* to this desolate place.

★ ★ ★

Prior to his trip to Esna, Bowen had spent considerable time with the French consul Paul Emile Botta in Mesopotamia, digging around the ruins of Mosul, and left the Egyptology—such as it was in those days—to the specialists. The French had been everywhere in the region, and there was even a graffito carved into one of the Esna stones by one Donnadieu: a name Bowen associated with a general involved in the Royalist conspiracy against Napoleon. Napoleon, of course, had been in Egypt nearly fifty years earlier. But something he had read in an obscure journal, badly printed on cheap paper and sold in several bookshops in Baghdad and Mosul, made him reconsider his position on Egypt. There was something he needed to see at Esna, something that connected to his work in Mesopotamia, and he could not rest until he had satisfied his curiosity on this singular point.

In Baghdad and Mosul, he had been interested in rumors that there had been an ancient civilization in the area before Babylon. In the Bible, it is referred to as Shinar. There were tantalizing references to it in odd scraps of old literature but the inability of contemporary archaeologists to decipher the cuneiform texts meant that any progress in identifying that civilization would have to wait. (Eventually, the translations would be made and the civilization identified as Sumer, but Bowen would have returned to the States and been well-advanced on his disastrous project long before then.)

It was the strange references to dark magic, and to a cult that worshipped the stars—or a pantheon that existed somewhere in deep space beyond the starry skies—that intrigued Bowen. There were scattered mentions of this cult in the pre-Islamic literature, and there was a sect or a clan of some sort in and around Mosul known as the Yezidi who were said to be in possession of secrets of this sort. They were characterized as devil-worshippers, but Bowen thought that was a lot of balderdash. He had met some of the Yezidi men and even one of their priests, and had come away from those encounters with a high opinion of the tribe. They had claimed their origin was more ancient than Babylon, and that they were the first people to inhabit the Earth. Well, that had to be mostly balderdash, too, but Bowen wondered if there was an element of truth to their tales: a clue to human origins.

And the Yezidis had a Book. A Black Book, they called it, a secret book which they showed to no outsider. And now he had heard of another.

It was 1843. There was a lot of evil in the world, and he had a suspicion things were only going to get worse. There was still slavery in the United States, and British and European imperialism could be felt everywhere from Africa to Asia. Europe would soon break out in the violent revolutions of 1848 as political, social and economic unrest threatened to fracture the monarchies. Bowen was aware of all of that, but his concentration was on finding evidence that a technology had existed since ancient times for communicating with spiritual forces, and rumors that details of this technology had survived in a few rigorously-suppressed texts. A single system for contacting the Divine—proven and scientific—was sure to unite peoples from many different faiths and cultures. Joseph Smith had used just such a system to contact the Angel who gave him the Book of Mormon not that long ago. Bowen had heard that, in India, people believed that such books were hidden all over the world, buried in caves or other inaccessible places by their authors or by stranger, more spiritual forces to protect them from being misused.

Somewhere in all that morass of myth and fancy Bowen knew there resided a kernel of truth. And now, even more than a blasphemous tome replete with forbidden knowledge of the kind that all "primitive" societies were believed to revere, there was physical proof of his belief that a powerful technology existed that would change forever the uneven dynamic that existed between the gods and men, the power equation that was always loaded in favor of the non-human.

He looked down at his battered notebook and studied its pages once again. He had carefully copied the signs and symbols he found on the walls of the half-buried temple, and, using the recent breakthrough on deciphering hieroglyphics made by the Frenchman Champollion, he was able to translate the most important sections relating to the god Tutu. While many of the symbols—which were largely astronomical in nature—resisted any attempt by Bowen to decipher them, the hieroglyphic passages were clear.

And frightening.

The descriptions of Tutu and the elaboration of his powers and characteristics made Bowen's hair stand on end. Partly this was due to his being isolated in the underground chamber, surrounded by unsettling images painted onto its walls that had not been seen for two thousand years. To read of personified evil in such a place was to make it seem all the more real and immediate. But the matter-of-fact recitation of the god's qualities was straightforward enough.

Tutu was a vanquisher of demons, and in Egypt that meant he had legions of demons under his control. As mentioned, he protected one from bad dreams and interceded between the Dream and the Dreamer. He was no stranger to the realm of the Dead, and ruled from the stars: specifically from a constellation that the archaeologists and Egyptologists could not identify for it did not appear in their star charts. But seemed to be located in the first decan of Taurus, in an unknown constellation of seven stars situated somewhere in Orion. There were other astronomical references, however, and at one point Tutu was believed to represent both the Sun and the Moon, or even other astral configurations that defied identification. Tutu had the shape of a sphinx, but with the face of a child and the tail of a serpent. He often was depicted as trampling on the arrows of the fierce lion goddess Sekhmet, carriers of disease, plague, and horror. He is even identified in one stela with the Greek term θεοδαίμων, or "divine demon."

But that was not the worst of it. In the writings on the temple walls Bowen found many scattered references to a Book: a Book that the hieroglyphics described as the *Book of Evil Things*, and also as the *Book of Death and Life*, or the *Book of Bad Things of Finishing the Lifetime*. In Greek: Νεκρονομικον.

Necronomicon.

The Egyptians had a "Book of the Dead" and it was rumored that the Tibetans had one, as well, but this text fell into a separate

category. The Egyptian references were specific: this was not the
same as the *Book of the Dead*, which was a collection of prayers
and rituals to facilitate the voyage of the spirit of the Pharaoh to
the stars. Rather, the *Book of Evil Things* was a collection of spells
and incantations designed to vanquish one's enemies, to summon
demonic forces—and to breach the barrier that exists to separate the
living from the dead, the gods from humans, the Earth from the dark
and forbidden realm of the distant stars.

His team was coming back from its noontime prayer at the small
mosque not far from the entrance to the temple. He thought about
that, the proximity of one religion's house of worship to the other.
The same people, the Egyptians, worshipped at both. The same
people, in the same geographical area, but separated by time. By
thousands of years. What was the relationship between geography
and time, between space and time? Bowen thought about these
things frequently. Can you stand in Egypt in 1843 AD and somehow
make contact with Egypt in 1843 BC? And was that even possible if
you were, yourself, not Egyptian? Was blood the fluid that connected
BC and AD on the otherwise arid soil of temples, ruined and living?
Was that the purpose of all that animal and human sacrifice? In
his mind's eye he could almost see time collapse in front of him as
the men who gathered in the shade of an old palm tree before the
temple entrance became the very same men who built that temple
during the Ptolemaic dynasty. And now they were digging it out
from the sands: pulling at the same stones they had laid millennia
earlier. These could be the same men, Bowen thought, who built
the temple and even the pyramids and who were now returning to
their work as if it had been only yesterday that they had walked its
halls and marveled at its decorated ceilings. Immortality had never
seemed more sinister.

He shook himself out of his reverie and turned his attention
to the dig. He was due back at Brown next Spring. He would not
return first to Mosul, preferring to leave that to the French for now.
What he had in his notes and in the copies he had made of the

inscriptions and designs of the temple was more than enough to occupy him for some time. That, and the object. Instrument. Artifact. Whatever it should be called. He knew what his next task would be, and of how he would use all the resources at his disposal—and those of Brown University, under its current president, Francis Wayland— to accomplish his greatest achievement and liberate humanity from its enslavement by the gods.

Providence, Rhode Island
June 27, 1844

Professor Enoch Bowen had returned to the States at last. It had taken him a year since the dig in Esna, but he had accumulated the books and treatises that he would need to understand the function and use of the device he had uncovered at the temple of Khnum with its brooding presence of the god Tutu. He knew that the device and the nature and character of the god were linked, for the designs on the box that contained the device were all of that deity and of the snakes and stars with which he was identified.

First, however, he needed an appropriate edifice within which to build his laboratory. He found it in an abandoned church on Federal Hill in Providence.

The writing on the cornerstone was in Greek, which Bowen took to be a good sign, all things considered. It was rendered ελευθερία θέλησης, or elefthería thélisis: Free Will. The idea of a church named for Free Will resonated with him. It reminded him of the sixteenth century scholar Rabelais, and his Abbey of Thélème: the "monastery" built by the giant Gargantua, a monastery whose motto was "Do What Thou Wilt." The French word *thélème* means "will," and was amplified in the church's Greek name, θέλησης or *thélisis*. The monastery as envisioned by Rabelais was not limited to men, however, but to "monks" and "nuns" alike, and was conceived as a palace of freedom as well as of lust. Bowen had heard that there were Asiatic sects that made of sexuality a kind of religion, and that in India there were groups—or circles—that met in cemeteries or charnel grounds to perform magical operations involving illicit sex as part of their rituals. As a scholar by nature, he easily could have spent many precious days and weeks working on all the ramifications of these coincidences and correspondences, but instead set himself to work to build his laboratory.

Once in legal possession of the church building, he had it sealed off for the time being and devoted most of his attention to its steeple. The first landing in the steeple had stained glass windows that were opaque, but the upper landing was completely dark. He set about cleaning and repairing it as best he could, doing all the work alone, and when he was finished he fashioned a kind of altar within which he would conceal the artifact he had brought from Esna, much the way the Israelites had hidden their Ark within the Holy of Holies. The past few months had taught him a great deal about the function and purpose of the artifact, for it had replaced the contents of his dreams with new sensations and impossible images that he could never quite shake, not even upon awakening.

He had discussed his findings with Francis Wayland, out of earshot of the university staff. Wayland was a Baptist minister, but a progressive thinker, who opposed slavery and who believed that there should be public libraries where average citizens could avail themselves of the learning of the ages, for free. Bowen relied upon Wayland's modern ideas as a bulwark against which to measure the force of what he was about to reveal; but that venerable and deeply moral man recoiled at some of what Bowen had to tell him, and shrank from the object that the professor had set so gingerly down on the desk before him.

"Why have you brought that here?"

"Why, to show you that I am not insane. That the object exists. Surely, you can see that this … this anomaly … is of tremendous historical significance?"

"Historical, yes. But you intend far more with this in your possession, do you not?"

"Francis, this could be the key to undoing thousands of years of human enslavement to the gods!"

"I truly believe you *are* insane, Enoch. Like your namesake, you are obsessed with occult powers and communication with non-human beings. I fear, though, that unlike your namesake you will not last the 365 years he was blessed to enjoy, nor will you walk with God in Paradise."

"You will take steps to stop me, then?"

The old president of Brown University was silent a moment as he considered his options, and his duty before God.

"It would be useless to try. This isn't Salem in 1692. We don't hang witches in this country anymore. And you know my views on slavery. But what you are suggesting is blasphemous! Humanity enslaved to the gods! It was Jesus who freed us from spiritual servitude, Enoch. It is up to each one of us, individually, to find redemption and liberation in the teachings of the Testaments. What you are saying is mere repetition of what the Serpent said to Eve in the Garden! 'Ye shall be as gods,' isn't that it?"

"No, Francis. We shall not be as *gods*. We shall be as *men*, as *human* beings, for once. Unshackled from the constraints that thousands of years of mindless blubbering at the altars of unseen and uncaring deities have bound us. Why do we enslave others, Francis? Is it anything other than doing unto other human beings *what has already been done to us?*"

In the end the two men could not agree. Francis Wayland insisted that he would not stand in the way of his old friend and colleague if he wished to experiment with the ritualistic prescriptions he had discovered in Egypt, as long as he did it away from the university and did not involve any of its faculty or students. This had to be an independent activity on Bowen's part. But if word of it got out to the world at large, then Francis admitted he would be powerless to protect him.

As Bowen left Wayland's office, there was a knock on the inner door and his daughter let herself in. Asenath was young and beautiful, in a New England Baptist sort of way, with severe features, light blonde hair, and penetrating eyes. She was engaged to be married to a famous Boston surgeon, one Charles Thurston, but she was interested in all things archaeological and anthropological. Brown University did not allow women as students until the end of the nineteenth century, so she derived her education in these matters from her father's extensive library and her conversations with her father's friends. She had overheard some of what her father had been discussing with Enoch Bowen and was intrigued.

"Whatever was Dr. Bowen going on about, father?"

"This is nothing that should concern you, dear. I am afraid that Enoch has spent too much time in savage lands among the godless and under that unrelenting tropical sun. It has gone to his head."

"But what was that ... that thing that he brought to the office?"

"You saw it?"

"I peeked around the edge of the door, father. I was dying of curiosity."

"I see. Well, it was a kind of idol or fetish, you might say. Carved stone of some kind, perhaps a semi-precious stone. Onyx? Maybe volcanic glass. Obsidian, perhaps. It was all sharp angles ... a very curious piece of pagan sculpture."

"It seemed to glow, somehow. The little I saw of it. Like a crystal when you shine a light into it. Only ... only the light seemed to come from within it."

Wayland snorted in dismissal.

"There are many strange things coming out of Egypt these days, my dear. I am afraid that wasn't the strangest."

"Oh?"

"Enoch claims to have discovered some texts while he was out there. Dangerous volumes of superstitious nonsense, if you ask me. Dangerous because they can cause a man to take leave of his senses and start believing in the most fantastical things."

"Like a man rising from the dead and forgiving us our sins, father?"

"Don't blaspheme, daughter! Our Lord and Savior Jesus Christ was a perfect anomaly. He was living proof of the presence of the divine in the world! There was none such before or after Him!"

"An anomaly? Isn't that what Professor Enoch called that device he found?"

"Are you deliberately trying to provoke me, daughter?"

"I wouldn't think of it, father." She smiled at him, and linked her arm through his. "But you have to admit that Dr. Bowen's travels have delivered some very interesting results."

"How would you know? I doubt he has been speaking about his latest trip to Egypt and Mesopotamia in any detail, not in polite company."

"No, not in front of me. But he has been talking to my fiancé, and they have been comparing notes."

"I see. And what would a surgeon know of these matters?"

"I think Dr. Bowen has been in need of some scientific perspective on topics ranging from human consciousness to the phenomenon of spiritual conversion. At least, that is what I gleaned from being the perfectly brought-up lady and listening without speaking."

"Ah. I see. Well, at least Bowen has not abandoned his senses entirely and is seeking confirmation of his theories from men of science."

His daughter smiled at him, a little mischievously. Asenath knew far more about Bowen's travels than her father suspected. Her fiancé had told her a great deal about Bowen's interest in the faculties of the human mind. Thurston had studied in Leipzig, and had learned much from the theories of Carl Ludwig. He had tried to convince Bowen of Ludwig's theory that human beings were mechanical creatures, subject to the same laws that governed physics and chemistry. Bowen seemed receptive to these ideas but not for the reasons that Thurston promoted. To Bowen, humans were indeed machines: automata that had been created as servants by an alien race of beings. Thurston had recoiled at so outlandish and frankly blasphemous a suggestion and had told his fiancée so.

She took her leave of her father and left the university grounds. She had heard that Bowen had acquired the old Free Will Church in Federal Hill, and wondered if perhaps she would one day pay him a visit. It was unseemly for a young woman of her social position—and betrothed, at that—to drop in on single gentlemen without an escort, but Enoch Bowen was of an age that it would not be too scandalous. She was fascinated by his travels and by the rumors that he had dabbled in forbidden arts while abroad. She had also heard that he had amassed a library that contained books not to be found at Brown or in her father's study. If she could not go to university, she could at least read as much as she was able, and that she meant to do.

As she walked down the street outside the university she saw the front page of a newspaper had been pasted up on the corner for all to read. It seems Joseph Smith, Jr.—the founder of the Church of Jesus Christ of Latter-Day Saints, the Mormons—had just been slain by an angry mob.

It seemed like a sinister omen of things to come.

Federal Hill, Providence
New Year's Eve, 1844

It had been only six months since Enoch Bowen had acquired the Free Will Church, but in those six months a great deal had transpired. A few days earlier, Dr. William Drowne of the Fourth Baptist Church of Providence, son of the learned and influential Dr. Solomon Drowne, had sermonized against Dr. Bowen from the pulpit. Bowen had engaged upon a satanic pursuit, according to Drowne, and was threatening to drag all of Providence into the Pit with him.

Drowne was a colleague of Francis Wayland. They were both Baptist clergymen, and held some similar views on faith and politics. Drowne also was aware that Enoch Bowen was an old friend of Wayland, but he felt that the strange archaeologist had finally gone too far.

Within a month of acquiring the Free Will Church, Bowen had renamed it. He had the original Greek inscription on the cornerstone chiseled off and replaced with another Greek legend: *αστρική σοφία*, or *astriki sofia*: Starry Wisdom. And to make matters worse, he had begun to attract a weird kind of congregation.

These were men and women who had traveled some distance to share in whatever lurid ceremonies were taking place in the blighted church. There were scholars of some kind, from Boston and other towns in Massachusetts, as well as from as far away as Westerly, Rhode Island and Mystic, Connecticut. A strange old man from Whateley, Massachusetts was also in attendance almost every weekend that the "church" was open, dressed oddly in what appeared to be some kind of Oriental garb which excited all manner of speculation. Some of the people who showed up for services that began on Friday evenings, and which extended often all weekend until Sunday evening, were evidently of African background, and there were rumors that some of them were slaves who had escaped from the South along the underground railroad.

There were stories of strange smells coming out of the church, like the incense used by the Papists but with a more pungent, even acrid, odor. There were sounds of chanting, but they were in no language that Drowne had ever heard for he spent an hour one weekend lurking just outside a window of the church to see what he could make of it. It wasn't Latin, and it wasn't Greek, of that he was certain. It wasn't Hebrew either, and he doubted it was Aramaic. He knew that Bowen had spent considerable time in Egypt and Mesopotamia, so he thought the chants might be from one of those languages. If so, that meant that almost certainly Bowen was calling upon pagan gods.

It all had been too much for Drowne, who excoriated Bowen and his Starry Wisdom Church during a sermon on Sunday, December 29 of 1844. His congregation was scandalized by the implications of Drowne's description of the unholy goings-on at the new church in Federal Hill, and Bowen suddenly found himself

ostracized by polite society in Providence. He met privately with his
friend, Francis Wayland, who could do little more than shrug and tell
him that he had been warned. Starry Wisdom was being suspected
of harboring runaway slaves, which didn't bother Wayland at all, but
there were stories that the slaves were bringing their own pagan
beliefs and practices with them to the church and that Bowen was
incorporating them into his own strange rites.

Bowen tried to explain what he was doing, but Wayland was
having none of it. He knew that it all centered on that strange
artifact that Bowen had brought with him out of that temple in
Esna, and on the books or scrolls or whatever they were that he used
to operate the thing and call down ... well ... whatever it was that
he was calling down.

Bowen made another attempt to convince Wayland that he was
not calling anything down, but that the artifact was a gateway that
allowed him to travel outside earthly space and time. It was, he said,
a geometric device, like an astrolabe or even a sextant, except that
the measurements and constellations of the device were not those
that could be made or seen from Earth. It was as if an astrolabe
did not only pinpoint one's location on the surface of the Earth
but actually transported you to another set of coordinates in some
other solar system. It was a trapezoid, he said. No. Not a trapezoid.
A trapezohedron. Its strangely asymmetric shape was the key to
its power. It was, Bowen said, a kind of mirror but a mirror that
reflected not the physical appearance of the one who looked into it
but the essence of that person in another dimension. The same, but
not the same.

"It's like a mathematical equation," he insisted, wild-eyed and
nearly frantic with the desire to make his friend understand. "Two
plus two equals four. But one plus three also equals four. When you
look into the trapezohedron you are two plus two, but what you see
is one plus three ... the trapezohedron is the equal sign."

The more he tried to explain it, the more insane he sounded. In
fact, Wayland thought he had become a raving lunatic and made the

decision that he would do what he could to close down the Starry Wisdom Church and have his friend committed to an institution somewhere for a rest cure. Before he could do that, however, he had to arrange for his daughter's wedding to Charles Thurston.

As he was busy with those preparations, the first of the disappearances had taken place.

Providence, Rhode Island
Spring, 1845

There was a rumor that a child had gone missing from a home on Angell Street. No one seemed to know which family, or which child. It was one of those persistent stories that began to accrete on the dark stones of the Church of Starry Wisdom like moss or rust stains. A missing child now, and a few months later another.

No one knew why the Starry Wisdom congregation would be responsible for children going missing. Certainly no one suspected that human sacrifices were taking place; the idea was too bizarre even for everything they had been told about Bowen and his cult. But still … there had been no missing children until Enoch Bowen had opened his church.

When Bowen had told Wayland that he was not calling anything down, but rather using the trapezohedron as a kind of magic mirror, he was not being completely truthful. The device *was* a kind of mirror, certainly, but a mirror that could work in both directions. One might see oneself in the mirror, but there were things on the other side of the mirror that could see *you*. The trapezohedron was a kind of portal or gateway and like any portal it opened in both directions: exit and entrance.

Bowen had started to notice this strange new function of the trapezohedron. The atmosphere in the church would change suddenly, as if someone else had entered and was standing just behind him when he was intent on studying the ancient volumes of esoteric instruction he had collected from all over the world. Noises that were not due to birds or rats within the church structure would nag at his consciousness, half-in and half-out, as ambiguous as memories. He found himself reacting to the strange sounds and unseen presences, driven to make modifications to the church's internal structure as if guided by an invisible hand. In fact, he believed he had discovered the real purpose behind the design of church steeples, and they were not for the ringing of bells.

Asenath Wayland had insisted to her father that Enoch Bowen be invited to her wedding that June, but Wayland refused. Bowen had gone off the deep end, he told her. He was disheveled and dirty, had lost a lot of weight, and was rarely seen in polite Providence company any longer. The stories about what was going on at the church were more and more bizarre, and Wayland was fearful that something terrible was about to happen and that it would affect the entire community. He just could not bear to bring himself to have his old friend committed. He knew what those institutions were like and he could not, in good conscience, consign Enoch Bowen to the hellish conditions of the local Bedlam. There had to be some other way, he said to himself.

But when the day of his daughter's wedding arrived, Enoch Bowen did appear. He was clean, neatly dressed, and seemed perfectly normal. Even prosperous. The change was startling, but Wayland was pleased.

"Enoch! You're looking well," he exclaimed, taking his friend's hand in his own.

"Thank you, Francis. I am well, as it turns out."

"Have you abandoned your obsession with the stone? What do you call it? The trapezohedron?" This was said in a conspiratorial whisper, so that the other wedding guests would not hear what was being discussed.

"The Shining Trapezohedron, I call it now. But to answer your question, I have come to terms with it and with the technology it represents." It was an opaque reply, but Wayland did not notice the ambiguity, so pleased as he was that Enoch seemed to have returned to some sort of normalcy after the past year.

"You have quite the congregation over at the Free Will Church, Enoch. Should I be worried?" It was said in jest, but Bowen considered the question seriously.

"I would not worry, Francis. We mean no harm to anyone, regardless of what wagging tongues would have you believe. We merely wish to be allowed to … to worship … in peace, just as you do."

"I apologize for the zeal with which Dr. Drowne had criticized you from the pulpit last year. I spoke with him about it and he has promised not to return to that theme, but he is concerned nevertheless. And about the missing children, of course."

Before Bowen could reply, Asenath—now Mrs Charles Thurston—interrupted them and welcomed Bowen to the gathering.

"I am so glad you were able to come, Dr. Bowen! It has been ages since we've spoken."

"I was pleased to accept your kind invitation, Asenath, and to put myself at your disposal should you wish to continue our conversations. However, I suspect that as a newly-married woman you will not have time for such pleasantries!"

He bowed, and she smiled and walked off to greet her other guests. Her husband, Dr. Thurston, stood slightly apart and stared at Bowen as if he had seen a ghost.

Francis Wayland turned to watch his daughter walk off and when he tried to resume his conversation with Enoch Bowen found that his old friend had disappeared into the crowd of guests.

Providence, Rhode Island
1846-1855

Although Enoch Bowen appeared, for all intents and purposes, a typical pastor of an average if slightly eccentric Protestant denomination in Providence the rumors about him and his congregation only got worse with every passing season. By the end of 1848, there had been ten disappearances of children and adults recorded in the town and the local neighborhood people began telling stories of human sacrifice taking place at the Starry Wisdom Church, although no evidence was ever found to substantiate these rumors. One would think it would be a simple matter for someone from the other congregations in town to attend services at Starry Wisdom to see for themselves if there was anything satanic or demonic taking place, but Starry Wisdom operated according to their own calendar and timetable. No one ever knew in advance when services would be held and, in fact, it seemed obvious that there were many Sundays when there were no services at all. Instead, one could observe lights in the church on odd days during the week and almost always at night. When these were observed, and some courageous soul dared to approach the building to gain access, it was revealed that the doors were always locked from the inside.

In happier news, Asenath Thurston became pregnant and gave birth to a son she named Francis Wayland Thurston, in honor of her father. The boy was born on the vernal equinox of 1846, and there was great celebration in the town. After all, the president of Brown University had now become a grandfather and all was right with the world. Young Thurston was certainly destined for great things.

Yet, there were whispers. Providence was, after all, a small New England town and prone to the gossips and jealousies of all small New England towns. It was averred that Asenath had been caught slipping into the Starry Wisdom Church from time to time, usually in the twilight hours, although it was never proven. It was also whispered that she had become a woman of loose moral character, although again there was no evidence at all to support such allegations. It would seem that her marriage to Dr. Thurston was a happy one, and she was prominent in local social circles. But the murmuring continued, especially among the residents of Federal Hill, and included the infamous claim that young Francis Wayland

Thurston was not really the son of Dr. Charles Thurston, but of the abhorred Enoch Bowen ... or even, it was said, of one of Bowen's racially-mixed congregation.

With more disappearances the rumor mill only grew more productive. Finally, an investigation was launched by the authorities in 1853. It was quiet, done with circumspection as the suspect was a learned man and a pastor, as well as a friend of the president of Brown University. Local people had reported strange sounds coming from the church, and all sorts of weird fantasies about what went on there. They mentioned the fact that the building seemed to be a magnet for former slaves—runaway and freed—and that often they went into the church but were never seen again.

The investigation turned up nothing. The investigators were allowed the run of the church building and while they agreed it was designed strangely with many odd details that they could neither identify nor explain, there was no evidence of foul play anywhere on the premises. That the church might have been a way station on the Underground Railroad to Canada occurred to the investigators, but abolition sentiments were running high and they neglected to mention this possibility in their reports.

In 1855, Francis Wayland stepped down as president of Brown, but kept a position as pastor of the First Baptist Church of Providence for a few more years before finally retiring from public life. That same year, Enoch Bowen—still running the Church of Starry Wisdom—entered into a lengthy correspondence with one Paschal Beverly Randolph.

Randolph had just returned from a lengthy sojourn in Europe, the Middle East, and Africa, where he met various masters of the occult arts. A man of mixed-race, he was born in New York City and left home early in his teens to begin working on board ships in order to make a living and see the world. His exposure to European, Persian, and African mystical practices transformed the young man into a celebrated spiritual leader. He was also—like Wayland and Bowen—a dedicated abolitionist; but he was not convinced there was any future in America for the slaves or the descendants of slaves after emancipation. In 1855, the same year he began corresponding with Enoch Bowen, he was quoted in the *Daily Illinois State Register* as saying during a speech to African Americans that "the Negro was destined to extinction" in the United States.

Bowen wrote to Randolph on a subject near to both of their hearts: magic mirrors. Randolph had studied the subject in Europe and the Middle East and would eventually write entire essays on the topic; Bowen had obtained his trapezohedron in a ruined Egyptian temple. But for Bowen the magic mirror was more than a device for seeing into the future or for contacting spiritual forces: it was a means of transport between two worlds.

They compared notes, and suggested other practices that might make more use of the mirrors. When Bowen described his device—albeit carefully and without a great deal of detail—Randolph was immediately intrigued and asked if Bowen would show it to him if Randolph was ever in Rhode Island. What happened next had a profound effect on the lives of both men.

In the meantime, Bowen had developed a technique for using the Shining Trapezohedron. He found that it reacted to sound, but that he had to hold it or face it in a specific way in order to achieve the effect he sought. The shape of the stone was so asymmetrical that it added to his confusion at first. That is when he realized that the box it was encased within held the key as to how it should be mounted and observed. The stone fit within the carved wooden container in such a way that only one set of angles was permitted. By matching the shape of the container within the box—custom built for the Trapezohedron's strange angles—he saw that images at each of the several corners corresponded to a mathematical formula for arranging the stone outside of the box.

His transliteration of the hieroglyphics associated with the Stone enabled him to duplicate what must have been the original chant. He had to experiment with the vowel sounds, but eventually he found the right combination of consonants and vowels in the right order, and when that happened the Stone began to glow with an unholy, mesmerizing light.

That was in 1845, when he was still working alone in the church. He then began to write to certain individuals he knew through his classes at the university—some former students, other lecturers in various antique or arcane subjects, and the occasional author whose work demonstrated an unspoken but vaguely hinted familiarity with the forces contained within the Stone—and these gradually formed the inner core of his congregation. He needed the minds to enable him to understand the Trapezohedron and of what it was capable—but he also needed the additional voices, for he found that the Stone reacted to volume as well as to the rhythm and proper pronunciation of the incantations.

When he added voices to the chant, a remarkable thing occurred. Forms began to appear in the Stone, and eventually seemed to leave the Stone and stand—unassisted—in the center of the church as if dragged out of the Stone. That is when one of the others he had recruited to the service of the Stone advised that they should begin taking careful notes of everything that transpired, and even attempt to communicate with the Beings that were being summoned out of the Aether.

Bowen naturally agreed, shaken as he was by the images—the hallucinations, he thought at first—that floated or crawled out of the Shining Trapezohedron. And that is when one of his associates noticed that every time some Thing left the precincts of the Stone, someone in the neighborhood went missing.

The archaeologist tried to reexamine the hieroglyphic texts as well as the mass of astronomical symbols that he discovered in the temple for a clue as to what was happening and how to avert future disappearances. So far the only ones who made the connection between the rituals of the Shining Trapezohedron and the missing citizens were members of Bowen's clandestine congregation, but he felt certain that eventually the authorities would come looking at the Starry Wisdom Church and things could go very wrong after that.

As the years went by and the 1840s became the 1850s, Bowen found that he was devoting every waking moment to the mystery of the Shining Trapezohedron, and even in his dreams he found himself walking the border between this world and some other. The figures that appeared within the Stone were not of this Earth, or indeed of any sensible realm of matter and spirit. The things that appeared, and which shudderingly left the Stone to roam freely upon the Earth, could not have evolved on any planet like his own. His colleagues had imagined they were from some sort of spirit realm, a place beyond the abyss that separates us from the kingdom of the dead, but Bowen shook his head at those suggestions. There was something else entirely taking place here, he knew, and with every new appearance—and corresponding disappearance—he felt more certain that the Shining Trapezohedron was not a link to the realm of the Dead or to the Heaven of the Angels, but a gateway between God's creation and the creation of some other ... Thing.

They did not gaze into the Stone or shout the chant every day, or even every month. They began to observe that certain arrangements of stars in the sky were more conducive, and anyway they were uncomfortable with the possibility that for every Being that oozed forth out of the Trapezohedron, another—a human being, often a child—was dragged into it, in a manner so far unwitnessed by Bowen and his comrades. Thus, they restricted their rites to only a few times every year. The rest of the time they spent in careful examination of every new Egyptian text that became available, as well as other forbidding scriptures from Mesopotamia, India, China and Eastern Europe. They began to accumulate a library of the esoteric arts, the equal of which would not be found elsewhere in North America. In addition, they began a correspondence with scholars and mystics throughout the world; but without revealing the treasure they had in their possession. Instead, they wrote of magic mirrors and the like, such as the shewstone of the Elizabethan magician Dr John Dee and his colleague, Edward Kelly, that was used to communicate with angelic forces.

Inevitably, however, word began to spread and friends and family of the original core group around Bowen began to attend the Church of Starry Wisdom. Bowen found that he would have to create a kind of orderly arrangement of persons so that only those closest to him and to his core group would have access to the deeper secrets of the Church. In this, he was no different than any new religion, for even Christianity had begun with a similar system of grades between those who were full initiates and those who were called catechumens. Thus, he and his core group formed the Inner Court, and those without were called the Outer Court. This, however, was not sufficient, for there were those of the Outer Court who were possessed of far greater acumen in these matters than many of the others, so a third grade or degree was added.

By 1860, this had changed yet again so that those around Bowen and his closest associates formed a separate Order, known as the A.A.—whose initials stood for a mystery connected to the Shining Trapezohedron and its power to bring its devotees to the stars. P. B. Randolph would eventually reveal its existence in a book he entitled *Eulis*, published the year before his death, and in doing so unwittingly exposed Bowen and the Church of Starry Wisdom (and himself) to great peril.

Before that happened, however, Paschal Beverly Randolph—the Rosicrucian, the Adept, the initiate of the Hermetic Brotherhood of Luxor, trance medium and healer—would pay a visit to the Church of Starry Wisdom and learn the truth about the Shining Trapezohedron ... and about the Church itself.

Providence, Rhode Island
1858

Having finally managed an invitation from Bowen, P. B. Randolph arrived in Providence just as summer was ending. He had rented a space in Boston's Beacon Hill district and was conducting séances there, and had set up a small alchemical laboratory in what he termed his "Rosicrucian Rooms." The journey from Boston to Providence was short and reasonable. The weather vacillated between summer hot and autumn cool, and that uncertainty in the climate lent itself well to the sense of liminality felt by the well-traveled teacher. He knew that feeling, having encountered it in North Africa and in the Levant on his travels to learn more of the mystical teachings of all races and ages. It was a noble impulse, but Randolph could not know at that time how dangerous was the desire to see behind the Veil of Isis.

No one was there to greet him at Union Station, so he made his way on foot to Federal Hill with some trepidation. The Fugitive Slave Act had been passed not long ago, and though he had been born free he harbored no illusions about his safety as a man half-African in blood and appearance. He was an arresting figure in any case, with his dark complexion, manicured beard, and intense expression, and several pedestrians remarked to themselves how elegant yet how sinister did the man appear.

He found the building that housed the Church of Starry Wisdom and knocked firmly on the heavy wooden doors. He noted the cornerstone with its Greek equivalent for "starry wisdom" and knew he was at the right place and at the right time, but there was no answer to his knock.

So he tried again.

"Dr. Randolph, I presume?"

The voice from behind startled the occultist. He turned around and saw an elderly white man, dressed properly but a little shabbily, hold out his hand.

Randolph took it, and looked the man over. "Are you Dr. Bowen? Dr. Enoch Bowen?"

"The same. Allow me," and the man pulled out a heavy ring of iron keys and unlocked the church doors.

"We don't take any chances around here," Bowen whispered. "I watched you come down the street from a place over there, behind those bushes." He pointed to a spot across the street from where they were. "I had to be sure you were not being followed."

They entered the gloomy interior of the church, which smelled from many burnings of incense as well as something else he could not quite identify.

"Is it that serious?"

"There have been … incidents … that cause us to be extremely careful."

"But you are a man of God, are you not?"

"Oh, indeed. That is not the question."

"Then what is the question?"

"The question, my dear Dr. Randolph, is 'which God?'"

The two men made themselves as comfortable as possible in the rear vestry room off the apse of the church that had been made into a kind of study with a sturdy desk. Bowen would glance up in the direction of the steeple from time to time, as if expecting something to happen there, or perhaps some assassin to crawl down the spiral staircase towards them.

From his vantage point on an old leather chair that had once served as a bishop's throne, but which had been dragged into the vestry as a guest chair of sorts, Randolph could see rows of fine leather books—some apparently quite old—in shelves. He was immediately drawn to them, but out of politeness kept his seat and attended to what Bowen was telling him.

"Our congregation is small, but by design of course."

"Of course."

"We don't advertise what we are doing here. We need the space, but we also need the privacy. What we are doing in this place has not been done in thousands of years to my knowledge, not since the Ptolemaic period, if then."

"Surely other magi and adepti of ages past have been engaged in similar, if not identical, pursuits?"

Bowen shook his head.

"What we are attempting here is so far beyond conjuring demons or speaking with angels, or mediumship with souls of the dead. The ... the mirror ... we have in our possession was not used for those purposes at all."

"Then ... to what purpose if not that?"

"I will show you presently. But for now, suffice it to say that the ... mirror ... is a gateway, a portal, to another realm entirely. I cannot say with any conviction that it is indeed a realm of spirits, of angels or demons, or even a realm of God. It is beyond those calculations entirely. What comes through the Stone has nothing at all to do with any part or fraction of God's creation."

"Stone?"

"Pardon me?"

"You called it a 'Stone.' Is that what it is? A kind of rock ... *tu es Petrus*, and all that ... or is it the Philosopher's Stone you speak of?"

Bowen merely frowned and shook his head.

"It is none of those things, and shares nothing in common with any of them. You shall see for yourself, but I must enjoin you to the utmost secrecy. You must swear an oath to me that you will never reveal what I am about to show you."

"I do swear."

Bowen nodded. "I sense you are a man of great integrity, and I trust your word. Come, let us approach the Stone."

Bowen led the way to the nave of the church, and then up the spiral staircase to the first of two landings within the steeple. This was a room about fifteen feet square, with a lancet window in each quadrant that had been fitted with opaque screens, giving the whole area a somber and quite gloomy effect. Bowen leaned over a small table in a corner and lit a kerosene lamp, which illuminated a scene such as Randolph had never seen before in his life, and he had traveled greatly.

There were seven chairs arranged in a rough circle around a central pillar or column. This column was roughly four feet in height, and adorned with strange symbols and sigils, such as had been found by Bowen at the temple in Esna. But that was not all.

★ ★ ★

Behind each of the seven Gothic chairs was placed a large, almost featureless statue as if a vulture or some bird of prey brooding over the chair or its inhabitant. Each statue was black in color, thus lending an even more sinister effect to the whole. Randolph could not identify the statues. They looked like nothing he had ever seen. They were not Egyptian, at least not from any of the known dynasties. They were roughly shaped, bulky, and protuberances on their backs seemed to suggest wings. There were faces, if such hideous expressions could be said to resemble a human or animal face, and these were rendered with care. In the flickering light of the lamp they seemed almost animate, each with a gaze so penetrating they seemed to follow him around. Each was different from the other, yet Randolph noticed a similarity between them that suggested they were related in some way, as if manifestations of a single infamous entity taken at different moments in its evolution perhaps. Randolph was certain there was more to these statues than the sculptor's art.

But in the center of this bizarre assemblage was the pillar, and on top of the pillar was an oddly-shaped box, carved out of wood that had been decorated with more of the strange and indecipherable symbols that were to be found on the pillar itself.

Bowen gestured towards the box.

"The Stone is contained within that chest. I brought them both with me out of Egypt, from a temple a little south of Luxor. You note the strange shape? Yes, it is not square, or rectangular in any way. Yet it was constructed most carefully, and with joints so tight they cannot be separated with a knife or a razor. You may approach the chest and open it, but do so with caution. The Stone within is as oddly-shaped as the chest that contains it."

Randolph hesitated. The entire scenario was so unsettling, and Bowen's demeanor now so vaguely mocking, that he felt he was being made a fool of at best, or being hastened down a dangerous and irreversible path at worst. But the pull of that very oddly-constructed box and its mysterious contents was too strong to resist.

He walked between two of the Gothic chairs and stood before the pillar. He reached out with both hands and lifted the box. It was heavy, but not so heavy that he would need two hands to carry it. He put it back down on the pillar and opened the box.

Within he could see something faintly glowing, but by which fuel he could not imagine. He inserted his fingers and felt around the place where the Stone—as such Bowen called it—met the contours of the box. Finding purchase, he lifted it out of the chest, gingerly, and noticed that it seemed to emit a kind of heat for it was warm to the touch but in a way that tingled rather than burned.

He heard Bowen sigh aloud at the sight of the Stone.

"It is called the Shining Trapezohedron," he explained. "It is the center of all our work here, in this room."

"It does shine, but what is a trapezohedron? Is that not a geometric shape of some kind?"

"Indeed. A trapezohedron is a solid version of a trapezoid, a quadrilateral in which at least two sides are parallel to each other. In this case, it is a solid figure in which each of its faces is a trapezoid or a trapezium, which is a quadrilateral in which no sides are parallel to each other. You will see that both seem to be represented in this device."

★ ★ ★

Randolph marveled at the thing, and something about it made him want to hold it for as long as possible. Even then, he had strong misgivings about it.

"By its very nature, its unwholesome asymmetry, it mocks

Nature and the beauty of Creation. There is no Golden Section here, no balance between right and left, between up and down. It is a Stone that has no place to rest on the Earth, no square platform, nothing to suggest that human beings deliberately fashioned it."

"And no human beings did."

Randolph shuddered involuntarily and decided to return the device to its intricately carved container. He had some difficulty, since removing it from the box he had rotated it in his hands several times to get a better look and found that he could not figure out how to reinsert it. Bowen came forward and after a minute of moving and rotating the Stone was able to find the way to return it safely to the chest.

"You say no human beings constructed this device?"

"I do."

"How can you be certain?"

"The Stone itself has confirmed it, on more than one occasion."

"I admit that its appearance is uncanny, and defies description, but to claim that it is un-human ..."

"Non-human, I should say. And that is not to mean by an animal or other brute, nor by an angel or demon."

"Then ... what?"

"Do you believe that beings live as we do on other planets, Dr. Randolph?"

"I do, most assuredly."

"And that, in as much as they resemble us in some basic particulars, that they would have limbs and extensions of those limbs capable of making tools?"

"It stands to reason."

"And that those tools would have functions roughly similar to ours?"

"I agree with all of this, Dr. Bowen, but it seems you are trying to suggest that this Shining Trapezohedron of yours was made by some craftsman on Mars?"

Bowen smiled.

"No, not at all. Not even remotely."

"Then I am afraid I don't understand."

"The device you were holding just now was not made by a Martian or a Venusian or any creature or human-type being on any of the planets in our solar system, for all the reasons we have just been discussing. If beings live on other planets, they must be subject to many of the same physical laws as we do. In fact, *all* of the same physical laws, simply in different proportions as the environmental particulars of their planets may differ from ours in degree, but not in kind."

He pointed at the wooden box on the pedestal.

"That device, to which I refer as the Stone, could not have been made by men on Earth, nor by men from other planets in our solar system or, indeed, anywhere in our universe. It obeys no laws of physics that we may identify. It is of a shape that defies human requirements of design and function. It has come from elsewhere. Elsewhere entirely. And it serves as a conduit for beings from that Elsewhere to enter our world, at which point they seem to disappear."

"That is an outlandish claim, Dr. Bowen. I assume you have evidence to support it?"

"I do, but it will have to wait until more of us are present. I plan a demonstration this evening, to which I invite you to be my guest. This will enable you to see with your own eyes that what I attest is, indeed, the truth."

Later that evening

After a simple meal served in the vestry, Randolph and Bowen repaired to the upper room. Shortly after, they were joined by a procession of individuals who came in through the front door, which had been left unlocked. The individuals came in a scattered file, one or two at a time, so as not to arouse any notice from the neighborhood. The last one in locked and barred the door from the inside.

Randolph was getting an uneasy feeling about the arrangements.

They seemed familiar, yet somehow forbidding. Even sinister. They heard the participants trudge up the spiral staircase to the upper room.

Bowen was sitting in one of the Gothic chairs around the Stone, dressed in a simple black robe over his clothing. Randolph, as he was not a member of the group, stood to one side where he could see the proceedings clearly. A kind of circle had been designed in chalk to mark the sacred precinct. It was not one he recognized from Agrippa or Francis Barrett, or the other grimoires of the European magicians. This one had more in common with the *vèvè* of the Haitian *vodouisants,* for it was more angular than circular and contained unfamiliar sigils.

The kerosene lamp was lit, and one by one the other chairs were taken by members of the group dressed in dark robes, mostly men but including one woman. This last, he later learned, was the daughter of Francis Wayland, formerly president of Brown University. The presence of a woman at the ritual might seem shocking to most, but to Randolph it indicated a degree of sophistication where the machinery of esoterica was concerned. There were rumors in America and in Europe of the Black Mass, during which it was said women were placed on the altar in a state of complete undress as a mockery of the Roman Catholic ritual, but Randolph understood the requirement on a different level entirely for the role of sexuality and gender was central to his understanding of occult power and illumination: a point of view that was dangerous to hold much less to promote in the mid-nineteenth century, especially for the son of a former slave. When eventually he made those controversial assertions public, he would couch them in loftier language and associate them with the Rosicrucians or some other ancient Order with a suitably acceptable pedigree.

His ruminations on this matter, however, were interrupted by the arrival of a new group of people who did not appear to be adepts.

These individuals climbed the spiral staircase to the steeple room, and they took positions around the central circle of chairs. They were men and women, and several children. This astonished Randolph, who could not understand why children were allowed to witness—much less participate in—what could only be an unearthly rite. Then he noticed to his greater shock that the race of the newcomers was the same as his own, or as that part of himself that was reviled and despised by the men who considered themselves his masters. These were African men and women, and African children, and his heart went out to them even as he recoiled from the possibility that some harm would come to them, or that this white New Englander and descendant of slave owners himself would use this opportunity to enslave his people further. Or worse.

At that point a pall of silence fell upon the group, as heavy as an anvil. He noticed that the occupants of the seven chairs were dressed alike in their dark robes, simple of design, which further accented the gloom of the proceedings. The darkness of the robes seemed to blend into the chairs and the chairs into the strange large statues behind them, as if each making a single unit. Randolph began to understand that the statues were specific to the chairs, which were specific to the adepts. There was a connection between the adept and the statue, an identification with some sort of otherworldly power that he could not name, for these statues were not of Egypt that he could tell, nor of Babylon, but of some other culture that reminded him of nothing on this Earth. He regarded the whole scenario as the creation of some madman in an institution for the insane, drawing his disturbed fantasies on the wall of his cell.

The light from the lamp cast weird shadows on the contours of the room and made those large statues behind the chairs seem alive with floating grimaces and leers. The box containing the stone appeared to take on some of the light and the symbols and images etched thereon began to glow and dance in the shadows. He knew these were optical illusions, tricks of the light, but they unnerved him nevertheless.

Bowen began to speak in a low voice, barely audible to Randolph. The words were not in English. It would be a long time before Randolph would hear that language again, spoken by a Chinook Indian in San Francisco. He then would recoil in dread when he heard that fateful phrase, *Aqlō'kXulį* or "It is finished" in an opium den in that city. The language was called Aklo by Bowen, and eventually made its way into stories by Machen and later by H.P. Lovecraft. In the Lepcha language spoken by a few thousand souls in the Himalayas its archaic form—*A-klo*—means "language of the Fall." As Aklo, Aqlo or its cognates, the sense is of an ancient language no longer in use by humans as a vernacular but only as a sacred language or, perhaps, its opposite. Xul, as in the above declaration, was known as an evil spirit among the Babylonians and had negative connotations among the Mayans as well: a spirit of the end, of the finish. All of these traces pointed, in Randolph's mind, to the existence of a single ancient language that was spoken by humans before writing existed; but according to Bowen, the Aklo language was not a human construction at all.

Randolph could not make out separate words, but there rose around him a kind of hum as of the whirring of an infernal machine. The others in the chairs—evidently the elders or high priests of the cult—picked up Bowen's chant and were repeating it with greater volume, and an insistent rhythm all the more remarkable when one considers the lack of a drum or any other percussion instrument to mark the time.

A sudden feeling of horror descended upon Randolph as the vibrations of the chant rose up from the wooden floor to ascend his legs and torso. It was a feeling of drunkenness or the sensation one obtains from *ganja*, such as he had sampled on his travels abroad, but with a strong element of paranoia and even, he thought, despair. It was a feeling as if he had been condemned to death after an arrest and a trial of which he had no memory for a crime he did not know he had committed, *but was certain he had.*

★ ★ ★

That was when he heard the voice, a sound coming from all around him, like an insistent whisper in a language he did not speak. The words meant nothing to him, but each syllable uttered by the voice opened a world to his gaze and he tried to shut his eyes against it but it was no use. The visions were inside his head, along with the sound of that gibbering voice. He could feel the voice slithering through his organs, as if searching for something it knew to be there. He felt it move around his heart, and felt its pressure there, and through his lungs, and down his intestines. He felt a sharp pain in his private member as if the voice had exited his body that way, in a vile and monstrous display of disinterest and mockery. The whispering gradually gave way to a fathomless silence, and he realized in that moment that he had been visited by what Bowen had called the "Haunter in the Dark."

And from the floor above them, in the windowless chamber at the very top of the steeple, a footstep could be heard and felt through the entire structure of the church. Something was descending, but from what invisible place devoid of materiality in this world? Another step, a shuffling gait, a shambling …

He had not noticed who had opened the box, or when, but the Stone was there between them atop the pillar, glowing softly in a light whose color he could not identify, like something burned or charred. He felt that odd tingling sensation again, flowing up his arms and into his chest. There was a pressure on the wooden floor as if something large and heavy had just stepped onto it, although everything around him seemed the same. Then, the light from the lamp grew flat and two-dimensional and he was frozen in a nameless terror as if the only thing in the room, in the church, or in all of Providence that remained alive was the Stone itself.

Although the Stone was small enough to fit in one's hand, it was now the size of the entire room, or so it seemed to Randolph who could see nothing else. The thought "magic lantern" came into his mind as his reasoning sought an explanation in the real world for what was happening, but it fled from his mind just as quickly as it had entered. This was no magic lantern show. This could not be real, he thought frantically to himself, but it cannot be fantasy or illusion either. Was there a middle ground between the two? Or some ground entirely Other, entirely Outside the world—*outside even the mystical world*—that he knew?

From the Stone appeared a shape and a sensation at once. It was without edges, yet it was mobile and ambulatory, its color changing with its movement, a kind of mauve in various degrees of brightness. The sensation was one of disgust, as if one had suddenly ventured into a well-used latrine expecting it to be a delicately scented lady's boudoir. The thing floated or slid out of the Stone and through the assembled cultists and passed through the wall furthest from Randolph and presumably out into the street.

There then appeared a procession of vile and inexplicable things—creatures—objects—it was beyond Randolph's powers of description (which were considerable, as his published works attest) and he found himself transfixed by the sights even as he wished them to stop. He had to be hallucinating, he told himself. Perhaps Bowen had poisoned him at dinner, fed him some form of peyote such as the Mexican shamans were known to imbibe when they went on their terrifying journeys to the stars. He felt nauseated, and his limbs began to tremble, but the chanting continued as if the cultists were afraid to stop, and then the unspeakable took place.

★ ★ ★

One by one, the runaway slaves—for that is who they were, as Randolph discovered but surely knew, surely sensed at that moment without being told—approached the Stone in awe and in terrible trepidation. A few carried bags with them, but most just the clothes on their backs. The children among them were silent, too afraid—too absolutely terrified—to cry out or make any kind of sound. They were used to being silent, all along the horrible routes out of the enslaving South to the dangerous North, on their way to free

Canada. They were told to keep quiet no matter what transpired, and now those lessons learned the hard way had been too powerful to loosen their grip. They should be crying, thought Randolph in a moment of clarity. They should be *screaming*.

He watched them go past him, into the circle and, one by one—one by one, one by one—they walked up to the Stone and disappeared.

Randolph wanted to move, but he was frozen in place. He wanted to shout, to cry out, to stop them from going, but he was in the grip of something like a nightmare. He tried to open his jaws, to make any sound, but could not force his mouth to open, which terrified him the more.

As the last man walked up to the Stone, Randolph noticed the woman standing next to it. It was Wayland's married daughter, and she lifted her hands towards Randolph as if inviting him to take a voyage to the unknown country with the rest of the travelers. At that point, his mind no longer capable of recording all the unfamiliar scenes and impressions, and frightened almost to death because he knew he *could* make that decision, he *could* take that step and leave it, leave it all behind—the hatred, the persecution, the constant threats to his life, the emasculations, the utter and complete lack of God and hope and love anywhere in the world—he lost consciousness.

That morning

"*Tutulu*," said a voice above him. "*Tutulu*."

Randolph opened his eyes slowly and with great care. The inner lids felt like sandpaper and he was certain his irises had been scratched or scarred in some fashion for the pain that attended them with the incoming light from a window.

He was back in the vestry, and the sun was shining and the place was empty except for himself and Bowen.

"What ... what happened?" he croaked and tried to rise from a makeshift cot.

"Tutu happened, Dr. Randolph. Tutu. An Egyptian god, much ignored. Tutu is known as the 'hidden god,' Doctor. A gateway to the other gods. A gateway to the stars and the realm beyond the stars. The Haunter of the Dark. Certainly, you heard his voice last night? You felt his presence within you? The first time is always unsettling, I admit. In fact, I vomited the first time. Most do, or void their bowels uncontrollably. There is no shame in it, not the first time."

"Did I …?"

"Oh, no. Not at all. You dropped to the floor in a kind of fit or seizure. And then you were still. I thought we had lost you, but your vital signs were strong. When the ritual was complete, I had a few of the men help me bring you down the stairs to the vestry."

"That language …" It started to come back to him. "What was that language?"

"I transcribed it from the hieroglyphics I found at the temple in Egypt. Thank God for the likes of Champollion. I was never sure of the vowels, though. I had to crib that from the Coptic, but eventually worked them out. Trial and error, mostly. Not certain I have them all correct, even now, but the ritual seems to work and the Stone functions quite well, don't you think?"

"What … what do the words mean? What were you saying?"

"Oh, I have no idea."

"No idea?" Randolph stood up and felt his head for wounds or bumps, but he seemed to be intact.

"The pronunciation is the key, not the meaning of the words. They are strings of consonants for the most part. You have to guess at the vowels. A little like Hebrew before the pointing. You have a phrase like 'Fngh mgl wnf th Kth lh Rlh wgh ngl fht gn' and it is confusing, of course. Notice the letter 'l' in the syllables as well. As far as we know there wasn't actually an 'l' sound in ancient Egyptian."

He seemed to go on in this vein, with Randolph nodding absently at times and trying to rouse himself from his pallet. There was a cup of tea on a small table next to him, which he took to be for his own refreshment, but he hesitated. Had he been drugged with peyote or hashish or some other substance the night before? Bowen had been to many of the same places in the world as he had, and Randolph well knew from his own experience how hashish could influence and enhance the process of trance and spirit communication. It was entirely possible he had been made to ingest some noxious plant or fungus. But what would be the purpose of such a ruse? Bowen was not seeking celebrity, not desirous of impressing a stranger to no end. And what of the runaway slaves?

That seemed the safest way to begin his interrogation of Bowen.

"Dr. Bowen, I understand that you may be a stationmaster?" he asked, using the code word for someone who housed and fed slaves before moving them to the border. To Randolph's way of thinking, the Church of Starry Wisdom was a "station" in the Underground Railroad.

Bowen stopped his pacing and pontificating, and looked down at his guest, thinking awhile before responding.

"You know that is a serious accusation, Dr. Randolph."

"Of course, I do."

"You know my sympathies are with the abolitionists?"

"You have made that plain in the short time we have been acquainted."

"And you know that the Fugitive Slave Act has made it dangerous for us in New England to harbor runaway slaves, no matter how we may be sympathetic to their plight?"

Randolph nodded, and added "I also know that Rhode Island was a slave state to begin with, one of the most active in all the colonies. Even after the Revolution, your state was prominent in the trade. So many tens of thousands of slaves passed through Newport on their way to plantations all over the country. Thus, the sentiments of Rhode Islanders is problematic. You risk imprisonment and fines, Dr. Bowen, if in truth you are a stationmaster and this church is a station on the railroad."

Bowen was silent a moment as he lit a pipe. Randolph briefly wondered what manner of tobacco he had filled it with, but put the thought out of his mind as Bowen began to reveal more of the truth about the Church of Starry Wisdom.

"We do have a railroad running through the state from the private homes in Ashaway and Hopkinton of fellow abolitionists who act as conductors, to Providence, and from here to different locations in Massachusetts and up through New Hampshire, to the border with Canada. This is true. And this church is a station, as you rightly assumed."

"Then … what happened last night? To the runaways I saw in the ritual room? Where did they go?"

Bowen looked at him sternly.

"The road to Canada is dangerous and peopled with those who betray their neighbors to the Law. Not many make it all the way to freedom."

"No more dangerous, I submit, than the perilous road taken to reach this place from the South."

"True, but imagine the heartbreak—or worse—if one makes it all the way to Providence and then is captured a few miles from the border and sent back? It has happened, as I am sure you are aware."

"But still, people do it all the time, Dr. Bowen, do they not?"

"Yes, but what we offer is an option. Another means of escape. Another country to run to."

"Another … country?"

"Another … plane of existence, so to speak."

"You mean … death?"

Bowen stood back, alarmed.

"No! Not death! We do not *kill* those people. And neither do *They.*"

"I am afraid you will have to explain all of this to me. I have a terrible headache and my eyes are in pain, but I must know what happened last night and especially what happened to your passengers. I feel I may be in the grip of a cult of demon-worshippers and I must needs know the truth before I live many more hours on this accursed planet in ignorance."

"The pain in your eyes is from gazing too long at the Stone. I should have warned you. It will recede quite quickly. By this evening you will feel fine. As for your headache, that tea next to you will cure you of it."

Randolph looked suspiciously at the cup.

Bowen smiled. "It's only a blend of peppermint and chamomile. Two flavors that would normally clash, but in the right proportions they can be quite soothing."

Desperate, Randolph warmed his hands on the hot porcelain cup and then took a hesitant sip. Bowen had been telling the truth. The concoction was soothing, and it also helped to settle his stomach.

"The Haunter in the Dark is what we call the force that powers the Stone. It is only comfortable in the dark, when the sun has gone down."

"Comfortable?"

"An unfortunate term, perhaps. What I mean is that we cannot use the Stone in broad daylight. Something about the way the light interacts with its surface. Like a magnet which incorporates both a positive and a negative pole, it seems that light can also be polarized. Direct sunlight does not permit the Stone to work; but indirect lamplight—or no light at all—enables the Stone to function."

"And what, pray, is its function?"

Bowen shrugged his shoulders in a show of frustration.

"It makes no sense to say it aloud. I shall attempt it, however, in the hope that you will catch my meaning.

"It acts as a way to move matter from one state to another, from one existence to another. It is a mirror, as we have discussed in our correspondence, but not precisely the same as the magic mirrors of John Dee and Edward Kelly. The image you see in a normal mirror is yourself, in reverse. Your right hand now appears as if it is your left. In this mirror—in the Shining Trapezohedron—what you see is beyond imagining. It is an image but not the two dimensional image of the ordinary mirror. It is a multi-dimensional image, precisely the same as you are but … in a different arrangement, so to speak. And that image is not precisely what we think of as an image. It is whole. It exists independently. It moves and rises and appears on its own, as if moved by unseen winds and malicious waves on a distant star."

"The mirrors of Dee and Kelly were used to communicate with the spirit world, with the realm of angels and demons."

"Indeed."

"And this is not the same?"

"Not at all. It is, perhaps, used by the spirit world to communicate with *us*."

"Then this must be an engine whose controls are beyond our understanding! Communicating with angels and demons already requires tremendous circumspection, training, purity, preparation. How do you approach the Stone with anything less than that? Where is the guide book, the *vade mecum*, the grimoire? This is like no science or art ever discovered by man."

"Agreed. All I have is my notebook with the hieroglyphics and symbols copied from the temple at Esna wherein I discovered the Stone, and years now of practice, of trial and error, of experimentation, along with a small group of devoted colleagues. That is all I have. But it has borne fruit, as you saw last night."

"All I saw was a parade of monstrosities coming out of the Stone, and a desperate file of persecuted human beings going into it! I imagine sitting at the feet of Moloch would have been no different!"

"Dr. Randolph, imagine for a moment how we would appear to a race of Martians. I agree, the appearance of these beings is unsettling and …"

"What did you tell them?"

"Excuse me?"

"What did you tell them, the people you sacrificed to the Stone? For that is what it was, a human sacrifice, if anything I witnessed is to be believed. What did you tell them to make them go willingly and quietly into the Stone?"

"I assure you, they were not sacrificed …"

"Do they live?"

"What?"

"Do they *live*, Dr. Bowen? Are they *alive*? And if so, *where*?"

And that is when Randolph knew that he had been tricked. There was something in the tea, something that robbed him of mobility. He felt his limbs go limp and his head heavy upon his neck. He dropped the teacup which shattered into pieces on the floor. He tried to open his mouth to speak but the effort cost him his consciousness.

CHAPTER FORTY-FIVE

The Rosicrucian Rooms
Boston, Massachusetts

RANDOLPH HAD FLED PROVIDENCE and indeed the North altogether. The so-called "Free States" seemed as dangerous to him, if not more so, than the slave states of the South but for different reasons. In the South, the enemy was clear and the dangers mortal. There was no ambiguity, no trickery or pose. The African man was not human, but a commodity, a kind of machine. African men and women had but one purpose and that was to satisfy their masters. His own mother had been raped by her owner, and he was the unfortunate product of that crime, a visible reminder. In the North, the perils were dressed in the masks of polite smiles and supercilious phrases, but the sudden almost imperceptible shift of an eye would reveal the presence of ulterior motives, barely-suppressed hostility, and perhaps imminent capture. While many in the North professed a hatred of slavery, they did not acknowledge a love of the African man except as a symbol of their own generosity. In the North, Randolph still was not human, not an independent identity, but simply an expression in a larger equation that had more to do with white self-satisfaction than his own African humanity. Slavery had poisoned the entire country, one way or another, and the only solution seemed to be to wish it away and to wish himself away in the process.

He remembered the last scene at the Church of Starry Wisdom, just before he left, and Bowen telling him, "But you yourself said that the Negro was destined to extinction in the United States!" as if that had been rationale enough for what he had witnessed that night. All those well-meaning abolitionists with their rheumy eyes and scraggly beards and the spittle flying from their lips as they screamed about equality and dignity, while marching the Africans *out of the country* to Canada or—as in Bowen's case—to some immeasurable Abyss. The force that held them all in thrall was invisible; a set of laws that

were made by men and could be changed by men with the stroke of
a pen, but no one had the courage to do so. And what of the force
that held Bowen in thrall, that invisible power emanating from the
Stone? Was it any different, he wondered? Another set of laws, sent
down upon the Earth by another set of masters?

Asenath Wayland Thurston had arrived just before Randolph
had taken his leave. He had been drugged again, that pleasant-tasting
tea had been designed to render him unconscious, while Bowen
decided what to do with him, if he had seen too much since he had
been allowed to penetrate the mysteries. But Asenath had interceded
for him. What danger could Randolph do to them, for none would
believe what he had seen? And he certainly would not expose their
Station on the Underground Railroad, for that would be to betray
his own people.

Truth be told Bowen had wanted more from Randolph, for
Randolph was an initiate of several mystery schools, including the
Hermetic Brotherhood of Luxor: named for the very region where
the temple at Esna was located and most likely the repository of
important secrets that would illuminate further the nature of the
Shining Trapezohedron. Randolph had access to people and to
organizations, in America and abroad, that Bowen no longer had
except through written correspondence, which was dangerous.

During that last afternoon to evening, Randolph noticed a
familiarity between the elderly Bowen and the younger Asenath, and
understood that their intimacy was related to their ritual practices.
Her husband would not have approved, of course, had he known
and furthermore they had a son, named after her father—Francis
Wayland Thurston—who already was deep within his studies at
Brown. He recognized the calm assurance and power of a woman
who understood the nature of her gender and her sexuality, and of
how it could be marshaled to ceremonial purpose. He knew she
had lain with Bowen in that very church, and that some of the light
he saw emanate from the Stone had been generated through the
same techniques that he himself had discovered in Oriental lodges

in North Africa. For all their suffocating self-involvement, they were adepts and he recognized them as such. They were creating a dynasty of their own, of scholars and occultists, in this northern city with its heritage of religious refugees, slavery, and revolution.

So, after making many promises to keep in contact and to tell no one of what he had seen, and although his first inclination had been to throttle Bowen to within an inch of his life for having drugged him and tricked him, and quite possibly tricked the runaways as well, he decided to leave quietly and without display. Asenath's presence had soothed the atmosphere considerably, and he found himself drawn to her. He felt he could have offered her more of what she was seeking than old Bowen, but knew that was not to be.

Instead, he gathered himself and his bag and left the Church of Starry Wisdom.

But not before having stolen a book from the vestry shelves.

★ ★ ★

Randolph traveled the world and made contact with a wide variety of spiritual teachers and occultists. While he made progress in the study of western forms of Tantra and became famous for insisting that western, European systems of magic were based on an initiated understanding of sexuality—a position that would be adopted decades later by the German Ordo Templi Orientis founded by Theodor Reuss and Karl Kellner, and which would eventually number Aleister Crowley among its members—his fascination with what he had seen and experienced at Bowen's Church of Starry Wisdom stayed with him and inspired his research into magic mirrors, and in ways of "charging" those mirrors to obtain the same results as Bowen's Shining Trapezohedron.

The idea that bodily fluids such as blood and semen could be used as ointments to transfer creative energy and power from human beings to inanimate objects such as talismans, amulets, and even magic mirrors was crass and unsophisticated—the result of a too-literal interpretation of the Tantras—but it came close to mimicking the actual process. However, Randolph was never able to obtain the same results as Bowen did with his Trapezohedron. His attempts while in London to acquire the shewstone of Dr John Dee and Edward Kelley were similarly unsuccessful.

Randolph reportedly committed suicide with a pistol in Toledo, Ohio in 1875: the same year as the founding of the Theosophical Society in New York and the birth of Aleister Crowley in England, and a few weeks before the death of French occultist Eliphas Levi. While there is some doubt that Randolph killed himself, and the death eventually was ruled an accident, there were witnesses that claimed another person was in the room when Randolph died and that he was killed during the commission of an attempted robbery by the assailant. Said assailant was believed to be searching through Randolph's collection of books when he was surprised by the victim in the act.

Randolph left behind a number of unpublished manuscripts and works-in-progress. One of the volumes found among his papers by his widow was a handwritten manuscript taken from the collection of Dr. Enoch Bowen of Providence that eventually—after many detours and misadventures, including a stint in a library of the Third Reich being examined by Julius Evola, and some time in the hands of a cult called Dagon—made its way into the knapsack being held by one Professor Gregory Angell of Columbia, descendant of Professor Emeritus George Gammell Angell of Brown University, and presently being dangled on the concourse of Terminal One in Frankfurt Germany in May of 2015, 140 years later.

CHAPTER FORTY-SIX

Interrogation Room
Frankfurt International Airport

GREGORY ANGELL SAT AT A DESK in a room usually reserved for the examination of potential smugglers and people whose identification documents were obvious forgeries. Angell satisfied both requirements.

Just hours earlier, the woman who had occupied the window seat next to him on the plane from Singapore had been sitting in that same desk having her belongings examined, although he had no knowledge of this, or of her.

His knapsack similarly had been emptied out in front of him, with its cache of money wrapped in underwear, handwritten notes, and a very old manuscript written in an alphabet that was unrecognizable to the German security personnel, but which was the object of their fascination anyway.

All of these objects just sat there, on the desk, without a word of explanation or inquiry. Angell looked at the man and woman—both Americans—standing in front of him on the other side of the desk in the too-bright interrogation room and raised his eyebrows.

"Well?"

"Well what?" answered the woman, who seemed to be in charge. About forty. Short blonde hair. Navy slacks and windbreaker. Sensible shoes. Badge. Her ID said her name was Prudence Wakefield. It sounded phony.

"What's up? What's going on?"

"Professor Angell ..."

"I don't know to whom you're referring. My name is Richard Raleigh."

"Your name is Gregory Angell, a professor of religion at Columbia University ..."

"I am Richard Raleigh, like my passport says, and ..."

"I wouldn't go there, Dr. Angell. Your passport is an obvious forgery."

"Well, the quality of work at the State Department is not up to its usual excellence, I admit, but …"

"There's really no use to argue. We're not here to interrogate you, just to hold you for the time being."

"Why? What have I done?"

"Here? In Germany? Nothing, as far as we know. Except assaulting that guy outside the bookstore. Ouch."

"He pressing charges?"

"Nah. Not gonna happen."

"Then …"

"But you're wanted by some very powerful people in Washington. We don't know much more than that, however. Hence, the wait."

"Wait for what?"

"For whom."

"Okay, for whom, then?"

"You'll find out soon enough. It's not like you have a plane to catch, right? There are no reservations made in … well … any of your names."

"That's offensive."

"You're telling me."

"How do you know Maxwell Prime?"

Whoa.

"Who?"

"The man you struck with your backpack just now."

"It's a knapsack, not a backpack. I'm not twelve."

"Your knapsack, then."

"I don't know what you're talking about."

"We have it on videotape, Dr. Angell. This is Germany. There are CCTV cameras everywhere."

"Surprise, surprise. And I'm not Dr. Angell."

"So, what's your beef with that guy?"

"I never met him until today." Which was true.

"So why did you hit him?"

"It was an accident. I must have hit him when I turned around. I'm clumsy that way."

"We have the tape."

"Okay. You're right. He was coming on to me."

"Seriously?"

"Well, he was stalking me, wasn't he? First the restroom … I mean, come on."

That was Maxwell Prime? *What the hell was* he *doing here? Who was he working for?*

"This is getting nowhere. Do you want some coffee? I want some coffee. How do you take your coffee, Dr. Angell?"

"In a Starbucks. I'll pick some up for you if you like. And I'm not Dr. Angell."

"Starbucks? In Germany? There are better options."

"Surprise me."

She nodded to the large man next to her who so far had not uttered a word. He sighed, and left the room.

Prudence was alone with Angell. She sat in the chair opposite him and leaned across the table, shielding her face on either side with her hands, letting her hair fall in such a way as to create a kind of curtain.

"We're being recorded," she said, in a low voice but with a smile.

"I figured as much," he whispered back.

"They want you *and* the Book, you know that, right?"

Uh oh.

"What do you mean?"

"The Book is good but it's not as useful without you. They need both."

Angell rested against the plastic seat back and exhaled.

"*We* can take the Book, and leave you behind."

"Or vice versa?"

She shook her head.

"We want the Book. We kinda need it."

"Who's 'we,' Kimo Sabe?"

She shook her head again.

"We have the *magica materia maxima* thing worked out on our end. They don't."

What the holy fuck …? What did that mean?

"You're expendable to us. We don't need you at all. But they do. Both. They need both. You *and* the Book."

Another player. This had to be another player. Where was that coffee?

"So, if you don't need me then why are we having this conversation? Just take the Book and run."

"Can't do that. They don't know who I'm working for. I have to play nice in front of the others. They would never permit me to walk out of here with the Book."

"So …"

"So I need your cooperation. You need to help me help you escape. Your freedom for the Book."

"How do I know you'll keep your end of the bargain?"

"You don't. But I need to get out of here, and so do you. Time is running out. You know that, right? I can see it in your notes."

"What do you mean?"

"The timetable. You have almost figured it out. Isn't that why you came here, to Frankfurt?"

Angell stared blankly at the woman.

"The *twins*? At the *cathedral*?"

"I'm sorry … I don't know what you're talking about."

"Well, there's no time to explain now. If we wait too long you'll wind up in US custody and the Book, too. They're coming for you, you know. That little trick with your friend in New York has them all rattled."

"That was the intention. I had to let them know …"

"So you *do* know what I'm talking about."

"No! I mean, I know about half of it. Enough to realize that we have to act fast if we want to stop …"

"Stop what?"

"How do I even know I should be talking to you?"

"Look at it this way. Who else do you know who would understand a single word?"

"You have a point."

"You know that they will try again. What they did the last time. And the time before that. They're running out of options. The Gate will close and they will have lost any hope of getting it open again in the near future. That much you do know. And if they fail, well … the penalties are rather burdensome. So they will try harder now."

"They tried damned hard the last time."

"Listen. We don't have any more time. My colleague will be back with the coffee any minute. And your people are arriving on the next flight from DC which should land in about an hour or so. So … are you in or out? Last chance."

"If I don't agree?"

"I'll simply find a way to take the Book and leave you here. You'll either wind up with your friends back in DC, or with the Adversary. The ones you met in Nepal. The ones they rolled up in Florida."

"Florida?"

"Wow. You don't know, do you? You really have been off the grid."

"What about Florida?"

"I'll tell you later. In, or out?"

She handed him his passport. He took it and slipped it into his jacket pocket.

"I thought you said it was an obvious forgery?"

"I lied."

★ ★ ★

The security officers at Frankfurt International Airport carry a variant of the Heckler & Koch MP5 submachine gun. The two American intelligence officers, however, were unarmed. The large American man—whose name he never learned—brought coffee, and then told them he had orders to go to another part of the terminal to wait for Aubrey to show up and to brief him on the situation.

So, Aubrey is coming, thought Angell to himself. He had wanted to warn Aubrey, not fly home with him and risk going to some kind of secret prison. He had no illusions about Aubrey or his people. They had sent him into harm's way, and then sent trackers to find him and snatch him when he didn't play ball. He was expendable to them. Hell, he was expendable to everybody. But if Dagon was neutralized there was a good chance he would be allowed to live out his life in peace in some other country. Or, if not peace, then with a clear conscience that he had thwarted what they were trying to do. He had to roll the dice.

He caught the woman's eye and nodded.

After a few sips of coffee, there was a knock at the door and two German airport security guards—*Polizei*—were waiting outside. They were wearing Kevlar vests and carrying the HK MP5s.

Angell was not in handcuffs or otherwise restrained. He was to be detained and questioned, but not arrested. Those were Aubrey's orders, but his plane had not landed yet.

It was decided to take Angell to a more secure location in another area of the airport to await Aubrey's arrival from DC. He got the impression that something was up, some new wrinkle that made them change the venue. They got up, and shuffled out of the interrogation room.

What was really making him crazy was the fact that it was Maxwell Prime who had been trying to snatch him from the restroom, and that Prudence Wakefield—if that really was her name—was working for someone else, not the American intelligence services (or not *only* the American intelligence services). There were suddenly too many players and he was getting a headache trying to figure it all out.

Angell had been given his knapsack to carry, minus the Book. His money was still in the knapsack, replaced there after they had counted it. They could find no reason to confiscate the cash since he had not brought it out of the United States or violated any US or

European or Singaporean laws. His notes were likewise intact. They knew that Aubrey would want to discuss those with him at length.

Scary Lady Prudence had the Book. He didn't know what she was planning, but she had to know he was not going to leave the airport without the *Necronomicon*.

As if reading his mind—and why not?—she shifted the Book from the arm closest to him to the one on the other side of her body.

Suddenly she stopped in midstride and held her hand to her ear. She had an earpiece with which she was in contact with the rest of her team in the airport.

"Say again?"

Everyone stopped and waited for her instructions.

She turned, as if to go back the way they had come.

"Are you certain?" She said into her wrist mic.

She lifted her head and looked at the three man escort, and twirled her hand in the air as if to say "we're going back."

It was a narrow corridor. There was a single guard in front of them now, the one who had been taking up the rear. He turned to lead the way back.

At that moment the corridor in front of them filled with smoke. The guard in front fell back and tried to cover his face. Angell and Prudence did the same, turning to run back in the other direction. The guard behind them shouted something in German that Angell did not understand. Prudence yelled back, and the guard nodded, rushing past them to help his colleague who seemed to have inhaled something noxious.

Prudence grabbed Angell by the arm and propelled him down the corridor.

"This way, and quickly."

"What did you tell the guard?"

"That we were going back to the interrogation room and lock the door."

"Are we?"

"Hell, no."

"Where did the smoke come from?"

"A friend. Stop asking questions and haul ass!"

★ ★ ★

Airport workers have their own entrance and their own means of getting to the areas on the other side of Immigration and Customs. They have to pass through security checkpoints as well, but once inside they are able to move between the areas a little more freely. Obviously, they don't have to show their passports and get visas.

That was the channel Prudence was using to get out of the airport without going through the formalities. Angell was glad for the chance to move, but wary of having his fortunes tied so tightly to this complete stranger. As soon as he was able, he would cut her loose and find himself a way to get out of the country on his own.

But not without the Book, which she was carrying in a tight embrace.

They were suddenly outside, in the fresh air. It was the middle of the night, but it felt refreshing to be away from the processed air of the terminal.

"Where are we going?"

"To the cathedral."

"Why the cathedral?"

"To see the twins, of course," she winked.

★ ★ ★

She led the way, and in moments she was getting into a parked car. Angell just stood there and looked at her, wondering what he was getting himself into.

"Are you coming or not?"

He hesitated only a moment before getting in and slamming the passenger side door after him.

CHAPTER FORTY-SEVEN

Monroe's Office
Fort Meade, Maryland

MONROE WAS NERVOUS. He hadn't heard back from Aubrey. The news story out of New York that a university professor, Gregory Angell, had disappeared somewhere in Asia and was believed to be the victim of foul play, had gobsmacked him. It was Steven Hine who was the source of the story, and he was interviewed by the local NBC affiliate as saying that he had received word of Angell's surfacing in Singapore only to disappear again. There were hints of human trafficking, and a possible terrorist connection.

There was nothing there that pointed back to Monroe or Aubrey, but the implication was clear. If anything happened to Angell, Hine would see to it that reporters knew where to look. He had to hand it to Hine: he had thought carefully about all of this and was sending him a clear message.

Of course, the news media would start looking into Angell's background in earnest anyway. It was only a matter of time before someone talked to the landlords at Angell's apartment in Red Hook, or to other faculty at Columbia and discovered that Angell had spent time embedded with US forces in Afghanistan and Iraq. They would probably come up with some kind of story that Angell had fallen in with a terror group—Al Qaeda, maybe, or ISIL—and that the former university professor had now gone the way of Anwar al-Awlaki: the American born Yemeni terror leader. That would piss of Hine no end, probably, and inspire him to start causing trouble for Monroe.

Sylvia had watched the news report with Monroe and was surprised. She had not been involved in the original mission to send Angell to look for the *Necronomicon* in Iraq although she had heard a summary of the project when she got involved in the Dagon affair along with Harry and Simon. Now she was able to flesh out the story a little more, with some clarification from Monroe.

"There's one unintended consequence of this story, of course," he added, when he had answered her questions about how Angell had been recruited and why. "Now Dagon has more information about Angell's background than they had before. They have Hine's name and university affiliation, too, as well as Angell's old apartment in Red Hook. I think Angell's friend might have done more harm than good, in the final analysis."

"But, Dwight, it was you who started this whole thing. I understand the reasons. I understand that finding the Book—or at least making sure Dagon didn't get it—was very important, and that Angell was the best person for the job. But there were aspects of this you didn't tell him. He was operating blind."

"There were things he couldn't be told. It was need-to-know. And, anyway, the premise was so strange, even for a religion professor, that I doubt he would have believed any of it and just written us off as crazy or deluded."

"This was all done through Aubrey?"

Monroe nodded. "He recruited him in Brooklyn, a year ago now. A little more, maybe."

"So you've never met?"

He shook his head. "No. Everything went through Aubrey."

"Do you trust him?"

Monroe was shocked. No one had ever asked him that before.

"Aubrey? Of course I trust him! I've known him for decades. We've worked together under some very tough circumstances. In the field and off."

"What I mean is do you trust him to handle Angell the right way? I know you're as dedicated and committed as they come, and so is Aubrey, I'm sure. But don't you worry that he might bend a little, give Angell some breathing room to figure things out for himself, maybe ... I don't know ... give him some slack. Let him ride this out a little. Find a place to hide? Wait until it blows over?"

Monroe's expression was hard to read. He looked at Sylvia, and then away, towards the safe where he kept the Lovecraft Codex.

"Gregory Angell is the missing link to all of this. For so many years I've been trying to piece together, to understand, the background story. To this. To all of this." He waved his hands over the office but clearly intended everything one could see in any direction. "We live and work in this country, in this world, day by day. We have a certain set of assumptions we live by, stories we tell ourselves about who we are and why we do what we do. We never sit down and question any of that because it would be fatal. We would lose our edge. This is not a profession where self-doubt and second-guessing is valued, although that is probably what we all need the most."

"I don't understand."

"It's like this. We don't have a *context* for anything we do. We don't remember our history, much less understand it. We don't understand science, or math. We don't appreciate art, or literature. We are not aware of our own psychological states, the underlying structures in our brains that determine so much of who we are and why we react the way we do. We are expected to do a job, to follow orders, obey the law, wake up, eat breakfast, go to work. Come home. And eventually die. And we don't know why. We don't know where our DNA comes from. We don't know the meaning of our gods, our religions. Why we slaughter each other on our way to our respective heavens. Something is fundamentally wrong here. A mistake was made, Sylvia. Long, long ago. Before any of our civilizations sprang up in Mesopotamia or Turkey or Asia or Africa."

He stopped, running out of breath. Sylvia was shocked at his passion and the utter despair in his voice.

"Jesus, Dwight …"

"No, no. It's not … look, I'm an old man. I remember where I was when Kennedy was killed. And now here I am, more than fifty years later. And nothing has changed. Beneath all of the data, all of the timelines and stories of wars and presidents and kings, the genocides and homicides and fratricides, there are forces at work and they operate according to principles and agendas we can only guess at. Fifty years ago, Kennedy was assassinated and today there are still children starving around the world, children being trafficked for sex and slavery, people dying of thirst because there is no water or dying of disease because their drinking water is poisonous.

"There is an evil in this world. Something ancient and eternal. Something beyond our understanding. Lovecraft knew that, maybe better than any of us for he predicted the world we have now. He was a racist bastard, fussy and elitist, but that didn't stop him from piercing the veil and seeing the truth. We make fun of him because he saw space monsters in a world where we had real evil: Nazis and the Soviets and mass murder on an epic scale. We thought he was looking in the wrong place. But he wasn't. He saw the monsters, alright. The ones who were blind were us."

He stopped to take another breath. Sylvia just looked at the floor and remained silent.

"And Gregory Angell has the Book, the centerpiece of this mystery, and for some reason he contains within himself—his own genes, his blood, his DNA, whatever—some key to unlock the rest of it. At least, Dagon thinks so. If we let them have him, we are giving up on ourselves. We might as well throw in the towel, because it means we have stopped believing in anything, in anything at all."

Simon's Apartment
Crofton, Maryland

★ ★ ★

Monroe and Sylvia were let into the apartment building by Simon's buzzer. When they entered the apartment they could hear Harry and Simon still arguing the way they had been when Sylvia left them, over two hours ago.

★ ★ ★

"I've got it. The Tunnels of Calabi-Yau. They're not some kind of occult thing. They refer to modern physics." It was Simon, walking into the living room with a sheaf of printout.

"Physics? Seriously?"

"Calabi and Yau are the names of the two scientists who discovered it, Eugenio Calabi and Shing-Tung Yau."

"Discovered what?"

"Extra dimensions of space-time. A six-dimensional Calabi-Yau manifold is what gives us mirror symmetry."

"Mirror symmetry …"

"It's actually quite cool. Mind-blowing, if you want to know."

"So … mirror symmetry means …?"

"It's like this. Imagine that there are two objects that have the same properties, are identical in every respect, *except* appearance. In other words, you look into a mirror and you see yourself, except it doesn't look like you at all. It freaks you out."

"Oh, *that's* clear."

"No, really. It's … it's like the math is the same … I mean, the same result … but one side of the equation looks completely different from the other side. The mirror is what is between, like the equals sign."

"Except it's not, right?"

"Okay, look at it this way. It has to do with quantum mechanics and string theory. In quantum mechanics, you have something called duality. You can have two different classical models, different shapes, different … ah … topologies, but they share an equivalence at the quantum level. You see that with string theory. You have a model and then its mirror. Two seemingly different models but at the quantum level they become more and more equivalent so that a complicated formula describing the first model becomes a less complex formula in the mirror."

"I have no friggin' idea what you're on about. Break it down for us, man. How does any of this even apply to our problem?"

"Well, it wasn't me who brought this up, right? It was the mysterious sender of that cryptic statement about the Tunnels of Calabi-Yau. I'm just trying to explain the context."

"So what are the Tunnels?"

"They're what connect the original model with its mirror. The equivalence formula."

"Nope. Still in the dark."

"Okay, let's try this. You know that Dagon uses its own calendar and its own ... topology, right?"

"That word again."

"For a reason. The topology of Dagon shifts constantly. It's never the same twice. The hot points—the *points chauds* of the message—keep moving, as if the latitude and longitude on the planet is in flux. The time and space formula they use has nothing to do with the modern world. It's a legacy formula but we know that, no matter what, the rituals take place on this planet. Just not the way we're used to. Seas become mountains, mountains become seas, and like that. Right?"

"Following you so far."

"Okay, good. The key to understanding Dagon's system is mirror symmetry. That guy that Bertiaux was talking about—P. B. Randolph—he was always on about magic mirrors that would let him see other worlds, other planets, angels, demons, and all of that. Right?"

"Okay..."

"And then there was that short story by Lovecraft about a stone, the Shining Trapezohedron, right?"

"Aha."

"See? They are all talking about the same thing. In fact, there really *is* a Shining Trapezohedron except it's called an Amplituhedron."

"Getting lost again ..."

"An Amplituhedron is something that was recently discovered, about two years ago. It's described as a 'jewel-shaped geometric object' that challenges what we believe about space and time as being fundamental to reality. It's really a challenge to quantum theory as well, a way of saying that geometry itself could be used to describe the real world."

"You said 'a jewel-shaped object'?"

"Yes. Just like the Lovecraft story, right? About the Shining Trapezohedron. But this is an Amplituhedron and it is, well, a multi-faceted jewel just like the Shining Trapezohedron."

"So Lovecraft was talking about a real thing?"

"Well, 'real' in a mathematical sense, maybe. It might have been his way of describing something in plain English that you would need a whole hell of a lot of math to begin to understand. I don't understand most of it, myself."

"That's refreshing. *Anything* that humanizes you …"

"If you look at the rest of that message, it talks about the *Poteau mitan*, and discs and spheres … I think the message becomes a little clearer. In the Lovecraft story, ritual magic is a major component of the plot. The Shining Trapezohedron is a gateway to another world. Randolph's magic mirrors were, too. In vodoun, the spirits from Africa rise up the central pole—the Poteau mitan—to arrive on this side of the planet, possessing the devotees. Mirrors. The hounfort or the peristyle as the mirror of Africa, or as the mirror of the spiritual realm represented by Africa. A meeting place between two worlds. The Poteau mitan is the Tunnel between the two formulas. Like the Tunnels of Set, which are on the opposite side—the mirror side—of the Kabalistic Tree of Life."

"So, the demonic forces represented by the Tunnels of Set …"

"Are mirror images of ourselves. Hideous, maybe. Frightening in appearance. But nevertheless our twins."

★ ★ ★

Monroe and Sylvia just listened. They were lost from the first mention of the Calabi-Yau manifold and had to concentrate hard just to keep up. It was Monroe who finally broke in with more direct questions.

"What does all this have to do with the message about the Tunnels of Calabi-Yau?"

"The message is about quantum mechanics. It's about string theory and mirror symmetry, which are almost impossible for non-specialists to understand, but whoever wrote that message compared these concepts to vodoun. The Poteau mitan, the *points chauds*. These are all vodoun. The author of the message was telling us that Dagon is using some very sophisticated physics. Remember the Pinecastle ritual? The little girls trained to look into magic mirrors?"

"Unfortunately, yes."

"And we have those mirrors, right?"

"We have one being analyzed by the FBI at Quantico, and another by a lab at MIT. So far, all we know is that they are polished obsidian. Volcanic glass. Except for one mirror which seems to have been made of steel. That one seems to be no more sophisticated than a garbage can lid. But it had a gemstone fixed in the middle."

"I don't remember that. What gemstone?"

"Ah, it was red. A garnet, I believe."

"That's interesting. And possibly relevant."

"Why is that?"

"The crystal structure of a garnet is … wait for it … a trapezohedron."

"Seriously?"

"I kid you not. The 'crystal habit'—in other words the appearance—of quartz crystals is generally hexagonal, diamond crystals are octagonal, and analcime—a version of garnet—and often garnet itself is a trapezohedron. You know there are a lot of New Age stores that sell crystals for various purposes. There's one in Boston called Seven Stars. It's quite well-known. They have a large collection of the things. They're believed to have certain properties depending on type of crystal, color, size, and so forth.

"For instance, there is a long and venerable tradition concerning magic mirrors. You will even find them in the grimoires. And the English magician and mathematician John Dee used similar devices—

he called them shewstones—as did Joseph Smith, who started the Latter-Day Saints. Hey, John Dee's shewstone was polished obsidian! Anyway, the magic mirror is a pretty common technique for seeing the unseen. For penetrating other worlds. Or, you know, so they say."

"So what does that tell us that we didn't already know?"

"The way the mirrors are being used. Most people who study this sort of thing figure it's like crystal gazing, that old standby of the fake fortune teller in the carnival booth. Gazing into a crystal and gazing into a magic mirror are related ideas. The real magic mirror is a two-way street. You look into it, it looks into you."

"So the big metal mirror with the garnet …"

"Is Dagon's interpretation of the Shining Trapezohedron from the Lovecraft story."

"Why didn't they just use a big slab of garnet?"

"Because such a thing doesn't exist. It's hard to find a garnet that's larger than a few inches, max. There have been one or two that were larger, but they fetch huge prices at auction. Anyway, from that weird message we received about the Calabi-Yau tunnels, I think that Dagon has found a way around the problem. They are applying modern theories of quantum mechanics, string theory, and mirror symmetry to their requirement for a way to set up a bi-directional 'magic mirror.' They have found a way to apply quantum mechanics to magic. And what did Arthur C. Clarke say?"

"*Any sufficiently advanced technology is indistinguishable from magic,*" they all replied, in unison.

"There you go. Anyone hungry?"

CHAPTER FORTY-EIGHT

St Bartholomew's Cathedral
Frankfurt am Main, Germany

THE SPIRAL STAIRCASE LEADING UP the steeple was like something out of a horror film, or at least it seemed that way to Angell. He was thankful he got some sleep on the plane from Singapore, otherwise he would not have been in shape to make the climb. It was after midnight Frankfurt time, and he had been awake for hours. He was hungry, too, but there was no time to waste.

For some reason, one he didn't know.

Prudence drove to the cathedral and parked as close as she could. The place was closed, but for reasons he did not understand she had access.

On the short drive there from the airport she explained about the twins.

"Back in the 1990s, a coffin was found underneath part of the cathedral that contained the body of a young girl and the cremated remains of another child. Two children in a single grave. The girl was covered in jewels and finery. The other body, gender undetermined, was dressed in Nordic attire. From what archaeologists have been able to determine, they were of the same age and there is a good chance the cremated child was a girl as well, if the clothing is any indication."

"Why is this discovery relevant to the Dagon calculations?"

"The cathedral was built over the grave. In fact, the cathedral was aligned perfectly with the site. You know that churches were often built over the relics of saints?"

"Of course."

"But these bodies were buried sometime in the Merovingian period, or before. It was a time when Christianity and paganism were coexisting, side by side. Perhaps the two children were twins, one being raised as a pagan and the other as a Christian? To cover their bets? Perhaps the location of the cathedral was somehow connected to that fact?"

"The Merovingian period? Seriously?"

She smiled.

"I know what you're thinking. *The DaVinci Code*, right?"

"Well, I was thinking more of *Holy Blood, Holy Grail*, but yes, you're right."

"There's a lot of resonance between the stories of the Merovingian kings, the spread of religion throughout Europe and the Americas, sacrificial rites, and all of that. Dagon is steeped in it."

"I thought they were mainly Middle Eastern pagan types?"

"Don't let their name fool you. They belong to an ancient tradition, older than Sumer, older than Egypt. And more … global than either of those."

"You sound like you admire them."

"They are … formidable, I guess you could say. Deeply committed to their cause."

"I saw an example of that commitment in a mountain cave in Nepal."

She was silent at that, and concentrated instead on finding a parking space close to the cathedral.

"Let's go," she said, finally, and let them into the small museum attached to the church.

★ ★ ★

"I still don't know why we are here."

"You will, once we get to the top."

"The top?"

"The steeple. You can see all of Frankfurt from up there."

"Nice, but … I'm kinda being hunted by cultists and, like, secret agents?"

"No difference between the two, really."

They passed through the darkened museum which housed a lot of religious artifacts, such as vestments, chalices, and ciboria.

Charlemagne had once held a council on that very spot. The dim lighting was a little spooky and unsettling, especially in the middle of the night. The silence was palpable, as if the whole building was holding its breath.

They entered a small courtyard. She led the way to an entrance to the cathedral proper, with spiral staircase that reached up into the steeple at the top of the building.

"Why do you say there's no difference between a spy and a cultist?"

"Both have secret names, secret identities, traffic in secret power, believe they know the truth about the world through its secrets and mysteries. They have passwords and initiations …"

"Spies don't have initiations."

"Modern day versions. Polygraph examinations, for instance. Physical fitness training, surveillance techniques, how to withstand interrogations, and all those other things they teach you at The Farm."

"You seem to know a lot about it."

"I've been around."

They went around and around on the staircase. It was an exhausting ascent. Eventually they came to a landing at the top. It had been a narrow climb of more than three hundred steps to the top of the 95 meter high edifice. Through the mesh-covered windows on the way up and over the metal fencing at the top Angell could look out and see the lights of the city. Whether it was the sight or the climb itself that was breathtaking, Angell could feel the strain of the past twenty-four hours in his chest.

"Quite an expedition."

"Beautiful, though, isn't it?"

"Still don't know why I am here."

"Look out in that direction." She pointed to a distant cluster of buildings to the northwest of where they were standing. He could hardly make them out in the dark and with the towers of the city's business district in the way.

"That's the university. It was named after Goethe in 1932, but it used to be known as the 'citizens' university when it was founded in 1914."

Angell thought about that for a second.

"So, it was founded the same year as the outbreak of World War One, and then renamed in honor of Goethe just before Hitler came to power."

She gave him a wry look.

"There is virtually nothing in modern Germany that you can't bracket with the war years. You're bound to see connections that seem meaningful to you, but which really aren't to the rest of us."

"Wait a minute. You're German?"

"I was born in this city. My father was American, but my mother was German. She was the granddaughter of one of the scientists who worked at the university. You may have heard of him. Otmar Freiherr von Verschuer." She pronounced the name with pride and in a fluid German accent.

Angell shook his head. "No. Sorry. Never heard of him."

She sniffed. "No worries. You probably heard of his most promising student, though. Josef Mengele?"

"Mengele? *The* Josef Mengele? The Angel of Death at Auschwitz?"

"The one who specialized in twins research. Yes. That research began here, in this city, at that university, with my great-grandfather the Baron von Verschuer. He was a prominent eugenicist before and during the war. After the war, though, he got religion and began writing about applying Christian ethics to the practice of genetics."

Angell was stunned. This was too much to take in all at once. The guy on the plane. Maxwell Prime at the airport. And now this. What the hell was going on?

"That was after he got rid of the most incriminating documentation, of course, which included the reports that Mengele was sending him on a regular basis. From Auschwitz."

"Jesus."

"I'm sure he thought so. He died, my great-grandfather, in a car accident before I was born. We never spoke about him, never acknowledged our relationship to him. Even though he was denazified after the war and was never sent to prison, we were still a little afraid of the notoriety. And then, of course, Mengele turned up dead in Brazil ten years later and that threatened to open the old wounds again. That was in 1979."

Her voice became softer, and she gazed out over the city without really seeing it, or perhaps seeing it in a different time, with different eyes.

"The documents, the research work. All the papers from the Kaiser Wilhelm Institute of Anthropology, Human Heredity and Genetics, passed to me when my mother died a few years ago. I never knew she had them. They were in boxes marked KWiFA, the abbreviation for the institute during the Nazi era. And it's all there. Mengele's notes on his twin research. It's in those boxes. All of it."

She turned to face him, still holding the *Necronomicon* tight against her chest.

"And we are standing over the site where the most famous twins of Frankfurt were buried about 730 AD, at the same time and probably the same year that Charles Martel defeated the Muslim armies of the Umayyad Caliphate at the Battle of Tours. You see, our people tell us the twins were sacrifices made to defeat the invaders.

"Two small children, four years old, just like Mengele's favorite subjects. One covered in jewels, the other in bearskins. Different in costume, but identical in essence. The relics on which this church was built. The power in those two little bodies, reaching out over the centuries. Informing this whole place. Inspiring the work of Mengele and von Verschuer. The ambitious attempt to understand this whole thing about twins. About genetics. About mirrors. And symmetry. The key to understanding reality.

"The key to opening the Gate."

"Oh, my God. You're Dagon!"

CHAPTER FORTY-NINE

Simon's Apartment
Crofton, Maryland

MONROE SAT AT THE DINING TABLE in Simon's apartment, surrounded by the usual suspects: Harry, Sylvia and Simon himself. He was secretly grateful. The past few months Monroe's meals had been mostly whatever he managed to scrounge on his way home from the office. Aubrey was missing because of Angell in Europe, but otherwise it was the same group that had solved the Pinecastle case last November.

Simon had been busy with a beef goulash, made according to strict Hungarian guidelines. The paprika was imported from Hungary, and no potatoes or tomatoes were involved. Simon used cuts of beef shank that were heavy in collagen, and cooked the dish in a large Dutch oven rather than the traditional *bogrács* or cauldron: his only nod to modernity, because he had no open-air fire to hang the cauldron over.

To accompany the goulash, he had selected an Egri Bikaver, or "Bull's Blood" wine, also imported from Hungary.

"Did you know that the name 'bull's blood' for this wine came from Suleiman the Magnificent, who laid siege to Eger in the sixteenth century? He claimed that the Hungarians added blood to the wine which explained their ability to resist the siege," he explained—somewhat pedantically—to Monroe as he poured the thick red wine into an old-fashioned cut crystal goblet with gold trim.

Monroe raised his glass and silently toasted Simon, who returned the salute.

"The goulash smells amazing," he said.

"It's the paprika. Normally you wouldn't get much of an aroma from grocery store paprika, but this is *rózsa* grade. I have Aubrey to thank for it, actually. He has the most amazing contacts in the former Iron Curtain countries."

Monroe smiled. "That he does."

Simon ladled goulash into some china plates that looked like they had been stolen from some old Slovak lady's estate and passed them around. Harry was starving, and Sylvia could not resist the aroma.

"I am still trying to nail down the Dagon macrocosm, though," Simon said to the table at large.

"Macrocosm?"

"Well, their world-view. As you remember, we discovered they use a different calendar than the rest of the world, and a different geographical system as well. Time and space, but from an off-planet perspective where time scales are different, constellations are constructed differently, and even the topography of the Earth is different. Their slogan—'when the stars are aright'—hints at a deeper understanding of how our solar system is arranged than our own. Of course, their mythology states that the Old Ones—their gods, for better or worse—came to the Earth from elsewhere and brought their systems with them. So we are dealing, potentially, with a completely different and virtually incomprehensible system of measurement of time and space and until we know where the Old Ones came from (or where Dagon believes they came from) we are working blind."

Monroe could no longer resist sampling the goulash.

"Oh, there are egg noodles, if you like." Simon passed him a bowl. "Purists would not use starch in this dish at all, but I find noodles useful for soaking up the broth."

"This is amazing," said Sylvia. "It has layers of flavor to it. Just when you think you know how it tastes, it surprises you."

After a few bites, and the second bottle of Hungarian wine, it was Monroe who got them back on track.

"Do you think it is possible that there is more than one Dagon out there?"

Simon set down his fork and looked up.

"That sounds ominous."

"It's a possibility that has come up."

"You mean another group, working in tandem with Dagon?"

Monroe shook his head, and spooned another taste of the goulash before answering.

"No, not in tandem. Maybe working against them."

"An anti-Dagon? I suppose it's possible, but the implications …"

"What do you mean?"

"They would have to know at least as much about them as we do. Probably a lot more. How is that possible? Dagon is pretty much off the grid. If someone else has been tracking them, they are at least as much of a danger to us and to global security as Dagon."

"That's what I was thinking. You would have to contend with two groups operating from the same … what did you call it? macrocosm? … totally outside our frame of reference. Outside any Earthly frame of reference."

"And you believe such a group exists?"

"There's evidence that they have been mopping up Dagon cells on their own, without our involvement. I figure a rival group. And besides, where did that Calabi-Yau message come from, and why was it sent? We haven't been able to trace it, which seems impossible to me."

"Do you believe the maxim that the enemy of my enemy is my friend?"

"Not really, Simon. Sometimes all you get are two enemies. It's like the Middle East. A problem we always seem to make out there is to believe that we can choose sides, and that there are only two: pro-US and anti-US. But the ground keeps shifting, and your friend today is your enemy tomorrow, and you never saw it coming."

"So this new group may present the same challenges," suggested Sylvia.

"Unfortunately, we have to consider the possibility."

"That's all we need. Dealing with Dagon has been tricky enough.

We succeeded last time, but just barely. And if this other group is rolling up Dagon networks we didn't know about ..." Harry was getting paranoid. Or maybe it was the Bull's Blood.

"Yes. There's no telling how much we don't know about all this."

"And your Professor Angell?"

Monroe finished the last of his goulash and took another sip of the wine.

"I'm not sure he would be any help here. We'll know soon enough, though."

Simon ladled more goulash into Monroe's bowl, ignoring his half-hearted protests, then ladled more into his own bowl as well. Harry and Sylvia had already helped themselves.

"I will work on the problem. I can use whatever data you can give me, but if you can't I'll still try to figure out how an anti-Dagon would work and if they use the same system of correspondences. You know that the god Dagon in the ancient Middle East was not really a fish-god as has been depicted?"

"Yes, I gathered that from my own research over the years."

"But Dagon *was* a god of death. There were a lot of blood sacrifices made to Dagon, sacrifices for the dead, and it is believed by archaeologists now that Dagon and Enlil—the Sumerian deity— were versions of the same thing. Enlil's temple in Sumer was called the "mooring rope of heaven and earth," meaning that he was the connection between the Earth and the Stars. That Dagon would be considered cognate with Enlil brings a whole new dimension to the cult. They could see themselves as fulfilling the role described in the ancient stelae and cuneiform texts. And they do that with blood sacrifice."

"So, the question remains ..."

"Yes. If there is an anti-Dagon, how 'anti' are they? Do they also believe they are a channel between the Stars and the Earth? And do they also employ blood sacrifice to facilitate that connection?"

It was Sylvia who said, "I hope you have dessert after all that gloom and doom."

"Yes. A very nice *rigo jancsi*, freshly made, and of course some coffee. Or tea, anyone?"

As everyone cleared the dishes from the table Monroe got a call on his cell. It was Aubrey, calling from Germany.

"We got him," was all he said.

CHAPTER FIFTY

St Bartholomew's Cathedral
Frankfurt

"You know that this church is named after Saint Bartholomew, right? One of the apostles?"

Angell could only nod, dumbly. He was immobilized, and groggy. He had no idea what had just happened, only that someone—a man—was standing in front of him and smirking. The woman—what was her name? Hope? No, Prudence—had left. This guy who looked like her … why did his head hurt so much? Why was he nauseous?

"You know how he died? Bartholomew? How they *said* he died? He was a martyr. They think he died in India, but they also have him dying in Armenia. Or, anyway, what used to be Armenia. The site is in Turkey, now. You know Turkey, right? You were there not long ago? Oh, I'm sorry. Too soon?"

"Fuck you," he managed, with a croak.

"Brilliant. You should write for television. Anyway, as I was saying. Bartholomew. He died having his skin sliced from his body. Did you know that? Some statues and icons show him holding a flensing knife. You know what that is, right? A flensing knife? It's for flaying the skin off a body, usually a dead whale. Except in his case he wasn't a whale and he was still alive when they did it.

"Now that kinda corroborates the whole dying-in-India story, since there are villages in India where they used to do that. I dunno, maybe they still do. They would flay the skin off a living human being in order to insure a good harvest. They'd stick the poor bastard in the middle of a field and remove his skin in strips. Or her skin. I forget. You're a professor of religion. You should know this stuff."

He pulled out an instrument from his black bag. It was a flensing knife. An antique from the whaling days out of New Bedford.

"Now, we chose this location for its … its whaddaya call it … its

380

resonance with the Bartholomew skinned alive story. Oh, you noticed my little toy? Yeah, it's a gem. Ha ha. A gem. It's an inside joke, but you'll get it soon enough. One of our guys, name of Vanek, sourced it for us. He's missing, you know. Probably in the bottom of some hell hole your people built in some third-world puppet-state somewhere. Anyway, where was I? Oh, yeah. Old Saint Bart. We chose this place because, well, it fit with our worldview. What do you call a worldview that includes planets and stars and shit? A cosmic view? A macrocosmic view. Anyway, Saint Bart, Black Bart, and getting skinned alive. It's because—and this you may or may not know—the ancient Mexicans actually worshipped a god who was depicted as wearing human skin. Yeah, weird, right? They worshipped him by killing prisoners or whomever and then flaying their skin from their bodies and offering the skins to the god. His name was Xipe Totec. The "Flayed God" they called him. You see, they did this as an act of *devotion*! With *prayer*! Religion is fucking weird, man! Right? Am I right?"

Angell stared out at him with hollow eyes.

"But this is the thing. It's not the flaying or the flensing or whatever you call it that is the central aspect of this act that concerns us. No. It's how the ancient Mexicans, the Aztecs, performed the ritual. The details. The rubrics, liturgics, whatever. The key is there. It's the same key that is known throughout the world. Like everywhere. But just out of sight of the rubes. And that is *how* they offered the sacrifices to the Flayed God."

He walked back and forth, manic, in front of Angell, waving the flensing knife in front of his face like a hypnotist with a gold watch on a chain.

"They had statues made of the god. Okay, everybody does that. But they had a hole made in the torso of the statue. A big old hole. Drilled sort of in the belly-button region. Dead center. Why? Because into that hole they would insert a gemstone. That gemstone would *activate* the statue. Make it come *alive*. Make it function as a gateway between this world and the world of the gods. Can you dig it, man? A *stone*. A Shining fucking Trapezohedron. To open the *Gate*. They would kill these people, slice off their skin, and make a body suit out of it like that sick fuck in *The Silence of the Lambs*. And the statues would be awash in fresh blood and the stench of the kill, and the skin would be draped over the statue with its shining gemstone in its belly and the gods would rise, move, and appear.

"And who were these gods, you ask? Who *were* they, these bloodthirsty, sick, perverted serial killing scumbags who wanted nothing more than the pain, blood and suffering of their followers, their devoted fans, their fucked-up Facebook friends? The Old Ones, man! The Old Ones! Cthulhu! And Yog Sothoth! And all the rest of that merry, shuffling, shambling band from the stars.

"The stars. Yeah, man. The stars. The stars are aright. You know that, yes? The stars are a-right. They are. They truly are. We are the Aztecs of the modern world, you know. Dagon? We're putting the blood back into baptism. We're putting the Christ back in Christmas, replete with all the nails and the torture and the blood running down his face from the crown of thorns. Merry Christmas little Jenny or Davey. Here's the reason for the season: wholesale fucking slaughter on a scale you wouldn't believe unless you ran the death camps for awhile and saw the potential. The Inquisition! The murder of the Cathars! Of the Knights Fucking Templar! Of the witches! Merry God-Damned Christmas to you, little boys and girls! Are you excited? Can't sleep? Want to see what's waiting for you under the tree?

"But you know what happens before we open those particular presents under the Tree of Knowledge? A psychic transformation in the consciousness of the planet. When the stars are aright the mind starts playing tricks. Dreams. Nightmares. A slight shift in perceptions. We don't know the cause-and-effect relationship, and we don't fuckin' care. It just works. The doors open, the locks fall to the ground. Shit happens.

"And it's happening now. Look around sometime. You'll see it."

★ ★ ★

The Polizei traced the car Prudence used to drive to the cathedral. They fanned out around the area, quietly and without sirens or lights. Aubrey, exhausted from the flight and from long days tracking Dagon, had arrived in Frankfurt less than an hour ago and had started raving when he discovered that Angell was gone and the people he sent to pick him up were gone, too. But they didn't have that much of a head start and once they had traced the car to the cathedral using traffic cams and snitches he had begged the locals to keep the operation as silent as possible because they needed the element of surprise. He did not want to encourage the perpetrators to finish the ritual quickly. He had no idea what would happen to Angell or the Book if they were rushed.

The caretaker was brought in to give access to the police. This he did, unlocking locks and giving them the layout of the place, and the team quickly but quietly moved into the cathedral and spread out around it using flashlights affixed to their weapons. They did not know if Angell was being held in the church proper or in some other area, so they moved swiftly through the nave, the apse, the choir. They checked the museum and saw nothing amiss.

But the sound of metal on concrete made everyone freeze in position. Aubrey stood in the main entrance to the cathedral and looked around, and then up.

He motioned to the team leader, pointing at the steeple.

The leader nodded and motioned to his men. There was a brief, whispered discussion and it was decided to send some of the men up the spiral staircase and to hold the others in reserve. It was tight quarters at the top, not a lot of room to maneuver, and it was possible that there would be casualties from ricochets off the stone walls if someone started shooting.

They would throw in a flashbang grenade and then scramble the rest of the way onto the landing at the top where visitors usually looked out over the city. They were probably there, as there was really nowhere else to go that was accessible to foot traffic after that.

The other members of the team fanned out around the site and set up a perimeter. It was not known how many Dagon members were in the church or the vicinity and they were not taking any chances. Aubrey was confident that the Germans were taking this seriously as he had presented it more as a terrorist organization than anything else. When it came to terrorism, no one in Europe had a sense of humor.

Aubrey would take up the rear and follow the team going up the staircase. At least, that is what he had planned until he learned that there were more than three hundred steps to the top. One of the Germans had a vest camera and he gave Aubrey a video receiver so he could watch the operation unfold from ground level.

The security personnel were quiet, but they had to ascend slowly. They could work with ambient light coming in from the city, so they kept their flashlight use to a minimum. From across the street came the sound of organ music. Aubrey couldn't tell if it was a recording, or if someone was awake at three am playing the organ in an apartment, but he recognized the piece. It was Bach, *Ich ruf zu dir.* "I call to you." He couldn't tell if it was sinister, or somehow oddly appropriate.

The movement of the police in the darkened church; the sound of the organ music soft in the background; it was like a ballet or a performance of some kind and Aubrey felt a little disoriented. Maybe it was the flight from DC. Maybe it was the stress. Maybe Germany did that to people. He didn't know. But he seemed to be watching everything through a scrim, and hearing everything through a thick wall of cotton and silk.

About halfway up, they began to hear voices. He stared at the video screen, but all it was showing thus far was steps and more steps and stone walls.

The organ music stopped.

There was a scream coming from above. Startled, Aubrey held out a hand to stop himself from falling and dropped the video receiver. He thought the scream came from Angell, and that it was too late to save him.

The team rushed up the stairs no longer caring about making noise and threw in the flashbang as soon as they were close enough to the landing. Aubrey heard a lot of yelling in German from the security officers, and he reached down to retrieve the video unit. It was not broken, but the screen appeared scratched. He tried to get a clear look at what was happening and all he saw was a lot of smoke and what appeared to be a body on the floor.

CHAPTER FIFTY-ONE

Upper West Side
Manhattan

As a sniper she was used to waiting patiently for hours, even days, on end.

There were benches on Broadway in islands in the middle of the avenue, and she picked one to sit on. She wore her hair back, covered in a scarf, and had a pair of cheap sunglasses on to hide behind. She knew that the police were still looking for the woman who killed the Butcher of Sinjar, and she had to be careful. But the news program that showed the photo of Angell had the name of his friend, a college professor, and the name of the university. So there she sat, within walking distance of Columbia University.

She had already walked inside the campus, and wandered around between the buildings. She didn't want to attract anyone's notice, so she would divide her time between the campus and Broadway. There was a Middle Eastern café close by, and she was able to get bread and hummus, and some thick hot coffee from time to time. They let her use the restroom, but she only did that maybe once a day.

On the second day, she saw him. She was sure of it. The man called Hine. He would lead her to Angell. And she would learn what had happened to her that day in Nepal.

★ ★ ★

As she stood up from her bench to walk over to him she suddenly froze in place. There, standing across the street and waiting for the light to turn green, was the man from the student dormitory, the one she saw when she made it to the street after the assassination. The man with the gun.

Wasserman.

★ ★ ★

The old detective had seen the same news report she had. The same news report Monroe had seen. This guy Hine was some kind of connection to Angell. And Wasserman was determined to ask him what else he knew. So he phoned him, and made an arrangement to meet at a coffee shop on Broadway, near Columbia.

So far, he hadn't spotted Jamila who was glued to her position in front of the park bench. And Hine wouldn't know either of them by sight anyway. He was walking to the coffee shop to be on time for his appointment with the detective. They were both heading uptown. When their backs were to her, Jamila began to move. She would follow them and wait for an opportunity.

How did these two know each other? How was it possible in a city of seven million that three people could suddenly find themselves on the same street at the same time? Was New York really just a small town after all, where everybody knew everybody else?

Jamila knew that could not be true, but there was something that was bringing the three of them together at the same time.

She picked up her pace.

★ ★ ★

She followed Wasserman and Hine uptown to a busy coffee shop that her guidebook said had appeared in a popular American television show of decades ago. It was small and there were a lot of customers. She would stand out if she went inside so she stayed outside and kept watch.

Wasserman and Hine were deep in conversation for more than an hour. Hine had a lot to talk about, for it seemed Wasserman was mostly listening and not talking except to ask questions.

Finally, they got up from their table and paid their bill. They walked out of the coffee shop, still talking, and Jamila had to decide which one to follow once they split up. Hine would know about Angell, but Wasserman had been the one to see her after the assassination. She should probably steer clear of Wasserman for the time being.

Wasserman headed towards a subway station, but Hine stayed on the street and seemed to be walking back downtown. She decided to follow him, being sure to stay far enough behind so he would not get suspicious.

He slowed down in front of an apartment building and she guessed that is where he lived. She stood across the street from the building to give him enough time to reach his apartment, then she crossed over and looked at the names on the doorbells. She found Hine's name. She knew the address, and now the apartment number.

She would come back later in the evening.

★ ★ ★

As she turned to go further downtown before finding a subway line that would take her back to Queens, she heard a voice speaking a familiar language.

Looking around, she identified the voice as belonging to someone in a yellow bus. She knew that yellow buses were school buses here in America, but this one had wire mesh in the windows. It was stopped at a red light.

She walked closer to the vehicle and heard it again. A small, plaintive voice asking for its mother. In Kurmanji.

The side of the bus was unmarked. No identification at all. But the rear of the bus had writing on it. She tried to sound it out before the light changed to green and the bus disappeared forever.

Children Charity Center of New York. She knew "children" and she knew "center" and of course she was in New York. She did not recognize the word "charity." She would look it up later. But right now she had to find out why a child was in a bus that looked like a prison and why the child was speaking her language.

With a Yezidi accent.

CHAPTER FIFTY-TWO

St. Bartholomew's Cathedral
Frankfurt, Germany

THE BODY ON THE FLOOR WAS UNKNOWN to the Polizei and equally unknown to Aubrey. It was not Angell, so that was a good thing.

As the smoke cleared, Angell was found. He was sitting on a folding chair, strapped to it with duct tape around his wrists and ankles, and with a tourniquet on his left arm. He was groggy, probably from the smoke of the grenade, and was unable to answer any questions at first. He was able to walk, so they unstrapped him from the folding chair and led him slowly down the three hundred plus steps of the cramped staircase.

When they reached the bottom, Aubrey was there to meet them.

"You look like hell," Aubrey told him.

"I see you got my message."

"You've given us a lot of trouble, professor."

"I'm not a professor anymore."

Aubrey nodded to the policemen who were holding him up. They let him go and Aubrey wrapped his arm around Angell's shoulders and walked him slowly out of the cathedral and over to his vehicle.

"We're going to take you home."

Angell pulled away.

"No! You can't do that. Not now."

He tried standing on his own but he was still weak in the knees. Aubrey caught him before he fell to the ground.

"I don't believe we have any plans to prosecute you …"

"It's not that. The operation isn't over yet. What they were doing now, to me, was a preliminary rite. They were collecting … genetic material from me. To use later. Blood and … and skin."

"Skin?"

"You'll find a special knife up there. It looks old. Was supposed to be used to cut the skin off whales. It's a ritual implement."

"Who was … the other guy?"

"See, that's the thing. That's why I can't go back. Not yet. That guy is … was … a twin."

"A twin?"

"Of the woman who picked me up at the airport. The one posing as one of you guys. Prudence, her name was. Prudence Wakefield. She had ID and the local German cops showed her a lot of deference. But she was Dagon. And so was he."

He leaned Angell up against the side of the SUV as he unlocked the door.

"Where is she now?"

"She … she left. She took … she took the Book with her."

"Oh, crap."

They got into the car. Aubrey made sure Angell's seat belt was fastened. He didn't have a driver. At the moment, he didn't know whom he could trust. He watched the Polizei clean up the situation at the cathedral for a few moments, then started the car.

"Crap indeed," said Angell, continuing the conversation. "Her twin was waiting for us up there. In the shadows. When she started talking, I realized she was Dagon and as soon as I blurted that out, I was taken from behind and drugged with something … Hey, how did you find me?"

"Cameras. We saw you leave the airport with a blond woman and get into a car. We were able to trace the car. It took a little while, but I had just landed from DC and started throwing my weight around. The Germans weren't having any, and you can't blame them, but my own people started doing their damned jobs. I have no idea how Dagon infiltrated our crew …"

"Wait. There was another guy. Prime. Maxwell Prime was there. He was there first. He tried to grab me …"

"Yeah, we know. We saw all of that on the CCTV system."

"Did you pick him up?"

"I'm still waiting for an update on that, but we figure he left as soon as he saw … Prudence. As soon as he saw Prudence. He must have figured it was out of his hands by then."

"So Prime works for them?"

"He does now. I don't know how they got him out of where he was being held by us, but they did."

"She mentioned something about Florida."

"Professor, you don't want to know about Florida."

"You're probably right. What I need right now …"

And a moment later Angell was asleep in the passenger side of Aubrey's car. And Aubrey still didn't know the answer to one question.

Who screamed? And how did the twin brother die?

CHAPTER FIFTY-THREE

Simon's Apartment
Crofton, Maryland

As she was helping Simon clear away the dishes from the goulash, everyone in a buoyant mood as they celebrated finding Angell
and maybe getting closer to solving the problem of Dagon, Sylvia's
phone buzzed. She excused herself and went to answer it privately.
She didn't have much of a social life—none of them did, obviously—but she wanted to preserve what there was of it, anyway. She
had been dating, on and off, an analyst over at State and she hoped
he was calling because he was free that weekend. Instead, she saw a
number she didn't recognize.

When she answered it, she heard the voice of Devata, the
administrator in charge of the Florida children.

"I just wanted to let you know. The children have been taken."

"Taken! What do you mean?"

Her voice could be heard in every corner of the apartment.

"Just what I said. People came from the Marshal's Service with a
bus and paperwork. They said they had been authorized to take the
children to a foster care facility in New York City."

"What are you talking about? I never authorized such a thing!
When did they leave?"

"About two hours ago. Maybe a little more."

"Oh, God. Why didn't you call me earlier, when they were *there*?"

"There wasn't any time. We had to get the children ready, and of
course we have the pregnant ones, and the ones in isolation. It was
a madhouse here. And, anyway, they cautioned me not to contact
anyone. They put a man in my office to make sure I didn't make any
calls. I'm calling you right now from my car."

"Jesus, this is outrageous. Do you have contact information for
them?"

"I have their paperwork, the authorization. It came right out of their headquarters here in Virginia."

"Read it to me."

Sylvia sat down on the floor with the phone held closely to her ear as she listened to Devata read out the authorization for the transfer. When she was done, Sylvia thanked her and hung up. She remained sitting on the floor silently and motionless until Harry came over and knelt down next to her.

"What happened? What's wrong?"

"The children. They've been taken."

She looked up at him with dry eyes.

"I hope we made the right decision."

★ ★ ★

Back in New York City, Jamila's contact got a strange request from the Yezidi sniper.

She needed a rifle. Any rifle. But preferably her Dragunov. She had a new mission.

CHAPTER FIFTY-FOUR

Hilton Hotel
Frankfurt Airport

"She said she was the great-granddaughter of some guy called Ottmar something. A university professor during the war years in Frankfurt. He was working with Mengele."

"Josef Mengele? Auschwitz?"

"That one. She claimed that Mengele would send reports to Ottmar something ..."

"Ottmar Freiherr von Verschuer."

"Yes! How did you know?"

"I know stuff..." Aubrey said, pretending to be a little hurt.

"Well, I didn't know the name until she said it. Anyway, she's a relative. Her father was American and her mother was German. Her mother was the link to the Ottmar guy and to Mengele."

"I know Prudence Wakefield. She has been with us for about ten years. I knew about her father and the fact that she was born in Frankfurt, but I didn't know about the Mengele connection. How did we miss that?"

"Anyway, she said she has the Mengele files. The medical files he compiled on his work with twins at Auschwitz. It ties together with the selection of the cathedral, because of something to do with twins buried underneath the church or something. Something to do with the year seven hundred something, Charles Martel, and like that. I don't remember all of it. Just that ... oh, and there is a connection to Saint Bartholomew. The flaying of his flesh ..."

"Yes, there's a very unsettling statue of Bartholomew without his skin. I think in Italy."

"Gross. Anyway ... flaying the flesh, some Aztec god, an Indian ritual for the harvest ... just a lot of stuff thrown at me. The twin told me that Dagon considered itself the new Aztecs, just bringing back that old time religion, if you know what I mean."

"Well, all of that is very helpful. It should enable us to find Prudence Wakefield and recapture the Book. I don't imagine she was able to leave the city yet, not by plane anyway as there aren't any flights at this hour ... but there will be soon."

Aubrey made a number of phone calls with all the data he had on Prudence as well as the new data related to him by Angell. There was the German equivalent of an APB for Prudence's car, but they were sure that was a dead end. Her photo and particulars were sent to every airport, rental car agency, train station in Germany and throughout the Schengen region. They developed photos showing her with red hair and black hair, just in case she changed it overnight. But one thing was certain: she had the Book and she had to give the actual, physical Book to someone connected with Dagon. There was a very good chance she was waiting for her twin brother to show up with the material she believed was taken from Angell. The blood had been taken, and was in a small vial now in police custody. The twin did not have the chance to remove Angell's skin, however.

"Which reminds me. I didn't ask you before. How did the twin wind up dead? And who screamed?"

Angell became quiet and refused to return Aubrey's glance.

"What?"

"You're not going to believe me."

"Try me."

He swallowed.

"The scream? That was me."

"That I believe."

"Fuck you, too, very much."

"Sorry. It's been a long day, and I'm an old man."

"Anyway, I did the screaming. It was because of what I saw."

Silence.

"Saw? Saw what?"

"Something came out from behind the twin. I thought it was Prudence coming back for a second, but couldn't figure out how she got back up there without us seeing her. But it wasn't Prudence.

I don't know what it was. All I saw were what I thought were eyes, but now I'm not so sure."

"Eyes."

"Just eyes. Like little flashlights or LEDs or something. The twin turned when I screamed and saw what I saw and before he could scream he was making these gargling sounds, like he had been poisoned maybe? And then he fell to the floor. At that point, there was a loud explosion and all that smoke …"

"That was us."

"Yeah. Maybe. Anyway, I was out of it. They had drugged me, and I figured I was hallucinating. There was this shuffling noise, and a kind of vibration through the floor and walls. And I blacked out, I guess."

"Probably whatever they gave you. Sodium pentothal is one guess."

"Yeah, probably. Then what killed him? What killed the twin?"

"I have no idea. I know they're doing a tox-scan. We'll probably have an answer in a while."

"Okay, but then how was he poisoned? What was the delivery system? It sure as hell wasn't me. Who did it?"

Aubrey had to think how much to tell Angell, but figured the poor fool deserved the truth.

"We think maybe Dagon has an opponent out there somewhere."

"An opponent?"

"Another cult, another secret society. Like CIA and KGB in the old days. Except we're not too sure if the opponent is on our side, or not. Maybe they're like two mafia organizations fighting over the same turf. Anyway, that is the current theory. If it's true, it might explain what happened in that steeple. Whoever is following Dagon may be one step or two ahead of us."

CHAPTER FIFTY-FIVE

Dubai International Airport
Dubai, United Arab Emirates

THEY WATCHED MOODY GET OFF THE PLANE in Dubai but not out of the airport. He waited around at a small coffee counter and was met by another man, who passed him an envelope without a word.

Moody looked around, did not spot the tail sent by Aubrey, and opened the envelope which contained yet another air ticket and a hundred dollars spending money. When Moody saw the destination on the ticket he almost fainted.

His tail followed him to the Iraqi Airlines ticket counter. It became obvious that Moody was checking in for a flight to Baghdad.

Iraq.

That was all they needed to know. They had their orders. Once Moody had his ticket, he wandered off to see how he would spend his hundred dollars. As he was standing in front of a magazine display he was braced by two burly action officers who took him by the upper arms and spoke softly into his ears. Had there been other onlookers, they would have seen Moody slump, with all the energy draining out of his body and pooling on the floor around his ankles, only to evaporate like smoke.

He was in the custody of a US intelligence service, and he never knew which one. He had never heard of Monroe, and was unaware of the Florida debacle. In fact, Monroe's orders to pick him up had saved him, for Dagon was sending him to Iraq to die.

CHAPTER FIFTY-SIX

Babylon Warwick Hotel
Baghdad, Iraq

THE DARK LORD SAT IN HIS HOTEL ROOM overlooking the Tigris River. The Babylon Warwick in the Karrada district was considered five-star for Iraq, a luxury he insisted upon in what was still a war zone. And even with Dagon's excellent connections with the terror organization ISIL—known as the 'Caliphate,' which he found amusing—there were still suicide bombers abroad in the land and all sorts of possible dangers. As a man with only one arm now, he could not afford to wander around the city and take in the sights.

He had arrived a few days early, as requested by the leadership. Most of that time he spent in his room or in the hotel's restaurants. The rooms are dark and there are very few electrical outlets in the rooms, but that was okay for his purposes. There is a sky lounge with beautiful views, but no alcohol is served in the hotel at all, anywhere, which was an inconvenience but then you paid for the hotel's legendarily tight security. To stay elsewhere was to risk life and, well, limb—and he was running out of those.

There was wifi, of course, but he was loathe to use it. There was no sense in advertising his presence to the intelligence agencies of the world. Of course, as a man with one arm he was noticeable but he was traveling on his fake passport with the fake name that no one would associate with him.

When he checked in, there was a hand-written note waiting for him in the usual code. He was told to wait patiently. A few more individuals had yet to arrive. Once everyone was gathered, there would be transportation provided to the ritual site. Of course, everything depended on the timing of the ritual. The hot point was passing over the Persian Gulf and would soon hover over the city sacred to Dagon and to Dagon's avatar, Enlil.

The Gate would be opened, once and for all.

And the best news of all?

They had the Book! It had been seized early that morning in Frankfurt. The *materia magica* was also in the process of being obtained according to the ancient rites. Everything was coming together, finally.

There was a knock at the door.

He got up from his post looking out the window and stood, waiting. The knock came again. He smiled, and went to the door and opened it.

A young girl, an Arab of about thirteen with dark eyes and long dark hair, stood there with a shy smile. She wore no makeup, but that was okay. No point advertising what she was doing in the hotel even though the staff was well aware. She was nervous, obviously, but they all were: otherwise, what was the point?

He waved her into the room and shut the door behind her. There were two days until the movement of the point over the ancient city.

He had all the time in the world.

CHAPTER FIFTY-SEVEN

Contact in the Desert
Joshua Tree, California

GLORIA MADE HER WAY BACK TO THE UFO conference on the final day of presentations and lectures. It was sunny, hot, and dry as always in the desert. People milled around, holding bottles of water and brochures, or wearing hats with alien-themed buttons on them. There was a vegetarian food stall, a pizza stall, a coffee counter, and little pop-ups selling trinkets like crystals and scarves.

Jean-Paul had disappeared, and the day before she was able to sit down and talk with her new friend, Alexander Ferguson Blair. He was as good as his word. He did some research and discovered that her New York doctor had been murdered shortly after she left the city. That news stunned her, and while she didn't really know the doctor that well she felt overwhelmed by the fact that someone had actually killed him.

Then Blair had made a few calls to friends of his in the UFO community and found out that her doctor had also been involved in a subset of the community that was focused on the whole "missing twin" phenomenon. Blair felt that it was not worth the kind of wild speculation that it seemed to generate, but he couldn't convince Gloria of that.

He walked up to her and they sat down on a bench outside one of the pavilions. He tried to tell her that the missing twin situation was a medical condition without any other, stranger, cause.

"Look, you know why I'm here. You know about my experiences. And my missing kids. How can you claim there is no connection?"

"Because correlation is not causation."

"What does that mean?"

"It means that just because two events seem similar or happened at the same time it doesn't mean the one caused the other. Missing Twin Syndrome is a real thing, but it's not caused by space aliens."

"Weird thing to say around here."

"But it's true, though. What is relevant is that your doctor was evidently studying the UFO aspect. We just don't know why."

"Okay, but that still doesn't help me. It doesn't explain Chromo-Test. You're not going to say that all this weirdness is coincidental, are you? My genetic anomalies. My abduction experiences. *My missing children.*"

"You have a point. Any one of these things taken separately doesn't suggest anything … well, paranormal. But taken together …"

"That's what I'm saying. There's a pattern forming, and I don't know what to do or who to call. That's why I'm thinking to go to Chromo-Test like they asked. Maybe they know more about this than they're telling me."

She stopped and took a deep breath as she held her stomach.

"Are you okay?"

"It's … it's fine. Just the pregnancy. The little creature is sure making its presence known."

"About Chromo-Test …"

"What?"

"How will you explain showing up without your children? Aren't they the ones they wanted to test?"

"What else am I going to do?" she wailed, attracting attention from some passers-by.

She lowered her voice and grabbed Blair's arm.

"I've been in this situation since November. My kids are missing. I'm pregnant with what used to be twins and what is now, I don't know, a creature from another world? I've got genetic anomalies, whatever the hell that means. I'm a friggin' test tube for somebody, or something, else. What do you want me to do? What do you expect me to do? The only one who ever told me what to do was that guy in the parking lot in Whately, Massachusetts! And right now, he's the only one who's making any sense. He knew I was pregnant the moment I knew. He knows what happened to my kids. And I have no idea who he is or why this is happening, and I can't go to the goddamned police and file a fucking missing persons report!" Her voice had risen an octave, so she lowered it again.

"*I'm a test tube, and test tubes don't have any rights.*"

★ ★ ★

Alexander Ferguson Blair would one day write a paper on the theme that people who experience alien abductions demonstrate a lack of agency and autonomy over themselves, their bodies, and their place in the world. That it was the ultimate symbol of invasion. An alien force from outside the power structure suddenly appears and rearranges reality, without consultation or compromise or an agreement of any kind. That the power differential was the same as in a case of rape or murder. He would opine that the paranoia over alien abductions was generated by feelings of white guilt over the colonization of people of color in African and Asian or indigenous societies; or slavery; or a misidentification with the civil rights movement. He would also suggest that it was a subconscious feminist reaction against the male power structure that claimed political, social, and economic control over female bodies, a way of bringing that conflict into the public discourse. The aliens were not really aliens from this point of view, but human men, doing what they have always done.

It would be a learned paper, full of academic citations and dispassionate argument, but it would be fueled by the first-hand experience of the emotional trauma undergone by one Gloria Tibbi, of Providence, Rhode Island.

★ ★ ★

In the meantime, though, he had to do what he could for this woman. He felt obligated, now that he knew the background. This was not your typical person claiming a close encounter of the third kind. This was a woman in serious trouble, and moreover one whose backstory checked out.

What he had not counted on was the fact that his Internet search for Gloria Tibbi had raised red flags back in Washington, DC and up the corridor to New York. That it wasn't just Chromo-Test that was looking for Gloria, but agents of the federal government. Monroe finally was advised of the Internet search and made a few phone calls. He found out that whoever had been doing the search was located in and around Twenty-Nine Palms and Joshua Tree Park. A few more calls and it was determined that Gloria Tibbi was indeed herself in the vicinity, presumably on her way to Chromo-Test by car. That didn't make a lot of sense, but he had to go with it.

The fact that she was a possible suspect in the murder of her ob/gyn made the rest of Monroe's task a little easier. All he had to do was phone in the information to the NYPD and they would have local police pick her up and hold her for them. This would give him the opportunity to question her, too. But Aubrey was in Germany, or would be soon, and he had no one else to send. He couldn't go himself, not until Angell was back in custody in the US. And then there was the confirmation out of New Orleans. Seems a birth there generated some controversy. More inexplicable genetic anomalies. And the connection to another murder as well. In fact, the New Orleans case made the Providence case seem positively tame by comparison. But the acceleration of strange births with bizarre genetic components was an indication that something very big was happening, or about to happen, and NYPD had come no closer to finding out who killed the ob/gyn, if the news reports were to be believed. The case in New Orleans was also unsolved. It meant what Harry and Sylvia were worried about had some basis in reality, something he could not tell them yet until he had more data.

Things were getting out of control.

★ ★ ★

In the meantime, Blair and Gloria had a long discussion about what to do next. He had another presentation to do that afternoon, but after that he was free and they could drive to San Diego and get to Chromo-Test in the morning. He would stay with her until he found out what was going on. It might make a good anecdote for another presentation some day. And, anyway, she needed a friend and he wasn't doing anything special.

★ ★ ★

All of that would have been great except for one thing. While Blair was giving his presentation in one of the smaller pavilions he saw Gloria suddenly stand up and leave the room in a hurry.

Probably had to pee, he thought to himself. *Weren't pregnant women always peeing?*

What he had not suspected was what really happened.

Her water broke.

She was having the baby *now*.

BOOK FIVE

DIE REGIERUNG DES HIMMELS

(THE GOVERNMENT OF THE SKY)

If, before I pass over the river to the better shore, I am permitted to write further concerning the SPIRITUAL KINGDOMS OF FARTHER SPACE, I shall amplify the points here merely touched upon, not for want of inclination, but of means to give what I write to the world ... Around both these foci and the galaxies they control, encircling the entire ellipse like a belt of molten silver, is another zone: and on that zone is the scene of the seventh grand stage of human existence. ... The final zone, I may here say, however, crosses our "Milky Way" at right angles.

    —P. B. Randolph, *After Death*

CHAPTER FIFTY-EIGHT

In the Aether

IT BEGAN, AS DOES EVERY GOOD AND BAD THING, WITH DREAMS.

A Dogon woman in Mali had a dream about something—a machine—descending to the Earth from the heavens. The machine spoke to her about the origin of life. It dazzled her with lights and music. She felt an unspeakable, indescribable welling up of every good thing within her. Every love she ever felt or imagined or wondered about. Movie stars and next-door neighbors. Gods and angels and athletes. Her mother. Her brothers. The embrace of her father. Her embrace of her children. The men who had possessed her, entered her, filled her and robbed her, and emptied her of hope. That love was so unendurable, she wandered out into the lane in front of her house with a machete and an old Bible printed in a language she could not read, and she prayed aloud and screamed incomprehensible words and knelt down before a speeding truck, begging to be allowed to travel back to the government in the sky.

In Mexico, in the Yucatan, fabled land of the Mayans, two children ate hallucinogenic mushrooms and found themselves diving into a cenote that they knew contained a tunnel that led to the Other Side, the Sitra Ahra, the backside of God, the Tunnels of Set, *per vas nefandum*, the Tunnels of Calabi-Yau, the Mirror of Orpheus, and they were never seen again. But they did see Robert Barlow, who greeted them in their indigenous dialect and then spent an hour vomiting speedballs in the corner.

On the West Bank, a mother awakens from the dream of her son: a suicide bomber who killed himself, and an Israeli soldier at a checkpoint months earlier. She awakens from the dream of every bad thing that ever happened to her, but her son is still there, standing beside her bed, a ghost. "No!" she screams. "This can't be!" He should have entered paradise immediately after the explosion, immediately after becoming a martyr. That is what they have been told. Paradise and virgins. Virgins for her virgin son. There cannot be ghosts of suicide bombers, for the implication ... is too painful to bear. If there are ghosts of suicide bombers—specters of men and women, boys and girls, in shredded vests and torsos, mutilated by the C4 and the det cord and the shrapnel, roaming the Earth with hideous moans—then there cannot be a paradise for martyrs. It would mean they lied: the imams and the mujahidin, with their pious furies and their obscure hadith. But the pain for her son is a sign to the mother that she still feels love. That there is still love in her, and therefore love in the world. It is the endless Pietà, enacted every hour in every country on Earth, of mothers holding their dead and murdered children. Only this time, the Old Ones are watching; the Gate squeaks on rusty hinges.

The conflagration went unnoticed by virtually everyone else on Earth, with a few exceptions: people whose reputations as psychotic preceded them. The phrase "touched by God" had lost all meaning by the twenty-first century, and was replaced by "borderline personality disorder." The only truth in that diagnosis was the word "borderline," as in "liminal," as in peeking around the doorframe to see the unimaginable about to take place on a scale impossible to comprehend. Imagine a conflict between sub-atomic particles, photons permanently entangled, taking place at far distances on opposite sides of the universe. Battles that would not be seen with the naked eye. They would not be seen with an Earth-based telescope, nor with a space-based telescope. These clever devices all look in the wrong dimensions, and in the wrong directions. The war is taking place at the Planck scale, spin vectors all askew, polarities dancing on the head of a pin register in an FBI van outside the Lincoln Memorial as Honest Abe tries to make a trunk call. What hath God wrought, Toto? Why, this is Kansas, nor am I out of it.

In a darkened Catholic Church in Pittsburgh at midnight, the officiating priest intones the ancient Latin canticle in perfect Gregorian cadence: "*Orchides forum trahite,*" he sings.

"*Cordes et mentes veniant,*" comes the response.

(*When you've got them by the balls, their hearts and minds will follow.*)

"Amen," agrees the congregation of black-clad pedophiles, thinking to themselves, quoting Ignatius Loyola or maybe Aristotle: *Give me the child until he is seven and I care not who has him thereafter.* Thus far the words of the Gospel.

Dreams and fantasies. "A dream to some, a nightmare to others!" cries Merlin in the movies.

It starts to happen, the phenomenon that CIA and the US military and the Soviets and the Chinese all tried so hard to make happen in the 1950s, the 1960s, the 1970s. It's happening now, with regularity and frequency, and among unauthorized personnel, you know, regular people, and it cannot be stopped. It started when a wife had the strong, inescapable feeling that something bad had happened to her husband. You know the story. You've seen it a hundred times. At that very moment, her husband is in a traffic accident or his plane has crashed or someone came to his place of work and shot it up. She doesn't know how she knows, she just knows.

Only this time, *everyone* is getting it. The feeling that one's spouse, child, parent, lover is in danger, is cheating, is robbing a store, is stealing paper clips from the office, is jerking off in a public park, is shooting someone in the back. Everyone is getting the vibes, man. Everyone is freaking out. And it's all true. It's all happening at once. Everyone's a goddamned psychic, and everyone is dreaming wide awake.

And with every new revelation, every sudden mental image of an unauthorized penis or vagina, every private climax, every unapproved liberation of a toy from a store, or supplies from an office, or even just the fantasy of sex with a supermodel, the ugliness of love and need and desire is revealed. No one wants to know how the sausage is made (no pun intended) but everyone is in the back room of the butcher shop, eyes taped open like Malcolm McDowell in *A Clockwork Orange*, forced to see what love costs them. *Love and Death*, maybe. Or *Love in the Time of Cholera*. Magic works when magic is not seen. Now we see it all.

Now we know how we've been had. We've been dreaming all this time. And we just now realized that we have also been dead all this time. Dead but dreaming: our natural state. Just ask Gurdjieff. Ouspensky. Lovecraft.

Giggles in the after dark, after party, afterbirth. What rough Beast …? We haven't had that spirit here since …

★ ★ ★

Smiley Face Guy isn't having any. He knows there are two sides to every coin, and in his universe sometimes five or six. (Try sleeping a yoyo with superstrings.) He knows humans, and he knows that they ain't as simple as all that. Humans are the interface between dimensions, that's why they're so fucked up. They live in one state but are conscious of more. God hath given you one face and you make yourselves another … Alright, stop that. Hey, is Shakespeare still a pop culture reference on this planet? What? No? That's fucked up. All that Great Work for nothing.

★ ★ ★

Smiley Face Guy sees what's happening. He's the needle that stitches these worlds together. Sure, the Dagonites or whatever the hell they call themselves these days, know the score and use it to their advantage but that's stolen data. Dagon hacked the Server a million plus years ago and their Trojan Horse has been corrupting files ever since. But Smiley Face Guy has the original data in its original form. What Dagon stole, he created. And has made tremendous strides since then. Dagon's operating system is not up-to-date, to borrow a metaphor. It's past its sell-by date, to borrow another. That's what happens when you leave your Server in the hands of the mehums. (That's "mere humans" to you and Robert Anton Wilson.)

The tubes. The tunnels. They're the key to it all, ain't they, guv'nor? The cenotes of the sky, ¡que maravilla! Tunnels in the air.

Here they come! Heads up! Can you see it? The Hummer of the skies!

CHAPTER FIFTY-NINE

From Joshua Tree to Baghdad

IT WAS CALLED THE DESERT MEDICAL CENTER, and was about twenty minutes from the Contact in the Desert conference. A man with long, grey hair, deep wrinkles, and a leather vest studded with alien buttons offered to drive her there in what appeared to be a VW Bug. He made it to the hospital in fifteen.

Gloria was rushed to the emergency intake and then, when it became obvious she was going to deliver on the floor, they got her a gurney and pushed it into an OR for the delivery.

They kept trying to get information from her—her name, if she had insurance, if there was someone they should call, etc.—but all Gloria could do was scream. The nurses noticed she seemed to be crying, really crying, but they thought it was in pain.

They were wrong.

A doctor in scrubs arrived and after ascertaining her vital signs nodded to the nurses and they prepped for the delivery. She was concerned about Gloria's blood pressure and knew they would have to act quickly. She felt around and determined that the baby was indeed ready to arrive and that all seemed perfectly normal. She would have preferred to have the mother's medical records in front of her, but if she had, she might have had second thoughts.

Alexander Blair finished his presentation and wandered over to the entrance to see what had become of Gloria Tibbi. That is when he learned that she was rushed to the hospital in the throes of labor. He got the address of the hospital and drove there at once.

"Excuse me. Has Gloria Tibbi been admitted?" The woman behind the admissions counter looked up at him and then down at her terminal.

"Are you the father?"

"Ah, no. Just a friend."

"I see," she said, a little incredulous. "Well, she's in labor. That's all I know right now. You can sit in the waiting room if you like, but I don't know how long it will be."

"Who brought her here, by the way?"

"I have no idea. She was just dropped off, I think."

"I see. Okay, thanks."

He looked around and found a plastic chair to sit in and a pile of magazines that were so old the covers were faded. He had his shoulder bag with him, and some files and a tablet so he was set for the time being.

He looked up at the clock. It was just after three pm.

★ ★ ★

Three pm in California meant five pm in New Orleans. Detective Cuneo was just finishing up for the day. As he was leaving the office he ran into Lisa Carrasco who was ending her shift as well.

"Hey, Lisa."

"Detective."

"Half day?"

"Ha."

"Listen. I was about to go over to the hospital to check out the Boy in the Box. Wanna come with?"

She thought about it for a moment. He looked so forlorn at the prospect of going there alone that she couldn't say no.

"Sure. Why not? I haven't seen him in months."

"Great. Thanks. Let's take my car."

Cuneo drove, and Lisa listened to him talk about his meeting with the houngan and before that with the professor from Tulane.

"So it sounds like you two really hit it off, huh?"

"Me and Hervé?" he asked, mischievously.

"Very funny. No, I meant you and the prof."

"She was nice, I admit."

"Sounds like she was a little flirty."

"Oh, no. Not really. She was very professional."

"I see."

"No, really."

"Okay," she said, not believing him for a second. "What did you learn from those meetings, though? All that voodoo stuff?"

"They call it *vodoun*."

"Sounds very French."

"More like West African. But I learned a lot about more recent versions, and some stuff I hadn't heard of before. You know, my Mom was into that stuff, too. She came from Haiti originally. All that obeah and wanga was right down her alley."

"Wow. What did your Dad think of that? Wasn't he Italian?"

"Yeah, well, the Italians have their own version, too. They call it *strega*. Means 'witch.' They burn candles, hold novenas. My father's mother used to pray to the saints and if she didn't get what she wanted, she'd turn the statue of the saint upside down and keep it in the closet until it behaved."

Lisa thought that was funny.

"I would have liked to know someone like that. She sounds like a wonderful lady."

"Oh, she had a lot in common with my Mom. I guess that's what Dad saw in her."

"Yeah, right. A lot in common between an Italian grandmother from the old country and a Haitian woman from Voodoo Land."

"Well, you're looking at the result, *cher*. Hell, this whole city is like that."

They arrived at the hospital and parked. They flashed their shields and wandered off in search of the ICU. The nurses had moved the baby from neo-natal ICU to the one where they usually put adults.

It was after five, and the nurse he usually spoke with wasn't around. He asked the first nurse he found on staff that evening about the baby.

"Well, he seems to be doing a little better now. He's stopped wandering the halls at night after pulling out the leads from the monitors. He's still trying to speak but we can't understand a word. And his appetite is very strong. Are you sure you don't want to speak to a doctor? I can see who's available who knows about the case."

"Maybe later. For now, I just want to take a look and to show my colleague here what we're up against. She was involved with the case from the beginning."

"Sure. Okay, follow me."

They walked behind the nurse towards a room that was closed off with glass walls and doors. They could see an array of monitors for each patient. At the moment, the baby was in a separate section that was closed off by more glass doors, more for the comfort of the other patients than anything else.

There was a nurse already in the ICU with him, and when she looked up Lisa almost fainted on the spot.

"Jesus. It's … it's *her*." She tried to raise her finger to point at her but suddenly didn't have the strength.

The nurse lifted her head and stared right back at her.

It was the Asian woman who had been standing in the living room over the crime scene in Belle Chasse; the same one who had stood outside the Galvez home the day the murder was discovered, and screamed, and then disappeared.

★ ★ ★

Five pm in New Orleans meant six pm in New York City.

Detective Lieutenant (Retired) Wasserman just got off the subway after meeting with Professor Hine. The scholar was more than happy to talk about Gregory Angell with him, but still seemed reticent when it came to some details. Hine had evidently been in contact with the same DC spooks that Wasserman had spoken with, specifically this guy named Aubrey.

Hine told Wasserman that he had been in China when Angell had surfaced after being MIA from Columbia for more than six months. Angell had told him some of what he had been through in the Middle East and Nepal the previous year, but without going into a lot of background. There were terror groups, weird cults, and a Book. Angell was freaky when it came to the Book. It was a handwritten text, in an old form of Greek but with lines in Arabic and some other language or languages as well. It seems that the Book was the center of the whole issue with Angell and the intelligence agencies and, well, all of it.

Angell had contacted him and told him to send a message to Aubrey. He, Hine, didn't understand the message at all. It was a lot of gobbledygook, phrases that made no sense but that Angell assured him would mean something to Aubrey. Angell said it was urgent.

Then Angell contacted him a second time and gave him more data. That was the last he heard from him. Maybe two, three days ago.

Wasserman had asked him some more questions, mostly background stuff, then gave him his card. He scratched out the office phone number since he didn't work for NYPD anymore, but wrote down his cell number. Since they both knew Aubrey, and since Hine knew Angell personally, he figured they should stay in touch.

Now, back in his apartment, he wasn't so sure he had done the right thing. Maybe he should have phoned Aubrey first. But if he had, he was sure Aubrey would have told him to forget the whole thing.

"Ah," he said to himself, kicking off his shoes. "Fuck it."

That's when his phone rang, and it was Danny.

"Hey, remember me? We used to work together? Or, I did the work and you just farted around waiting to put in your papers."

"Whaddaya want, Danny?"

"A brief moment of your valuable retiree time, Detective formerly known as Loo."

"Can we do this on the phone? I've had a long day."

"No sweat. I just wanted to fill you in on my discussions with a baby doc over in the Bronx about how they figure out about the DNA and the twin thing and so on. He was very helpful, but scary as hell."

"Lay it on me."

Danny started reading to him from his notes, sounding like he was lecturing at the Academy.

★ ★ ★

"They use amniocentesis, usually, but it depends on the circumstances. There is a danger of miscarriage, even if slight. What happens is they insert a needle into the amniotic sac and withdraw the amniotic fluid which contains the DNA. Or they do a CVS—that's chorionic villus sampling, to you—which uses tissue from the placenta, reached through the cervix. Both are invasive, and a little dangerous for a mother who maybe is older than thirty-five or so because it can result in a miscarriage in some cases. A less invasive measure is to take some blood from the umbilical cord. That doesn't harm the fetus in any way, but the results are mixed: that is, the baby's DNA is mixed in with the mother's. It still can be used as a general way to test for congenital defects, Downs Syndrome, and like that. You following me so far?"

"Sure. Go ahead."

"Okay. So I ask him, what about the DNA, doctor? How is it tested? I mean, does the doctor do that in his office, or what?"

"*Oh, no. The samples have to be sent to a lab for analysis.*"

"I see. So ... how long would that take?"

"*Oh, not long. You see they are looking for specific markers for specific illnesses or defects. It's not like when you guys send DNA to the lab for testing in a murder or rape case, which can take weeks or longer. This can be done in a few days or so.*"

"Expensive?"

"*Insurance covers some of that but, yes, it can be expensive.*"

"Who has access to those results?"

"*Well, the lab of course. The doctor. Presumably his patient.*"

"No one else?"

"And that's when it gets even more freaky. This guy tells me, '*Look, Detective, we all know how vulnerable data is these days. I suppose it is possible that a lab's computers can be hacked. In fact, we know they can.*"

There was a case just now of some computer types working in a genetics lab. They actually inserted a computer virus into some DNA, and sent it off to another lab for analysis. When the lab started testing the DNA, the computer virus infected their system. It was harmless, just a test to see if it could be done, but … well, there you go."

"So I say wait a minute. You said they inserted a computer virus into some DNA? How is that possible? DNA is, like, organic, right? A computer virus is digital, zeroes and ones. How the hell …?"

"'*DNA is digital, Detective. Do you get that?'* DNA is digital. That's what he told me. '*It's as digital as computer code. Just four proteins code for everything in the double helix that makes you, and me, and the houseplant. The DNA helix is like a software program itself. And these people proved it.'*"

"I mean, Loo, that's fucked up. Pardon my French."

"No worries. I'm fluent."

"So I finish by asking him where would an ob/gyn like my victim have sent the DNA samples for analysis?"

"So he says well, he's in New York, right?"

"Was."

"Was. Okay. So there are a few likely candidates. Are you ready? I'll give you their names and phone numbers."

"So the doctor read off a small list of three labs, and that was that."

"You're right. That's some scary shit."

"Right?"

"What about those labs?"

"Well, that's where it gets even scarier. I call all three. The first two, nothing. The last one is based out in California, so I had to wait until they were open. A place called .." he flipped through his notes. "Chromo-Test. Out in San Diego. They're the guys who do these family DNA tests, you know, you spit in a tube or something …"

"Yeah, I know. I've seen their ads on TV. But, wait, they do more serious work for baby doctors?"

"Yeah, it's a separate division. They have an office in the City, but the labs are sent to San Diego for testing."

"Okay. So?"

"So this. I call it in, identify myself, say we're working on a homicide, mention the murdered doc's name, and suddenly I'm the center of the fucking baby doc universe. Yeah, they know the vic. Know all about him. He had a bug up his ass about something to do with twins. I knew that already, right, but I let the guy go on and tell me something I don't know.

"Loo, they want first crack at his files. The secret ones. I tell him, listen, that's evidence in a criminal investigation, blah blah blah, but they don't care. They are so friggin' unimpressed it's not funny. Then they put another guy on the line, and this guy is scarier than the last. Former CIA, former State Department, former Santa's Little Helpers for all I know. He may be former everything but he's currently a something. He has all the right codes, you know what I mean? They ask me if I know a guy called Blair who's been phoning around, asking the same questions, only this time ... sit down, Loo ... you sitting down?"

"I'm falling down. What? Tell me."

"This time this Blair guy is calling them about our missing witness. Gloria. Her name is Gloria Tibbi and she is, at this moment, in California. In some hippy-dippy commune or something. Some UFO thing."

"Jesus. UFOs? Wasn't that what the vic was into? About the missing twins?"

"Exactly."

"Fuck me. Who's that Blair guy?"

"Oh, man. Another one. Some kind of UFO researcher or something. Guy's got a low profile, which is surprising for that crowd, and has published some papers and I think a book. I'm working on getting a complete profile of this guy without breaking too many laws. He's low on the social media totem pole but there's stuff around. He's in California now, too."

"State's like a friggin' magnet."

"You got that right."

"Nothing else on the shooter, huh?"

"The skirt who wasted the ... the whaddaya call it ... the diplomat? Nah, nothing so far. CT have been all over the ports, the airports, bus stations, looking at facial recognition software which is like reading fucking Tarot cards. They're going over traffic cams. Bupkis. They're looking at everyone who entered the country for, like, up to two weeks before the hit. They think they can narrow it down from there."

"Danny, this whole DNA thing has got me wondering."

"About what, Loo?"

"The way the doctor was mutilated. The staging of the crime scene. And now these UFO types all over it. What if this was the work of some kind of cult? The skull, the missing fluids ..."

"Well, we considered that, remember? Because of the weird crime scene. But when we found that he was keeping secret files on the missing twin thing, we figured it was someone who was pissed they lost a twin, or something. In other words, something personal. Like the crime scene was just forensic countermeasures—to throw us off."

"Yeah, but what if it wasn't? What if the crime scene is the whole point? What if it was a warning to other people looking into the same thing? To stay away? Not look too close?"

"But why? Everybody I talk to tells me the missing twin thing is normal. Freaky, but normal. Why warn somebody away from something that happens all the time?"

"Danny, nobody would go to all that trouble to stage the scene that way unless they were trying to make a point. Where's the blood? The fluids? The skin off the vic's skull? That's not just overkill. It's like the killing was an afterthought, or maybe just a by-product of what they were trying to do."

"You mean, like a side effect?"

"Yeah. Like that."

"If that's *the side effect* …"

"Yeah, yeah. I know. Have you compared the M.O. to other cases?"

"First thing we did. Nothing. There was this old punishment from the Middle Ages or the Renaissance or something where they would skin people alive."

"But the doc wasn't completely skinned. Just his head."

"There was that, too. Beheading and skinning as part of the same punishment. The Aztecs did that, too, but they were crazy bastards who did a lot of sick stuff."

"Been watching the History Channel again, Danny?"

"Shit, who's got the time? Nah, this was from some report compiled by some nerd in the department once we started looking at the M.O. like it was a serial killer or something."

"But no connection between skinning people alive and missing twins, right?"

"Not that we could find. Not even in California."

"Try New Jersey."

Danny, laughing, said goodbye and hung up.

Wasserman sat in his living room, shoeless, and thought about what Danny had just told him, and put it against what he had heard from Steve Hine an hour earlier. There was a cult involved somehow with that whole thing, with Angell and his spirit bowl and the whole rigmarole about a Book. And now, this.

He remembered the Son of Sam case vividly. That was really the last time there were rumors of a cult operating in New York, murdering people. Oh, there were individual cases that had cultic overtones, but nothing as organized as Sam. Not until now, anyway. There was no evidence at all that Angell had anything to do with what was happening in New York City today, but still …

Pondering all this, he closed his eyes for a minute.

And then was fast asleep.

★ ★ ★

She had the address. She was sure the bus was going there. It was headed in the right direction when she saw it going north on Broadway. All she had to do was get there and scout the area so she knew what she was getting herself into.

For the moment, she forgot all about confronting Professor Hine about Angell. There would be time enough for that later. Right now, Jamila had to know why there were Yezidi children headed for the Bronx.

★ ★ ★

It was after six pm in New York and the same time in Crofton, Maryland.

Sylvia and Harry were in a huddle in the living room while Monroe and Simon were looking at something in Simon's study.

"They've been taken to the Bronx. The pregnant girls are all okay. The other girls, too. The only ones that worry me are the two in isolation."

"Wasn't it dangerous to move them, any of them?"

"Harry, what else could we do? We had to move them. By moving them we made them more visible to Dagon. That was the whole point, to draw them out once and for all. And we had to put them all together. If we separated the pregnant girls from the others, Dagon would rescue the pregnant ones and kill or abandon the others the way they had originally intended. This way, we force them to go after all of them at the same time. We couldn't watch two or more separate groups. We don't have the resources. Now they're all in one place and Dagon will have to do what they can to keep all of them alive, at least in the short term. Once they make their move, they will have walked into a trap. An ambush. This was the plan you agreed to, remember?"

Harry nodded, but was miserable nonetheless. He was not an operational sort of guy. He was an analyst who romanticized about being a field agent. Now he was not so sure. He wanted to save the girls, certainly, and give them a better life than the one they were leading in wire cages. But it wasn't as simple as all that. It never was. The goal was simple; the mission was complicated.

"How do we know that Dagon is aware of the move?"

"Oh, we know. We know because we've been compromised. Aubrey's team in Germany was penetrated by Dagon. That's what Monroe was trying to tell us just now. Maybe it was Angell who got doubled. Maybe someone else. But right now we have a chance to put an end to this once and for all. Aubrey's on his way back, with Angell. This could all be over in forty-eight hours."

In Simon's study, which looked like a cross between a hacker's lair and a medieval sorcerer's library, Monroe was staring down at a chart made of pieces of paper taped together to form a sheet about six feet long and two feet wide.

Simon explained, "It was the idea of hot points—*points chauds*—that Bertiaux described to Aubrey plus the diagrams that Bertiaux drew for him that helped put this together. Hot points move; they are the interface between our topology of space and time and the way the Old Ones (or, at least, Dagon) understand the terrain.

"Imagine that we all left the Earth today and then sent ships back a million years from now. Where would they find Stonehenge? Or the Great Pyramids? Possibly under water. The *space* would change with *time*. Our space travelers would bring maps and globes with them that were created on the Earth today, not in a million years from today. The disconnect between the two would be considerable, making the old maps useless. And remember, even the technology we use today to draw up our maps and globes would be hopelessly antiquated and obsolete in a million years, but it would be the only data available to our future visitors. They would have to superimpose the new maps over the old ones to see where everything used to be. Are you with me so far?"

"Yes. I never thought of this in such detail before, although the concept is not new to me."

"Dagon uses the equivalent of the old maps," Simon went on, pulling out something that looked computer-generated and recent.

"This is how our geologists think the world looked like a hundred million years ago. You can see different continents, mountain ranges, etc. All of that land mass is still there—here—but in appearance it's quite different, of course. There is an ocean where Tibet should be, for instance."

"This is just … fascinating. Really."

"By calculating the dates, times and places of the previous two rituals—the one in Nepal and the one in Florida as the centerpiece rituals, even though there were others—we can triangulate Dagon's unique GPS system. If we look at those locations, for instance, and understand what used to be there millions of years ago, we can begin to predict where and when the next rituals will take place. What is Nepal today, for instance, was under water then. Hence the story of Cthulhu lying 'dead but dreaming' in an underwater city, even though the ritual took place on dry land, under a mountain."

"Yes, we more or less figured that out when it happened."

"But we were not able to figure it out in *advance*, to predict it. Then Pinecastle gave us more information because we began to understand how Dagon thinks. There was no landmass where Pinecastle is now, another indication that millions of years ago something else was there. It also hints at the idea that maybe the mythology of Dagon really is a half-human, half-fish kind of creature even though the original Dagon was not. That maybe there is a tradition within Dagon that the Old Ones are underwater deities."

"As much as I hate to admit it, Ingo Swann used to tell a story about UFOs coming up from under the sea. The whole alien-human hybrid story that goes around in UFO circles may have some relevance to the idea that the Old Ones were here before us, seeded this planet with DNA, and have come back to … I don't know … harvest the results? If the UFOs originate under the sea rather than in the sky, that would have given the Old Ones a means for monitoring the situation here."

"Damn, Dwight. You're starting to sound like an episode of Ancient Aliens!"

"I don't mean to, believe me! In a way, this whole discussion is a means of trying to understand something that is just out of our reach. Not all UFOs come from the seas, and not all of them come from the skies. Either there are two modalities for the same group of Old Ones, or two entirely different species. The underwater version needs the UFO to travel in our oxygen-rich environment because they can't breathe out of water. It's their version of a submarine. And the others who are coming to this planet from elsewhere have the same problem, but in a different way. Just as we would have to wear space suits going to their planet, or deep sea suits going beneath the waves. It comes down to the same basic problem: beings interacting with environments that would be hostile to their organisms. Some fish have evolved to being amphibians, but that takes millions of years. We have learned to do that in a lot less time."

"Lovecraft described these Old Ones as being amphibious. The ancient historian Berossus wrote of Oannes as a fish-man coming up from the sea to bring civilization to the Sumerians. He was described as never eating or drinking anything on the surface of the Earth, but only returning to his underwater realm every evening."

"I wonder."

"What's that?"

"If Oannes was bringing civilization, or weapons."

★ ★ ★

Six-thirty pm in Maryland is two-thirty am in Baghdad.

The smoke from the car bomb in the parking lot of the Babylon Warwick Hotel could be seen for miles. There were two simultaneous bombs, one at the Babylon and another at the Cristal Grand Ishtar.

The Dark Lord was furious. He was told that ISIL would not attack any targets in Baghdad for the next two days while Dagon was present. Somebody didn't get the memo.

The girl he was with was cowering under the sheets. She had already been frightened of his missing left arm, not to mention his particular … proclivities … but now this? Bombs going off in front of a nice hotel where there had been a wedding party that night?

He looked down at her. He was told she was thirteen, but he was sure she was older. That wouldn't do. But there wasn't much he could do about it now. The security forces would be knocking on his door soon to make sure he was okay. It wouldn't do to have a young naked girl in his room.

He pulled her out of the bed rather roughly with his one arm and told her to get dressed, quickly. He would have to get her out of the room. He hated to lose the opportunity to have her again, even if she was actually sixteen and not thirteen, but he couldn't take the chance that someone was not paid off or otherwise taken care of.

"*Igri!*" he shouted at her, through clenched teeth. *Hurry up.*

Trembling, she pulled on her clothes, her eyes downcast and not daring to meet his gaze.

It was precisely this reaction he had been hoping for all along when he hired her.

He went over to her, stopped her getting dressed, and made a quick calculation. He had a good ten, fifteen minutes before things got dicey.

He turned her around and pushed her roughly onto the bed, looking at the time on the bedside clock as he did so.

He would keep it under fifteen minutes.

CHAPTER SIXTY

In the Aether

ACCORDING TO EARTH SCIENTISTS IN THE early twenty-first century, there is a distinct possibility that at least two universes exist simultaneously—ours and another one—and that they are perpendicular to each other. Normally, one does not experience the other universe at all, except perhaps vicariously. And then, only by mediums, mystics and magicians. The occasional acid head. The odd schizophrenic. And novelists. Mostly novelists.

This is not to be confused with the "many worlds" theory, or with string theory. The Old Ones do not entertain the types of mathematics they view as virtually indistinguishable from Kabbalah, especially the Frater Achad version with the paths on the Tree of Life all fucked up and backwards. And don't get me started on William Gray.

No, the Old Ones understand the relationship between mass and energy to be reciprocal in ways we can only guess at, restricted as we are to mathematical systems that have inherent flaws and which flaunt axioms that cannot be proven.

That is how, even now, they are massing on the other side of the Gate. Their inherent volume is in flux: pulsing greater and lesser, bigger and smaller, in indirect proportion to the energy expended. As they grow larger in mass, they absorb energy which is translated into mass; they then grow smaller and the resulting increase of energy exerts simultaneous pressure on the Gate.

They cannot open the Gate from their side; it's a problem of physics. All they can do is ensure that the optimum conditions are met so that when someone from the other side—our side—exerts pressure the polarity of the two sources of energy/mass is sufficient to blast the Gate wide open. Like a collapsing star creating a black hole.

It happened several times in the past, most notably in 1947 when the hot point passed over the Pacific coastline, but the Gate slammed shut again on each occasion. In 1947 it had been opened by a competent magician with the experience and the knowledge to maintain an open Gate for an extremely limited period of time, measurable in nanoseconds. But that was enough to bring forth Maury Island, Roswell, and the Dead Sea Scrolls, and to put Aleister Crowley in his grave. It was also the same year that gave us the invention of Reynolds Wrap, with its resulting meme of tin foil hats.

Jack Parsons, on his own, was able to do that with a little (very little) help from L. Ron Hubbard. All of Dagon, with tremendous resources at its disposal, was not. Not so far, anyway. Why? Well, there are several theories but the most important factor is the continuing opposition from Starry Wisdom. It was Starry Wisdom who blew the whistle, dropped the dime, jumped the Snark … whatever … in New Orleans in 1907 to get the Dagon ritual broken up in the bayou with its missing children, orgiastic rites, and the summoning of Cthulhu . (See "The Call of Cthulhu" for details.) True, it was Monroe and his crew who were able to do that when Dagon tried *exactly the same thing* in Florida in 2014. And before that, in Nepal, but that was mostly Angell. That they had help from Starry Wisdom was never revealed because, well, Monroe was unaware of it himself. He had never heard of Starry Wisdom, except as a possibility described in the Lovecraft tale about the Shining Trapezohedron.

There is a throwaway line in that tale—"The Haunter in the Dark"—about the number of congregants in the Church of Starry Wisdom in Providence. It reads:

"200 or more in cong. 1863, exclusive of men at front."

In other words, you had a sizeable congregation at the Church during the Civil War that did not include the men serving at the front. So, there were Starry Wisdom members in the Union Army in 1863. Oops. At that time, P. B. Randolph was recruiting black soldiers to fight alongside the Union Army. How many of those black soldiers were also members of the Starry Wisdom congregation? Was Randolph a recruiter for the cult? He jump-started so many occult lodges and secret societies in his lifetime that one has to consider the possibility, *n'est-ce pas?*

In the end, it didn't matter. The Church closed its doors in 1877 due to enormous pressure from the community (or that was the cover story anyway; it was also two years after the death of Randolph which might have been more to the point). Its members fled Providence. Our sources indicate that they wound up in the one place they would feel at home: New Orleans. Randolph had been writing about magic mirrors and magnetism, and had referred to "Voodoo" as powerful but sinister: all topics that could just as easily have referred to his experiences at Starry Wisdom as anything else. But it would be wrong to conflate the Church of Starry Wisdom with Dagon. Dagon had been in New Orleans since at least the time of Jean Lafitte and the War of 1812.

There was a deeper agenda underlying Starry Wisdom's breaking up of the 1907 Dagon ritual.

In August of 1877, the astronomer Asaph Hall III discovered the moons of Mars: calling them Deimos and Phobos: the Greek words for "terror" and "horror" respectively. His discovery was due to the urging of his wife, Angeline Stickney the mathematician and abolitionist, who was born on November 1, 1830: All Saints Day. It was the discovery of the two Martian moons—and their terrifying nomenclature—that convinced Starry Wisdom to decamp from Providence. After all, "the stars were aright."

Asaph Hall would die on November 22, 1907, only three weeks after the Dagon ritual in the Louisiana bayous and only one week after Aleister Crowley and George Cecil Jones created the Argenteum Astrum: the initiatory body known as the A∴ A∴, on November 15 of that year. The Dagon ritual had been unsuccessful due to the police raid detailed in Lovecraft's account of the incident. The evidence that was collected at the scene—including eyewitness accounts and interviews with suspects—was largely ignored by law enforcement except as a curiosity in conferences. It was not analyzed, and the circumstances were considered so weird that no one really wanted to be associated with its investigation except for the redoubtable Inspector Legrasse.

Most importantly, the reason for the police raid—the reports of missing children—was never pursued, and today no one knows who the missing children were or what became of them. The initial police reports were either destroyed or simply never made it to the archives. Coincidentally, Golden Dawn initiate and Crowley secretary Francis Israel Regardie was born that same month—on November 17, 1907—but obviously would not have been one of the children. And for those who think that all of this timeline analysis may be stretching the point, remember that Aleister Crowley himself pointed out the relevance of his having been born in 1875: the same year that the Theosophical Society was founded in New York, and the same year that Eliphas Levi died (of whom Crowley believed himself the reincarnation) and, of course, the death of Randolph. By that logic, the A.'. A.'. is a reincarnation of the Dagon cult that was raided in Louisiana the same month and year.

★ ★ ★

(Kenneth Grant, wandering open-mouthed in the Mauve Zone, suddenly stops and goes "Whoomp! Whoomp!" like a crazed audience member in the Arsenio Hall studio. Or a backup dancer for a Tag Team video. Sorry. Too soon?)

★ ★ ★

Why did Dagon choose the Pinecastle Bombing Range for its ritual in November, 2014?

Because of the historic connection to the ritual site in Louisiana. The indigenous tribes that lived and built earthen mound temples south of New Orleans were in frequent contact with the tribes that lived across the Gulf of Mexico in Florida. Archaeological evidence demonstrates that both groups maintained trade with each other and shared some ... shall we say ... *spiritual* concepts in common? The mound culture in southern Louisiana was the equal of anything one would find further north, in Ohio or West Virginia for instance. Large, pyramid-shaped mounds in complexes totaling as many as twenty-four in a single site; elaborate burials reminiscent of ancient Egypt; and high priests evoking spiritual forces from the skies. Dagon needed to maintain the occult link between the indigenous American practices and their present incarnations. Like would-be Druids cavorting around Stonehenge on the summer solstice, Dagon initiates sought out the centers of a darker power, the ley lines of the intergalactic magnetic fields passing through the core of the unsuspecting Earth.

One impulse from a vernal wood ... and like that.

But there was another problem, of which only Dagon was aware.

All those ancient sacred sites—Stonehenge, Macchu Picchu, the Filmore East—are located on hard ground. On the land. Dagon knew of other sites, not so conveniently situated. In other words, sacred sites below the waves. Below the oceans. That is why Lovecraft wrote about the sunken city of R'lyeh. Of Cthulhu dead but dreaming in that sunken city. So Simon and Monroe were right to that point.

The key to locating the undersea sites has to do with plate tectonics, and with an ancient, prehistoric sea the geologists refer to as the Sea of Tethys.

The Sea of Tethys existed two hundred million years ago—at about the time the Old Ones were on the Earth—and separated what is now India from the rest of the Asian continent. (India at the time was located off the coast of Australia.) Over the next 150 million years India gradually moved towards Asia, and the resulting pressure created the Himalayas with Asia on the north side and India on the south side.

When Dagon held that ritual in the Himalayas—in Nepal, beneath the mountains, in a place called Khembalung—they were standing right above the spot where one of the ancient sunken cities was located according to maps that had been drawn up when India was an island continent all its own. In fact, archaeologists have located pink sandstone deposits in the Himalayas containing magnetite, thus demonstrating that (a) the region was once flooded by the Tethys Sea, and (b) that the magnetite itself shows how the Earth's magnetic poles shifted, even flipped, over time.

The ritual was designed to raise Cthulhu straight up from the sunken city—now the buried city—and into the cavern. And it almost worked.

Just for giggles we should probably mention that the origin of the name Tethys goes back to a Greek goddess of the oceans, a name borrowed from the Sumerian: *Tiamat.*

Everyone knows geologists love a good joke.

CHAPTER SIXTY-ONE

Hilton Hotel
Frankfurt Airport, Germany

ANGELL WAS RECUPERATING NICELY IN THE HOTEL. The drugs were leaving his system, and he was more coherent and eager to put an end to all of this and get on with his life. First, though, he had a lot of unfinished business with Aubrey.

The old spy knocked on his door around seven am local time to join him for breakfast. There had been two German Polizei stationed outside his room the entire night, and they had just been spelled by a new pair.

Aubrey himself wheeled in the breakfast cart, not taking any chances with the hotel staff. Just in case. After all, his judgment of personalities hadn't been too sharp when it came to Prudence Wakefield.

"Her twin didn't have any information on him," he said, after the usual pleasantries. "No ID. Nothing. But we are having better luck with his sister. Prudence Wakefield was born here, as she claimed. She was born a twin, and her brother's name is, or was, Joseph."

"Like Mengele."

"Could be. There was a definite Nazi connection to the Dagon cult, and to the theft of the *Necronomicon* and its winding up in an SS library during the war. You know, the whole Julius Evola thing. Mengele was SS, of course. And we have a lot of detail now on their mother and grandmother, and working backwards to Ottmar von Verschuer. The German police have just raided Wakefield's home and found some of the Mengele files. But that's not the worst part."

Aubrey took a triangle of toast and poured himself a cup of coffee.

"They also found references to a human trafficking network being run by a neo-Nazi group out of South America. Seems they were working with Dagon in that regard."

432

"For the sacrifices, like the one you were telling me about that happened in Florida?"

"Actually, no. Not exactly. This group was trafficking in human beings as part of a genetic testing project using Mengele's research. Now that we have CRISPR, scientists can apply some of Mengele's theories concerning twin research in pretty much real time."

"What does that mean?"

"It means the new breed of eugenicists doesn't have to wait around for twins to be produced naturally. They can create them in the lab. They still have to gestate, etc. using surrogates, but they can control the outcomes fairly easily. There is a geneticist in China who's doing this now with twins, and bragging about it."

"What's Dagon's interest in all of this? I don't see the connection."

"You should brush up on your Lovecraft, then. He wrote about this in 'The Dunwich Horror.' Twins that were alien-human hybrids. Fraternal twins, in that case, not identical twins. But still."

"So the real goal is not to produce a human master race but an alien-human *hybrid* master race? Are you serious?"

"As a heart attack."

"But where do they get the alien DNA?"

"That's just it. To Dagon, there doesn't seem to be much difference between the idea of 'aliens,' popularly understood, and the Old Ones. Gods, angels, demons, aliens … it's all the same to them, evidently."

"So you're saying they're not waiting around for a flying saucer to land to donate eggs or sperm. The whole 'Opening the Gate' thing is to call them here, and they will do the rest?"

"That's what they were doing in Pinecastle. And in New Orleans before that."

"New Orleans? Oh, 'The Call of Cthulhu.'"

"Right. And now Monroe has evidence that they've been at it again in New Orleans. There's a very weird case going on there right now that has connections back to the 1907 episode."

"Okay, but one thing still escapes my understanding. Why did they need me, personally, and not just the Book?"

Angell moved over to the chair opposite Aubrey and poured himself coffee. He looked at the breakfast Aubrey had ordered— eggs, sausages, baked beans, tomatoes, a real English fry-up—and decided he wasn't feeling quite that well just yet and settled for toast.

"Monroe and I have discussed that. A great deal, actually. Our theory is that there is a lot of nonsense written about the *Necronomicon*. Many scholars and academics reject outright the idea that the book was ever real. Lovecraft insisted it was invented, possibly to disguise the fact that he had been involved in the theft of the Cthulhu Cult file. I don't know."

"Got it. My family has despised the name of Lovecraft for a hundred years, for that reason."

"Understood. See, it doesn't matter that a physical version of it exists and that cults are fighting over it and almost caused a global catastrophe because of it. It almost doesn't matter what it *says*, what's in it. But putting the Book together with a very real descendant of the original scholar who studied the Cthulhu Cult—your George Gammell Angell—makes it all just as real, just as powerful. Your blood spattered on that Book closes the circle. It's the history of the last hundred years collapsed into a single artifact, one that teaches its followers how to walk on the stars. How to open the Gate. Your ancestor was alive at a time when the Gate had been opened once. His experience of that was imprinted on his DNA. We know now that environmental factors can affect the genetic code and also that strong emotional experiences are transmitted via the DNA as well. Your ancestor was murdered on the Providence docks almost 100 years ago. Before that, he was intensely involved in the study of the Cthulhu Cult and was in conference with other learned individuals who entrusted him with the files. He was analyzing a young man, an artist, who had violent dreams about the cult, and about Cthulhu. Hell, your ancestor even had a statue that was carved by the student, a small piece depicting Cthulhu's appearance. All of this information and experience is locked, they believe, in your DNA. It's a key to opening the Gate."

"And my skin? They needed that, too?"

"I think that was just the twin's personal fetish, but who knows? Maybe all that stuff about flayed gods is relevant. Or maybe they wanted to bind the Book in human skin. There have been instances of that in history, you know."

"Wonderful. I feel so … so special."

"You'll get over it."

"So, what's the word? Any chance of finding Prudence any time soon?"

"Well, everyone's working on it. In the meantime, we picked up your friend Moody in Dubai."

"Who the hell is Moody?"

"Oh, you never knew his name. The guy who followed you from Indonesia to Frankfurt."

"The guy who tried to steal my knapsack?"

"The same. We found him on the CCTV feed, being accosted by your friend Prime. Prime gave him a ticket to Dubai, and when Moody got to Dubai he found another ticket waiting for him. This time to Baghdad."

"Baghdad! That's a war zone!"

"Yeah. In fact there was a double car bombing there just now, a few hours ago actually. And right in front of the hotel where he was supposed to stay."

"What's that all about?"

"There has been movement of Dagon personnel to Iraq. We've identified some low level types, all heading in that direction."

"Wait. That reminds me of something. Dagon, or Dagan as it is sometimes spelled, was a more modern version of the ancient Sumerian deity Enlil. That's a Mesopotamian god, associated with the ancient city of Nippur."

"Aha."

"There used to be a ziggurat there, a temple to Enlil. It would be considered a sacred site to the Dagon cult. The ultimate sacred site. The place where Dagon would have actually been worshipped in the open."

"So if their members are headed there …"

"That's where the next ritual will take place. That's where they've taken the *Necronomicon*."

"And the vial of your blood."

Angell got up from his chair, still a little shaky. "Where are my notes?"

"They're safe," replied Aubrey, a trifle sardonically.

Angell whirled around on him.

"What do you mean, 'safe'? What did you do with them?"

"Relax. You were out like a light. I had to transmit them back to my people in DC. There wasn't time to waste. I have them here."

He reached under the breakfast cart and withdrew Angell's knapsack.

Angell reached for it, then stopped.

"Is it all there?"

"If you mean the money, yes, it is. We're not thieves, Gregory."

"Yeah, right." He grabbed the knapsack and rummaged through it. His notes were there.

"She didn't take them. Prudence. She took the Book, but really had no interest in the notes."

"Why would she? She already knew the system. She didn't need your notes."

"Still. You would have thought she would steal them and destroy them herself so that they wouldn't fall into the wrong hands."

"Who would understand them if they had? I looked at them, and I didn't understand a word."

"I guess you're right."

"You're annoyed!"

"What do you mean?"

"You're annoyed! You wanted someone to look at the notes and marvel at how bright you are to have figured it out! You academics are all alike."

Angell wanted to punch that self-satisfied smirk off his face, but then realized that what he was saying was at least partially true. So he relaxed and sat back down.

"Yeah, well. Maybe you're right. But it does raise one question, and that is: did I really figure it out? Or am I completely wrong in my calculations?"

"I have no idea, but I'm pretty sure our people back home can verify it one way or another."

"If my notes are right, though, we have a problem."

"Which is?"

Angell looked over the papers, which were slightly out of order, and rearranged them again.

"Maybe we know the place for the ritual. Nippur. And I think I know the timing. You said they're all moving into Iraq now?"

"Yes, why? I assume that means the ritual will be held very soon."

"Soon, yes. If you're going to a war zone for any reason other than taking part in the hostilities, you'd want to get in and get out, fast."

"Sure."

"That idea reinforces what I was thinking about the timing. If my calculations are correct, and the stars are aright as they say, then I believe the ritual will take place tonight."

He looked up at Aubrey's surprised expression.

"And that means we are almost out of time."

CHAPTER SIXTY-TWO

Children Charity Center
Bronx, New York

NALIN SAT IN HER CORNER AND REMEMBERED.

Her isolation cell was probably the wrong place to put her, but how would they have known? She had been unable to communicate with her keepers. She spoke only a local form of Kurmanji—the Kurdish dialect that was common among some Yezidi—and she had been so traumatized that speaking at all was a struggle for her.

She liked the way the two walls of the corner felt, as if they were giant arms hugging her, protecting her. She squeezed herself into that corner as tightly as she could and closed her eyes. She remembered the smells of her village near the sacred mountain in Iraq. The sound of her family chatting. The scraping of pots for dinner.

And then the machine guns.

She watched helplessly as strange men came and dragged away her father and her two brothers. As they came to take away her mother and her three sisters and her aunt. She watched them shoot her father and brothers in the road outside their house. They didn't even have time to beg for their lives. There were bullets flying everywhere and holes opened up in her father and her brothers and blood came out and pooled in the dirt.

The men pawed at her sisters, ripping off shawls and skirts. She saw that her sisters were ashamed and crying. One, her oldest sister, was taken behind the house and she heard screams. One by one the men went behind the house and did something to her sister, and then came out and other men would replace them.

She wanted to run to her sister, but one of the men held her by the arms and wrapped string around her wrists. They threw her into the back of a truck.

As the truck started up and went down the road they passed her house and she could see behind it, see her sister spread out on the ground, bleeding, and one of the men standing over her and shooting her in the head.

Nalin thought: my sister's last moments on this world, in this life, was of men raping her—for she learned that was what it was called— one after another, and then a man shooting her dead. Those were her last moments. A day before, she had been expecting preparations for her wedding to a boy from the next village.

Nalin thought: how to make room in your head for all those things of their village, the cooking and the cleaning, the laughter of your family, the eyes of your fiancé; and in the next moment you are being raped and you are only living from one second to another, in the spaces between the thrusts of evil men inside you, being defiled, being shamed, being hurt, and as you take your next breath, as the last man pulls out of you, he points a gun to your head and you wonder if that will be your last image, the last thing you see, the last thing you feel, and before you can finish that thought you are dead.

Nalin thought: they wanted to do the same to me. They wanted to sell me to another fighter, another murderer and rapist, and then another one after that, but another man came and said no. Another man came and said we need this one. Another man came and said we will get more money for her if she is a virgin. Money from abroad, not local money. Not goats or shoes. But real money, enough to buy a hundred weapons or many thousands of rounds of ammunition. Keep her apart from the others. Keep her in a cage. Do not let her escape.

So they kept her in a locked room. They gave her some food and water and a bowl to relieve herself. And she stayed there for days. For weeks. Men would come and look at her. But no one touched her. And then one day she fell asleep for a long, long time and when she awoke she was in a big room in some foreign place with other girls, girls she did not know, and she fell asleep again for a long, long time and then she was in a secret place on the other side of the world. And a man came and told her what she must do.

Nalin thought: this is what they taught me. To think in pictures and not in words. To dream while being awake. To be awake while dreaming.

Nalin thought: they made me look into a dark, dark mirror until I could see the things they wanted me to see. They held my arms and legs. They touched me with sharp things that hurt. They put me in water. They held me before the fire. They buried me in the ground. They suspended me in the air. And all the time my eyes were open and then I began to see what they wanted me to see, to hear what they wanted me to hear.

Nalin thought: and then, and then …

Nalin thought: and then I wasn't here anymore. I was somewhere else. I was outside of my body and looking at it from heaven. Is this death? I thought. Will I see my mother and my aunt and my sisters and my father and my brothers and my cousin? And I saw my body shaking. I saw my mouth open and words come out even though I was not speaking. And all the horror I had seen was in front of me once again. My father and my brothers. My mother and my sisters. My aunt. And my cousin. And the men who killed them. And … and something else. Someone else. Something disgusting. It was made of the bits and pieces of my family's broken bones. The bits and pieces of my memories. The bits and pieces of rent flesh, spilled blood, and broken minds. And It was pleased. I shouted and screamed from somewhere inside of me but no words came out, no sounds could escape. My sounds and my words were like me: in an isolation cell. In a locked room.

Nalin thought: and I saw the men smiling. And I saw the men trembling. I saw the men worshipping the memories of my murdered family, memories that became a single Monster. And I saw that my pain and my sickness had pleased the men.

Nalin thought: and I saw that my nightmares had become their dreams.

Nalin thought: now I am alone in another room. Now they will use me again.

CHAPTER SIXTY-THREE

The Road to Al-Diwaniyah
Iraq

THEY HAD TO TRAVEL BY DAYLIGHT on the main road, Route 1, south of Baghdad. There was safety in numbers, and confidence in the light. The Dark Lord was in the second car. The first car was filled with men holding automatic weapons. So was the third car. The fourth car had more Dagon members but not as many as he had expected and none that he knew personally. Others were already at Afak, waiting for them. From Afak they would proceed to the ritual site at Nippur.

There were road blocks, of course. US military and Iraqi Army. Some mercenaries as well. The mercenaries were better-equipped. Most of the fighting was going on in the north, in and around Mosul and Tikrit. There were the occasional IEDs in the south, but right now ISIL had its hands full dealing with American and coalition forces in the north.

Ordinarily the ride to Afak would take two hours, more or less. But the road blocks and the traffic slowed them down and if they made it in four hours that would be good time. The car bombings outside the hotels made everybody on edge.

They traveled in a convoy, but tried not to make it too noticeable. They did not want to attract the attention of ISIL forces or sympathizers. They had to make it to Afak and then back to Baghdad early the following morning, before dawn if possible, so they could get out of this godforsaken country before all Hell broke loose.

Literally.

They would open the Gate tonight. The stars were aright.

★ ★ ★

The Dark Lord had not met with the new high priestess and high priest since the day his arm was removed, and even then it was only the briefest of views. They wore masks, as per the requirement of the ritual, so he never saw their faces. They were the ones who were selected to replace the sister-brother team that died in Pinecastle. He did not know their names.

One piece of good news that he received just before leaving the hotel was that the surviving seers and breeders had been located. They had been in US government custody somewhere in the States all this time, and now they had been moved to New York City. He had been informed that a team of Keepers of the Book were on their way to the site. They would snatch the breeders, some of whom were pregnant and due within a month or so, and take them to a safe place to give birth. Everyone was freaking out about this! A new litter of hybrids always made everyone giddy with anticipation. The last successful group consisted of only two live births: the now-deceased priestess and priest, and before that the accursed Vanek and his twin. Word had it that Vanek was rotting in some black site prison. He knew that the bitter thug was trying to contact him using the Tantric methods they had all been taught, but he ignored the attempts. He was in no mood to do anything to help that psychotic screw-up. Let him rot. He lost an arm because of Vanek. Fuck him.

But the ritual they were holding tonight was far more powerful than anything they had done before, at least in his lifetime. They had tried to raise Kutulu in Nepal, and that had failed even though they had the Book in their possession at the time. That was because that timid interloper Gregory Angell had interfered and seized the Book for himself.

Then they tried to open the Gate wide in Florida. What an elaborate operation! And costly, too. But that ritual was thwarted because American law enforcement became aware of the human trafficking angle. At least, that is what he was told. And Vanek had been the weak link in that network and was captured.

This time, though, they were not taking any chances. They would conduct the ritual at Nippur, for that is where the hot point would be positioned in a very few hours. How fortunate that the *point chaud* would hover over the exact same spot it had inhabited five thousand years earlier when Enlil was worshipped and Dagon was yet a dream. And only the initiates of Dagon were aware that Nippur marked the spot on the Earth under which an ocean once existed that concealed the sunken kingdom of Ur Il Yah.

His reverie was disturbed by the annoying voice of his fellow passenger, the irritating subhuman known to the world of men and losers as Maxwell Prime.

"Jesus Christ, man. I've spent a lot of time in hot countries in my career, but it's gotta be ninety-five in the shade right now and it's not even noon. It wouldn't be so bad if it wasn't for the dust. And the smell of … what is that? Camel shit?"

"Are you certain you are not the source of the odor?"

"Hey, well, it's true, I spent a lot of time in stir in that black site you got me out of, your people I mean. It takes a long time to get rid of the smell. It stays with you, you know what I'm saying? You smell it every once in awhile. Catches you by surprise. What did you say your name was?"

"I didn't."

"Right. Okay. No problem." He shut up for awhile then and concentrated on looking at the passing countryside.

Prime had been in Iraq before, something he had not shared with his colleagues. When they brought him out of the airport after he had been hit in the face by Angell, he was taken to a car and driven out of Frankfurt and out of Germany to France where they got a flight to Dubai. He had no objections, figuring this was all part of the master plan to take down Monroe and Aubrey.

Up ahead he could see the first car with its load of AK-47s and rocket launchers. They had some kind of military pass that would whisk them through the checkpoints along the way, no questions asked. He used to work with Blackwater out here, and they had a similar arrangement. Or maybe it was Blackwater that issued the passes. He forgot.

He had the sudden urge to start singing the Mister Rogers song about a beautiful day in the neighborhood but at the last moment decided it would be … unappreciated by the one-armed bastard sitting next to him. So he remained quiet but in his mind he played the song to himself to pass the time.

"Another hour to al-Diwaniyah," their driver announced. "And then from there we go to Afak. *Inshallah.*"

"*Shukran,*" said the Dark Lord.

"*Afwan.*"

CHAPTER SIXTY-FOUR

The Bronx
New York City

SYLVIA AND HARRY HAD TAKEN AMTRAK from DC to New York, and hailed a taxi to get them to the staging area. The communication they received from Aubrey, still in Germany, was that the ritual they all feared was due to take place that night, Iraq time. That meant a good eight hours earlier, New York Time. If the ritual took place at midnight in Baghdad then that meant four pm in New York. Most likely, if there was going to be an assault on the foster care facility in the Bronx it would happen this morning or afternoon, to give Dagon enough time to add the little seers to the sacrificial roster and probably to snatch the pregnant girls and take them to a place where they could give birth under Dagon auspices.

They were not sure about any of this, of course. They weren't exactly flying blind, but close to it. What if they had the dates and times wrong? What if Dagon was uninterested in the girls, or hadn't learned of their sudden vulnerability? There was a lot they didn't know for sure, but oddly enough Harry was convinced that today was the day. When asked why, he simply shrugged and said he just knew.

That made Sylvia nervous, so on the train ride up to New York she asked him again.

"I can't describe it. I feel … different. Uneasy, anxious, but also as if I can see what's going on through their eyes."

"Whose?"

"Not sure. But Dagon, anyway."

"I don't like the sound of that."

"No, I don't mean that they're using me somehow. How would that work, anyway? It's just this weird feeling. I've had it for a few days now. The feeling that something very important is about to take place. Anticipation. That's the word I'm looking for. Anticipation. I have this feeling like, it's okay, just go with the flow. It's gonna be great."

"I really don't like the sound of that. Look, let's try something. You've heard of cognitive interviews, right?"

"Wasn't that an Eighties kinda thing?"

"It's still used in some cases, but mostly for memory retrieval. I want to try it with you. I want you to relax and try to get back in that frame of mind where you're doing all this anticipating."

"Um, okay."

"Just close your eyes and breathe deeply. Relax."

"Okay. Relaxing … relaxing …"

"Okay. Think of anticipation. This feeling. Try to get it, to feel it inside of you."

There was a pause. Harry was breathing deeply, and it seemed as if he was concentrating.

"I feel good. Almost happy. Or something."

"Okay. Can you see anything? Sense anything around you?"

He frowned, still with his eyes closed.

He was quiet for a few moments, and then seemed a little more animated.

"I see … I don't really see it … I kind of remember it but it's not a memory I recognize …"

"Don't intellectualize it too much, just tell me what you see. Or remember."

"An apartment. Small. Cold. Kind of grungy. Dark."

"Okay, let it flow. Let it take you. Follow the good feeling. The anticipation."

"That's just it. It seems to be concentrated there."

"Can you see anything else? Words of any kind? A sign? A picture?"

More silence for a moment, then "No, not really. But the place does seem familiar somehow."

Another few moments.

"It's two places."

"Pardon?"

"I'm seeing two different places. Both small. Cold. Dark. Dirty, sort of. Dank. They're superimposed on each other."

Sylvia was becoming convinced that this wasn't going to go anywhere, when Harry suddenly opened his eyes.

"Shit. I do know that place. The first one. The apartment. It's from when I went up with Dwight to Whately."

"Massachusetts?"

"Yeah. Except I never went to the apartment because it wasn't there, it was … it was in New Bedford, and I've never been to New Bedford."

"I am totally confused."

"What I mean is, the place I saw was in New Bedford, but I only ever saw photographs of it. When they tossed that guy's apartment, the one they arrested in Whately. I was there with Dwight. It was Aubrey who went to the apartment and searched it.

"The guy was this cultist name of Vanek. Dwight interrogated him. I was seeing Vanek's apartment. Why would I associate that with happy anticipation?"

"As far as I know, Vanek's in prison somewhere."

"That could explain the second place I saw. It was much worse than the first."

"What do you think this means?"

"I dunno. Probably nothing. Some conflation of what happened last year with what's happening now. I mean, it's connected, right? The girls again? Dagon."

They got out and hailed a taxi and wound up in the Bronx, a few blocks away from the Children Charity Center. When they got to the staging area—an old warehouse near Arthur Avenue—they found that they had been stiffed.

Instead of the SWAT team they were expecting, they got two uniformed police officers about four seconds from retirement and a detective who seemed to be their supervisor.

"Sorry, Ma'am. Sir. But the team got called away on a hostage situation near Yankee Stadium. This is all you've got right now."

"This isn't acceptable! We may have a few dozen bad guys here at any time ..."

"I understand this is for a foster home?"

"A care center, yes."

The detective looked around at the two uniforms and back at the two feds.

"I think we can handle it."

"You don't understand, Detective ..."

"No, Ma'am. All due respect, but you don't understand. We don't have the staff right now. You can't give us any kind of information on this case. You won't share any details. How can we organize the kind of response you tell us you need, on a fucking whim? Pardon my language, but you see where I'm going with this. If it turns out a whole gang of bad guys shows up, you'll get your overwhelming response, I guarantee it. But right now, we have a hostage situation and a CT situation as well."

"CT?"

"Counter-Terrorism, Ma'am."

"What kind of counter-terrorism?"

"I can't say. You understand."

"What ever happened to inter-agency cooperation?"

"Once again, all due respect, but your operation doesn't come with a whole hell of a lot of justification. Since when does NSA conduct raids in the Bronx? Or at all? You see what I mean?"

"We're not conducting a raid, Detective! We just want to be ready to arrest a lot of very dangerous individuals who want to break into that facility and harm those girls."

"I promise you. We see those dangerous individuals and I'm on the horn right away getting a couple dozen squad cars and shotguns. No one is getting through us."

The other two policemen nodded vigorously.

"Well," said Harry. "I guess we're fucked, then."

"It sure explains Vanek feeling happy, though."

CHAPTER SIXTY-FIVE

Monroe's Office
Fort Meade, Maryland

MONROE TOOK THE CALL FROM AUBREY in his office. Harry and Sylvia had already left for New York, and Simon had been burning the midnight oil looking for confirmation of Angell's calculations in the mass of documentation he had accumulated over the past few months.

"Dwight, do you still have any juice with the Joint Chiefs?"

It was an honest question. They had blown through a lot of regulations, not to mention expense, with their operation in Nepal and then their Pinecastle op. Of course, both operations were net successes, but it brought a lot of light onto Monroe and his motley crew from a number of individuals who saw in Monroe and his ad hoc team a threat to their own hegemony.

"Maybe. Could be. What do you have in mind?"

"Nothing much. Just a drone."

"You're kidding? For a strike?"

"No, I don't believe that will be necessary. Just for surveillance. We think that the opposition are regrouping around the old site of Nippur tonight, Baghdad time. Can we task one with an overflight of the area, say around ten pm local or so?"

"I'll work on it. But if we find out you're right, what's to stop us from dropping a Tomahawk?"

"It's an ancient archaeological site, Dwight. We're not the Taliban."

"How else to stop them, though?"

"That's my second request. Can we divert a fire team from up north? They can help light up the site for the drone and then move in if we're right and they're up to something there."

"How big a gathering are you expecting? A fire team may not be enough. And that's a lot of terrain to cover."

"I wish I knew more. We're basing everything on a chain of conjectures here. But if we get confirmation that the bad guys are assembling on the hill at Nippur, then at least we know they are all in one place. We can decide whether or not it justifies a tactical response then."

"It would take time to get a team down there."

"We've got roadblocks and checkpoints along Route 1, though, right? We can use them as choke points, make sure no one is getting very far after they do whatever it is they do."

The conversation went on in that vein for another few minutes. Monroe said he would do what he could to task a drone for surveillance over the Nippur site, and in the meantime would work on logistics for either stopping a ritual or dealing with its aftermath. It was true that the intelligence they had so far—from Angell's capture by Dagon agents to the arrest of Moody at Dubai—pointed to something happening imminently, and happening in Iraq. With their human trafficking networks seriously compromised, Monroe was fairly certain that a replay of Pinecastle was not in the works. Angell was trying to be more helpful in predicting what form a ritual would take, how many people would be involved, and so forth but he was working with limited resources as well. The Book had been taken by Dagon and was presumably on its way to Baghdad if it wasn't there already. Angell had his notes, which had been scanned and sent to Simon, but that was about all.

Monroe hung up and started making his calls.

CHAPTER SIXTY-SIX

Desert Hospital

GLORIA WAS STILL IN LABOR.

She had been in the delivery room for hours, and the staff was getting worried. They wanted to perform a C-section but the baby's vital signs were still good and Gloria resisted. You would have thought she would welcome some respite from the painful contractions and just ask to be knocked out and get it over with, but she had been down this road before and knew what to expect.

As for Gloria's own vital signs, she was strong and determined. Her blood pressure had been all over the place for awhile and they feared eclampsia but suddenly she stabilized and seemed to mellow out. While the contractions were still painful, as always, Gloria seemed to be in another world. She was lucid, and was able to answer their questions from time to time, but she appeared unnaturally serene. The nurses and doctor exchanged worried glances, but her vitals were good.

Blair had remained behind in the waiting room until about five pm. Someone came out and told him it would be a while yet, and to get something to eat, for which he was grateful. He really didn't know what he was doing there, anyway. He didn't know Gloria very well, after all.

So he returned to his motel room near the Joshua Tree site and when he opened his door he found himself surrounded by law enforcement, looking for the woman he had just left at the hospital.

They wanted to speak to Gloria about a homicide in New York. Blair professed to know nothing about that, until they produced evidence that he had searched her name two nights earlier. They had her credit card record for a room in another motel, but when they went there she was missing.

And her car was in the lot at Joshua Tree.

Blair had to think quickly. They seemed to know everything, but they didn't seem to know she was in a local hospital, giving birth. The last thing she needed was a bunch of cops showing up and demanding to talk to her while she was in labor or, God forbid, handcuffing her to her hospital bed.

At the same time, he didn't want to be accused of aiding and abetting but those were the noises the cops were making. They were local, but they were waiting on a detective from New York to arrive and conduct a real interview. At least they were calling it an "interview" and not an "interrogation," but Blair knew that could change. He was not technically under arrest yet, just a person of interest.

But they were sitting in his motel room and taking up positions outside. *They must really think she killed that doctor in Brooklyn*, he thought to himself.

★ ★ ★

"Fuck! Did you see that?"

It was one of the cops from outside the motel room.

"No, what?"

"That thing … it passed right over us!"

"I didn't see anything. What the hell you talking about?"

"Seriously, you didn't see it?"

As that weird conversation went on outside, audible to everyone in the room, one of the cops—the one who seemed to be in charge—asked Blair what he was doing at the Contact in the Desert conference. Wasn't that about UFOs and such?

"Yes, mostly, but my interest is more along the lines of exobiology and that sort of thing. You know, if aliens existed what would they look like and if communication with them would be possible. I'm not really a flying saucer guy."

"Uh huh. So … little green men and all that?"

"Not really. But … yeah, I guess you could say that."

"And this Gloria Tibbi, she was into that, too?"

"You'll have to ask her."

"Oh, I will. When I find her. I have to ask you again, do you know where she is?"

"I have nothing to tell you about that, officer."

"Uh huh. Well, I guess we'll just have to wait here with you until that New York City detective shows up. Could be hours and hours. You get any sleep last night?"

And it went on like that for awhile. By seven pm Danny had arrived from New York and was already complaining about the heat, but by then it was too late.

CHAPTER SIXTY-SEVEN

Afak, Al-Qadisiyyah Governorate
Iraq

Maxwell Prime was once again in restraints.

The Dark Lord was in the next room, talking with a woman who seemed to be in charge. Prime himself had been taken roughly from the car when they arrived in this small town below the Nippur site and had his wrists tied with a plastic tie. He began to realize that he was a pawn in some larger game. Again.

In the next room, the Dark Lord and several other people were sitting on carpets on the ground, sipping very strong and sweet espresso from little porcelain cups. Prime could hear some of what they were saying, and it made him start to panic.

"The ritual will culminate with the rising of the Sun," the woman said. "But it will begin much earlier, of course. The point will be above us in a few hours. We have to be ready by then. That means the usual preparatory rites should begin soon. We need everybody on site in an hour. Is he ready?" She pointed with her head to the room where Prime was being held.

"He has not been told what is to take place."

"Fine. He has no need to know. What I mean is, will he give us any trouble later?"

The Dark Lord smiled.

"He will not be a problem. I will see to it."

"See that you do. We don't want this to fall apart like last time. We have run out of opportunities. Another one will not come along for a century, or more."

The Dark Lord had the grace to look contrite, and unconsciously touched the place where his left arm should be with his right hand.

"It will succeed, my Priestess."

Then she laid a bombshell in the middle of the room.

"My brother and consort was sacrificed in Germany a few days

455

ago. I believe he was taken out by either a member of the German
security services or by those who have opposed us since the dawn
of time."

Everyone was aghast at this news. There was murmuring around
the circle of devotees. While his absence had been noted, it was
believed to be related to some secret ritual preparations.

It was the Dark Lord who addressed the issue.

"Do you mean that Starry Wisdom is conducting operations
against us again? I thought they had elected to stay out of our way?"

"The situation has changed. Once they knew that we had lost
the Book, they saw us as weakened and vulnerable. I have remedied
those circumstances, but I believe they see no reason why they
should relax their opposition."

"They want to keep to the slow way, the gradual replacement of
humans by the pure seed of the Old Ones."

"And how has that worked for us in the past?"

"It has not, my Priestess."

"Even as I and my brother were born of the mixed seed of
humans and the Old Ones, and even as the previous high priestess
and her brother were the same, our goal has always been to take
extreme action and open the Gate once and for all, to end this
charade of gradual genetic manipulation that is the fascination
of our enemies. This planet, and all who live on its surface, *must
be cleansed*. Physical pollution is spiritual pollution. Let us call the
hybrids of Starry Wisdom what they are: mutants! They are unclean
things, creatures composed of both natures who have forgotten their
real birthrights.

"They do not understand, or do not accept, that the pain we
inflict on our victims has the intended effect of polarizing the
microtubules, of using the physical brain to enter into and control
the quanta, as we control the direction and intensity of the operation,
using the victims as devices to entangle them with the Old Ones.
When we open the Gate, all of humanity will be subject to that
polarization. The world will be renewed.

"With this ritual tonight we will stare into the mirror and see our true selves. Our twins on the Other Side will pass through to greet us, and embrace us, and our human natures will be burned away in their sacred gaze. The Old Ones were, the Old Ones are, and the Old Ones shall be, the Masters of this World."

Prime was listening to all of this and realized that he had made a serious mistake. One of many, but most likely the fatal one.

These people, his new friends, were batshit crazy.

★ ★ ★

There was movement in the room next door. The High Priestess, known in the world of men as Prudence Wakefield, great-granddaughter of Ottmar Freiherr von Verschuer, the mentor of Josef Mengele, stood up and surveyed the assembled initiates. They were not many. Dagon lost initiates at the last two rituals and was down to a skeleton crew. While they had many followers in all parts of the world, the inner circle was necessarily small but entirely—fanatically—devoted. Blood would be spilled in the course of the rite, the Opening of the Gate ceremony that had always been the core ritual of Dagon, but that was to be expected. They had Maxwell Prime, who had lost them Angell and the Book, and he would do nicely. His screams would charge the vibratory matrix even as they flayed the skin from his body. ISIL was afraid of Dagon, for their cruelty was tightly controlled and never used to satisfy a baser instinct, fetish, or lust. It was a means to an end. ISIL was learning that, but had a hard time controlling their followers. Dagon had no such trouble. They had been doing this for thousands of years.

Her people in New York would obtain the missing girls at the same time as the ritual was taking place in Iraq. They would use the seers one last time before their throats were cut. And as for the breeders, if they could retrieve them and bring them to safety, so be it. If not, they were to be sacrificed as well. Either way, the Old Ones would be satisfied.

She reached into the cloth bag she kept at her side and touched the vial of Angell's blood. A necessary instrument that would charge the Book and bring the ritual of 1907 full circle to the ritual of 2015. One hundred and eight years, the sacred number in the religions of India, the number of beads in a *mala*, the Buddhist and Hindu rosary. It is said the number 108 refers to the twenty-seven constellations and their four elements, or the twelve signs of the Zodiac and the placement of the nine planets within each of them. In either case the number refers to the heavens. To the stars. And there is an extra bead in the Hindu rosary, and it is called the *sumeru*. How fitting!

And eighteen is the number of "life" in Hebrew. How appropriate that this day would give life back to the Old Ones on Earth. That the ritual would bring them back from the stars.

Spirit of the Sky, Remember!

CHAPTER SIXTY-EIGHT

Children Charity Center
The Bronx

THE CHILDREN WERE STRANGELY QUIET. It was like a forest when a hunter approaches and all the wildlife freezes in place. They stood up and seemed to sniff the air, as if aware of the approach of a predator.

The circumstances of their life in the charity center in the Bronx were not much different from their stay in the federal facility in the DC area. In fact, the Children Charity Center was funded by federal dollars anyway. They had several isolation rooms for the problem children and an open area for the mothers-to-be and the other children. It was not much different, and the Pinecastle kids were the only guests currently housed at the center. It was not known how long they would be there, and Sylvia was hoping that a way could be found to get them into different—friendlier—facilities once the threat aspect had been removed.

Sylvia and Harry were sitting in an unmarked car within sight of the building, along with the lead detective. There was another car on the other side of the street with the two uniforms. They had started to pass the time with idle conversation, but that soon ran dry and they just found themselves reduced to silently looking at the building and thinking their own thoughts.

They hardly noticed when two young men in hoodies wandered past the building at a slow walk, and then reappeared a few minutes later, walking back. Harry followed them with his eyes, not worried yet that they might be Dagon, or sent by Dagon. The two men did not seem that interested in scoping out the building and why would they? It was called Children Charity Center. Nothing particularly alluring about that.

The two hoodies disappeared again and Harry lost interest. He lay back in his seat and closed his eyes.

Sylvia kept watch, however. She was nervous, and worried about the kids. If they had miscalculated in any way ...

That is when she heard the singing.

★ ★ ★

Inside the building, the girls started to chant something in a language no one at the center could identify. It was the second day of June, and a full moon.

Half a world away, atop what was left of the ancient city of Nippur, the ritual of the Opening of the Gate had just begun.

CHAPTER SIXTY-NINE

Nippur
Iraq, formerly Sumer

WITH A RISING VOICE, THE HIGH PRIESTESS and Queen of Dagon calls her people to the service of the Old Ones and the Opening of the Gate:

★ ★ ★

With words and sounds we imbue life into the dead thing, the ambitious but still rotting corpse. When we opened the mouth of the mummy in ancient Egypt, we enabled it to eat but also *to speak*. If it can speak, it can live. We did not open the ears, for hearing is passive. A drum can hear. A stone can hear. But Kutulu—dead Kutulu—must speak in order to live, and we must open our mouths as instruments for Kutulu so that he may rise, and move, and appear, and so that we may live in the vibrations of the sounds that gush forth like the vomitus of plague and the sentiment of fever from the gorge of his stricken, diseasèd throat and through the tendons and chords of our own.

He has spoken to us in dreams, and in nightmares, and in delusions, and in all the many and delicious schizophrenias of our tortured minds. He knows how we have fooled ourselves into thinking we were free, that we had free will, that we moved across an Earth that we thought we owned, of which we thought we were Lords. That was never so; but as in the howling asylums of our hideous cities which house the mad and the insane who think they are gods, or kings, we live on the surface of this planet like so many strait-jacketed maniacs, covered in our own filth and soiled with the fairy tales of our fathers.

All dreams come from the Dreamer, and the Dreamer is Kutulu, the High Priest of the Old Ones. In quaking fear, the faithless appeal to the doctors of the mind to release them from the horrors of their nightmares, not knowing that their dreams are not the royal road to the Unconscious but the widdershins path to the subterranean Crypt in R'lyeh where Great Kutulu lies dead but dreaming. How they would scream in despair if they ever realized that every dream they ever had was generated from one single, blasphemous, crepuscular source! Every dream of standing naked before crowds, or running desperately from a mob, or fucking one's mother or father or terrified cow … every single one, every dream wet or dry, every nightmare and night terror and paralysis, every bed wetting fantasy, every kick of every blanket over every emaciated frame in the world, comes from a single putrescent corpse squirming in a stone sarcophagus older than any civilization on Earth, covered in indecipherable hieroglyphics whose very pronunciations would drive the dullest mind insane.

For it is written:

Ph'nglui mglw'nafh Cthulhu R'lyeh wgah'nagl fhtagn.

All those consonants, and those mysterious, errant vowels! The credulous believe that the pronunciation is there, but it is not. As in the unspoken, unutterable name of the Jewish God, there are only consonants. The words must be spoken in a sigh; the vowels are the spirit, the breath, the pitiless weeping between the consonants and not the broad, braying vowels of the modern, insensate world.

In the original, it reads:

Ph'ngl mglw'nfh Cthlh R'lyh wg'ngl fhtgn.

But the meaning is clear, and has been for millennia:

In his house at R'lyeh dead Kutulu waits dreaming.

Dreams. Pictures. Speech. Words. It is all about the *words*.

Let us say the words.

CHAPTER SEVENTY

The Hounfort Marasa
Lower Ninth Ward, New Orleans

HERVÉ STOOD BEFORE THE *poteau mitan* in her temple, her hounfort, in the Lower Ninth Ward. She was alone, in a prayerful frame of mind. There were various bottles on an altar in the rear of the hounfort, each one containing a spirit she had summoned or controlled in the course of her career. Spirits of the dead. Servants. Some of these she had managed to bring with her to the United States after the hurricane, only the most important ones. Others had been created here in New Orleans. She knew each one, by name and power and history.

In another area, behind a hanging flag, the Twins were represented: two dolls of indeterminate gender looking identical, for they *were* identical in some parts and dissimilar in others. The *Marasa Dosou Dosa.* They were her loa, her special spirits. They were Twins, and she was Twins. This was a mystery that was not easy to reveal to the average person. Only an initiate such as herself, *ounsi agowe*, a spouse of the spirits, could begin to understand. Even then, there were those of the vodouisants who had ostracized her once they knew who she really was. When they called her "he/she" or "shim" in an attempt to denigrate her, they spoke her secret names and did not know it.

But what that detective had told her had shaken her, regardless of the strong front and proud attitude she showed him in the Waffle House. The war between Dagon and Starry Wisdom had returned to New Orleans after a long hiatus. She knew all the stories, had heard of them from vodouisants who had been here forever. Moreover, she knew of Dagon from the tales told around the *peristyle* back home, in Leogane and Port-au-Prince. The bokors would always get excited talking about Dagon. How their eyes would shine! The other *nanchons* would shrink in fear at the mention of their name and of the hideous rites they would conduct in the cane fields and in the mountains near the border with the DR. Dagon was not Haitian. It had nothing to do with vodou. But it could be found everywhere from Cap Haitien to Jacmel, but only on certain days according to a calendar no one understood. In the old days, some of the tontons macoutes were said to be Dagon initiates, but Hervé was certain that was a story told to make them seem even more frightening.

Tonight she would call on the loa. She needed to feel them. She needed to talk to them, to hear what they had to say. She needed the direct contact, to feel their breath on her cheeks before she succumbed to their intense ministrations.

In Haiti she went to the Catholic church for Mass on Sunday as is expected. She had to avoid the touch of the young priest who was sent there from Venezuela. When she was a child, she knew she was different and that she could arouse the interest of men and women, of boys and girls. She felt that gave her power, but the others said it made her weak. But she liked the Mass, the idea of the Mass. The big naked Christ on his cross hanging over the altar, and everyone eating his flesh and drinking his blood. No wonder the priests were lustful, for how could one serve such a god without being aware of flesh, and blood, and of the vulnerable, tortured man with the perfect body always in front of them? The carefully-delineated muscles. The provocative loin cloth. The eyes full of surrender. There was a sexuality in the Mass that made her aware of herself and her own body. Then there were the conflicting signals of the grown men dressed in flowing robes. The congregation kneeling before those men with their mouths open, tongues extended, to receive the Sacrament. Men and women alike. And children. Always children.

And now Hervé was sometimes priest, sometimes priestess, in the Mass of the Loa. Sometimes Mercury, sometimes Salt. Sometimes Sulfur. Sometimes the Lion, sometimes the Eagle. Sometimes both at once as the *prima materia* moved in her body, through the channels along her legs, her spine, her arms, her torso, up to her head, to the vault in her brain, to the *thalamus*: a word that means the bedchamber, the marriage bed. She gave, and she received. She was penetrated by the loa. And, secretly and known only to her, *she penetrated them herself.* Fecundity. Procreation. She had internalized all of that, like the Tantrikas of India or the Daoists of China. Her spine fucked her brain, over and over. Endlessly. *She was the flesh made spirit.* Unless you can reverse the process and draw the power inside you, conceiving a fetus in the center of your skull, alone except for the caress of your secret Twin, you cannot know sex or love or the power of creation.

And the starving mothers with their ten children apiece thought they knew all there was to know about birth and the making of life even as they lay on their backs: the mindless tools of a force they could not see. The spirit made flesh. Machines of meat and blood. Eat of this … drink of this …and remember me.

And the loa laughed.

★ ★ ★

The devotees began to arrive, rousing her from her reverie, from her sweet memories of Haiti and its warmth and smell and sounds, like an old lover from the past who still has the power to arouse passion even if it is only bittersweet, familiar and comfortable rather than the burning urge of lust and fever. She had enjoyed her lovers then, when her bare feet walked the hot soil of her homeland.

"*Nou pral antre nan sabagi a la,*" she intoned in Creole. We are going to enter the sanctuary.

M'ape rele mètrès ki sati anba dlo." I will summon the Mistress who comes from under the Water.

★ ★ ★

But as the drums started and as she petitioned Legba to open the Gate to permit the loa to enter the peristyle, she felt something else crawl up her thigh and into her deepest, darkest places.

She opened her mouth to scream, to stop the drums, but it was too late and she lost consciousness.

CHAPTER SEVENTY-ONE

Children Charity Center
The Bronx

Sylvia pushed Harry on the arm.

"Wake up! Do you hear that?"

The detective was sitting in the driver's seat and he rolled down his window to get a better look at the place and to hear what they were singing.

"That's not singing, Ma'am. I don't know what that is, but it's not singing."

★ ★ ★

From inside the building, the staff was worried and standing around waiting to be told what to do. The girls in the common area had all stood up, except for some of the pregnant ones who remained seated, rocking back and forth and humming.

Nalin was in her new isolation cell, not much different from the old one. But she was standing up, too. And chanting. The staff had not realized that until they passed her door and heard it, clear and loud, coming from that tiny little thing.

Yasemina, the one who had tried to kill a guard at the previous location, was likewise alert and attentive. Her chant was almost sub-audible, but it was there. They looked in on her and withdrew quickly when they saw the look in her eyes.

Meyan, who smelled so bad the last time, now smelled like a mixture of incense and flowers.

The mothers-to-be were picking up the chant now, too. Had Devata been there, she would have recognized it at once. The local staff, however, had never heard this before and they were unsettled by how all the girls had seemed to start in on it at once, as if they were programmed.

The head administrator picked up the phone to call somebody, anybody, and then realized she had no idea whom to contact. Who do you call when you're confronted by a case of mass demonic possession?

★ ★ ★

Harry opened his eyes. He felt really groggy, which was unusual for him. Sylvia shook him again.

"Wake up! I think we have a problem."

"What? What is it? How long have I …"

"Listen! Can you hear it?"

Harry looked out the window towards the building.

"Yeah, I do. It's the same, isn't it? Like the one on the tape?"

"Yes, exactly. The girls are all inside, chanting. This can't be good."

The detective turned around in his seat.

"Detective, have you ever heard singing like that before in your life?"

"Well … no, but these are foreign kids, right? Different kids, different songs."

But Harry was already getting out of the car. He looked both ways before starting to run across the street when bullets started flying from all directions.

Sylvia screamed.

The detective pulled out his weapon and tried raising his two uniforms by radio.

Harry hit the ground, but was unhurt. He scrambled back towards the car.

"They're shooting at us!"

Sylvia yelled at the detective, "They're here! Call for backup! Now!"

And she opened the car door and dragged Harry back inside.

★ ★ ★

The two hoodies from before withdrew Ingram Mac-10s from under their jackets and began spraying the street with 9mm rounds.

But they were only the diversion. The real assault was taking place from the rooftop.

There was a puff of smoke first, and then the sound of a bang as someone blew open an access door. Sylvia craned her neck to see up but then pulled back inside as the hoodies began to concentrate on their vehicle.

Harry pulled the door open on the other side and dragged Sylvia out. The detective was returning fire at the two men and simultaneously trying to call it in. No one knew where his two uniforms were, but they feared the worst.

Just as the two men with the machine guns started crossing the street in their direction first one, then the other, fell to the ground as if struck by the hand of God.

"Where the hell did that come from?" yelled Harvey.

"Must be my guys," claimed the detective.

"I don't think so." He pointed to their car where they could just make out blood spatter on their windshield.

"Shit. Ah, shit. Those were good guys."

"No time for that now, Detective. When is backup getting here?"

"I called it in, but got no response from dispatch."

"Keep trying. Are there any more weapons in the car?"

The detective reached over and popped the trunk.

"If you can get to the trunk, there's two shotguns and ammo there."

"Good enough."

Harry crab-walked out of the car and around the back to the trunk. He found the shotguns and a couple boxes of shells.

He gave one shotgun to Sylvia.

"Do you know how ..." but stopped when he saw the look on her face. "Okay, okay. So, what do we do now? Rush the place?"

"We have to save those kids. And we seem to have a guardian angel around here, or whoever or whatever took out those two Ingrams. Let's do it."

Without thinking—because they knew if they stopped to think

they would lose courage immediately—they began a run across the street, over the bodies of the two fallen hoodies. They braced for bullets coming from whoever shot them, but there was nothing.

As they got closer to the building they heard the chanting again. It had never stopped.

Across the street from the building, on a rooftop, Jamila sighted another man trying to use the access door to get inside the building where the children were housed. She picked him off easily.

When she could see no more men, she reloaded and then started down the stairs to the street.

"I'm coming," she said.

CHAPTER SEVENTY-TWO

All around the world
Universe A

As the chanting intensified in the Bronx, it grew in urgency and volume on top of the hill in Nippur.

Maxwell Prime was staked out and spread-eagled in the center of the temple area. He was terrified but couldn't make a sound. His mouth was taped up to the point where he could barely breathe. He was naked, and his body had been marked with lines and sigils like the diagram of a cow showing where all the different types of beef come from.

The chanting picked up speed. It was the same chant as that being sung by the children in the Bronx, although Dagon could not know that yet.

Ph'nglui mglw'nafh … Cthulhu R'lyeh wgah'nagl fhtagn.
Zi dingir kia kanpa! Zi dingir anna kanpa!

Fires had been set all around the perimeter. They were standing on the highest point of the ruin and above them the Great Bear hung from its tail in the sky, though it could hardly be seen due to the brightness of the full Moon.

Armed sentries had been posted around the edifice to ensure no one disturbed the ceremony.

The High Priestess invoked Cthulhu, using his Sumerian name, Kutulu; Kutulu the intermediary between the Old Ones and the human race.

She invoked Shub Niggurath.

She invoked Yog Sothoth.

And as she did so, there was a chorus of energetic response as from thousands of miles away the Pinecastle girls yelled out:

N'gai, n'gha'ghaa, bugg-shoggog, y'hah'; Yog-Sothoth! Yog-Sothoth!

★ ★ ★

470

Sylvia and Harry, each carrying a shotgun, ran across the street to the building expecting at any moment for bullets to come from behind them, but none came. The detective finally moved and followed them, scanning the rooftops to see where the sniper had come from.

They stood on either side of the door and waited. They could still hear the rhythmic chant of the children, like some satanic nursery rhyme, and they nodded to each other. Now or never.

They tested the doorknob. The door was open. Harry pushed open the door and Sylvia followed with her shotgun raised and pointed as if she had been doing this all her life.

She went in first, and Harry followed. The detective walked in backwards, his weapon pointing at the street. For the first time, he wondered why there was suddenly no traffic and no people he could see, anywhere.

Jamila did not know who those people were, but if Dagon was shooting at them they had to be friendlies. She recognized one of the men she shot as having been at the Nepal ritual. He escaped, then, only to be gunned down in the Bronx a year later.

She heard the chanting, too, but tried her best to ignore it. She knew the chants, had been taught them by Dagon on the run up to Nepal, and sometimes she heard them again in her head when she started to lose consciousness during one of her 'episodes.' She had to remain clear, now, because she had no faith that the people running into the building had any idea what they were up against.

She walked calmly across the street to the building, chambering a round.

★ ★ ★

"He's crowning."

In a desert hospital on the other side of the world, Gloria was giving birth.

At that moment a man walked into the main entrance of the hospital. There was nothing unusual about his appearance except for his broad and engaging smile.

And in New Orleans, in another hospital room, Lisa Carrasco looked down at the Boy in the Box. The Asian nurse had been detained by Cuneo to answer a few questions. The hypodermic syringe in the nurse's possession had been seized and the contents analyzed. It was a potent combination of amphetamines and a hallucinogenic agent. A check of the hospital's records showed that the nurse had been hired a few weeks before the discovery of the baby. A few weeks before the murder of Mrs. Galvez.

Cuneo was still trying to get his head around all of this when he received a phone call from his commander.

There was some guy in DC trying to get a hold of him.

He made his apologies to Lisa and to the uniforms he called to arrest the Asian nurse on suspicion of the attempted murder of the baby. He would charge her for the murder of Mrs. Galvez later when the evidence secured from her apartment proved enough to convict her.

But Lisa wasn't listening. She was staring at the baby with the strange covering of hair and the tortured whimpering and thought it was the most beautiful thing she had ever seen.

CHAPTER SEVENTY-THREE

Nippur
Iraq, formerly Sumer

As the ritual atop the hill continued, growing in intensity, it was captured on film by a Predator drone outfitted with a camera specially designed for night-time recording and onward transmission.

It was being controlled from a control room in Creech Air Force Base in Nevada, just outside Las Vegas. The video was seen by Monroe at NSA and by Aubrey in Germany. Angell was pacing the room, nervous as hell that it was happening again and that he wasn't there to stop it the way he had the last time. Aubrey had to remind him that they had managed to stop the Pinecastle ritual—and the other, diversionary rituals of last November—just fine without Angell's help.

But Dagon had the Book again. They had the *Necronomicon*. And his blood, for chrissakes.

"Well, then," said Aubrey. "It's just like you're there anyway, isn't it? So please sit down and be quiet. Watch this, if you want to be helpful."

He had Monroe on the phone.

"Do you want to stop this? Say the word and we launch."

"No, Dwight. Like I said, we can't blow up a world treasure like the ruins of Nippur."

"Then we go with Plan B. We pick them up when it's over and hope they haven't done any actual damage."

"I do see someone on the ground there. Do you see it? A body?"

After some muffled conversations on Monroe's side, the camera was able to zoom into the scene a little better.

They noticed the body of Maxwell Prime.

"So that's what happened to him," muttered Aubrey.

"Is he gone?"

"He's not moving."

"What a way to go. As a sacrifice to the gods of Sumer atop their most ancient city."

"You sound wistful, Dwight."

"In my case it will probably be in a hospital bed with tubes attached to my body, peeing into a bag. Tell me which one is better."

"Jesus, you're morose."

"I have reason to be. We got word from New York. The operation there is underway. And with virtually no assistance from NYPD so far. Jurisdictional issues, or something."

"I hope Sylvia had sense enough to stay out of it. I know how she feels about those kids."

"She's there. They're both there. Harry, too."

"Crap. What can we do?"

"I've got people on the ground now. They'll be there to assist in about ten."

"Look at your monitor. Something is happening."

★ ★ ★

At Nippur, the tension was palpable. A tremor ran through the assembled devotees. The Dark Lord was assisting the Priestess and he could see that her eyes had become unfocused, her breathing harsh, and her body rigid.

Another tremor ran through the devotees and this time each one stopped moving and became equally rigid, wide-eyed and terrified.

The pages of the *Necronomicon* began flipping back and forth, as if an invisible Being was paging through it. But it was probably just the wind.

The Dark Lord raised his right hand, the one holding the dagger as prescribed in the Book, and began to intone the chant preparatory to the offering of the sacrifice. The Gate was above them. The light of the Moon was darkening, as if from an eclipse.

He knew that as soon as he thrust the blade into the body of Maxwell Prime that the Gate would open and the Old Ones would gush forward like sewage from a broken pipe. The world that he had known all his life would begin to die. And it would begin here, in the middle of a war zone, in the country that started it all thousands of years ago. Sumer. Babylon. Ur of the Chaldees. The land of Abraham, and all those religions that flowed from his loins. The Old Ones would correct that. A new religion and a new science would flow from their loins and the loins of the new people they would create. Everything he knew or had ever known would disappear into the great Maw of the Earth Monster known as Kutulu.

This is what he had wanted all of his life. This is why he had trained. This was why he had lost his arm.

Why, then, did he hesitate?

The Moon darkened … darkened … and disappeared behind a disk vast and silent and hovering over the temple of Enlil, of Dagon, in Nippur.

The Gate was straining at its hinges.

CHAPTER SEVENTY-FOUR

In the Aether

YOU LAMENT THE DESTRUCTION OF THE HUMAN RACE? You have been praying for an end to your misery for centuries. For millennia.

You create scenarios of death in your media. Films about catastrophic events that wipe out entire cities, entire countries, the entire planet. If the human race is a psychiatric patient, its movies and books and music and art are the dreams and psychoses and neuroses that reveal the truth. You *want* to die. You *want* it to be over.

A little girl in another country—never your own—watches helplessly as her mother and sisters are raped repeatedly by religious fanatics over days. Then they are hanged in front of her. The little girl is sold to traffickers who take her from town to town, even out of the country, to be 'married' over and over again to different men, some as old as sixty and seventy.

Do you believe *you* deserve to be spared death and destruction?

Poor people in another country—never your own—die from starvation, from thirst, and from disease. Needlessly, in a world awash in food and medicine. Parents watch their children die. Other parents sell their children into slavery, to gain money for themselves and to guarantee their children another few years on the planet even as they are beaten, subjected to indescribable torments and sexual abuse.

Do you believe the human race should be spared?

You slaughter each other in the name of God. You find justification for murder and rape in your scriptures. Then why do you object when *our* scriptures give us justification for slaughtering *you*? Our scriptures *are* your scriptures. The only difference is, we are more honest. We have taken your religions to their logical conclusion: Armageddon, followed by Apocalypse.

You punish human beings for being women; or children; or gay; or transgender; or black; or brown; or Asian. We punish all of you

476

equally, without regard to race, ethnicity, religion, or gender. We start with the best of you and work our way up to the worst of you.

You murder babies in their cribs. So do we.

You abuse prepubescent boys and girls. So do we.

You torture prisoners, people under your control. So do we.

We murder the murderers. We rape the rapists. We torture the torturers.

What you cannot accept is that you are all guilty of the same crimes in the eyes of our Gods. Those who perform the acts, and those who support them, and those who look the other way. You have always suspected that this was so, hence your dreams of genocide and racial annihilation. Your dreams of apocalypse. Your *Independence Day*, and your *Towering Inferno*, and your *Planet of the Apes*, and your *Mad Max*. Your *Day After Tomorrow*.

You *want* the world to end. You want all this to be over.

We're here to make that happen.

Open the Gate.

CHAPTER SEVENTY-FIVE

Children Charity Center
The Bronx

SYLVIA, HARRY AND THE POLICE DETECTIVE walked down the corridor leading to the main room from which they could hear the chanting.

They heard footsteps running down into the building from the upper floors, probably the roof.

When they got to the main room, they stood on either side of the door. It had a glass window that they could see into. The girls were still alive, still standing upright and chanting, like a weird choir. Or a road show of *The Sound of Music* ... in hell.

And, to her horror, Sylvia saw one of the children on the floor, a pool of bloody water around her. She was giving birth.

She had no time to react, however. There was a shot fired, and a bullet screamed close to her head. She ducked, and another shot went wide.

Someone from upstairs was trying to block them, and was firing from a staircase they had not seen.

★ ★ ★

Jamila calmly entered the building and slipped into her awareness mode. That's not what she called it, but that was what it was. She had learned it from Rabten, the dear old Tibetan monk in northern India at Dharamsala, and it always worked for her in times of stress where she had to be alert and react without conscious thought.

But the chant was getting to her anyway.

She struggled to maintain her hold on her mind as she felt her body react to the sound and the rhythm, the cadence and the ancient language of the chant that was used to summon Kutulu, using her as a vehicle and medium. The old days, the old ways, still had a hold on her even as she knew they would kill her. She was in an abusive relationship with her own history.

She breathed deeply and pulled back from the abyss. She had nearly gone over the edge and if she had she would not have survived long enough to help the children. No. In fact, she would have become one of them. One of the victims, not a survivor.

I am not a vehicle, she told herself. *I am the driver.*

Yeah, came a voice in her head. The voice of an abuser: her history. *Keep believing it.*

That was when someone or something tugged at her sleeve.

She shook herself awake and looked down, her hold on her rifle still strong.

It was Nalin, free of her cell, and she spoke to Jamila in their shared language.

"Sister, in the name of Melek Ta'us. Help us."

CHAPTER SEVENTY-SIX

Nippur
Iraq, formerly Sumer

HE RAISED THE DAGGER at the highest pitch of the chant and as the darkness overwhelmed them all. He was standing over the body of Maxwell Prime, but swerved instead on his heel and drove the blade into the chest of the High Priestess, of Prudence Wakefield, of the great-granddaughter of Josef Mengele's mentor and teacher. He drove it in and held it against her breasts, holding her up with his one arm before allowing her to fall gently to the ground.

He thought he had done what he had to do. When he was at the brink of destroying everything, of the shared history of the human race—its wars and its campaigns, its art and its music, its murderous evil and moral blindness—he knew that he couldn't do it. The Old Ones were their history, too. Human history was a deformed and debilitated creation of these monstrous Beings from beyond the stars. Why permit them a do-over? Why collaborate in our own destruction? To let the Old Ones back through the Gate would be like allowing parents to murder their grown children. Their children, who are mirror images of themselves.

He was wrong of course.

The murder of the High Priestess was still a sacrifice.

When Monroe and Aubrey and Angell saw the act on the video feed, they thought they had won. They thought the Gate had been kept closed. They did not realize that human reasoning does not work really well when it comes to the things of the Other Side, the Sitra Ahra, the Tunnels of Set.

Angell felt uneasy. He had the sense that something was wrong but could not put his finger on it.

Simon, at his apartment which he never seemed to leave, ever, jumped up from his chair in the study, the mass of calculations—his and Angell's—in a disorganized pile on his desk.

"Oh, shit," he said, to the empty room, the empty apartment.

★ ★ ★

Before anyone could react, the Dark Lord left the ritual. The other devotees were still standing, still chanting, and seemed not to have seen what he did. Instead, their eyes were fixed on the vast dark disk hovering over them, between the Earth and the Moon. He left Maxwell Prime tied up on the ground. He picked up the *Necronomicon* and the vial of Angell's blood. He could use the blood as a negotiating ploy if he needed to.

He got his clothes from the pile at the entrance and covered himself as best he could. He had only one arm, and he was afraid to let go of the Book.

He scrambled down the hill to the first armed sentry he saw. Their cars were parked close by and the keys were in the ignition.

"Can you drive?" he asked the sentry.

He nodded.

"Good. Let's go. We have to get back to Baghdad immediately."

They could still hear the chanting from the top of the hill, but the sentry knew who the one-armed man was and knew he had to follow orders.

They set off on the long drive back to the Babylon Warwick Hotel, with the Dark Lord in the back seat cradling the *Necronomicon* and wondering if he did the right thing after all.

The darkness hovered over the site. The hot point was fixed and staring like a wall-eye on the blood pooling around the body of one of their own, a half-breed Priestess who had been sired by Yog-Sothoth on a thunderous evening in Berlin as the Wall was coming down. She and her brother, named after the man who murdered twins for a living.

The Gate was a disk, intercepting a sphere. Between them, the Tunnel of Calabi-Yau as it is known among the mathematicians.

Or the Tunnel of Set as it is known among the magicians. The disk continued to hover over the sight as one by one screams were heard, screams replacing the chants.

The signs and seals drawn on the body of Maxwell Prime burned bright and hot in the Sumerian night. The Moon had become dark, and disappeared below the horizon. The Sun was about to rise.

The sentries went to the cars and turned over the engines. They were expecting the devotees to come down from the hill and begin the journey back to Baghdad.

But the only one left alive was Maxwell Prime.

CHAPTER SEVENTY-SEVEN

Children Charity Center
The Bronx

As the Dark Lord made his decision in Nippur, the children in the Bronx started shouting and singing in a frenzy. Blood was blood, and blood called to blood. And blood was all these children ever knew.

Jamila grabbed the hand of Nalin and spoke with her, asked her questions in a hurry, received answers, nodded. She tried to leave Nalin behind, in safety, but Nalin told her that her safety was with Jamila, and the *jin*. She nodded. She moved Nalin behind her and told her to hold onto the back of her shirt.

She moved down the corridor.

Ahead of her, she saw a woman with a shotgun. The woman turned and aimed at her, but all Jamila had to do was shake her head, and pull Nalin out from behind her. Somehow Sylvia understood. She nodded back, and then made the sign for "two" with her fingers and pointed to the staircase ahead of them.

Jamila nodded back, and motioned for Sylvia to get close to the wall. Sylvia motioned to Harry to do the same. The detective was on the other side of the corridor and aiming at the staircase with his 9 mil.

There was a creak from the staircase, and before the detective could get a clear shot a rifle fired from behind him causing him to drop to the floor and cover his head. Jamila had watched the Dagon killer through her scope come down a single step. She adjusted her aim and hit him high. He screamed, but did not die. Instead he fell down the stairs and was shot and killed by the police officer.

Then someone killed the lights.

It was about ten pm and dark as hell in the old building without lights. And eerie, as the chanting and shouting from the children continued unabated.

The Gate opening in Nippur was the turning of a key in a lock. When the Gate opened, it did not open only over the Enlil temple in Nippur but in sites all over the world at the same time. Time and space were measured differently by the Old Ones, and an open Gate in one place on Earthly topography meant an opening in another place in the topological system of the Stars, but that one place was large enough to swallow the globe. It would take a massive effort to shut the Gate, once opened.

And that is when Simon realized that there were two forces at work in the world that day, and that the Church of Starry Wisdom was already fighting to close the Gate. His calculations demonstrated that previous rituals had been affected by more than one operator, which didn't make sense at first but which suddenly came together when he remembered what Monroe had told him about two cults working against each other. Starry Wisdom was there in October of 1907. And they were there again, in June of 2015.

P. B. Randolph had said as much in his writings, and it was apparent that Randolph knew whereof he spoke. Randolph had an issue with both Starry Wisdom and Dagon, however, which is why he started a Rosicrucian Society in America. Something to mellow out the vibes and provide a Middle Way. Doomed to failure, perhaps, as evidenced by Randolph's violent death, but a noble sentiment nonetheless. Who was responsible for Randoph's death, Simon wondered. Starry Wisdom, or Dagon?

He went back to the calculations, on fire with the new knowledge and new perspective. Maybe one day he would find Dagon's goals more immediately preferable but right now he had to throw his support behind Starry Wisdom.

★ ★ ★

In the final analysis, though, it would be "a plague on both your houses."

★ ★ ★

Harry crept low along the wall, getting closer to the staircase. It was almost pitch dark in the building. There were windows, but they were covered in wire mesh, either to keep people out or keep the children in. Regardless, they let in very little light. He was afraid to fire his shotgun unless he was one hundred percent sure of his target as the flash would blind him temporarily.

Jamila had no such qualms. Her scope was made for this environment. She could see shapes move in front of her. There was the woman, a man next to her, and another man across the way on the floor who was crawling towards the man he had just killed.

At that moment, she saw another shooter creep down the side of the staircase. She didn't like this. It was too stupid. The man had to know there was a lot of fire power in the corridor. Why take the risk?

Which is when she realized he was only a diversion. Nalin pulled at her shirt urgently, and Jamila wheeled around and fired blindly into the space behind her. And then again.

Sylvia turned at the sound of firing but Harry kept his eyes on the movement he saw ahead of him. When he saw it was another shooter and not a kid wandering around scared and lost he fired directly at the shape, squinting his eyes against the flash. The boom from the shotgun was loud and commanding. Deafening in the narrow space. Harry moved quickly ahead towards the staircase, his eyes adjusting, and swept the area in front of him. He had blown a hole through the chest of the shooter on the stairs.

That gave Sylvia and the detective enough time to rush the main room and take charge of the children, but when they did so they saw two more shooters in the room with them, guns pointed at the heads of the smallest girls.

CHAPTER SEVENTY-EIGHT

Joshua Tree
California

BLAIR OPENED THE MOTEL ROOM DOOR to admit a homicide detective from New York City called Danny something.

There was a half-eaten pizza on the table and an opened two liter bottle of Diet Coke. There were two local cops in the room, and another two outside the door.

Danny showed Blair his shield, and then sat down on a corner of one of the room's two twin beds to ask him a few questions.

"Look, Mr. Blair, I don't want to inconvenience you any more than you have been already. I'm sorry for the interruption in your schedule, but we have reason to believe that you have been in contact with one Gloria Tibbi and her two children. Ms. Tibbi is a person of interest in a homicide investigation, as I am sure you are aware since you spent like two hours doing a web search for her a few nights ago. Now, not too many people know who she is. She has no social media profile to speak of, and she comes from Rhode Island which is, like, about the furthest from this neck of the woods as you can be. So, I want to ask you nicely in the hope you would respond in the same spirit. Do you know Ms. Gloria Tibbi of Providence, Rhode Island?"

"Do I need a lawyer?"

Danny feigned surprise, as if he had never heard that question before.

"Do you, Mr. Blair?"

"I'm not sure. I've never been in this situation before."

"What situation?"

"Having the police enter my motel room, hold me for questioning, invite visiting policemen from New York to ask me questions. Like that."

"Well, it's like this, Mr. Blair. You're not under arrest, so you don't need a lawyer. You're not a suspect in the homicide. Not yet, anyway. All we want is Gloria's current location and some kind of understanding as to why you two would be acquainted."

Blair looked nervously from the pizza box to the detective.

"Did I interrupt your dinner, sir?"

"No. It's not that."

"Then what is it?"

"How much do you know about UFOs?"

★ ★ ★

In the hospital room, Gloria had given birth to a healthy baby girl. Her first girl. Seven pounds, eight ounces. Not bad for about six weeks premature. She had no idea what to name it at first, but then decided on Hope. Hope Tibbi. Kinda weird, but nothing really goes with Tibbi.

She was exhausted, as was the delivery room staff. They left her alone after they cleaned the baby and cut its umbilical cord. They wrapped the infant in a blanket and handed it to her for a few minutes. The attending marked the date and time of the delivery and left to get something to eat.

★ ★ ★

They left Gloria, tired and relieved, in Recovery. They brought the baby to the Neonatal Unit. Gloria fell asleep.

★ ★ ★

When she awoke a few hours later, she found the staff standing around her bed, worried looks on their faces.

"Oh, no. What's happened? Is my baby …?"

"As far as we know, your baby is fine."

"As far as you *know*?"

"Little Hope was taken away. We don't know by whom. We assume it was her father? She was there one minute and somehow she was gone the next. We did a sweep of the facility but she was nowhere to be found. Then we saw this."

A nurse handed her a tablet. On the tablet was a video, taken by a CCTV camera outside the main entrance. It showed a man with a baby walking off towards the highway. Walking. With the baby in a carrier. Just before he disappeared out of camera range he turned to face the camera.

And smiled.

"My kids!" she said. "My kids!"

The staff was confused.

"There was only one baby, Ms. Tibbi." .

She turned to them and smiled.

"No. You don't understand. My kids are coming back."

The staff thought she was obviously delirious, but as they were discussing all this the police arrived. They had notified the police of the baby-snatching, but another car arrived with some smart-alecky New Yorker in it.

He barreled his way through the main entrance and made straight for the maternity ward, pushing his way through the cops who were trying to get information on the baby-snatching.

He saw the crowd around a woman in a bed, and figured her for his target.

He held out his hand. The one with the shield.

"Ms. Tibbi? Ms. Gloria Tibbi? My name is Danny Dugin. I'm a detective with the New York City Police Department. You may have heard of us? We've had a hard time finding you, Ms. Tibbi."

CHAPTER SEVENTY-NINE

Children Charity Center
The Bronx

SYLVIA DIDN'T MOVE. She stared at the men who had picked up two of the smallest girls and were threatening to shoot them. The girls themselves seemed unconcerned, as if it was some kind of adult game that was being played. Or maybe they had been through this before, back in Iraq, back in Mosul, on the day that ISIL came to town.

The chanting was winding down. The girl who was giving birth on the floor was making a keening sound. Another girl, Yasemina, was standing outside what had been her locked isolation room and just stared at the two men as if she had seen them before.

Jamila saw what was happening from a distance. The two men had entered the main hall from a different entrance and Jamila knew she had to find it quickly and come up behind them.

Sylvia was loathe to release her grip on the shotgun, not knowing what would happen if she did.

Harry was edging around the door behind her, his weapon pointed at one of the two hostage-takers but so far not seen by them in the near total darkness. The mesh-covered windows in the main room let in a small amount of street light, enough that the two shooters were backlit.

So far, no one had said a word.

Outside, however, there were sounds of activity. A real SWAT team was setting up a perimeter and preparing to enter the building, being kept at bay by their team leader who got word that there were friendlies inside and that they were armed. With the lights off and no means of communication with those inside, it was decided to wait one and see what transpired.

"Put down your weapon," one of the Dagon men ordered, breaking the silence. He had an accent that Sylvia recognized.

"You first," she replied.

"If you do not, then this girl will be the first to die."

"If you harm her in any way, I will kill you myself. You don't want that to happen, do you? Because then, you will never enter paradise. You know. Killed by a woman."

Sylvia saw the briefest of movements behind him. She kept her eyes trained on the first shooter, the one doing the talking, and hoped that Harry had the second shooter covered.

Where the hell was the detective?

★ ★ ★

The detective had heard the commotion outside on the street and crept back to look out the doorway. There he saw a number of vehicles with their lights off and a SWAT team deployed and waiting for the order to begin the assault. There was an ambulance down at one end, and the EMTs were trying to figure out if his two uniforms were still alive.

He only had another year left on the force before he put in his papers. He didn't need this crap.

He looked down at his chest where he saw red dots moving over it. The assholes were going to shoot him!

Then he heard a voice telling them to stand down, that he was one of theirs.

"No more," he told himself as he went back inside. "This is it. It's over."

And as he moved back down the corridor he heard the weirdest sound he had ever heard in his entire life.

It was an ululation, and it was coming from Yasemina.

★ ★ ★

An ululation is the unique vocal cry, a kind of trilling sound, used by Middle Eastern women to signify woe or mournfulness. It is often heard at funerals. It is sometimes used as a gesture of defiance, a warning.

Yasemina's ululation was picked up by one of the other girls cowering in the main hall. It was then picked up by Nalin who appeared out of nowhere. It was the creepiest thing the adults had ever heard, with the exception of Jamila who took advantage of the cover the sound gave her to move closer to the shooters. She wanted to be sure she did not hit either of the girls they were holding. She was an expert sniper, and had rescued girls from Daesh many times before, but this was a strange land with strange people and strange adversaries. She wanted to be sure.

The ululation picked up volume and the two shooters from Dagon started to panic.

"Shut up!" the second one yelled, first in Arabic and then in English. "Stop it!"

He lifted the girl he was holding higher on his chest and held his weapon next to her skull– another Ingram Mac-10 whose rounds would have obliterated her entire head—and threatened to shoot unless the sound stopped.

There was a single pop! and the man lost hold of the girl who slid down and onto the floor. He remained standing for a second, and then dropped to the floor himself. Jamila had hit him in the back, severing his spinal cord.

The other shooter threw the girl he was holding to the side and turned to face the new threat from Jamila. Before either of them could get off a shot, Sylvia fired her shotgun straight at him, missing his torso but shooting his legs out from under him. The sound of the shotgun was enormously loud and the flash as bright as fireworks. Harry rushed in after Sylvia to cover the two shooters in case either one was still a viable threat. They didn't even notice the SWAT team storming the building now that the worst was over.

She came to her senses quickly and yelled for an ambulance. She had a girl giving birth on the floor and what seemed like a few more on the way.

She saw Yasemina and recognized her from Devata's isolation cell. She ran up to her and held her for a long time.

As for Nalin, she was gone.

And so was Jamila.

CHAPTER EIGHTY

Babylon Warwick Hotel
Baghdad

THE DARK LORD HAD MADE IT BACK to the hotel without incident. He wasn't sure about the others. He hadn't waited around to find out.

There was a flight leaving Baghdad in a few hours and he would be on it. He was back in his room, and admiring the *Necronomicon* that he was now holding in his hand after all this time. He placed it in his carry-on bag and answered the knock at the door.

It was the last time he would be able to enjoy the flavors of this country for a long time. The young girl in the doorway was easily fourteen or fifteen at the most. In no mood to quibble, he asked her inside. She appeared terrified, which was what he wanted.

She stared at him. He was missing an arm, and that made her all the more frightened and therefore all the more desirable.

He took her by the hand and brought her over to the bed. He patted the sheets and asked her to sit.

She complied. He asked her if she wanted anything to eat or drink. She declined, in polite and heavily-accented Arabic.

"Ah," he said. "Are you a Maslawi?"

She nodded, yes, she was from Mosul. The sing-song Maslawi accent is particular to that region. *How delightful*, he said to himself. *I wonder how she will sound when she is under me?*

He kept his shirt on with the left arm flap pinned to his sleeve. He undid his trousers slowly, taking the girl's hand and passing it over himself so that she could feel him growing harder.

He pushed her down, a little roughly in order to see the fear fill her eyes, and then reached between her legs. She whimpered, and he closed his eyes in pleasure.

And felt the sensation of hard steel being driven into his chest.

He drew back, his hands on the hilt of the blade and tried to remove it from his heart but she had aimed true.

"Yes," she said, in Maslawi-accented Arabic. "I am from Mosul. But I am Yezidi, and YPJ, and this is the day of your death. You will no longer defile my sisters with your filth." She pushed against him, hard, her hand on the hilt of the knife so that it drove in deeper, but he was already dead.

She got up and went to the bathroom to wash herself off and to remove her clothing and replace it with the chador she brought with her and had left outside the door. As she was leaving the room she spotted the *Necronomicon* sitting in his open carry-on.

CHAPTER EIGHTY-ONE

New York, New York

SYLVIA WENT TO BELLEVUE with the pregnant girls and with Yasemina, who would not leave her side. One of them almost gave birth in the ride over. The others made it to the hospital in good time. Sylvia waved her ID around and made noises about "national security" and a terrorist threat that had been averted. NYPD followed close behind and confirmed everything Sylvia said, even if only about half of it was true.

A nurse came out to greet Sylvia and to tell her that they would all be taken care of in the best possible way, not to worry. They were in good hands.

"Hi," she said. "My name is Stacey. What's yours?"

The babies that were born that day were all perfectly formed.

And they were all twins.

★ ★ ★

Harry eventually caught up with her, after giving the locals his report and his contact information. They would want to talk to both of them later, and Harry wondered how they were going to handle it from DC. He had no doubt that Monroe had a lot of ability and contacts in that regard, but he was wondering if maybe that well was running a little dry. That, and the fact that the old man didn't look too good these days. But he kept those concerns to himself.

"Who was that woman?" he asked Sylvia, when they were alone with Yasemina sitting on the floor between them.

"I don't know. I never saw her before. I don't even know if she spoke English. We communicated with signs. But she was a helluva shot. I think she was the one who took out those two Ingrams on the street, one bullet each, rapid-fired."

"Sniper training, maybe."

"But she's only a kid. Hardly more than a teenager."

"What are you going to do with this one?" he asked, looking at Yasemina.

"Well, there are protocols and rules about this sort of thing. I can't just pick her up and bring her home with me."

"Do you want to?" he asked, surprise in his voice.

She looked at the girl who had been through so much, and who had even tried to kill a security guard! She looked completely vulnerable now, though. Like a normal little girl.

"I don't know. I kinda do. But what am I going to do with a kid, with my job and my schedule? What would any of us do?"

Harry looked at her slyly. "We could split the work between us."

On the floor, playing with an old and slightly dirty doll that had been in the kids room at the hospital, Yasemina thought back to the day she was captured. She remembered the men with guns, vividly. She remembered being taken away from her family. She remembered her training at the hands of Dagon.

Go with them, a familiar voice told her, in her head. *Go with them. There will be a chance to escape later. There will be a chance of revenge.*

Be quiet, Nalin, she answered. *Go away.*

I will never leave you, Yasemina. They will. But I never will.

★ ★ ★

In Brooklyn, Detective Lieutenant (Retired) J. Wasserman had turned on the late news. He couldn't sleep. He knew Danny had gone to California on the Richard Hill case, the murdered baby doctor, and wondered what he had turned up. Instead, he tried to anesthetize himself with talking heads and "breaking news."

He saw a story about a shootout in the Bronx. *Car 54, Where Are You?* he sang to himself.

He saw the videotape out of one eye, hardly paying attention. SWAT team. Possible hostage situation. A foster center for girls. All's well that ends well. A shot of the girls being led out of the building, surrounded by SWAT and being taken to an undisclosed location to be examined by medical professionals. *Probably Bellevue*, he said to himself.

Body bags. Spent cartridges. Was that a Mac-10? That detective. He looked familiar. Couldn't place him, though. Started to turn off the television.

And then he saw her. Briefly. A flash of light in the back of the shot. A woman, hardly more than a girl, holding another girl. Moving away from the others. Couldn't anyone see her?

It was her. The shooter from Feil Hall. The sniper who took out the terrorist.

"Ah, fuck it," he said aloud. "I'm not going into that wasps' nest again. Fuck it. Let her go."

CHAPTER EIGHTY-TWO

Hounfort Marasa
New Orleans

HERVÉ CAME TO IN A PUDDLE OF PERSPIRATION and clairin. The devotees were standing around her, frightened at the sudden transformation of their houngan. Although she was no stranger to possession by the loa, this time was different. It was no loa they recognized and whatever it was it did not respond to any of the methods used to free a horse from its rider.

They helped her to sit up. She looked around and spoke to the people in Creole, asking them what had happened.

"The Mistress rose up from the Waters," they said.

"The Mistress laughed at us. Then the Master came."

"This was not our Master. This was *le Baron.*"

Baron Samedi was not of their rite. The Baron was Ghede, only appearing in Ghede rites, which were concerned with Death. Something was wrong. Hervé had been possessed by Baron Samedi, and that was frightening indeed. *Les points chauds* were out of whack, or ... or the Gate had been opened.

The Gate had been opened.

The Gate had been opened.

The more she said it, the more she believed. Not the Gate opened by petitioning Legba. No. This Gate was the one that kept the two worlds separate. The veil between them. It would be as if Guinee had suddenly become Baton Rouge, and the loa were marching down North Street. When the loa start riding people at random, taking over while they work or sleep or make love, then something bad has happened.

There was one authority to whom she could appeal. One authority that it was forbidden to contact under any circumstances. But she knew that in a case like this she would have to take the risk.

Anyway, what did she have to lose? If what happened today started happening again, she would lose her hounfort and the reason for her life.

She would have to contact the A∴A∴.

★ ★ ★

This was not the Argenteum Astrum of Aleister Crowley. This was the original, the one mentioned by Randolph in a book published long before there was an Aleister Crowley. This A∴A∴ stood for *Amor Artis*. There was only one member of this Order known to reside in New Orleans. There were maybe only five in the United States, and less than twenty worldwide. But they controlled all the *nanchons*, the rites, the rituals, and it was all they did. Their oath did not permit them to hold jobs or identify themselves or each other in any way. But they could be found if one knew how to look.

Hervé put on her best outfit after bathing in scented water and making offerings to the Marasa. She set out on foot, for they had to be approached on foot. And she looked up at the sky and prayed that it would not rain.

★ ★ ★

She found the Magister where she knew he would be. He was sitting on a stoop in the Lower Ninth, in front of a house that had been destroyed during Katrina and not rebuilt.

She came and sat down on the sidewalk in front of him.

He pretended not to notice her.

She spoke.

"The Gate has been opened. Everything will change. The Old Ones will come from the skies. From the stars. I can feel it changing now. My dreams will change. My nightmares will change. My vodoun … it will change, too."

He looked out onto the street as if he had not heard a thing she said. But that was how it had to be.

She got up and bowed, and put a coin on the stoop next to him.

After a moment of walking, she turned around to see him. He got up from the stoop and walked into the ruined house.

It began to rain.

★ ★ ★

A∴A∴. It stands for *Amor Artis*.

In English, that means Love Craft.

EPILOGUE

In the end, Danny couldn't hold her.

Gloria had receipts for every place she ever stayed since leaving Providence. A check against her credit card and ATM records showed that she left New York at least a week before the murder of the doctor in Brooklyn. Her friend corroborated the alibi. They could have eliminated her as a suspect if they had only known her name earlier. Her absence from the city around the time of the murder made her look suspicious and, anyway, they didn't have any other leads.

Before he left to get back on a plane for New York he asked her one last question.

"Your kids. I don't see them. Where are they?"

Gloria simply smiled at him.

"They're waiting for me. In San Diego. I had to stop here first."

"What about the baby you just had?"

"Oh," she said. "She'll turn up."

★ ★ ★

She drove to San Diego with her new friend, Alexander Blair. He wanted to see the end of this story play out. He wanted to talk to Chromo-Test himself. He wanted to see if her two kids really were waiting for her there, as she seemed to believe without a shred of proof.

But mostly he wanted to stay with her a little longer.

Something was in the wind. Something had changed in the world. It made him nervous, but it seemed to compel him to take more chances.

He would take this as far as it would go.

★ ★ ★

Cuneo figured the Asian lady—who had a series of aliases and who seemed to have lived a lot of places—was the perp. She had killed

501

Mrs. Galvez. She was working for someone else though, he was sure of it. If Lisa was right, and Galvez was Starry Wisdom, then maybe the Asian was with this Dagon group that Hervé knew about. Two cults fighting it out in his city. That's all they needed. But he had to get some answers out of Asian Lady fast. Like, how the hell did the baby get in the box?

Lisa had applied as a foster mother for the baby, something Cuneo could not fucking understand. But she saw something in him that no one else did, and the fact that she was single and gay meant that it might be more difficult for her to adopt a baby otherwise. But this particular baby? They would be more than happy to have her take him off their hands.

It was a late night, but Francine had said she would be happy to have a drink with him. They would meet in the Quarter like a couple of tourists and pretend they were from somewhere else.

He liked that idea. Liked it a lot.

★ ★ ★

Vanek was found hanged in his cell at Gitmo. It was written off as suicide. The walls were covered in indecipherable writing using his own blood and feces. They took a photograph of the writing, and filed it along with the death certificate.

Maxwell Prime was found wandering the streets of al-Diwaniyyah. How he made it that far from Nippur was anyone's guess. Especially naked. He couldn't find his clothes, but his skin was covered in so many scars and weird markings that it looked like clothes. At least, from a distance. There were ligatures on his wrists and ankles but he had torn himself free and now was babbling nonsense syllables.

As he seemed to be an American, some troops came by to pick him up and clean him off and try to identify him. They ran his fingerprints, and they came back with all sorts of "need to know" identifiers. So they contacted military intelligence, who passed it on to the Pentagon and eventually to CIA. He was identified as an escaped high value prisoner.

Which is why Maxwell Prime wound up back in a black site. Only this time, instead of counting his steps in German or Mandarin he was talking to the walls in a language they did not recognize.

Ph'nglui mglw'nafh … Cthulhu R'lyeh wgah'nagl fhtagn.
Zi dingir kia kanpa! Zi dingir anna kanpa!

★ ★ ★

Jean-Paul woke up in his own bed in Whately, Massachusetts, without a single clue as to how he got there. His mother was passed out in her bedroom, so all was right with the world. In a small pile of snail mail on the plywood desk in his basement lair was an acceptance letter from some local university he had never applied to. He was to start in August.

★ ★ ★

Their plane landed at Andrews Air Force Base. Monroe had managed to wrangle a C-130 for their ride home.

For the first time in more than a year, Gregory Angell set foot onto American soil. He had nothing but the clothes on his back, and a knapsack with some incoherent notes and a wad of cash.

A car was sent to meet them, and took them directly to an apartment in the town of Crofton, Maryland. Simon had agreed to let them use it for the homecoming and to help with the transition.

The door opened and Angell walked into a room filled with a number of individuals he had never met or heard of before, but they all seemed to know him.

An old man in an expensive suit approached him, and held out his hand.

"Dr. Angell, my name is Dwight Monroe. I am very pleased to meet you, indeed."

ACKNOWLEDGEMENTS

Thanks to all the usual suspects—Yvonne and Jim at the top of the list—but also special thanks go to Michael Bertiaux, who permitted the use of his name and work in this book, however bowdlerized it became in the execution, and to Ariock Van de Voorde who acted as intermediary.

Thanks also to Linda Moulton Howe, who kindly provided some information on Richard Neal and his work in trying to solve the mystery of the missing twins.

And my regards as well to Contact in the Desert, where I have been giving presentations the last few years, much to my surprise and occasional consternation.

And to those mysterious individuals at To The Stars Academy of Arts and Science who in themselves provide the perfect mix of science, Ufology, and the intelligence community.

As always, any errors are mine alone and this is a work of fiction. Kinda.

Afterword
by Simon

Also the mantras and spells; the obeah and the wanga; the work of the wand and the work of the sword; these he shall learn and teach.

—*Liber AL*, I: 37

As this trilogy involves the *Necronomicon*—and as I was the editor of what occultist and author Kenneth Grant referred to as the "Schlangekraft recension" of the *Necronomicon*—I was asked to contribute some thoughts on the story and especially on the occultism as described in the three novels.

There are certainly several major themes to be found in these pages and even some of the less obvious ones deserve more exploration than I could give in a short essay. So I will restrict myself to the one area that I think best describes the thread running through all three of the books, and that is the relationship between the works of H. P. Lovecraft on the one hand and the various iterations of the occult renaissance that was inspired by the works of Aleister Crowley on the other. After all, the *Necronomicon* contains a dedication to Crowley.

While there are those on both sides who disavow any direct connection there certainly has been a lot of foot traffic between these two neighborhoods. For instance, there is a real Esoteric Order of Dagon (not to be confused with the fictional Order of Dagon of the trilogy), which was established with the idea that Lovecraft's works should be taken seriously by modern, Western European occultists in the Aleister Crowley—that is to say, "Thelemic"—tradition. This was an idea put forward repeatedly by Kenneth Grant in his Typhonian Trilogies, and in that series he references not only Lovecraft but also and specifically the version of the *Necronomicon* with which I have been identified, and from which some ritual details have been adapted in the *Lovecraft Code* (such as the requirement that the ritual of Opening the Gate takes place when "the Great Bear hangs from its tail in the sky").

You will find a lot of these references in *The Lovecraft Code, Dunwich,* and *Starry Wisdom.* There are several mentions of Crowley, of the secret societies he led such as the OTO and the A∴A∴, and of some of the personalities that are associated with the Thelemic tradition, such as Michael Bertiaux, as well as some intellectual celebrities such as Umberto Eco and Alexander Grothendieck. Easter eggs abound in these books, and those who have read deeply in modern Western occultism will appreciate them.

But these novels are not concerned with ceremonial magic—ancient or modern—in a purely general way. There is a specific purpose behind the rituals described in the trilogy, it seems to me, which is its emphasis on non-Western, non-European forms of esotericism, spirituality, and magic. This emphasis is wedded to the central obsession of H. P. Lovecraft: the threat to humanity posed by extraterrestrial forces and the existence of human agents in the world who understand how to make contact with these forces to the detriment of civilization; and as a corollary, the use of sexuality and sexual rituals as methods for making this contact. This both conceals and reveals a central mystery of occult theory and practice and, truly, all one needs to know and understand about magic—or "magick" as spelled by Crowley—is contained here.

For Lovecraft, the cults that traffic in interstellar magic are by and large composed of individuals who come from those parts of the world that he viewed as savage, backwards, lustful and dangerous. From "The Call of Cthulhu" to "The Horror at Red Hook" these cults are composed of individuals who are Middle Eastern, African, and Asian (and Native American) in race and ethnicity. In his other stories they are depicted as human beings who have interbred with non-human species, as we find in "The Dunwich Horror" and the "The Shadow over Innsmouth," to give just two examples. These are not the charming aliens of *The Day the Earth Stood Still,* or *E.T.,* or *Close Encounters of the Third Kind.* These are hideous beings, generating foul smells and gibbering speech. Even dread Cthulhu himself has an octopus for a head (a characterization that today has some unexpected relevance as represented by such modern works as *Other Minds: The Octopus, the Sea, and the Deep Origins of Consciousness,* by Peter Godfrey-Smith).

This idea of interbreeding between humans and non-humans—represented in the UFO community by the concept of alien-human "hybrids"—is not new. In the novels, NSA alumnus Dwight Monroe points out the relevance of Genesis 6:1-4 that mentions intercourse between the "sons of God and the daughters of men": a situation that seemed to inspire God to send a Flood to wipe out humanity. Much of Lovecraft's oeuvre can be seen as a riff on this basic Biblical concept. In fact, his obsession with this idea—illicit sex with non-humans and the resulting destruction of the world—may stem from his own personal history.

Sexually, Lovecraft is a cipher. He was married for all of two years, and during those two years he frequently was apart from his wife. There were rumors of his possible homosexuality even including a same-sex relationship with a teenager, the future anthropologist and Lovecraft's literary executor, Robert Barlow: a rumor for which there is no direct evidence—although Barlow's suicide in 1951 was due to the threat of his being outed as gay. Lovecraft's published fiction betrays an almost adolescent view of sexuality, with an orgy in "The Call of Cthulhu" and the sly allusions to incest in "The Dunwich Horror" as only two examples. Yet, it is important to realize that Lovecraft associated sexuality with occult practice: an idea that was promulgated by the visionary African-American author of occult works, P. B. Randolph, an idea which was disseminated by groups such as the German Ordo Templi Orientis or OTO (which Aleister Crowley would eventually come to dominate), the Fraternitas Saturni, and many others since then. How, then, did sex become associated with rituals and with "non-humans" in Lovecraft's mind?

That Lovecraft was a racist is a given. Modern scholarship tends to admit that this is the case, and his published writings and his correspondence support this view. There have been attempts to soften this accusation by saying that Lovecraft was simply a product of his era; that racism was endemic in American society at the time. This is clever, but a closer look at American society when Lovecraft was writing reveals that there were many who famously and openly opposed racism. For instance, the National Association for the Advancement of Colored People (NAACP) was founded in 1909 and included many prominent white activists among its founding members, even as Jim Crow laws and lynchings of African-Americans in the South provided a deadly counterpoint. There were, obviously, abolitionists in America at a time (pre-1865) when slavery was considered normal, a product of *its* times. The point is: we expect more from our artists and our spiritual leaders than merely echo chambers for whatever cultural or political narrative is current or popular.

Prophets are no exception, yet sometimes prophets do get it right even when their followers get it wrong. That may be because the deeply-unnerving experience of spiritual contact with alien, i.e., "non-human" or "super-human," forces tends to focus one's mind in an unrelenting way. Certain statements are made. Certain philosophies are underlined. And then, quite often, they are forgotten when they become too uncomfortable or indigestible. The result is conflict, even among those who claim allegiance to the greater good; and religious sects and secret societies are notorious this way, for the messages of their prophets are designed for those who have attained higher initiations and who are expected to understand them. When those initiations are obtained by fraud or artifice, or when the required spiritual work is not done, then the initiates—realizing that their lack of qualifications have rendered them powerless—turn on each other, as social acceptance and public elevation become substitutes for "Crossing the Abyss": that stage in serious spiritual practice in which one's ego is transcended.

In the novels, the cults of Dagon and Starry Wisdom are similarly in conflict even though they enjoy roughly the same level of spiritual understanding, having sprung from the same original cult. Their magical systems reveal an operating system that is far beyond the comprehension of most modern secret societies and occult groups, for they have incorporated knowledge of modern science (which is exactly what the ancient secret societies had done with the scientific knowledge of *their* times). They have switched their entire worldview from one that is Earth-based and thus pre-Galilean in nature to one that is Space-based: not an easy thing to do for most of us humans even though we have known for centuries that the Earth is not the center of the universe.

The conflict between the two cults is to be found not in their understanding of how the world "really" works, but in the way they use that knowledge. Their goals are different. They both recognize that the Old Ones want to open the Gate and flood into the planet, but Starry Wisdom wants to control that ingress, slow it down, and improve the genetic defenses of the human race at the same time. For Starry Wisdom, the human race is improvable and salvageable. For Dagon, that ship has already sailed. Both groups use methods with which reasonable people reasonably could disagree. Which group is the most advanced along the spiritual path? Which group's leaders have "Crossed the Abyss" in Western occult parlance, i.e., attained a level of non-duality having destroyed the superego and the ego in the process? Either of them? Neither of them?

And who can be trusted to make that judgment?

★ ★ ★

In 1904, an English magician, traveler, and man of many parts—Aleister Crowley—made contact with an extraterrestrial intelligence while on a kind of honeymoon in Cairo. The story is much too well-known to describe in detail here and there are many excellent biographies of Crowley to consult. We are concerned with the text that was received by Crowley at that time, dictated by the non-human entity known as Aiwaz (or Aiwass).

This book—*Liber AL vel Legis*, or simply *The Book of the Law*, known to its devotees as *AL*—is very short, divided into three sections or chapters, and contains the central thesis of this new religion of Thelema, the Greek word for "Will." (Thus, followers of Crowley are known as "Thelemites.")

The core dictum of this text—and of Thelema generally—is found in Chapter I verse 40 of *AL*:

Do what thou wilt shall be the whole of the Law.

A statement that is usually greeted by a response found in Chapter I verse 57:

Love is the law, love under will.

For this core dictum of Thelema to make any sense, one needs to know what the Will is: how to define it, how to discover it, and how to identify one's consciousness with it; and then to apply that understanding to the concept of Love (what the medieval philosopher and martyr Giordano Bruno called "the link").

It is by now well understood that "will" in this sense is not equivalent to "desire," or "wish," or "want." Will rather is understood to mean the spine of the organism: the axis around which it revolves. It is the core of the human being, and is identical to the core of the universe itself. We are not normally aware of "universal consciousness" or "cosmic consciousness." We are deaf, dumb and blind to it. We are distracted by sensory data that overwhelms conscious and rational thought. The closest many of us ever come to the type of silence required to hear the hum of the Will is through sleep; some of us can hear it in meditation.

The ego is not identical with the Will. Neither is the superego. The id brings us closer to the organic origin of the Will, for it is concerned with flight and fight, and with procreation. These concepts are all connected with ideas of survival: both for ourselves as individuals, and as members of the human race. These are unconscious instincts, and as such they can provide a pathway into the rest of the unconscious.

The problem with individuals raised in a modern Western society is that these instincts are often suppressed; when they are not, they are ornamented in so many theological explanations and cautions that they become unrecognizable.

Tantric practice, on the other hand, provides a mechanism for bypassing ego and superego in order to proceed directly to the id and from there to a direct knowledge of one's Will. This is all well and good, but it requires lengthy and strenuous training at the direction of a genuine teacher, and such is often hard to recognize if one could be found.

There is, however, a short path to this type of knowledge: a system for making conscious contact with one's Will in a more efficient and even more communal manner. *Liber AL* refers to this short path.

In order to make the type of breakthrough we are discussing it is necessary—to borrow a phrase from the French poet Rimbaud—to "derange the senses." AL is clear about this when it states in Chapter II verse 22:

> *To worship me take wine and strange drugs whereof I will tell my prophet, & be drunk thereof!*

This command could be understood literally, or figuratively. In either case, the derangement of the senses—the breakdown of the superego as a means of confronting the ego—is intended.

Drink, drugs and sex. All of these, approached in the right way, are methods of deranging the senses: of silencing the superego and permitting unconscious material to surface. In the novels we see Dagon take this idea to its extreme conclusion of utilizing sexual rituals incorporating unwilling victims as a mechanism for incarnating the Old Ones. It is conscious, deliberate, and carefully planned to take place at a precise location and time. And the novels are careful to point out that there are ethical and moral issues to be addressed which Dagon either ignored or dismissed as irrelevant to their cause. By contrast the trilogy's central protagonist, Gregory Angell, while rejecting God and religion entirely, could not abandon his basic decency. What, then, is the way to balance the requirements of extreme spirituality with those of social mores and conventions?

That there is a relation between sexuality and the Will is a core principle of Tantra and other occult practices and, of course, is a cornerstone of Crowleyan theory as represented by the two dicta mentioned above concerning the Will, Love, and Law, and represented in the Gnostic Mass.

Very few rituals or other practices of the secret societies under discussion were or are open to public scrutiny, of course. But the one ritual that is sometimes accessible to non-initiates is the Gnostic Mass. This Mass—a mainstay of the OTO, a kind of "gateway drug" to the religion of Thelema—bears some similarity to the Roman Catholic Mass. There is an altar, a priest (and a priestess) and the consecration of the Elements (bread and wine) and the Communion of these Elements with the congregation. The symbolism is blatantly sexual, which for the time the Mass was created by Crowley would have been seen as scandalous or even blasphemous. It would have satisfied Lovecraft's understanding of weird and orgiastic occult rituals, however, if for that very reason alone.

The concept of sexuality (whether of the occult variety or the average human variety) implies both biology and psychology. We have often heard the statement that the body is a temple; in fact, both the body and the temple are machines for attaining alternate states of consciousness and both allow a space for the attainment of one's Will. The role of the body—and of bodily functions, such as sexuality—has been degraded or downplayed in the last several millennia in the West, but has been recognized and emphasized in the East as well as on the African and South American continents, and has been referenced in *AL* itself.

The method is a simple one.

It appears in Chapter I verse 37 and thus right at the beginning of the text and even before the iconic phrase "Do what thou wilt shall be the whole of the Law."

It reads:

*Also the mantras and spells; the obeah and the wanga; the work of
the wand and the work of the sword; these he shall learn and teach.*

Mantras and spells: Tantric techniques. *Obeah and wanga*: Afro-
Caribbean religion and esotericism.

This verse remains the missing piece of the puzzle for many
western occultists, with the notable exception of Michael Bertiaux
who single-handedly promoted the idea of a kind of Thelemic vodoun
that incorporated the Haitian *loa/lwa* as well as other predominantly
Haitian religious concepts. Bertiaux, of course, appears as a character
in *Starry Wisdom* which should attract the attention of the careful
reader.

Aleister Crowley from all available evidence did not "learn and
teach" the "obeah and wanga." He did not incorporate African
religious systems into, for instance, his compendium of occult
correspondences known as *Liber 777* although there are columns
devoted to Daoist, Buddhist and Indian deities and ideas. The
published instructions to aspirants of his A∴A∴ or Argentum
Astrum in his breakthrough text, *Magick: In Theory and Practice*, do not
include specific references to African or Afro-Caribbean religious or
magical practices but, again, do include several recommended (and
basic) Buddhist, Chinese and Indian texts. His systems do include
numerous Egyptian references, but these were based largely on
the kind of Egyptology he learned while an active member of the
Golden Dawn. Of Sub-Saharan Africa or the Caribbean, Crowley
knew very little and taught none at all.

What did he miss, then?

★ ★ ★

Liber AL vel Legis contains elements that are Afro-Caribbean in
nature which Crowley—due perhaps to "white gaze"—did not recognize, which ironically makes *Liber AL* more important than even
he was able to understand, thus perhaps validating its nature as a

genuine "received text" for it speaks explicitly of what the receiver is perfectly unconscious. The passionate disdain for other religions expressed in the infamous Chapter III of *Liber AL* (III: 49–55) can be considered as the outrage of the slave caste against the power systems that oppress them. Yet, Crowley specifically and clearly is instructed to teach "mantras and spells" and "obeah and wanga" ... and then doesn't, especially where obeah and wanga are concerned. His resistance to this indicates his own inner struggle; he was perfectly content to resist monotheism, Christianity, Judaism, even Buddhism and Hinduism, in an open and flagrant fashion. But he avoided Afro-Caribbean religions and cultures.

Ironically, there is a precedent for introducing non-European concepts into the Western occult narrative in the person of Paschal Beverly Randolph: an African-American occultist and author who traveled in the Middle East and claimed initiations there and who was also a resident of New Orleans and an observer of Afro-Caribbean religion and vodoun in that city. It was Randolph (also mentioned at length in *Starry Wisdom*) who created the first Rosicrucian society in North America, and whose writings on the importance of sexuality in esotericism influenced the founders of the OTO in Germany and many other groups besides. While Aleister Crowley claimed to be the reincarnation of the French occultist Eliphas Levi who died in 1875—the year Crowley was born—Randolph also died that same year and Crowley could have claimed him as his previous incarnation had he realized how much they had in common philosophically!

Interestingly, there is a strong transgender element in vodoun. The lwa of any gender can possess the devotee of any gender. Men are possessed by "female" lwa, and vice versa. (See the character of Hervé in *Starry Wisdom*.) Crowley would have appreciated this— he experimented with gender fluidity himself—but vodoun with its drums and orgiastic rites would have frightened him, I think. His knowledge of Afro-Caribbean religion seems derived from his conversations with travel author and adventurer William Seabrook and the other popular accounts (largely embellished when not outright invented) published in the newspapers and books of the period. It was Seabrook, after all, who popularized the idea of the Yezidis as "devil worshippers" with their Seven Towers of Satan arrayed from Iraq to Mongolia, a fantasy with which one assumes Jamila would have disagreed … perhaps violently!

This is not the world of the Rites of Eleusis as Crowley performed them at Caxton Hall. The very Englishness of the Golden Dawn is represented by the insistence on the correct performance of the rites according to almost mathematical rules that eliminate any possibility of spontaneity or passion. Theirs is a distinctly Masonic atmosphere. One is expected to generate power through the rituals, but it is institutionalized power: much like the type of power passed on to the newly-ordained priest by his bishop, it is believed to be there even if it is not experienced, either by the priest or by the congregation. It is there because canon law says it is there.

This is the antithesis to the possession of the voudouisant by the lwa (*loa*) which is accomplished through ecstasy, drumming, chanting, large communal rituals, etc. While the rites of vodoun have their own system, internal logic, and precision these are not so easily codified in textual form as those of the Golden Dawn or the other English and European groups with which Crowley was familiar. He could not "teach" obeah and wanga because there is no way to do so within the safe confines of the European secret society (and, anyway, he never bothered to learn them). Yet, ironically, it is the Afro-Caribbean cultus that holds the secret and a key to unlocking *Liber AL*.

While "the rituals of the old time are black" according to *AL*, II:5, and while the Abrahamic religions are attacked in *AL*, III: 49-55, Crowley is exhorted to teach "obeah and wanga" in Chapter I. This, taken together, would seem to indicate that genuine Thelema should be based on a re-evaluation of Western, European occult practice from the point of view of vodoun and the other Afro-Caribbean societies and, in fact, suggests that religions such as those of the Yoruba, the Congolese, and other African communities are what have been emphasized by *AL* but in such a way as to have slipped past its most prominent and vocal prophet.

Michael Bertiaux came closest of all published followers of Thelema where this position is concerned, and he understands that the Western systems can and should be melded with the Afro-Caribbean systems. His process was discussed at length by Kenneth Grant, who also appreciated this contribution and who linked it to his own interest in Tantra, a field to which he had much more exposure than had Crowley. Tantra, with its emphasis on experience over intellectualism, is closer to vodoun than to the kind of drawing room occultism of the Golden Dawn. Both Tantra and vodoun are "messy" in that they incorporate physicality and biological processes to a much greater degree than is found in the Western secret societies. While the OTO professed to understand this linkage in early twentieth century Germany, in practice they present no actual ritual processes in which this physicality is experienced directly. Instead, these specific "secrets" are hinted at, represented symbolically, in a manner suggestive of misdirection rather than discretion. It is as if the Western audience is considered too vulnerable or sensitive to be exposed directly to the actual praxis. This might have been true in Victorian times, and even as late as the 1950s in the US and Europe, but hardly can be considered operative today.

While Crowley recommends study of some of the relevant Tantric texts, largely out of context, he leaves it at that. There is no in-depth instruction in these texts in Crowley's writings generally. This may be due to the unavailability of Tantric texts translated into English at the time, or to Crowley's reluctance to accept a long period of instruction at the feet of a Tantrika. He was certainly a strong proponent of yoga as a technique, and was a close friend of Allan Bennett (Bhikkhu Ananda Metteyya): the initiate of the Golden Dawn who almost single-handedly introduced Theravada Buddhism to England. That said, there has been no systematic attempt to integrate Tantric practices and techniques within the Thelemic context except for the approaches of Bertiaux and Grant. The same is especially true of "obeah and wanga."

At the risk of sounding like a social justice warrior, Crowley's occult systems such as the OTO and its affiliated structures are overwhelmingly white, Western, and male. Naturally, for such is the bedrock from which the Order and its associated groups (like the Golden Dawn, the British and American Rosicrucian Societies, and the A∴A∴) have sprouted. But that is an accident of history rather than an essential characteristic. The groups that will have the most effect in reproducing Thelemic ideas and principles in the world will not be these venerable institutions but the non-Western, non-European, and gender fluid spiritual experience represented by the Afro-Caribbean, the African, the Native American, the Middle Eastern, and the Asian cultures. They represent a political resistance against the very same Abrahamic mindset vilified by *AL*, but they do it in real time, in the real world.

Thelema is not quite so liberating for the modern American white male, because the institutions that were repressive for American white males are no longer a threat to them (if they ever were). Thelema, however, can be liberating for the oppressed of the Earth because it challenges the political ideology of the colonizers by challenging the assumptions on which that ideology is based. It is anti-missionary as much as it is anti-Western, and understands that the exportation of Abrahamic religions is the Trojan Horse within which an entire economic and political structure is concealed. Thelema glorifies polytheism, animism, and occultism, the judicious use of alcohol and drugs, and sexuality: the lived experience of the shaman, the houngan, the Tantrika.

An objection could be made that the work of Bertiaux (for instance) is syncretistic, an eccentric and very personal blend of Western occultism with selected elements of Haitian voudon that represents a kind of "cultural appropriation" at best, or a flagrant disregard for academic norms of comparative studies at its worst (see the ongoing controversies regarding the dreaded "universalism"). Unfortunately, the same charge can be leveled at Crowley for his own eccentric understanding of both Egyptology and Asian religions. In fact, this blending and mixing of cultural and anthropological

subject matter is a hallmark of many modern secret societies. It
was certainly true of the Golden Dawn and of the original OTO,
and the grimoire-based magic of the European Middle Ages and
Renaissance periods is replete with "cultural appropriation" in the
form of mangled Hebrew, Greek, and Arabic phrases and techniques.
While this practice may seem naïve or misguided by academics, in
fact this juxtaposition of the familiar with the foreign anticipates
a state of emotional trauma and shock. It represents an attempt to
unlock doors within the unconscious mind of the experiencer by
juxtaposing symbols of ingrained psychological and intellectual
training and education with those of a completely foreign—
"alien"—culture, as if insisting on an identification or similarity/
consistency of the native, the familiar, with the Other. It performs a
critique of the experiencer's own culture and education by taking it
out of its comfort zone of the familiar and the secure. This emotional
shock treatment is designed to stimulate new ways of looking at
the familiar world, and does so through bypassing the well-traveled
intellectual highways and slashing new, psycho-emotional pathways
through the jungles of the unconscious. Our psyches are designed
for survival, for creating barriers between the self and the Other,
to enable the individual to live and move and breathe in a "safe
space." These antinomian techniques are designed to sabotage that
safe space, not to destroy the experiencer but to introduce her to
new modalities of understanding, stretching new—as yet untested—
psychological musculature, and abilities and perceptions of the
world, outside the safe space, that have remained buried in a state of
potentiality her entire life. For instance, death is a symbol and a meme
of occult praxis because death is a metaphor for the unknown land,
for the state of knowledge on the other side of the liminal divide. It
is indeed a "country from whose bourn no traveler returns" because
there is no "unknowing" of what becomes known, no way to see the
world the same way again.

The non-"white" peoples of the globe have already experienced
the world of the European, the American, and the Western through

conquest and trade and evangelization at first, and then through media, propaganda, and more trade. It is perhaps an imperfect or incomplete experience, but it is nonetheless a true one. In fact, it is one that the European, the American, and the Western peoples have rarely, if ever, experienced themselves because they are the carriers of it and can experience it only through the observed reactions of the conquered.

But *Liber AL,* I:37 makes it clear that the time has come for the tables to be turned, and for those who practice the "obeah and the wanga" to evangelize their former conquerors even as they liberate themselves from centuries of the worst, most toxic elements of Western spirituality. Because these former conquerors occupy an incredible psychological construction made of religion, politics, economics, racism, and privilege it will be useful to evangelize them using some of the symbol systems with which they are already familiar—Kabbalah, alchemy, ritual magic—as gateways for the "obeah" and "wanga." Vodoun already does this by utilizing familiar Catholic saints as totems and place-holders for African deities. So perhaps it is indeed time to turn up the volume, and to "evangelize" the Western secret societies as the first step in the process: to liberate the European, American, Western occult Orders from their enslavement to monotheistic, Abrahamic, patriarchal narratives.

The work of the wand and the work of the sword; these he shall learn and teach. (*AL,* I:37)

Once that happens, the liberation of every slave in the world is in sight.

—Simon